Tony's Wife

Also by Adriana Trigiani

ADRIANA TRIGIANI

Tony's Wife

**SIMON &
SCHUSTER**

London · New York · Sydney · Toronto · New Delhi

A CBS COMPANY

First published in the United States by Harper Books, an imprint of
HarperCollins US, 2018

First published in Great Britain by Simon & Schuster UK Ltd, 2019
A CBS COMPANY

1 3 5 7 9 10 8 6 4 2

Simon & Schuster UK Ltd
1st Floor
222 Gray's Inn Road
London WC1X 8HB

Simon & Schuster Australia, Sydney
Simon & Schuster India, New Delhi

www.simonandschuster.co.uk
www.simonandschuster.com.au
www.simonandschuster.co.in

A CIP catalogue record for this book is available from the British Library

Paperback ISBN: 978-1-4711-3644-3
eBook ISBN: 978-1-4711-3645-0

Printed and bound by CPI Group (UK) Ltd, Croydon, CR0 4YY

MIX
Paper from
responsible sources
FSC® C020471

IN MEMORY OF THE PERIN SISTERS

Viola, Edith, Helen, and

Lavinia

CONTENTS

MY WORLD'S GONE TOPSY TURVY

(Lyrics by C. C. Donatelli, 1938)

You can outrun it
Deny it or test it
But you'll never best it
Baby that's love
You might want it,
Crave it — even need it
But you'll never beat it
Baby that's love

CHORUS:
Even as I sing this song,
My world's gone topsy turvy
As the notes dip and soar
Sugar I think you're nervy

If you love me, you should claim me
Stop pretending and never blame me
Baby don't you love me?
Cupid stuck you and got you good
Straight through the clouds from above
As if you could doubt it and why wouldja
(You big lug)
Baby that's love

REPEAT CHORUS

1

CHRISTMAS EVE 1932

Feroce

(Fierce)

Saverio Armandonada warmed his hands underneath the tin lunch pail on his lap as he rode the trolley from the Chester Street stop to the River Rouge plant.

The brown wool gloves his mother had knit for his sixteenth birthday and given him the week before were unlined, so the heat from the pasty, hot from her oven, wrapped in a cloth and tucked inside, was enough to keep his hands warm until he made the transfer to the flatbed truck that would take him to his place on the assembly line.

The trolley rumbled through the snowy streets of south Detroit in the blue darkness before sunrise, making local stops until every car was filled to standing room with the men who made automobiles for Henry Ford.

In the morning, the trolley cars held the clean scents of borax, castile soap, and bleach. The men's denim trousers, flannel shirts, undergarments, socks, canvas coveralls, and work aprons had been scrubbed and pressed by their wives or mothers at home or by the laundress in the boardinghouse. On the return trip, the trolley would smell like a locker room.

The mood was as solemn as high mass upon departure, but after a ten-hour day, the cars would explode in a kind of revelry, as the air filled with laughter and banter that cut through a thick haze of smoke puffed from hand-rolled cigarettes and nickel cigars.

Saverio was a relatively new hire at the Ford plant. However, after nearly a year on the job, the kid was well on his way to being savvy. He could sort the tile makers from the steel cutters, the parts men from the iron ore miners, and the dockworkers from the electricians.

A stoop in the posture gave away the men who stoked the coke ovens, hands stained by black metal filaments told the story of a tool and die man, while the glassmakers wore the mark of their craft on their faces with a permanent wrinkle etched on their foreheads where the rubber rim of the goggles hugged their skin. Saverio knew that particular mark well. His father, Leone, had been a glassmaker at Rouge since 1915.

If Saverio could match the job to the man by his appearance, he could also identify their skill sets by country. German immigrants assembled engines, while Yugoslavians had an affinity for installing them. Italians leaned toward woodworking and glassworks and, along with the Czechs, tool and die. The Poles handled steel bending, stoking the furnaces, and executing any operation with fire. Albanians worked the coke ovens, the Hungarians did heavy lifting, maintaining the conveyors and bridges. The Irish were adept at the installation of electrics, transmissions, and radiators. The Scots were perfectionists at hinging, soldering, and clipping.

Upholstery, floorboards, and running boards were the domain of the Finnish, Norwegians, and Swedes; the operation of the riverfront, including shipping, delivery, and boat launches, was handled by the Greeks. The Turks and Lebanese tailored ragtops and small-scale interior installations. Black men from the heart of the city worked in the cyanide foundry and maintained and operated the railways within the Rouge campus, an extensive system that had sixteen locomotives and one hundred miles of track. Incoming trains delivered coal and iron ore for making steel, while outgoing trains transported the finished vehicles out into the world to be sold.

Mayflower Americans of English descent were management. The men who worked the line called them *college boys* no matter how many decades had passed since their bosses had sat in a classroom. One hundred thousand men entered the iron gates of the River Rouge campus every morning, six days a week for workmen, five for management.

The gates rolled open as the lead trolley, carrying laborers including Leone and Saverio, pulled inside, followed by the caravan behind it. As a whistle blew, the trolley doors parted on the platform and men poured out of them, hastily crossed to the other side, and jammed onto open flatbed trucks to be shuttled to their stations.

Leone was the next to the last man to leap off the platform and onto the ramp of a crowded flatbed truck. Saverio's father had the strong, broad shoulders of a finisher, and the brute strength to lift a car carriage without assistance. Leone turned and lifted his son effortlessly from the throng on the platform into the flatbed truck as though his son were a sack of apples.

"You wait," Leone said to the remaining men on the platform, before he hoisted the grill shut and flipped the latch, closing off the full car to further riders. The workers who remained behind grumbled, though not one dared defy Leone directly.

Saverio was embarrassed that his father had favored him, making room for his son over the others. After all, when an operator reached his station, he punched his time card, and once he was on the clock, Mr. Ford was obliged to pay him. Every minute mattered.

As the open cattle car lumbered slowly toward the plant, it hit a pothole, jostling the men. Saverio gripped the grill to steady himself. He was not at ease with the factory life. Sometimes he struggled with the competitive nature of the place, the fight to get where he was going, the incessant grind of the workload. He wasn't comfortable in crowds, or hustling to grab a better position in line in order to seize a better opportunity for himself over another fellow. He wondered if he ever would. Being part of a pack did not come naturally to him.

Gusts of freezing cold wind blew off the river and swirled around them as snow began to fall. Saverio looked up at the thick white clouds as the bright red sun pushed through the folds at daybreak. The colors of the sky reminded him of his mother's *ciambella*, fluffy Italian biscuits doused in a compote of fresh Michigan cherries soaked in sugar, which made him long for the warmth of summer.

The cattle car stopped at the loading dock of the glassworks. As the men filed off, Leone dug into his lunch pail, removed a bundle of small ginger cookies his wife had placed there, and tucked them into Saverio's pail before jumping off the ramp. Leone did not say goodbye to his only child, and the son did not wish his father a good day.

Saverio watched his father walk through the doors, gently

swinging his tin pail like a lantern. It was a carefree gesture from
a man who rarely was.

The snow came down hard by midmorning, melting instantly
into silver rivulets as it hit the glass ceiling of the plant, warmed
by the intense heat of the electrics below. Overhead, through the
glass, the white sky illuminated the machinations of the assembly
line inside in crystalline clarity. Saverio quickly mopped his brow
with the red bandana his mother had pressed and placed in his
pocket.

Saverio stood on the line, without bending, turning, arching his
back, or lifting his shoulders to do his job. He bolted the driver's-side
door handle onto a 1932 Ford Model V8 at waist level as it passed
before him on the conveyor.

There was no time to marvel at the machine itself, though it
was a beauty. The carriage, molded of Michigan steel, was painted
midnight blue. The black leather interior with its curved seat
and covered buttons on the upholstery was, in his opinion, the
height of swank. He could see himself behind the wheel, wearing
a Homburg and a Chesterfield coat, driving the girl of his dreams
through the woods of Grosse Pointe.

Saverio's equipment, a Ford-designed wrench, was evenly
weighted, with a rubber-coated handle. The jaw was locked in
place, measured to the exact specifications of the bolt. He wore a
fingerless glove on his right hand to control the tool's movement.

The boy relied on the operator behind him to place the bolt and
ring. He attached his wrench on the bolt and, with one smooth
motion, spun the wrench around it until he felt the click that
meant the bolt had fastened. By the time Saverio lifted the wrench
off the locked bolt, he was ready to attach the tool to the bolt on

the next car, and so it went, bolt by bolt, minute by minute, hour by hour, 978 cars a day, ten hours a day, six days a week.

His operation seemed simple to him now, but at first the line had terrified him. During his first week on the job, Saverio remembered that he had been secretly thrilled each time the conveyor stopped, overwhelmed by his role and certain he couldn't keep up. There were taunts and jeers from the other men whenever an operator made a mistake. But soon, with determination and pluck, he had mastered the technique of the wrench, and now he resented any glitches on the conveyor, or any work stops for any reason whatsoever. He was on the line to do the job and do it well.

The operators took lunch in the break room filled with rows of picnic-style tables topped with smooth aluminum. Saverio squeezed in at the end of a bench next to the finishers. It always felt good to sit for the thirty-minute lunch break. He laid out the contents of his lunch pail: the pasty, ginger cookies, a thermos of hot cider, and, surprise, a fresh apple turnover.

He bit into the pasty. The crust was soft, and the filling was hearty, finely chopped rump roast with slivers of buttery onions, diced carrots, and minced potatoes, cooked until it was tender. He chewed slowly, savoring his mother's cooking, because he was hungry, and whenever he rushed a meal, it never satisfied.

As he sipped the warm cider, he observed a group of men gathered around an old Lebanese peddler at the next table. During the holidays, the management allowed peddlers to come through and sell their wares during the breaks. Saverio had purchased a linen handkerchief set for his mother the week before from a nice Romanian couple. He'd also bought his father a new pipe and a bag of Blackjack tobacco from a peddler out of Lexington, Kentucky.

"What's he selling?" Saverio asked the man next to him.

"Gold. You got a girl?"

"I don't have her yet," Saverio admitted.

"You will if you buy her something."

Finished with his lunch, Saverio wiped his mouth, folded the cloth, and placed it back in the pail before stacking it on the shelf with the others. He joined the men as they examined all manner of gold jewelry displayed in a black leather case that folded out flat like a chessboard.

Delicate gold chains shimmered in neat rows on flat velvet pads. There were various styles of links: some loose like lace, others hammered like the rim of a chalice, another with fragile intersecting circles like the chain between the beads on his mother's rosary. Smooth wooden dowels were stacked with rings. The peddler offered a variety of polished gold bands for brides and grooms, and other kinds, fancy rings that sparkled with jewels set in glittering filigree, all kinds of small agates, shiny gemstones in ovals, squares, and chips. It was a gypsy's treasure trove, but there were elegant selections, too.

In the center of the board, in the first box lined in black velvet, was a platinum ring with a circle of bright-blue sapphires. The light danced upon the blue like the sun on the tips of the waves on Lake Huron. Next to it was another eye-popping ring, sea-green emeralds clustered on a chiseled band. The third made Saverio long to have been born a prince. A dazzling ring in the shape of a heart made of pavé diamond chips seemed to catch every bit of light in the room.

"You like the heart?" the peddler asked him.

Saverio liked it very much. He was mesmerized by the simplicity of the shape and the sparkle of the stones. "If I worked here a thousand years I couldn't afford it."

"You're right. So. A pin for your mother?"

"I don't think so."

"So you're looking for someone else." He grinned. "Your girl?"

"Yes." Saverio sighed. "For my girl." Saverio felt guilty claiming a young woman who wasn't his yet, but maybe if he admitted his feelings, they would somehow make them true, and Cheryl Dombroski would be his at long last.

"What does she like?"

Saverio tried to think because he didn't know. Cheryl was the most beautiful girl he had ever seen, and had the most glorious soprano voice in the choir at the Church of the Holy Family. She was seventeen, the second eldest in a big Polish Catholic family. Her father was an electrician. Her brothers played football. She had auburn hair, a long neck, and blue eyes that were the exact color of the sapphires in the case.

"If she's blond, yellow-gold," said the peddler. "Brunette: platinum. Italian girls like all manners of gold, yellow or white gold as long as it's not plate."

"I don't think I have enough money for anything you're selling, sir."

The older men looked at one another and laughed.

"Abel will work with you," a man around his father's age assured him.

"You will?" Saverio looked at Abel, who nodded in agreement.

"How much do you have?"

"I can spend three dollars," Saverio said firmly.

"Five will get you this." Abel lifted a delicate gold chain that sparkled when it twisted in the light, like one of Cheryl's curls.

"Take it," another man advised. "Do you have another? For my daughter."

Abel nodded. "I do. Gold is the best gift you can bestow upon a young lady. It tells her that she is valued, treasured, cherished," he singsonged as he boxed the chain in velvet. The man gave the peddler a five-dollar bill before tucking the box into his pocket.

"I'll take one too." Saverio pulled his money clip from his back pocket.

Abel held a different gold chain up to the light. "Eighteen-karat gold. From the mountains of Lebanon, where I was born. This gold crossed two continents and an ocean to find its way to you. It has properties." Abel took Saverio's money before placing the necklace in a box. "Do you understand what I mean by that?"

"Nope," Saverio admitted.

"It means that this chain isn't just made of the earth's most precious metal. It means that it has powers. It will bring you and the young lady that wears it happiness. Are you pleased?"

"If she's pleased, then I'm happy."

The peddler grinned. "Everything on the earth that was ever made by man was created to impress a woman."

"Everything?"

"All of it. Every work of art, jewel, song, poem, or painting."

"Diego Rivera didn't impress anyone but Edsel Ford when he painted the murals," Saverio countered.

"Mr. Ford may have hired him to create the murals, but Rivera wasn't thinking of his benefactor when he went to work. There was a woman on his mind every time he dipped the brush in paint. You see, no statue, bridge, or building constructed of stone or automobile made of steel was ever built to glorify man. No, it was built to show a woman what a man could do. Never forget that man was born to serve her. If you remember this and trust this wisdom, you will live and die a happy man."

"I just want to get through Christmas," Saverio said before

tucking the velvet box deep into the utility pocket of his work pants. But he had to wonder, as he made his way back to the line, how the old man knew he saw Cheryl Dombroski sitting in the carriage of every car he bolted.

"Hey, Piccolo," a workman shouted from the back of the trolley— "little one," the workers' nickname for Saverio. "Sing something."

Saverio acknowledged the request, but declined. "I gotta save my voice for midnight mass."

"Some of us ain't making it to church," a steel cutter from Building 3 admitted. "Some of us have a card game tonight. So sing, boy."

"Hush, boys. Leone's kid is gonna make some noise," another hollered.

"Quiet! Shut up!" The tile maker banged his lunch pail on the trolley pole until the car full of men came to attention. "Go ahead, Pic."

Leone Armandonada closed his eyes and leaned against the back wall of the trolley. He was used to his son performing in public. The boy had a voice like velvet, and whether it was a wedding, funeral, or trolley ride, someone always wanted to hear Saverio sing. The men settled down. The clack of the wheels against the track and the intermittent wheeze of the wood as the men shifted their weight in the swaying trolley car gave Saverio all the accompaniment he needed.

The Italian boy closed his eyes and began to sing *Silent Night*.

As his son sang the old Christmas carol, Leone removed his hat and ran his hand through the thinning scruff of black hair that remained on his head, keeping his eyes on the floorboards.

Saverio gripped the center pole of the trolley car to maintain his balance, but from the point of view of the men, it looked like a microphone stand in any fine nightclub. The men of Rouge who had heard him sing believed Saverio had the comportment and talent of any lead act they'd heard on *Sing Out*, the most popular radio show in Detroit.

As Saverio serenaded them, they listened with quiet reverence. As the words sailed over them, especially the phrase *redeeming grace*, they were soothed. Saverio modulated his performance to match the dips and curves of the trolley tracks, feeling the rhythm through his feet. As he held the final note on *peace*, he sustained his breath, holding the note to a delicate fade, as if it had been recorded on vinyl. The close was so clean, it was as though it had been sliced in the air with a knife.

The men gave him a hearty round of applause with whistles and foot stomps, rocking the trolley car back and forth on the tracks.

"Another one!" one of the men shouted.

Saverio looked at his father.

"No," Leone said definitively. "He is done."

"We can pass a hat, Leone, if that's what's irking you."

The men laughed heartily.

"Keep your hat," Leone joked. "And your pennies."

Saverio practically sprinted from his home to Holy Family Church on Christmas Eve. His clean hair was still wet under his cap, and his face stung where he had splashed lemon water on his cheeks after shaving. There was no need for him to shave twice in one day, but he wanted to look sharp for Cheryl.

At the corner of Denton, a black DeSoto was parked with the back door propped open. A short line had formed and was moving quickly. Saverio poked his head into the back seat, which was filled with wooden crates of fragrant oranges.

"How much?" he asked the fruit man.

"Fifteen for a quarter."

"I'll take fifteen."

Saverio grabbed the brown paper sack and climbed the steps of Holy Family Church two at a time. He patted the pocket of his good trousers to make sure the box with the gold chain was safe. There was no greater feeling in all the world than knowing he was about to impress a girl he was nuts about and make her happy.

As he entered the church, he blessed himself with the holy water and genuflected. The gray marble walls streaked with striae of gold were festooned with garlands of fresh myrtle and evergreen. The main aisle was lit by a series of long candles topped with open brass caps that anchored the flames. The altar was dressed in white linens, lit by a row of shimmering votives in crystal holders. A crèche, with handpainted figurines of the Holy Family, tucked under the altar, was also lit by candlelight. Behind the tabernacle, the wall was lined with fresh, fragrant blue spruce trees whose tips grazed the ceiling. The branches were decorated with small white pouches of tulle filled with red berries and tied with lace. The scene was breathtaking.

Saverio wanted to remember every detail of this night, no matter how small. It wasn't every night of the week that he told a girl he loved her, and there would only be one first time. His heart was so full, he could not imagine space within it for anyone else. Cheryl was all he ever wanted, all he ever would.

As he climbed the steps to the choir loft, he rehearsed what he had planned to say to Cheryl before he gave her the necklace. He had gone over what he wanted to say to her so many times, on the line at the Rouge plant and on the trolley ride, he had practically memorized his speech.

Cheryl, we've sung in the choir together since the Christmas we were eleven, and the truth is, I've loved you since then. You were wearing a red corduroy jumper and white blouse. You said your shoes hurt because your older sister had worn them first for a year or two and her feet were smaller than yours but it didn't matter, the younger sister always wore the hand-me-downs. Well, you don't deserve hand-me-downs, you deserve the best and everything new and every wonderful thing that's just for you and just your own. So, I want you to have this gold chain because gold represents the most precious feelings, and you are to me a treasure more valuable than gold, but gold is the best the world makes, and I wanted you to have the best. Merry Christmas.

Saverio wanted the privilege of walking Cheryl home from choir practice and from school. He wanted to be the only boy who held her hand and kissed her. He wanted her to wait for him by the bus stop on Euclid, like all the girls who went steady with all the guys from his school.

Saverio wished he could sing these sentiments to Cheryl, but that wasn't possible. There wasn't a song written that really expressed what he was feeling, and besides, even if there was, he longed to tell her so there would be no mistaking his intent. When he reached the top of the steps to the choir loft, the singers were mostly in position. He scanned the benches. Cheryl had not yet arrived, so Saverio began handing out the oranges to the choir members.

"Merry Christmas, Constance."

"I'll save it for Christmas morning." She palmed the orange like a snowball.

"*Buon Natale*, Raphael."

"*Buon Natale*, Saverio. Citrus is good for the pipes."

"Merry Christmas, Beatrice."

"Thank you!" She tucked it into her purse.

"Merry Christmas, Mary. Not a lot of girls have a holiday named for them."

"Merry Christmas!" She shoved it into her coat pocket.

"Merry Christmas, Robert."

"Thanks." And so it went, to Kevin, Kimberly, Agnes, Sarah, Philip, Ellen, Eileen, Patty, Eleanor, and Rose, with one to the organist, until only two oranges remained in the sack.

Saverio took his seat in the first row of benches and picked up his sheet music. He perused it mindlessly, having memorized his parts, until the musical notes began to jump around on the paper like ladybugs. He didn't think he was nervous, but now that he was here, and the necklace was tucked in his pocket, he was afraid.

Fear.

There was no room in his heart for it, but here it was, overtaking his feelings of love. Soon the sister of fear, unworthiness, crept into his thoughts, and he began to question whether he should admit his feelings to Cheryl at all.

What did he have to offer a girl, anyway? Not much, he didn't think. He was average in every way, a kind of a loner, not too much of one that it made him an oddball, but enough of one that it was obvious he might be a little backward, maybe sheltered too much by his mother. That's what they said about only children, he guessed. But if a girl loved him as he loved her, if Cheryl returned his feelings, he knew how to make her happy. He would work hard to give her everything she wanted. His wife would have a nice house with all the modern conveniences. There would be an Electrolux vacuum cleaner and Oriental rugs with fringes to use it on and an *Encyclopedia Britannica* set in red leather bindings on the bookshelf in the living room. There would be a bed with a sheer curtain over it, and a matching coverlet with ruffles. There would be a proper bathroom with a four-legged tub, a sink with a mirror with lights all around it. They would drive a Ford V8 coupe, of course, though if he could choose the car of his dreams, he would rather have a Packard out of South Bend, Indiana. But it didn't matter; as long as she was by his side, he would drive anywhere, in any vehicle, no matter how far, to prove his love to his bride someday, the girl who would become Cheryl Armandonada.

Cheryl.

A name that sounded at once like a sweet summer fruit and a soft, silky fabric. He would buy her every outfit in Norma Born's Dress Shop window. She would have gloves to match every purse that matched every hat. Her stockings would be silk, and her hair would be done in a salon once a week. His girl would have all the things his own mother didn't, because he would pay attention to her desires and make good on her needs. He knew, just from observing, that girls like to talk, and if that was the case, the least he could do was listen, and care about whatever it was she needed to say.

Saverio knew exactly what kind of man he wanted to be, and what kind of husband that man would become. The gold chain was the rope that he would climb to win her, the first gift of many. Eventually he would fill a jewelry box for Cheryl, stuffed with more rings, necklaces, and bracelets than the peddler sold.

Cheryl Dombroski appeared at the top of the choir loft stairs at last. She did not make a sound, but announced her arrival by the delicious scent of her perfume. She waved at the choir with one of those short choppy waves and a smile so broad and full, it looked like it hurt. Saverio sighed; she was in a good mood, which meant it was an opportune time for talking to her—well, to any girl.

Cheryl was wearing a short green velvet jacket over a pale blue chemise that had a thin belt. The dress was piped in mint green, and the buttons were green jewels of some kind. Her gloves were pale blue, as was her hat, a cloche of off-white satin. Her auburn hair was clipped back under the hat in long, loose waves. Her eyes were so blue it was as if the roof of the church had blown off, and he were looking at nothing but sky.

"You look beautiful," Saverio told her when she sat down beside him. She smelled so good, like roses and lilies and sweet lemons.

Constance, an alto, leaned down, placing her head between them. "Saverio gave us all oranges," she told Cheryl. Constance smelled like a menthol cough drop.

"I have one for you, too." Saverio fished in the paper bag. "Here." He gave Cheryl an orange.

"You're sweet." Cheryl leaned so close to his ear to thank him, he could feel her breath. The nearness of her lips to his made his heart pound. He felt himself throwing heat.

"You all right?" she asked. "There's something going around. My sister Karol hasn't stopped hacking since Tuesday."

"Sorry to hear that. No, I'm fine."

"I have news," she said as she thumbed through the music.

"You do?"

"Come here. I want you to be the first to know."

Cheryl stood, taking Saverio's arm, and led him to the lip of the choir loft. The pews were filled for mass. It was close to standing room only.

"See him?" Cheryl pointed.

Saverio saw a young man from the back, in a gray Chesterfield coat. The fellow sensed the stare and turned around. He winked at Cheryl. He had blond hair and broad shoulders. She waved at him in that choppy way she had greeted the choir when she ascended the stairs.

"That's him. Ricky Tranowski."

"Yeah?" Saverio was confused.

Cheryl removed her glove and showed Saverio her left hand. "We got engaged tonight."

"Engaged?" Saverio's mouth was dry.

Cheryl wore a gold ring, with a diamond the size of the dot of the letter *i* in the word *diamond*. The smidge of a chip was elevated on four prongs. Four too many, Saverio thought. Cheryl straightened the ring with her right hand.

"I don't understand," Saverio said softly.

"When I was born, the Tranowskis and the Dombroskis would joke, Ricky is for Cheryl and Cheryl is for Ricky. Well, we see them every summer in Traverse City and every Thanksgiving in Dearborn, and this year something just clicked."

"Clicked?" Saverio was hopeless.

"Yeah. You know." Cheryl smiled, every white tooth in her lovely head gleaming as she silently snapped her fingers. "Clicked."

Finally Saverio got it. "I understand." He couldn't look at her, so he stared ahead, steadying his gaze on the empty crib in the crèche underneath the altar.

"I can't wait to get out of here. Ricky got a job at the Packard plant in South Bend."

"Packard?" Saverio's heart sank.

"I know! Your favorite car! I didn't know this, but Ricky told me when you work the line at Packard, you can get on a list to buy one at a discount. I want a Packard more than I want to breathe."

"Everybody wants a Packard."

"I know. It's a dream!" Cheryl squeezed Saverio's hand.

"Congratulations." Saverio felt his heart ache.

"Are you okay, Saverio? I really think you might be sick."

"I could be."

"I'm sorry. Should I send my brother for some Brioschi?"

"No, I'll be all right. I just need to sit down."

Saverio went back to his place on the bench. Cheryl sat down beside him. "We don't have to duet. I can sing with Constance, you know. You look green. You can lie down in the robing room until you feel better. That's where Father naps between masses."

"Cheryl, I need to tell you something."

"Sure."

He looked at her. She was as luminous in the pink-gold light of the organ as she was in his dreams, but now she would never be his. He knew for certain that no man could ever love her as much as he did, but he didn't know exactly how to say it, and the words he had gone over and over in his mind to say to her that evening were moot, and now that she wore another man's ring, they bordered on something akin to bank robbery. Saverio couldn't very well claim someone who was no longer available to him. But he had to say something before the moment came when she would no longer listen, so he blurted, "I think you deserve a better ring."

She sat back and thought for a moment. "That's a terrible thing to say to a girl."

"If I had to go down in the mine myself and dig until my hands bled, I would find a diamond worthy of you. And it's not that one."

"I don't care about the ring," she said defiantly as she twisted it on her finger.

"You should."

"Why are you saying this? Why are you trying to ruin my night?"

"I don't want to ruin anything for you."

"You certainly are! You certainly have."

"I'm sorry. I'm not saying these things to hurt you, but to make you think about what you deserve. Once you're married, Cheryl, that's it. Forever and ever. You and whatever lug you choose."

"I choose Ricky. And he's not a lug." Her blue eyes darted around furtively. "He's a good boy."

"I accept that," Saverio promised.

"It doesn't sound like you do." Cheryl began to fan herself with the sheet music to *O Holy Night*.

"A woman can only go by signs," Saverio said. "And that ring is not enough for a girl as wonderful as you. Now, maybe tonight you think it's enough, because you're caught up in the excitement of the proposal, but there will come a day when that diamond won't cut it, and you'll remember what I said tonight, and you'll think, I should've listened to Saverio."

"You don't know me at all," Cheryl whispered. "I don't care about things."

"We'll see. And I do know you. I've known you all your life, and you've known me."

"I mean in *that* way." Cheryl looked ahead.

"I wanted to know you better." Saverio felt emboldened, maybe because Cheryl could not look at him. So he said, "I wanted to be more than a friend. I had hopes."

Cheryl clenched her jaw. "Why did you wait so long to confess your heart's desire?"

"I'm a slow burn, I guess—an idiot. I should've known that the most beautiful rose in the garden goes first."

"Well, it wasn't to be." Cheryl folded her hands on her lap like Sister Domenica after she passed out report cards.

"So you never thought of me that way?"

Cheryl Dombroski had just gone to confession. She was a good Catholic girl, and it was Christmas Eve. She wasn't about to lie. "Sometimes," she admitted.

"But not like Ronnie."

"Ricky."

"Ricky. Not like him?"

"I can't have this conversation with you, Saverio. I'm an engaged woman."

Cheryl announced her status in the same way she might admit that she was a Democrat, a Salvation Army volunteer, or had type O blood if queried on a survey. She was resolute. Saverio did not believe her, but he could not convince her otherwise either. If he knew one thing about Polish girls, it was that they were stronger than the liquid steel poured at the Rouge plant to make cars.

He also knew that it didn't make much sense to stand on an assembly line and bolt cars for the rest of his natural life if there wasn't a girl like Cheryl waiting outside the gates for him. What would be the point? There had to be a greater purpose to his life. He needed an incentive to get up before the sun, and the only one that mattered was love. He didn't get excited on payday like the other fellows. Money in his pocket didn't fill him up.

What was Saverio's purpose anyway? What was he working for if not to make a girl happy? He couldn't imagine choosing anything less than a ring that sparkled like the stars in Orion for the girl of *his* dreams. Cheryl would have received the pavé heart set in platinum had he asked her to marry *him*.

Despite the heaviness in his chest, Saverio stood and sang the mass with the choir as he had done every Sunday, Holy Day of Obligation, and funeral since he could remember. It almost felt good to sing, to put his feelings out into the church instead of holding them inside.

When it came time to duet *Silent Night* with Cheryl during the offertory, the trill of her soprano looped around the full-bodied sound of his tenor like a twining vine. He could not look at her as they harmonized, and she kept her eyes on the altar.

Feelings expressed to the object of a young man's affection should free him of the weight of the secret, but when those feelings are not reciprocated, it turns a world of wonder into an awkward place. Saverio vowed that Christmas Eve that he would never admit romantic feelings to a girl ever again. It was too dangerous. It also meant the ultimate sacrifice: no more gazing at Cheryl. No more studying every aspect of her, from the curves of her breasts to the cut of her small waist to the smooth swerve of her hips to her ankles, all the way back up to the arc of her straight nose.

Cheryl was an architectural wonder all right. Tonight would be the end of their conversations and their long walks home. No more intense discussions about their mutual passion, swing music: Dick Haymes versus Bing Crosby, and Duke Ellington versus Cab Calloway versus The Dorsey Brothers. No more rehearsals in the cold choir loft on Wednesday nights, complaining that Father wouldn't turn the heat on for them. No more looking forward and hoping.

Saverio went to the railing of the loft and took a solo with *O Holy Night*. He poured his pain into the hymn, knowing that there was no other place for it on Christmas Eve. Music had always been a respite for him. Singing comforted him; it was a way to release emotions he held, and feelings he needed to express. When he hit the notes in the bridge of the song, his voice released in a fuller tone, more powerful and assured than the parishioners had heard before. He held the note *a cappella* as the organist poised her fingers above the keys of the organ, and waited for him to breathe. When he did, he sang the final phrasing as she gently pressed the keys. The lyric *divine* hung over the congregation like a lace canopy as Saverio held the note.

After he finished, the organist lifted her feet off the pedals and her hands off the keys. There was silence followed by a restlessness in the congregation.

Constance leaned forward as Saverio returned to his seat on the bench with the choir. "They want to applaud," she whispered. "In church." Her hot breath made his neck itch, but he nodded in gratitude.

Saverio barely felt the congratulatory pats on the back from his fellow choir members. His mind was elsewhere. He had hit the high note deftly, as though he had snatched it out of midair like a butterfly and held it tenderly by its fragile vibrato wings as it fluttered. He sang in hopes of getting Cheryl's attention and winning her with his technique. But she hadn't been listening, it seemed. Her focus was elsewhere, on the congregation below, on her fiancé in the Chesterfield coat.

There was one orange left in the paper sack at the end of midnight mass. Saverio remained in the choir loft alone, peeled the orange, dropped the shards of skin into the open paper bag as he watched Cheryl and Ricky (who would soon be driving a Packard) light candles and genuflect at the Shrine of the Immaculate Conception in the alcove beside the main altar before they turned, arm in arm, walked down the center aisle, out of the church and out of his life.

With his feet propped on the organ bench, Saverio leaned back in his seat and ate the sections of the sweet orange one by one as the last of the congregation emptied out into the cold night. He planned to hide until the church was empty.

"Hey, are you Saverio?" A man around thirty with a mustache, wearing a navy wool dress coat, stood at the top of the choir-loft steps. "Don't let me interrupt you and that tasty orange, brother."

Saverio swallowed. "Brother?"

"Just an expression. You're the kid who sang?" The man spun his hat on his fist with his free hand.

"Yes."

"The solo. You blasted the C?"

"That was me." Saverio blushed.

"You can sing, my friend. I'm Sammy Prezza. I play sax with the Rod Roccaraso Orchestra. You heard of him?"

Saverio sat up on the bench. "I've heard him on the radio."

"Pretty good, right?"

"I like him fine."

"Well, our singer fell out, and Rod is looking for a new sound. I think he'd like you. There's a little quartet he uses that's all right, but the plum is the singing gig. Fronting the band. I wouldn't set my heart on that, but the quartet is always on the spin. Here." Sammy handed his card to Saverio. "We're playing East Lansing on New Year's Eve. This card will get you in. And I'll get you to Rod."

"And then what?"

"Sing for Rod and see where it goes."

"Thanks." Saverio looked at the card with a gold embossed treble clef and black letters. It looked swell.

"How old are you?" Sammy asked.

"How old do I look?" Saverio shot back.

"Good answer." Sammy turned back before going down the steps. "No kidding, you got pipes."

Rosaria Armandonada laced her arm through her son's as they walked home from midnight mass. "You sang so beautifully," she marveled. "The people were crying. I was crying."

"I don't want to make people cry when I sing, Ma."

"No, no, that's good. They're feeling something." She squeezed his hand.

"I want to make them happy."

"You do. Even when they're weeping."

"How can somebody be happy when they're crying?"

"They think about their memories. What they miss, who they miss. That's better than all the silly music on the radio."

"Not better. Just different."

As they turned the corner onto Boatwright, the scent of roasted chestnuts wafted through the air. They looked at one another. Saverio grinned. "Pop."

Leone stood in the front yard of their house, roasting chestnuts in a heavy iron skillet over a fire he had made in a small pit in the frozen ground.

"Leone, you should've heard your son sing in church tonight."

"I heard him sing plenty."

"Tonight, though, he sounded like an angel. He had power. It was pure."

"I guess I made some folks cry."

"I can make them cry when I sing too," Leone joked as he gave his wife a copper bowl filled with hot chestnuts, their black shells split open, spitting fragrant steam into the cold air.

"I'll make a syrup and dress them." Rosaria went inside as Saverio helped his father put out the fire.

Leone used a trowel to throw ash over the flames. Saverio knelt down and made a mound of snow into a large ball. He handed it to his father, who placed it on the ash. Soon the flames sputtered to curls of gray smoke.

"Pop, a man came up to me after mass."

"For what?"

"Wants me to audition for a band."

"To do what?"

"To sing. I'll play a little mandolin, maybe." Saverio knew the mandolin held a special place in his father's heart. He'd played the instrument himself when he was a boy in Italy, and had taught his son how to play.

Leone was unmoved. "You're a bolter at Rouge."

"I know. But I could sing at night. Make a little extra money maybe."

"You can't do both."

"Why not?"

"You can't. That life is no life for you."

"Those guys do really well. They make money entertaining people. If I got good, I bet I could double my salary."

"It's a crazy scheme. Don't fall for it."

Saverio followed his father into the house. "It's all for real. They want to pay me."

"They tell you they pay you, you go on the road, they no pay you. I hear stories of show business. It's for gypsies. You work, the boss keeps all the money. You starve. He gets fat and he gets show-girls and you get nothing."

"That's not how it works."

"What do you know?"

"Because a man from the Rod Roccaraso Orchestra was at mass. He made it his business to talk to me. He sought me out. He said I had talent. He said I could make it in the music business."

Saverio followed his father into the kitchen. Rosaria stirred the syrup on the stove. She turned off the burner and ladled the hot syrup over the meat of the shelled chestnuts.

"His business is not your business. We don't know this man. Who is he anyway? What does he really want with you?" Leone raised his voice.

"Leone, just listen to him."

"Shuddup, Rosaria."

She turned back to the stove and stirred the large pot of mari-nara sauce simmering on a burner.

"Don't talk to her that way," Saverio said quietly.

Leone banged the table. The son had tripped the switch of his father's rage, and he immediately regretted it.

"You mind your own business." Leone hit the table again. "This is my house."

"It's all yours, Papa. But you don't have to tell Mama to shut up. This argument is between you and me."

"It's fine," Rosaria insisted.

"It's Christmas Eve," the boy said wearily, knowing that his father spoiled for a fight, no matter the occasion.

"You lose your job at Rouge, that's it. They never take you back." Leone raised his voice. "Men come from Missouri, Kentucky, Chicago—from every country with their sons, and some have many, many sons to work at Rouge. They take any job. Cyanide foundry, they don't care. Any job. You have a good job on the line, and you no want it. Only a stupid boy gives up a good position on the line."

"I have other things I want to do. Maybe try something else. I don't know."

"Life is not what you want to do. It's what you have to do."

"Why can't it be both?"

"It can," Rosaria said.

"I told you to stay out of it," Leone warned his wife before turning to his son. "You know what I had to do to get you a job at the plant? They have lists of names. I told them you would be good, better than me."

"But I'm not you."

"You have everything easy. You are a mama's boy."

"Okay, Pop." Saverio surrendered. His father was furious, and whenever it got to this point, it would be bad for the son and worse for his mother.

"Saverio has a talent! I want to see him use it," Rosaria said quietly.

"How do you know talent?"

"I know my son."

"You know nothing!" Leone thundered. He stood abruptly, flipping the straight-backed chair onto the floor, where it made a cracking sound, and shattered.

Rosaria and Saverio rushed to pick up the pieces. They cleaned up the rungs and back of the chair efficiently; this wasn't the first time something had been ruined by Leone. Rosaria left the kitchen. She carried the broken wood in her arms like kindling.

Saverio stood quietly by the sink as his father poured himself a drink at the kitchen table. It was this way every holiday, and lots of Sundays. Leone's temper would flare over nothing, and soon he would be in a rage, his mother would leave, and the house would be silent but never serene.

The scent of the gravy bubbling on the stove became pungent: the garlic, tomatoes, and basil were cooked thoroughly. Saverio turned off the burner, picked up the moppeens, lifted the pot of sauce off the burner, and placed it off to the side while his father lit a cigarette. Saverio stirred the sauce slowly. He thought about how best to talk to his father. "Ma got her hair done."

"So?"

"You didn't notice."

"So what?"

"When a woman does her hair, it's not for her, it's for you. She looks nice. You should tell her. She'd like that."

Leone puffed on his cigarette. "Never tell your father what to do."

"I'm making a suggestion."

"You no suggest."

"Okay."

"You watch the way you talk to me."

"Okay, I will. If you'll talk nicer to Ma."

Leone waved his son off with his cigarette. "I don't make bargains with my son."

"I'm not always going to be here to talk to her. You and Ma will be alone someday, and you'll have to converse. Talk to her nice. Like I do. Like Mrs. Farino does at the market. Like Mrs. Ruggiero does at the butcher's. Like Father Impeciato does at church."

"The priest always talks nice. He wants the *soldi*." Leone rubbed his fingers together, indicating the collection plate.

"Everybody in the world isn't after your money."

"That's what you think. And they after yours too."

"I'm going to leave here someday."

Leone laughed. "And go where?"

"I don't know."

"And do what?"

"I'm not sure," Saverio lied. He knew exactly what he wanted to do, but he thought it wise to keep it to himself.

"You waste your life."

"That's the thing about a life, Pop. You get one. You can work at the Rouge plant and save every penny and buy your girl a gold chain and the night you're going to give it to her, you find out she's gonna marry somebody else. So all those hours on the line, when you thought you were working for your dreams, to make a life with a pretty girl you're nuts for, you weren't, you were busting your ass for nothing but the sheer joy of locking a wrench on a bolt for Henry Ford."

"You got paid good money."

"Money's only worth something if you can spend it to make somebody else happy. That's what the peddler said, and I think he was right."

"A gypsy. You listen to a gypsy?"

"He seems pretty smart to me."

"Use your head. You need to eat. You have to buy food with something. What you don't grow in your garden, you have to buy."

"Necessities. I calculated them too. The freight on them only amounts to a couple of hours a day on the line in a week in the life of a man. What to do with the other eight? Where do those wages go? How are they spent?"

"The government."

"Some. And the rest?"

"You save it. Under your mattress. Never the bank. Because you don't know what's coming."

"I don't care about that. I wanted to see my paydays in gold around Cheryl Dombroski's perfect neck."

"She don't want you."

"No, she don't." Saverio was pained to admit it aloud.

"To hell with her then."

"Fair enough. If she loved me, I would have given her everything I had."

"You have the eyes of a fish for her." His father smiled.

"If I had a girl, I'd treat her good. That's why I give you hell, Pop. You got a girl. You should treat her good."

"You don't know nothing."

"I know a few things. I know when you love a girl and you don't show her, it's a sin."

"Agh." Leone waved his hand at his son to dismiss him.

"You don't know how lucky you are. Someday you will figure it out, and it will be too late."

Saverio left his father alone in the kitchen. On his way upstairs, he saw his mother in the living room, sitting by the radio. She was now forty, and there was barely any white in her black hair. She still had a fine figure and the face of a Venetian, with a strong nose and lovely brown eyes.

Rosaria had made the modest home as lovely as she could. The walls were painted a cheery yellow. The gray linoleum floor was waxed to a polished finish. She had sewn muslin curtains that, while plain, had a little flair, with ruffles gathered along their hems. The family Christmas tree was decorated with ornaments she had made herself, star-shaped spiderwebs of lace that hung from the branches artfully. Saverio noticed how hard his mother tried to bring some beauty into their lives.

"You okay, Ma?"

"Yeah, yeah." She waved her son off as her husband had.

"I'm sorry."

"I can't fix the chair," she said. "I don't think ten men could fix that chair. The wood is bad. It'll make good kindling."

"I'll buy you a new one."

"Save your money."

"I have, Ma. It's upstairs under the mattress. When I finally spent some money on something pretty, it didn't turn out so good."

"I'm sorry."

Saverio smiled. "Maybe next time." "I like the tree." Rosaria looked it up and down. "I'll be sad when Epiphany comes and I have to take it down."

"You did a nice job."

"Thank you, Sav."

"Did you buy me a hat?" Saverio picked up a large round box wrapped in brown paper from under the tree.

"You peeked!"

"Nope. It's the shape of the box."

"I didn't know how to wrap it."

"It's fine, Ma."

"I hope you like it."

"I need a hat."

"I know you do." She lowered her voice. "You can't go around in a wool cap and impress the bandleaders. I want you to audition for that orchestra."

"I'd like to, Ma."

"When you sing, you mean it."

"I believe the words," he admitted.

"That's what moves people."

Saverio sat down next to his mother. "Like *Sleep in heavenly peace*."

TONY'S WIFE   31

Rosaria put her arms around her son. "Written by someone who held a baby."

Saverio tried to pull away, but his mother tightened her embrace. "You'll always be my baby."

"Ma." He was embarrassed.

"I raised a good son. An artist. I want you to be one. You used to write poems. You could write songs, you know. Songs like that."

"I could try, I guess."

"You have to—you have to use your talent. It's a sin not to."

"I like singing in church."

"When the Peparetti family butchers the hog, Mrs. Peparetti always brings me a pork shoulder. And I like to make it in the pot with gravy. One year, she brought me the meat and it wouldn't fit in the pot. The bone was too big, too much for my old pot. There was no way to cook it. So I had to bring it back to her, or it would've been wasted. That's how I feel about you. You've outgrown the pot. The choir at Holy Family isn't enough for you. The festival in the summer in Dearborn, it's for amateurs. You need bigger, better, more."

"How will I know if I can do it?"

"That's the easy part. The people will let you know if they like you. And if they don't like you, you can always get a job back on the line."

"Have you talked to Pop about this?"

"No. It would hurt him. He doesn't see art, and he doesn't hear music. He's a responsible man."

"That's what you call him?"

"He's your father," Rosaria reminded him, though she didn't have to. Leone was the sun in their little solar system; there wasn't room for much more than them. "Papa is practical."

"Practical men don't dream."

"They do. But they're different dreams. His dream is to hold on to his job week after week, year after year. To get a raise once in a while. To have enough to pay the rent. To buy a coat when he needs it—or you do, or I do. His dreams are to provide the necessities of life. He grew up so poor, to him, food, clothing, and shelter, even at their minimum, are luxuries."

"So are children."

"What do you mean?" Rosaria asked.

"Ma, why just one? Why didn't you have more children?"

"I said, God, send me what you will. And he sent you to me, and that was that."

"I want eight children someday."

"Eight?" Rosaria beamed.

"I want a house full of noise and laughter and music and games and kids. It gets too quiet around here with just me. I want a big table and all the people I love around it. I want to be the father, the man in charge. I wouldn't be like him. I'd be happy with my lot. I wouldn't be miserable if I had a good wife, that's for sure. I'd want people around all the time. I want a family so big I can't keep up with them. I want to be like Mr. DeRea: when he calls for his children, he stutters because he can't remember all their names. I want to be that confused, that I can't remember who's who. I want Christmas to be loud. Everybody singing."

"That's how it was when I was a girl. But we celebrated the Epiphany, after Christmas. The Marasco family takes their time with Christmas. We sang the songs, had the mass on Christmas, and something special—a fig tart, a sweet. We didn't have much for presents."

"No presents?"

"We didn't have anything but each other."

"Was it enough?"

His mother thought for a moment. "I thought it was."

"Maybe that's why Pop is so unhappy. Maybe if he had more

children, he'd feel like the other men at Holy Family. You know, surrounded."

"You were enough for me. If God sent you to me and only you, you were enough. I couldn't have asked for more. Try and understand Papa. Your father left his home."

"That's not an excuse."

"It will help you understand him. Think about it. I taught him English. When I met him, I thought he was shy and sweet. I think I liked him so much at first because he seemed in awe of everything, and it made me think that meant he appreciated the world and people in ways that the Italians that were here already might take for granted."

"Ma, he takes you for granted."

"You let me worry about that."

Saverio stood. "I took the sauce off the stove and turned the burner off."

"You're a good one."

The boy kissed his mother on the cheek before going up the stairs.

Saverio hung his church clothes, his one good pair of wool pants and his white cotton shirt, in the closet. He pulled on his flannel pajama pants. Feeling a chill, he buttoned up the top and pulled a sweater on over it. He crawled into his twin bed and curled up his knees to his chest. He was going off to sleep when he heard a knock at the door.

His father stood in the doorway of his room, lit by the dim bulb in the hallway behind him. Leone looked as though he were in relief, light passing through him only to fall into shadow, a *chiaroscuro*.

"Pop?"

"You need to leave this house." Leone's voice was even. He wasn't angry—it was worse. He had made a decision. Yes, he had a bit to drink, it was the end of a long workweek, and he was exhausted, but there was no mistaking his command.

"What?" The boy sat up in the bed but kept the blanket around himself, as if a patch of wool could protect him from a man who wanted his only child banished from his home.

"You get out."

"What do you mean?"

"You don't like your job, it's not good enough. I no longer support you. You go out and find your own way."

Even with the sweater, the pajamas, and the blanket over him, Saverio began to shake. His teeth chattered. He knew his father, and his father meant what he said.

"But Pop . . ." Tears filled Saverio's eyes.

"Don't cry," his father commanded. "I was twelve years old when I left Italy. I don't cry. Not then. Not now. I had nothing. I made it here with no English, a few coins. Nothing. You have everything but you no grateful. Not to me. Not to God. Not your mother. You find out about life when you live it. You'll see."

"Do you want me to go now?"

"The morning," his father said. "You go. And you come back when you beg my forgiveness on your knees." He closed the door behind him.

Saverio got out of his bed. He stood frozen on that island of helplessness, where there is no one to come to your aid, and nowhere to turn. He did not know whether to move or stand still. He had to think, but he was numb.

He knew that it would be much worse in the morning. By then, his mother would intercede, and there would be a reprieve, perhaps, but soon, it would happen again. He and his father would argue, and he would throw him out of the house. Saverio didn't belong here. This was no longer his home, if it ever had been.

Saverio went to his closet and surveyed the contents. Two pairs of work pants. Two shirts. One pair of pants for good (church), one shirt for good (church), one suit jacket, a hand-me-down from his father, gray tweed with the wrong width of lapels, now woefully out of style, narrow ones. He hated wearing it and would leave the jacket behind. Shoes: one pair of work oxfords with rubber soles. He slipped his feet into them.

One pair of black leather lace-ups (for church) went into their cotton sleeves. One dress tie, black and white silk, striped. One black wool newsboy cap. No proper hat nor suit, vest, or jacket. Three pairs of white cotton undershorts, three white cotton undershirts, and three pairs of black wool socks. He pulled the olive-green canvas duffel that he used when he attended Holy Family School and carefully filled it with his clothes. He packed his rosary, a photograph of his mother, the book he won at the Dearborn festival, *The Three Taps* by Father Ronald Knox, along with the choir folder with the sheet music from church.

He sat on the edge of the bed and went through the contents of his billfold. In it, he had $17 and a River Rouge plant identification card. He pulled the envelope with his savings from under the mattress. His salary had been $25 a week at the Ford plant.

Saverio had spent $187 of his earnings to pay for half of the roof on his parents' home, the trolley rides to and from work, shoes and his work clothes (his Rouge apron and gloves), and of course, Christmas.

He tucked the box containing Cheryl's gold chain into the duffel before dressing. The dream of seeing her wear the necklace seemed like a hundred years ago. A desperate moment will bury a man more quickly than a happy one can save him.

He folded his only pair of pajamas neatly and placed them on top of the other clothes in the case before snapping it shut. He sat down and wrote his mother a letter.

DECEMBER 24, 1932

> *Dear Mama,*
> *Merry Christmas, my dear mother. Pop asked me to leave*
> *the house. I will write to you when I am settled. Don't*
> *worry about me. As you told me, don't worry, pray.*
>   *Love, Saverio*

Saverio made his bed and tucked the letter under the pillow. He stood and looked around the room, memorizing the details of the bed, coverlet, lamp, nightstand, and dresser. He remembered his mother again, fished the cash out of the duffel, removed $50, and tucked it inside the envelope with the letter, returning it to its place under the pillow. He lifted the mandolin in its case off the shelf over the closet, threw the duffel onto his back, and opened the bedroom door. He peered down the hallway. His parents' bedroom was dark, the house still.

He slipped down the stairs, through the living room, past the pieces of the broken chair and the Christmas tree. He thought he might take the package with his name on it from under the tree—he surely could use that hat—but he decided to leave it behind, with the gifts he had left for his parents. He had taken only what he needed.

Saverio quietly lifted his coat off the hook, pulled on the wool gloves his mother had made for him, and put on his old newsboy cap.

The only child of Leone and Rosaria Marasco Armandonada

of 132 Boatwright Street, Detroit, Michigan, opened the door and walked out onto the porch into a beam of clear, white moonlight.

The temperatures had dropped below zero that Christmas Eve, but Saverio didn't feel the bitter cold. Within him there was nothing but fire, a low-grade burning rage from an anger that had gone unexpressed for too long, stoked by the confusion he held from being misunderstood and fueled by the pain of his unworthiness. His father's rejection and Saverio's aspirations had created a combustible grenade that was about to explode and propel him out of this life into a new one.

The boy's heart raced at the possibilities as he followed the light.

2

❧

Risoluto

(Bold)

Chi Chi Donatelli's feet sank so deeply into the cool, wet sand, she closed her eyes and imagined them taking root below the silt, embedding themselves into the earth and spreading into tangled vines of curlicues, multiplying until they covered the ocean floor. That's the effect Count Basie's music had on her. His lush orchestrations filled the spaces of the world for her until there was nothing left as she listened to *Swingin' the Blues* on WBGO out of Newark. The factory girl held a transistor radio up to her ear and pressed it close, as though it were a dial and she were a safecracker. She would not miss a single note.

The Atlantic Ocean rolled out before her like bolts of silver lamé under the white sun. She swatted a fly off of her bare shoulder, which glistened and was hot to the touch. At twenty years old, Chi Chi was petite and limber, with a figure that turned heads.

As the trombone reached for the sliding note that blew high and clean in her ear, she stretched her free arm as if she, too, were reaching for the monumental rippling high C. When the entirety of the orchestra came in under the solo, she adjusted the red chiffon scarf that tied the long, shiny black curls off of her face.

"Chi Chi!" her sister Barbara hollered from the pier, but Chi Chi didn't hear her because the beach was noisy and the radio was cranked. It was a perfect day because it belonged to her. She answered to no one. She let that knowledge wrap around her like the warm breeze off the Atlantic. Chi Chi was off the clock, the sun was high in the sky and looked like the face of a stopwatch without hands or numbers.

The beach at Sea Isle City was packed with union families during the July Fourth holiday week, from the water's edge to the bluffs. This particular slice of the Jersey shore was punctured with poles anchoring billowing striped umbrellas of orange and white, navy and pink, and red and yellow; lolling beneath them were as many people as could fit. The remainder of open sand was a patchwork of beach towels and sunbathers.

From the pier, the colorful wedge of beach looked a lot like a jelly bean spill.

In the distance the boardwalk was packed, and beyond it the Ferris wheel was fully loaded, spinning in the light. The lines for Fiori's Funnel Cakes, Cora's Cotton Candy, Funzo's French Fries, and Isle Show You the Best Hot Waffles & Ice Cream were long, but the customers didn't seem to mind. Gumball-colored horses on the carousel cantered up and down as they revolved on a wooden platform painted in bold stripes of turquoise and gold.

The crash of the waves of the Atlantic Ocean drowned out the clank of the wheels on the wooden roller coaster as it looped over the buoys and pier; a peal of screams could be heard as the riders took the drop after the incline high in the air over the water.

Barbara Donatelli was twenty-two, wore a seersucker romper, and her long black hair in a braid. She had the face and figure of a young woman, but she carried herself with the posture of a put-upon matron. She marched toward Chi Chi and gave her a hard shove in the back to get her attention. Chi Chi reeled around and put up her fists, ready to belt whoever had dared put their hands on her.

"It's just you." Chi Chi released her fists.

"I've been hollering at you all the way from Fontaine," Barbara complained. "Gimme."

Chi Chi stepped back, holding the radio close. She closed her eyes and listened to the smooth clip of the final phrase before Count Basie signaled the orchestra to wallop the finale. When the DJ came back on the air, Chi Chi handed the transistor radio back to her sister.

"You could thank me for the loan," Barbara said as she spun the dial of the radio to Off.

"Thanks."

"Ma wants you home. We have company coming. She needs help," Barbara said as she tucked the radio into her pocket.

"You're there. Pop started the grill already."

"All the cousins are coming over."

"Where's Lucille?"

"She's helping Aunt Vi at the sausage and pepper stand."

"Ugh." Chi Chi swirled her foot in the sand. "I want to stay out. It's my vacation."

"Ma doesn't get a vacation."

Barbara knew that all she had to do was mention their mother, and Chi Chi would pretty much do anything she asked of her. Resigned, Chi Chi had turned to follow her sister back home through the maze of sunbathers when they heard a woman scream. Chi Chi turned back and scanned the water's edge. She saw a young woman wading into the ocean, reaching into the waves.

"My boy!" the woman screamed again. "Help! Somebody help me! My son!" Another woman grabbed the mother by her waist as she attempted to go into the water. The surf had churned up, cresting in white foam that hid the swimmers beyond the shallow water.

Instinctively, Chi Chi ran to her. "She can't swim!" the woman said, gripping the mother by her waist.

"There! Out there!" The mother pointed. "Help my son!"

Chi Chi looked out into the surf and spied an empty green raft floating in the middle distance. She dove into the surf and swam for it.

Barbara ran after her sister; shielding her eyes, she checked the lifeguard stand. No sign of him. "My sister is a good swimmer," Barbara said, trying to soothe the woman, but it was impossible. They heard the lifeguard whistle behind them, the bathers parted, and then he, too, dove into the surf with a red board on a rope.

When Chi Chi reached the raft, she dove under it but found nothing. She tried to flip the raft, thinking it might have gotten attached to something—driftwood, or an old railroad tie that loosened from the pier. Her heart pounded in fear—she could not move the cloth raft. She felt around its edges. The lead rope was submerged; only the loop attached to the raft floated on the surface. She dove under the water again, sliding her hands along the grooves of the tangled hemp and followed it.

Soon she found the boy, lifeless, his head directed to the ocean floor. The boy's ankle was twisted in the loop of the rope. Panic surged through her, but, focused on her task, she loosened the knot and pulled him to the surface. As she held him, a wave washed over them, dragging them under as he slipped out of her grip. She flailed in the surf as she reached for him. The force of the waves pushed his body toward her, and she grabbed him again. She pulled him to the surface using the thrust of the current.

Chi Chi gasped for air. With one arm, she clung to the boy and kicked, reaching desperately for the raft with the other, pulling the boy behind her as the lifeguard swam toward them. The boy floated on the surface as she held him. In her arms, he was cold and rubbery, like a doll. His lips were a faint blue, and his eyes were closed when the lifeguard reached them. The lifeguard spoke to Chi Chi, but she couldn't hear his instructions; it was as though she were floating inside a thick glass bottle, and the boy, the raft, and the lifeguard were outside of it.

"Hold on to the raft," the lifeguard instructed again as he lifted the boy and placed him on the safety board, turning him over, facedown. Instinctively, Chi Chi swam to the far side of the board to protect the boy. With the lifeguard on the other side of the board, they swam toward shore, steadying the boy between them, the raft trailing behind them.

Chi Chi saw salt water as it oozed from his open mouth. The boy couldn't have been more than seven years old. As they reached the shallow water, the young mother tore away from her friend and Barbara and ran toward her son. "Michael!" she cried.

"Hold her back," the lifeguard ordered.

Barbara put her arms around the woman and restrained her, with the help of the friend. It was as if the entire population of Sea Isle Beach had gathered silently on the shore to watch the lifeguard breathe into the boy, who lay still on the board on the cold sand.

Chi Chi knelt down next to the boy as the lifeguard pressed his chest and breathed into his mouth. "Come on, Michael," she whispered into the boy's ear. "You can do it. Come back."

The lifeguard pressed the boy's chest gently and steadily with his flat open hands, trying to open his chest so he might breathe.

The boy's face began to take on color around his nose, the pale blue skin became tinged with pink. He moved his neck. The lifeguard helped him turn his head when suddenly the boy threw up salt water and whatever else was inside him. The boy began to gulp air. Chi Chi and the lifeguard helped him sit up. The lifeguard gently tapped his back, and the boy leaned forward and spit up more water. Soon, the boy's throat burned, he clutched it, and he began to cry. His mother broke away and ran to her son, knelt in the sand, and held him. She wept as her son's chest heaved.

Chi Chi sat back on her heels and watched the boy and his mother. As Michael curled up in her arms, his pale back curved like a seashell. As the boy cried, his breath moved the clean line of his backbone fluidly, like the links on a chain.

The lifeguard gave the sign that the boy was safe. The crowd behind them cheered. The roar, Chi Chi was certain, could be heard down the shore as far away as Wildwood Crest. Chatter erupted as the crowd announced the happy ending: *He'll live. He made it. Poor kid, that was a close one.* Barbara kicked sand over the spot where the boy had been sick, until all evidence of it was buried. The lifeguard corralled the people back to their umbrellas and blankets. Relieved, they receded from the water's edge. Today would be an ordinary day after all. Chi Chi kept her eyes on the mother and son. She bit her lip, tasting salt water, not from the ocean but her own tears.

"What's the head count, Ma?" Barbara leaned out the kitchen window.

"I think twenty-five, but it could go to thirty if the Rapucchis show up." Isotta smiled from the backyard of their freshly painted Cape Cod home as she and Chi Chi unfurled a red-and-white-checked tablecloth on the long picnic table.

Isotta Donatelli was an Italian of Venetian descent who understood the ways of the Neapolitans because of her long marriage to Mariano. Now in her midforties, she had soft brown eyes, a pale complexion, and the prominent, straight nose of the Italians of the north. Her full smile showed off lovely white teeth, and like her daughters, she had long dark hair, though hers had flecks of gray at her temples and was worn in a braided chignon.

"How does this happen?" Chi Chi complained. "I thought you were going to hold the number down this year, Ma. I don't want to work on my week off. I want to take sun and relax." Isotta's middle child had tied up her wet hair in a topknot. She wore a two-piece red bathing suit that exposed a half inch of her tanned middle and grazed the top of her thighs; the bottoms were cut square, boy style. Chi Chi had hoped to spend the afternoon doing her hair. Later, she planned to put on a sundress and gold sandals and dance the night away at the pavilion on the boardwalk with the rest of the kids her age.

"This is the curse of living by the shore," Barbara said as she placed a stack of dishes on the table. "Family washes up on the beach all summer long."

"Who's coming anyhow?" Chi Chi asked as she set the table.

"We've got the cousins from Michigan," her mother began, counting the place settings as she went.

"Farmers," Chi Chi said.

"Steelworkers," Barbara corrected her.

"What's the difference?"

"One brings you baskets of fresh peppers to can, and the other brings the Ford catalog with the rollout of the 1938 line," Barbara said wistfully. "One gift is work to do, the other is my book of dreams."

"Cousin Joozy—you remember her, she's the daughter of my mother's second cousin—well, she's bringing her cousin Rosaria by marriage. The one that married the fella from Italy around the same time I married your father. Armandonada."

"So we're not related to Rosaria?" Barbara pondered.

"We should just open a restaurant. At least we'd be making money instead of feeding all these cousins and their cousins ten times removed for free," Chi Chi groused.

"Rosaria's son is a singer."

Chi Chi's eyes narrowed. "Does he have any records out?"

"You'll have to ask his mother."

Chi Chi placed the silverware on the table. "You know I will."

"I feel sorry for the girl who gets stuck with that name. It sounds like a barge from the days of Nero." Barbara followed behind her with the salad bowls, placing them on the table. "Why would anybody marry an Italian from the other side? It's Victorian."

Their mother smiled. "I don't know, Barbara. Maybe love?"

"Love has a different definition for every person," Chi Chi reminded her. "You ever heard the story of Monica Spadoni? Her parents made a match with a guy she had never met, from a village she had never visited, from a family she did not know, all based on a photograph sent via airmail from Napoli."

"Was he handsome?" Barbara asked.

"Extremely. But that was his only asset. Monica had no idea what awaited her except his gorgeous mug, of course. The guy landed in New Haven, Monica was smitten. They got married, it turns out he was mean, she felt hoodwinked; in due course he wiped out her savings, left her flat, and went home to Italy to his wife and kids."

"How romantic. Tell us another one, Cheech." Barbara folded

the napkins neatly and placed them on the plates. "Who doesn't like a good old potboiler bigamy story?"

"The moral of all that? Yes, Monica got saddled with a real bargain from Catania. But she learned her lesson. Eat from your own garden, because you don't know what you're getting when you don't."

"That's an exception, Chi Chi," their mother said. "Usually when the family makes an *ambasciata* they take pains to find a suitable spouse for their daughter. They don't just pick anyone off the street."

"It only takes one mistake to ruin your life," said Chi Chi. "Who taught us that, Ma?"

"I suppose I did."

"Where do you want the birch beer, Iso?" Mariano, Isotta's husband of twenty-four years, kicked the back gate open with his foot and entered the yard with a silver keg balanced on his shoulder. Compact and round, Mariano had the thick forearms of a stonecutter. He was bald and had recently grown a slim mustache like the movie star William Powell.

"Mariano, put that down. Girls, help your father."

"Dad, what are you thinking?" Barbara rushed at him. "Use the hand truck!"

"You're gonna break your back!" Chi Chi lifted the keg off his shoulder with Barbara's help. They placed it on a low fieldstone wall their father had built himself.

"Look at me. I didn't even break a sweat." Mariano held his hands up in the air in victory. "I'm as strong as the day you married me, Isotta." He pulled the tap out of his back pocket and handed it to Chi Chi, who attached it to the keg. "Have I got enough hot dogs?" he asked as he surveyed the table. "A lot of plates here."

"You have enough hot dogs," Isotta assured him.

"Ma, you want the trays in the oven?" Lucille asked from the kitchen window.

"Yes, honey, put it on warm. What did you bring?"

"I got four dozen fresh rolls. Two pans of sausage and peppers. One pan of pepper and eggs and one pan of eggplant. Aunt Vi sent three potato pizza and four *pizza alige*."

"We've got more than enough food," Barbara said as she set up the drink table.

"Who can help Papa with the gelato?"

"I will." Chi Chi followed her father down into the basement for the equipment.

Lucille emerged from the kitchen, eating a plain roll.

"Save those rolls for company," Barbara chided her.

"We got thousands," said Lucille with a full mouth. Lucille was the baby of the family. At eighteen, she was the most beautiful of the daughters, but she was completely unaware of her charms. "Do I need to change?"

Isotta and Barbara looked Lucille up and down. She wore work boots and denim coveralls splattered with grease from the fryer at the sausage stand. "Yes," they said together. Lucille rolled her eyes and went back into the house to change.

"If she knew how pretty she was, she'd be dangerous," Barbara said quietly to her mother.

"Don't tell her."

Chi Chi and her father emerged from the basement. He carried the ice cream maker, a wooden barrel with a hand crank; Chi Chi followed with a sack of rock salt.

"What flavor should I make?" Chi Chi asked as she set up the machine, pouring the rock salt into the outer tray.

"Vanilla," Barbara suggested.

"Bland vanilla? Come on, Barb, you can do better than that."

"Why do you bother to ask for suggestions if you don't like them?"

"I want to see if you're ever going to go out on a limb and come up with something daring."

"Vanilla goes with everything."

"Nothing wrong with that," Mariano said as he dropped chunks of ice into the bowl underneath the mixer. "Especially when you throw some rum into it."

"Great, Dad. Always fun when the great-aunts get tight on ice cream."

The Donatellis' Fourth of July feast spilled out of their backyard and onto the side porch, with some of the cousins taking their plates to the front porch and lawn. Up and down Sand Point Street, similar al fresco meals were being served, with shore families hosting their annual summer parties. The older folks sought the shade of the umbrella table, or the cool breeze beneath the grape arbor that canopied the walkway from the stone path on the side of the house to the backyard.

Isotta had trained her daughters well. Lucille and Barbara served the guests and made sure that their drinks were cold and their cups were full. In the kitchen, Chi Chi jabbed spoons into a series of glass cups filled with ice cream and fresh sliced strawberries. She placed them on a tray and, opening the screen door with her hip, went outside into the garden and served the oldest guests first. Chi Chi tucked her head under the umbrella and offered dessert.

"Cheech, did you meet my cousin Rosaria?" Joozy Fierabraccio lifted two ice cream cups off the tray, handing one to her cousin. "Mrs. Armandonada. She's from Michigan. Detroit." Joozy wore a sleeveless sundress that exploded in a print of palm fronds on her sturdy frame.

"Thank you for inviting me," Rosaria said as she tasted the gelato.

"Our pleasure. As you can see, we love a party." Chi Chi grinned. "Go easy on the ice cream. It's spiked."

"Liquor burns off in the sun," Joozy said, waving the spoon around before letting it land back in the cup. "You can't get pie-eyed in the heat. It evaporates off the human body through the pores."

"I was at the beach this afternoon—" Rosaria began.

"The weather has been perfect." Chi Chi offered ice cream to the guests as they passed.

"You saved that little boy."

Chi Chi blushed. "It was nothing."

"No, no, it was everything to the boy and to his mother." Rosaria turned to Joozy. "She just dove into the ocean to save a child. She didn't even think about it. She didn't wait for the lifeguard."

"I was close to the water," Chi Chi said softly. "Anybody would have helped."

"Hundreds of people were on the shore," Rosaria insisted, "but you went in and saved the boy!"

"I'm afraid of the water," Joozy admitted as she spooned up another bite of ice cream. "The ocean is entirely too perilous and mysterious for me. Ah, *Madone*. All kinds of squish and foam under and around you, and then the strange fish that swim around in the depths. Many have teeth. You never know what you'll run into. I don't like that feeling. Of the unknown. Of the constant movement. To tell you the truth, I don't even like boats. I stay on *terra firma* under an umbrella with a good book. That's my idea of the shore."

Chi Chi laughed. "Sounds like a fine vacation to me."

"You have to know what you like in this life," Joozy told them, "or you fritter away precious time doing things everybody else likes to do." She ate a delicate spoonful of the ice cream. "Don't be a follower, Cheech. Be a leader."

"Got it."

"Do you like big-band music?" Rosaria asked Chi Chi.

"Are you for true, Rose? The Donatelli girls are musical. This kid has an act with her sisters." Joozy pointed to Barbara, who was serving birch beer, and to Lucille, who was carrying empty trays up to the kitchen. "They're good, too. Sea Isle's answer to the Dolly Sisters. They sing at church and at the Holy Name Society Dance."

"We made a couple records, too," Chi Chi offered.

"How nice." Rosaria was impressed. "My son sings with the Rod Roccaraso Orchestra. They're booked at the Cronecker Hotel all week."

"Is he the lead singer?"

"Yes, they have a girl singer too. And they rotate specialty acts. Would you like to take your family tonight?"

"I think they'd love it."

"I'll arrange for passes."

"Thank you, Mrs. Arman—"

Joozy held her hand up. "Allow me. 'Armandonada.' It's a mouthful of macaroni plus a meatball. I don't know how your husband squeaked by with that one intact on Ellis Island."

Rosaria ignored her comment and looked at Chi Chi. "I'll make sure Saverio knows you're coming."

Chi Chi moved through the crowd, delivering the rest of the ice cream. She looked back at Rosaria with the impossible last name. She was one of those Italian ladies who could wear a linen shift, sandals, and a locket and look regal.

For her part, Rosaria recognized Chi Chi Donatelli as a kind of angel. How could a woman so young possibly understand what it meant to that mother to have saved the life of her son on Sea Isle Beach that day? Chi Chi couldn't know, but Rosaria did.

As they climbed the steps of the Cronecker Hotel, Chi Chi re-tied the bow of her dress on her shoulder tightly, as the strap kept coming loose. She had made the sundress herself, out of teal and pink madras. Lucille wore a blue cotton pique sundress with a large patchwork pineapple on the straight skirt. Barbara wore a sheer pink organza dress with a belt of embroidered daisies.

"Ladies, I'm here!" Charlie Calza called from the street below.

"Hurry!" Barbara chided him.

"Your boyfriend is never on time," Chi Chi complained. "If we miss this show because of him, I'll give him the business myself."

"I'll handle him. It has taught me patience," Barbara admitted.

Charlie sprinted up the steps, weaving through the crowd to join the girls. "I'm sorry. I had to set up the cash drawers for the box office." Charlie had been Barbara's boyfriend since they were kids. He was tall and thick and wore his dark brown hair parted on the side and slicked down with pomade, as though it were al-ways the first day of school. He was a bookkeeper for Sea Isle's boardwalk pavilion, which is how the Donatelli sisters had seen every band from Fred Waring to Glenn Miller. He looked around. "Fancy digs."

"Nice break from the pavilion," Barbara said.

The Cronecker Hotel was a sprawling Victorian mansion hotel and restaurant on Ocean Drive that took up most of a city block. Painted in stately gray with coral trim, the hotel was known for its superb seafood and its elegant ballroom, which hosted the great touring dance bands.

Chi Chi gave Rosaria's name at the door, and their party was promptly escorted to a ringside table at the front of the crowded ballroom. The large glass windows were propped open, allowing the night air to blow through, cooling off the crowd. The silk draperies billowed in the ocean breeze like ball gowns.

"Is that you, Cheech?" a familiar voice said behind her.

"Rita! What are you doing here?"

"I got a date. A real cutie." Rita Milnicki, Chi Chi's best friend from the mill, pointed to her table. "One of the Osella boys. You know them. Nice family. Saint Dom's."

"Yeah. I see. You got the good-looking one."

"I know. David. But he's not the rich one. Lynn Ann Minichillo nabbed him. What are you doing ringside? Are you gonna sing?" Rita adjusted her cocktail hat and straightened the folds of her dotted swiss tulle skirt.

"No, we're here to see the band."

"I hear they're very good."

"Shall we powder our noses?" Chi Chi asked Rita, taking her by the arm. "You need it."

"My nose is fine," Rita insisted.

"I'm as slick as a fried pepper. I'd like some company," Chi Chi said as the pair made their way through the crowd to the foyer outside the ballroom. She looked up and down the hallway. "I want to say hello to Mr. Roccaraso," she confided.

"Do you know him?"

Chi Chi didn't answer her. Rita followed her down the hallway and into the kitchen. "The kitchen is the center of everything," Chi Chi whispered. "You can even get to the stage from here."

"How do you know?"

"Maria Barraccini is a waitress here. Gave me the skinny."

"So you did your detective work?"

"I never miss a Myrna Loy picture."

Rita followed Chi Chi through the sweltering hotel kitchen,

a chaotic assembly line producing an opera of clangs, sputters, sizzles, and shouts as a row of cooks flipped steaks on the grill, tossed shrimp in pans over bursts of flames, and fished clams in delicate nets out of aluminum steamer pots while servers loaded trays with white dinner plates holding the finished prix fixe dinner specials. The busboys were so busy that they took little notice as Chi Chi and Rita slipped through the dishwasher's station.

"I hope I don't smell like grease." Rita fanned her sleeves. "I'm wearing Houbigant. I think the steamers might cancel it out."

"You're fine. We didn't linger," Chi Chi promised her as they walked down a long hallway lined with posters from past dances on one side and a series of closed doors on the other. Chi Chi touched the doors as she passed them, as if to sense who might possibly be behind them. As they reached the end, they heard the band warming up their instruments. A handwritten sign marked BAND was taped to the door. Chi Chi leaned in and listened to small trills and scales on horns over their conversation inside. Straight ahead was a door that led to the veranda marked SINGERS.

"I bet he's out there having a smoke with the singers," Chi Chi whispered, pushing the screen door open. The wraparound porch was empty except for a small table with a mirror, set for touchups, a few rattan chairs, and two figures, a man and a woman who were sharing a private moment.

The woman was perched on the railing of the veranda as the man held her close, wrapped around her like a weed choking a rose. He kissed her neck urgently, his brown curls tumbling forward; she brushed them away. Her hands moved down to his neck, to his shoulders where she massaged them like macaroni dough. Chi Chi and Rita looked at one another and back at the couple.

The woman giggled and pulled away when she saw the girls staring at them. Her leg, which had been artfully wrapped around the man's waist, slid down his leg, as her pale green kid leather dress shoe fell off and hit the floor. The young man looked down at the shoe, then over his shoulder at Chi Chi and Rita.

"Sorry!" Chi Chi blurted before pushing Rita back through the screen door and snapping it shut.

"Let's get out of here!" Rita ordered.

The girls broke into a run and tore down the hallway, through the kitchen and out the galley doors, making tracks until they were safely back in the ballroom.

"How awful." Rita was breathless. "I hope we never see them again."

"We're about to see them onstage."

Chi Chi slipped into her seat at the front table while Rita joined the Osella family at theirs. Chi Chi fished her lipstick out of her purse and, using the butter knife on the table as a mirror, quickly applied a fresh coat to her lips. She placed the tube back in her bag, adjusted the straps on her sundress, and sat up straight.

There was something compelling about that young man even though he was obviously already taken. She liked his confidence. The way he put his arms around the girl was romantic, not handsy like some of the fellows she had dated. He had the swagger of a sheik, but she liked that he was an Italian kid, just like her. He was around her age, too, which made her feel like her own music career was possible, or maybe it meant that she wished it was she in the arms of such a man. She quickly erased the image from her mind. He belonged to someone else, and she would never set her cap for some other girl's fellow. That kind of danger wasn't something she knew. Yet.

Chi Chi shivered. She wished she had brought her cashmere shrug. Sometimes shore nights got cool, even in July.

As the lights went down, Rita snapped open her compact. If she hadn't needed to powder her nose before she took off with Chi

Chi, she certainly did now. She delicately patted her face with the chamois puff as the Osellas shifted their seats to get the best view of the stage from their table.

Buzz Crane, the master of ceremonies and the most famous DJ on their strip of the Jersey shore, took the stage in a beam of peach-colored light to introduce the Roccaraso Orchestra. The musicians filed in and took their seats to a round of applause. As they launched into their opening tune, Chi Chi thought the band could swing. Barbara nudged her when Rosaria Armandonada took her seat ringside with her cousin Joozy.

Rod Roccaraso emerged from the shadows, took the microphone center stage in the spotlight, and introduced the band. The brass section stood up and blew a fizzy jazz riff as the drummer tore up the skins. Two spotlights intersected. In one of them was the young lady on the banister, a cool blonde, and in the other was the masher Chi Chi and Rita had caught on the veranda. He was a handsome Calabrese kid. He pushed his thick curls back with his hand. That fellow could be any good-looking Italian American boy from any family in Sea Isle.

Chi Chi craned her neck to catch Rita's eye. Rita winked at Chi Chi.

Gladys Overby and Saverio Armandonada had a smooth act: strictly love songs, a romantic pas de deux that was musically light, but perfect fodder for a dance band. Couples took the floor as the lights lowered. Chi Chi could feel the wooden floor sag under the weight of the couples as she watched them glide past in their ice-cream suits and sundresses. She closed her eyes and listened to Saverio's vocals. He had an original sound, a lush tenor. Gladys was a typical whiskey alto. Their voices didn't mesh particularly well, but they were good enough for this level of orchestra and entertainment.

Buzz took the microphone. "Ladies and gentlemen, I've been told we have a lot of Italians here on the Jersey shore, so we brought along a little marinara to spike the evening. Say hello to the Gay Sisters, all the way from balmy North Providence, Rhode Island. Don't miss their recording of *Pistol Packin' Mama* on J & J Records."

Three of the most glamorous young women Chi Chi had ever seen stood before the microphones. In their chic, fitted Greek-style cocktail dresses of gold lamé, anchored with an enormous bow on one shoulder, they looked like three platinum swizzle sticks. Chi Chi felt ten years old and about as chic as a dinner napkin in her homemade madras sundress.

"I'm Helen DeSarro," the green-eyed blonde introduced herself.

"I'm Toni DeSarro." The petite comic redhead waved to the audience.

"I'm bored." The sultry brunette looked out over the crowd as they laughed.

"Maybe we should sing *Marie*," Saverio offered.

"Only if it's about me. By the way, it's Anne. Anne Stasiano."

"What about Gladys?" Helen asked.

"She's taking a Lucky Strike break."

"Oh, okay." Helen shrugged. "It's just the Gay Sisters and Savvy."

The girls gathered around Gladys's microphone stand as Saverio stood before his. The band hit the downbeat to the introduction of *Oh Marie*.

"Ladies and gentlemen," Rod said into his microphone, "let's swing."

The Gay Sisters tapped out the beat with a slight shimmy onstage as the patrons moved away from the bandstand. This go-round, the couples were so tightly packed on the dance floor that they resembled canned peaches. Saverio led the tune, and the girls followed with a repeat verse and provided the echo in perfect three-part harmony.

Barbara danced with Charlie, while Lucille took to the floor with the youngest of the Osella boys. Chi Chi shook one of Charlie's cigarettes out of the pack he'd left on the table and lit it off the candle on the table. She could take cigarettes or leave them, but tonight she needed the distraction. The sight of the Gay Sisters had given Chi Chi the pea greens, a Donatelli-style stomachache that came from plain envy.

After all, the Donatelli Sisters had sung this old chestnut, too, at least a hundred times, in their share of wedding halls and Sons of Italy lodge meetings, and at more than a few church celebrations up and down the shore. Chi Chi's sisters knew their harmonies and sang together on key, whether the piano was tuned or the saxophone player was missing half his pads. Why couldn't they get a shot singing with a big band? Why couldn't they get fancy dresses, decent hairdos, and lacquered nails, and travel with a band that had brass and sass?

Chi Chi decided that nothing would ever come between the Donatelli Sisters and a hit record. Everything mattered when it came to their act—the song choices, the arrangements, the costumes, and especially their sound. Every song Chi Chi wrote had the potential to catapult them from obscurity into the spotlight. Chi Chi perspired as she schemed. It was as though she were pulling stones to build the pyramids alone.

Chi Chi observed Saverio, who was at ease onstage. He stood back and allowed the Gay Sisters to do the heavy lifting. He tapped his foot as he looked out over the dance floor, assessing the level of interest in the song, putting just enough effort into it when necessary and holding back when it wasn't. The lead singer could always afford to relax onstage. Not the girls. They had to emote, move, and draw the crowd in.

Rosaria moved through the crowd as the orchestra wrapped up *Oh Marie*. She took Chi Chi by the hand. "I want you to meet my son," she said.

"Oh, that's all right, Mrs. Armandonada. He's busy."

"He has a break."

"I'm sure he wants to relax."

"He has time for that. Come with me."

Chi Chi was mortified as Rosaria pulled her through the crowd. Chi Chi was convinced she had on the wrong dress and sandals. The curls in her hair had gone limp. Her nose had gotten sunburned that afternoon when she was cleaning up the yard. This wasn't how she had planned to look when she made her big break into show business. Plus, there was no polite way to tell a mother that her son had been making love standing up to the girl singer in the band shortly before the show started.

"Saverio, this is Chi Chi Donatelli," said Rosaria. "I was at her home for lunch today."

"Hi, Saverio. Lovely set."

"*Grazie.*" Saverio was pretty attractive when he smiled. His brown curls hadn't gone limp. His nose was a little off-center, but it didn't matter. He was gracious and polite, every Italian mother's dream. Rosaria returned to her table as Chi Chi took her seat to watch the rest of the show.

Saverio stood at the microphone as the band fired up for the final set of the night. Chi Chi watched intently when Gladys joined him in the spotlight. She had changed her costume and it was a high-style confection, a diaphanous off-the-shoulder gown of honey-colored silk shantung, gathered at the waist with a waterfall of crystals that sparkled in the light. Saverio extended his hand to her. She accepted it. He bowed, and when he straightened, they belted *By the Sea* into the microphone.

Chi Chi was interested in the crooner and girl singer's stagecraft. She paid attention to the songs they chose and how they made specific tunes work in the overall show. There was an alchemy in the way they fronted the orchestra. It wasn't simply a matter of their sound and delivery. They weren't shiny objects in a shop window, intended to lure the customer in to listen to the band; they were, in youth and beauty, the essence of the message. Gladys and Saverio were in love, and that helped the act; their connection was as smooth as a silk stocking. Their chemistry was part of the show.

Chi Chi walked home alone from the Cronecker under a moon that slipped in and out of the low fog like a half note. The time gave her a chance to think about all she had heard and seen that night. She begged off when Mrs. Armandonada invited her to stay for dessert with Joozy and her son. Chi Chi wasn't in the mood. She was practically the same age as Saverio, and she still hadn't made the leap from amateur to professional. Sometimes, and this was one of those nights, it felt as though her music career might never happen. The last thing she wanted to do was spend time with someone who had the career of her dreams.

As she pushed open the screen door on the front porch, she could hear her family talking in the kitchen. She threw her purse on the sofa and slipped out of her sandals. The scent of fresh coffee, cinnamon, and butter coffee cake filled the house.

Every seat at the kitchen table was filled. Her mother, father, sisters, and Charlie Calza were having a robust discussion about the parking lot going in at the pavilion. Chi Chi pulled the work stool from under the sink over to the table and squeezed in between Lucille and her mother.

"Where were you?" Barbara poured her sister a cup of coffee.

"No doubt she was working over the singer." Lucille passed Chi Chi a slice of cake and a fork.

"I was properly introduced. Sort of."

"I knew it." Lucille sipped her coffee. "She worked him over."

"If we want to get on the radio, we need to make connections."

"He's kinda cute, that Saverio," Lucille admitted.

Barbara dug into her pound cake. "Awful skinny."

Charlie patted his stomach. "I'm happy you like a little meat with your potatoes."

"And your pound cake." Mariano passed Charlie the cream for his coffee.

"Thank you, Mr. Donatelli."

"I need you girls up bright and early to rehearse in the morning." Chi Chi picked the topping off the cake with the prong of her fork. "I want to try to cut another record before the orchestra leaves town. It would be nice to have the Donatelli Sisters on that bus when they pull out—at least in vinyl."

"I'm out, Cheech." Lucille propped her face in her hands. "I'm tired. I have burns from Aunt Vi's grease fire, and we just got the backyard cleaned up from the family party. Let's rehearse on Friday."

"I need your vocal for the harmony."

"Pop, make Chi Chi cut it out," Lucille groused. "Tell her it's a hobby."

"Not to me." Chi Chi stood firm. "We'll never get to the big stages if we don't rehearse."

"Give the kid a break," Barbara said to Chi Chi. "Not all of us are as ambitious as you."

"You should be. You girls are good," their father reminded them. "You'd be better if you listened to your sister and practiced on the weekends."

"Sister acts are like grains of sand in Sea Isle," said Barbara. "They're everywhere. And they can even import them. Those girls tonight were wonderful. They travel all over the place and pick up work wherever they can get it. I'm sorry, I'm not cut out for that kind of a life. I like to be home."

"We're so close to getting noticed, all we need is a little more practice and a break," Chi Chi pleaded.

Lucille cleared the dessert dishes. "All we do is work hard. Ever notice that? Maybe I don't want to spend my weekends moonlighting."

"So what," said Chi Chi. "We work hard at the mill anyway. If we can hit it in show business, it's better money. And then we can have all the things in life we really want. Barbara wants a Ford coupe, you want to go to secretarial school."

"What do you want, Chi Chi?" her mother asked.

"The world."

"It's already taken by the rich people. Don't be greedy." Lucille ran the water in the sink.

"I'd like to be greedy with my time and work at something I like to do. Okay, I like nice clothes and shoes. What's wrong with that?"

"Enjoy those things while you're young, because when you get to be my age, you don't want them anymore."

"Is that really true, Ma?"

"You want other things as life goes on," Isotta assured them. "And it doesn't come in a jewelry case or a hatbox."

"Like what?" Chi Chi asked.

"Time."

"Oh, that. Well, we have plenty of time." Chi Chi gave her mother a quick hug. "I can account for every minute when I'm working at the mill. But I think there's more to life than working the line at Jersey Miss Fashions."

"It's good to have big dreams," her father said.

"And to back those dreams up with a weekly paycheck," Barbara reminded her.

"Barbara is practical," said Charlie. "It's one of the things I love the most about her."

His declaration of love sounded like the beginning of an important speech. The Donatelli family sat back and waited.

"Charlie has something he wants to say." Barbara jabbed her boyfriend with her elbow. "We waited for you to get home, Cheech. We wanted to have the whole family together."

Chi Chi folded her arms. "So, what's the story?"

"It's not a story . . . Well, it will be a story." Charlie took Barbara's hand. "Our story. I spoke with your father tonight, and he's given me permission to marry Barbara."

"That's wonderful news!" Lucille left the stack of dishes at the sink and embraced her sister and Charlie. "I'm going to be a bridesmaid! Please choose blue. And I'd like to wear a picture hat with ribbons! June Allyson wore one in the picture I saw last week."

"Give your sister time to think and time for me to sew!" Isotta chided her youngest daughter, but she looked elated.

Chi Chi was stunned. The announcement seemed to come out of nowhere, but she knew what it meant. Her heart sank.

Isotta leaned over. "Congratulate your sister."

Chi Chi's legs could barely move. She used the wheels of the stool to propel her back a few steps before standing up; she went to her sister and Charlie and embraced them as her father poured a round of sweet wine to toast the couple. Her mother handed out the full crystal glasses.

As they raised their glasses, Chi Chi raised hers, too, and forced a smile. She was happy for her sister and Charlie; she knew they loved each other.

Going forward, Barbara would devote herself to the planning of her wedding and, once she was married, to her husband, like every other Italian American girl in New Jersey. The hobby that had been their singing act, with its costumes and props, would be packed away with the books and dolls of their childhood, stored in an old trunk in the attic where their efforts would be remembered only when their children needed an outfit for a school play.

Chi Chi could see the future and it was grim. Barbara would move out and take her lilting high soprano with her. Lucille had other interests; she was determined to go to school and get a desk job. Her smooth alto would benefit the church choir at St. Joseph's and not much more. Chi Chi's show business dream would remain one on the night of her sister's engagement. If Chi Chi wanted to write, record songs, and sing them with a band, she would have to go solo and come up with another plan—just when she was sure nothing could stop them.

"Do not antagonize, Chiara," Mariano said quietly to his daughter.

"Too late, Dad."

"Your sisters aren't going anywhere. You'll see."

Chi Chi wanted to believe him but she knew how the world in Sea Isle worked. Every girl she knew made a trade for the diamond ring. She vowed she would never be one of them.

3

UNION VACATION WEEK 1938

Capriccio

(Whimsical)

Chi Chi and Rita found a patch of clean, rippled gray sand below the bluffs on Sea Isle Beach. The expanse of the shore filled quickly on the Thursday morning of the union vacation week as families trudged past, chose their spot, and staked a claim by plunging the long poles of their beach umbrellas into the sand and opening them.

Underneath the canopies, the routine was the same for vacationers up and down the shore. Blankets were unfurled, picnic baskets placed, and transistor radios played as folks settled in for a day of sun, surf, and amusements on the boardwalk. The girls could not remember a holiday week with such excellent weather. The days had been deliciously long, under a glittering sun that punctured the cloudless sky like a brass button.

"You are so brown, Chi Chi," Rita marveled as she rubbed coconut oil on her legs.

"It's the suit," her friend assured her. Chi Chi wore a white cotton pique two-piece bathing suit. The top tied halter-style behind her neck in a bow that showed off the glistening tanned skin on her shoulders and back. "It'll fade the minute we're back to work."

"Don't say that word. Ugh." Rita tightened the belt on her black maillot. Rita was trim, with a heart-shaped face and sweet smile. Her dark brown hair was chopped in a bob, and the sun had streaked it with strands of gold.

"We have three days until we're back on the machines," Chi Chi said as she rubbed the oil into her legs methodically. "You know what I love about the job?"

"I can't imagine." Rita reclined on the beach towel.

"The paycheck. And I really like it when I've done piecework and there's an extra two dollars on the gross. I get giddy."

"What do you do with the extra money? Besides buy bathing suits?"

"I save it up and buy government bonds."

Rita sat up. "What are you talking about?"

"Government bonds. Not the US savings bonds. Those are fine too, but *government* bonds. Been buying them since I started working four years ago. I get a three-percent return at the top of the market, and no lower than two-point-one when it craters."

"How do you know how to do that?"

"Invest?"

"Yeah. My dad told me to put my money under the mattress."

"All you'll get from that is a poor night's sleep. No interest earned. That's medieval. That's off-the-boat thinking." Chi Chi rubbed suntan oil on her feet. "Put your money in the bank. If I could, and eventually I will, I'll buy real estate too. Oceanfront. Right now, the safest place for extra dough is in the bank. Earning interest."

"My dad got spooked by the crash."

"That's too bad. An investor should never take the whims of the stock market personally," Chi Chi advised.

"Says who?"

"The *Wall Street Journal.* I read it at the library."

"Get out."

"Yep. On payday, I go home, endorse my check, reconcile my checkbook, then Dad and I go to the bank. I take whatever cash I need for the week."

"I do that."

"I fill an envelope for my folks."

Rita nodded. "Me, too."

"I check my account. I always compare the bank's figures against my own arithmetic. I ask the manager about the market and current instruments. And when I've saved up enough, I buy a government bond."

"I don't do any of that. Geez."

"I could teach you."

"No, thanks."

"You're gonna rely on David Osella?"

"He hasn't asked me to marry him yet."

"But he's gonna."

"If he does, I'll give him my money. Why not?"

"You can give him your money, but you should know where it's going."

"Does your mother?"

"There's not a lot of extra money lying around at my house," Chi Chi admitted.

"You girls are hard workers."

"And Ma. We do all right. But four girls can't make what one man can pull in. We know. We add it up. I think about that sometimes. I don't know a man who could do what my mother does— she cooks and cleans and takes in sewing *and* works the line at the mill. She takes care of us, and Dad, and her parents. She just goes about her business. I wish she would have had a couple of sons. That might've helped."

"Sometimes it only makes things worse. They get married, their wives steal them away, and they make like ghosts," Rita complained. "You can't count on the boys."

"You could if my mother would've raised sons. She holds us close."

"Jim LaMarca was asking for you."

"That's nice."

Rita sat up. "That's nice? Are you screwy or what? He's a college man. He's tall and gorgeous—a genuine sheik, if you ask me. And he's rich, or he will be when he inherits the family business. You couldn't do better."

"How about he couldn't do better than me?"

"That goes without saying, Cheech."

"Where was he asking?"

"At the pavilion. He's going to summer school to pick up extra credits, so he won't be around. He'll be back at Christmas. Maybe he'll write to you."

"I'll wait by the mailbox like a *bombolone*."

"Maybe you should." Rita laughed. "You wanna go in the water? I'm burning up."

"You put on too much oil. You're frying like a *zeppole* over there."

"I'm going in." Rita stood, adjusted her suit, and trotted down to the water. She waded in slowly before diving into the surf. Chi

Chi watched her swim out to the pier by the safety net, where the lifeguard pedaled by in a paddleboat. She opened her rattan beach basket, pulled out her manicure kit, and filed her nails.

"Lady of leisure." A young man stopped in front of her, blocking the sun.

Chi Chi looked up. "Mr. Armandonada."

"Can I?"

"Can you what?" she teased.

"Sit down?"

Chi Chi made room on her blanket.

Saverio sat down and took her in head to toe. "That's some color you got."

"It won't last," Chi Chi said as she dusted sand off her foot.

"It's only July. There's plenty of summer left."

"Not for me. I go back to work next week."

"Where?"

"The blouse mill. It's a grind, but we don't complain. You wouldn't know about working the line."

"Yeah?" Saverio looked out to the sea, where the locals bobbed in the surf like tub toys. He had longed for hot summer days like this during the long Michigan winters. "What would I know about factory life?"

"You're not missing anything. Consider yourself lucky." Chi Chi buffed her fingernails. She opened the case to return the manicure kit to her basket. Before she did, she took Saverio's right hand into her own. "Your nails are a mess. Want me to clean them up for you?"

"Sure."

Chi Chi took out a nail file and began filing Saverio's nails gently. "You got nice hands."

"So do you."

"Then why are you staring at the ocean?" she flirted.

"Because I can't get enough of it. I was raised near the Great Lakes, and they're swell, but they are nothing like this."

"Is this the first time you've seen the Atlantic Ocean?"

"No. We've worked the Eastern Seaboard pretty good. I've seen the ocean from Florida to Maine. But I never get tired of it. It's always different."

"The shore is the only place I've ever lived."

"You're the lucky one."

"Summer is nice, but winter in a shore town is like winter anywhere else."

"What's it like?"

"It snows. It's gray as far as you can see. You can't tell the horizon from the water. And the sun gets lost behind the clouds for months. It makes me sad, if you want to know the truth."

"Lake Huron and Lake Michigan get fierce in the winter. Whitecaps."

"On a lake?"

"Yep. But they're . . . I don't know how to describe them."

"Majestic?" she offered. "Majestic whitecaps."

Saverio broke into a wide grin. "That's it. Majestic. You got a way with words, you know that?"

"Yeah, yeah, yeah," she joked.

"You do. That's the sign of a writer. So says Rod Roccaraso. He gets songs submitted to the band all the time, and he says a great songwriter is someone who can write a tune about a girl he's never met in a place he's never been about a broken heart he's certain to endure."

"I'll remember that."

"You should."

"I like writing about ordinary things."

"Like what?"

"Love. Family. Home. The things people want, well, the things everyone wants. Everybody wants love when they're not in it. Everybody misses home when they're away from it."

"Not me."

"You're a tough guy. Even though your mama follows you around on the road."

"You must like me. You're being awful mean."

Chi Chi tilted the umbrella to cover herself. "I'm just teasing you. And I like you all right. But, you've got a girl. And I respect that."

Saverio scooted under the umbrella and into the shade with Chi Chi. "The other night when you walked in, that was . . . unfortunate." He said the word carefully, as if he were getting used to the idea of it.

"I was snooping around trying to find Mr. Roccaraso to introduce myself on behalf of the Donatelli Sisters. It's one of the perks of living on the shore. A lot of bands come through, and I try and take advantage of the proximity."

"To get your foot in the door?"

"Sure."

"So you've seen a lot of bands?"

"Oh, yeah. And met some of the players. I got Artie Shaw's autograph. But that was just for fun. I try to meet the business managers mostly. Let's see. I've seen the orchestras of Wayne King, Gus Arnheim, Ted Blade, Jack Hylton, Jimmie Grier."

"No kidding. Name bands."

"You stack up just fine against them."

"Did I ask?" Saverio was curt.

"You did not," Chi Chi admitted. "However, I have yet to meet a man who didn't want to be the best at whatever it is he does. You want to win, whether it's marbles or the number one spot on the *Music Hit Parade*. You can relax. You're right up there."

"Thanks. Where do you find the guts to go right up to them?"

"I go up *before* the show. After the show, it's no longer about business, if you know what I mean. I learned that right away. Too many fans around. Their minds are not on the music."

"It's the time to blow off steam."

"If that's what you call it. For me, at that hour, a girl approaching a bandleader looks funny. Yeah, my father worries—but I don't tell him anymore. I just go. I conduct myself professionally, and that's that."

"You've got moxie, I'll give you that."

"When you want something bad enough, you find courage. Or it arrives. However you want to look at it."

"Tell me about your act."

"I sing with my sisters. We started out singing at mass, and from there we were asked to sing weddings, so we did standards. And now I write songs for us."

"You're all pretty. That helps."

"When you're singing, pretty doesn't get you past the first verse."

"Pretty can get you through the night," Saverio said with authority.

"I don't think so. You have ten seconds to look good, and then you have to sound good or you don't deserve to be on the bandstand. You have quite the set of pipes."

"I'd better. I get enough practice. I sing seven days a week."

"I'd love that! I wish I could get my sisters to concentrate. I know we'd make it if they would just pay attention."

"Why don't they?"

"Different dreams, I guess."

"Why do you want to perform?"

"I love to sing. And I love to write songs just as much."

"I'd like to hear you sing sometime. You and your sisters."

"That can be arranged. We're not as sizzling as the Gay Sisters, and even if you dipped us in gold, we couldn't pull that off."

"I bet you could," Saverio flirted.

"You don't know me."

"I'm getting an idea."

Chi Chi waved the nail file like a magic wand. "What do you think so far?"

"You're funny."

"That's what a girl hopes a nice guy will say to her." Chi Chi made a face. "Top of my list."

"You don't know what a compliment that is."

"Is it?"

"You're pretty, but you don't believe it, and I'm not spending the afternoon convincing you. Let some other guy hammer that one home. You'll realize it in time."

"By then I won't care." Chi Chi cracked herself up.

"Maybe not. But men do. A pretty girl on a man's arm is everything to him."

"Because it makes him look good."

Saverio nodded. "Sure. Or maybe it's the same reason a painting or a sculpture draws you in. It makes a man feel good to look at a beautiful woman. A man appreciates line and form—the elements of art and aspects of beauty."

"I had no idea men looked at women like paintings."

"It's about feelings, too, don't get me wrong. You think about what she might mean to you as you get to know her—and the idea of solving that riddle gets you."

"Sounds like a line of bull to me."

Saverio laughed and took his hand away.

"Hey, I'm not done." Chi Chi took Saverio's hand again and examined his cuticles carefully. "Pretty or not, funny or boring, you either like someone or you don't. And that can turn to love, or it doesn't. If it does, you decide to be true or you don't. And from that foundation, you build a life with her or you don't. But the way I see it, no matter the progression of the romance, there's not much in it for the girl."

"You believe that?"

"We all end up the same—maids who serve the king. A man can be anything he wants in this life, anything at all. He has no obstacle but himself between where he stands and getting his dream. But if you're a girl, there's always a man between you and your happiness, or he is the one responsible for providing it."

"A man wants to make a woman happy. It gives him a sense of purpose."

"But what about *her* sense of purpose? Where is she supposed to find it? When you're a girl, you can't even buy a government bond without your father or your husband along to sign for you. Don't you think that's wrong? That's my paycheck, money I earned and saved, and I still have to have my father with me to buy a bond."

"Nothing about life is fair," Saverio said. "But maybe the rule protects you."

"From what?"

"Maybe if your father is with you, you got a second set of eyes on your money."

Chi Chi considered the notion. "That's only slightly reasonable."

"No, it makes sense. Think about it."

"You don't understand. Moving through life as a girl is like riding in a contraption that's jury-rigged, held together with string, cheap glue, and fingers crossed."

"What do you mean?"

"We have to get lucky to find happiness. Nobody is pulling for the girl to win. I know. I'm in the middle of three sisters. My aunts married nice boys who did all right, and they felt nothing but relief because they were treated well. Relief is the sister of luck. But then I have a cousin who married a guy who hits her, and she has to take the beatings because she has nowhere to go. Her family tells her she made her bed, but she had no idea what was in that bed before she climbed into it. Bad luck."

"Anything can happen."

"And it does. My dad lost his job, and my mom, who already has enough to do, had to get a job in the mill alongside Barbara and Lucille and me to help out. The women always step in when there's a problem and fix it in every family, including mine. I see it all the time. Maybe that's why I want to sing. I figure I have a talent, and why shouldn't I spend my life doing something I love instead of settling by making a series of decisions that might, just might turn out all right if I happen to choose a good guy who will do the right thing by me? I don't want to base my future happiness on luck. If I were gambling, I wouldn't place a bet with those odds."

"Awful grim."

"You said I was funny," Chi Chi said in mock defiance.

"I take it back. You sound like Margaret Sanger on the radio. My head is about to split open."

"No time for humor, my friend. We have a limited amount of time, and I want to tell you everything that's on my mind."

"Lucky me. Why's that?"

"We're simpatico."

"We are, aren't we?" Saverio agreed. "But the sun's out, and we're at the beach. Can't we just have fun?"

Chi Chi laughed. "I thought we were!"

Saverio noticed her mouth. He could practically taste Chi Chi's lips as he looked at them. There was something different about this girl, unexpected and appealing. She was pretty and smart, but funny, too, the rarest of confluences in the traits of people, especially women. The more she talked, the more interested he became in what she had to say. Saverio wanted to kiss her, but remembered the circumstances of their first meeting, an unfortunate moment when she found him in the arms of another girl. If only she hadn't seen him with Gladys Overby. Chi Chi almost read his mind, he figured, because she moved away from him slightly as the bright sun illuminated everything else about her—her perfect pins, those curves, and her shoulders, smooth like gold.

"You ever been to the track?" he asked, scooting closer to her.

"Nope."

She smelled good. Her hair had the scent of coconut and vanilla.

"I saw Eddie Arcaro win the Kentucky Derby. He's one of us, you know."

"Slight of build?"

Saverio laughed. "Italian, you goof. 'Attaboy Eddie' he's called."

"How's that headache?"

"Still got it."

"It might not be me and my yakking. It might be the heat that's making your head hurt. Maybe you're hungry."

"Want to go to lunch? I know a place."

Chi Chi buffed his nails. "Where is Miss Overby?"

"Doing laundry. The first thing she does in any town we play is find the Laundromat. And after that, the beauty parlor."

"Smart girl." Chi Chi whistled. "And what a Sheba."

"You got a fella?" he asked shyly.

"Several."

Saverio laughed.

"That sounded stuck-up, didn't it? Well, it's my vacation week, and I left my humility at Jersey Miss Fashions on the looping machine."

"So, the fellas line up for you?"

"It's more of a rotation. But between us pals, none of them are serious contenders. They aim awful high for what they offer in return."

"What are they putting on the table?"

"If I am longing to be the wife of Brielle's best tailor, or the wife of Manasquan's butcher in line to inherit the shop, or the wife of the man fourth in line to the son of the man who runs Jersey's largest trucking company out of Passaic, the world is my oyster and I'm on my way to a string of pearls with a diamond bale."

"Sounds like it."

"But that's not what I'm looking for."

"What do you want?"

"You have the life I want," Chi Chi said sincerely. "I want to work at music full-time."

"I wouldn't mind your life," Saverio admitted. "We could do an even-steven exchange."

"You say that." Chi Chi examined his fingernails.

"I want to live by the ocean with my family."

Chi Chi looked at him. "I think you mean it."

"I want to know what it's like to wake up happy," Saverio confessed.

"You don't?"

"I wake up confused."

"Get you."

"Sad, isn't it?" Saverio looked at his nails, which now were even, round, and buffed. "Nice work. Thank you. Now my hands go with my dress shirt and cuff links."

"I'm not done." Chi Chi gently took Saverio's right hand into hers. She squeezed some coconut oil from a tube and massaged his hand. "This protects the cuticle."

The warmth of Chi Chi's hand in his relaxed him. He closed his eyes as she worked the oil into his skin.

"Hey, what's going on here?" Rita peeked under the umbrella, dripping wet. Cold droplets fell on Chi Chi and made her shiver.

"Your towel is right behind me," Chi Chi said.

"Thanks, Cheech." Rita grabbed the towel.

"Is that what your friends call you?" Saverio asked.

"I don't believe I've had the pleasure, officially." Rita smiled as she rubbed her hair with the towel. "I'm Rita Milnicki. Or Millix, if you go by the name on my dad's garage. They changed his name on Ellis Island."

"We met at Cronecker's," Saverio said. "Right?"

"We barged in on you," Rita admitted. "It was an accident."

"Oh, that was you? The other one. With this one?" Saverio joked.

"Meet Saverio Armandonada," Chi Chi introduced him. "His name was not changed on Ellis Island."

"I figured. You give a good show," said Rita. "How do they fit your name on a marquee?"

"They haven't yet."

"How did you find us?" Rita sat down on the blanket next to them.

"I was walking on the beach, and I saw Chi Chi."

"You weren't looking for her?"

"Gosh, Rita," Chi Chi admonished her friend.

"I'm always looking." Saverio grinned.

Isotta's kitchen was run with her version of military precision. She taught her daughters how to cook simple dishes before they could read. Her garden was a source of pride, but it also sustained the family. Baskets of fresh lettuce, cucumbers, tomatoes, and peppers picked that morning were stacked in the window seat. A warm breeze ruffled the café curtains as the scents of fresh butter, garlic, and tomatoes filled the air as they simmered in a skillet on the stove.

The first of the tomatoes had ripened on the vines. Isotta plucked them and made fresh gravy for macaroni, or salads with herbs and mozzarella. The entire family would can the bounty of tomatoes at summer's end to last through the winter.

Isotta lifted the pot of macaroni off the burner, carried it to the sink, and strained it in the colander. She shook it before pouring the pasta into a large bowl. She folded a cup of fresh ricotta through the macaroni before adding the pomodoro sauce from the stove. She sprinkled Parmesan cheese on top, followed by fresh basil.

The picnic table was set in the Donatellis' backyard for lunch al fresco. The girls had dressed the table with fresh linens. Fragrant pink geraniums in a terra-cotta pot served as the centerpiece. Isotta carried the macaroni outside. Barbara added a place setting for Saverio. He stood back as Barbara made room for him at the table. "I don't mean to be any trouble."

"The unexpected guest is always welcome," Isotta said as she placed the bowl of macaroni on the table.

"Told you," Chi Chi said in passing as she went into the kitchen.

Saverio took a seat at the table and observed the Donatelli family work together to put a delicious meal on the table. This is what he imagined a happy family life to be, an abundant table with many place settings, overflowing with platters of good food, everyone pitching in, laughing together in the garden, on a lovely summer day under the sun. Even Mr. Donatelli contributed, which had never been the case in Saverio's home when he was growing up. The men were served by the women without exception.

"Where's your mother today?" Mariano asked him

"Her cousins took her for a drive to Spring Lake. My ma likes to look at houses."

"That's the town to do it," said Mariano, as Chi Chi emerged from the kitchen carrying a jug of homemade wine. Her sisters followed with the bread and salad.

"I make the wine in New Jersey but the grapes come from California," Mariano explained.

"A truck comes from Mendocino around Labor Day loaded with crates and crates of grapes. Dad looks for color and firmness." Chi Chi gathered the glasses as her father poured the wine.

"And I use my nose. Scent is very important with the grape." Mariano tapped his nose.

"I always throw Papa's wine into the sauce," Isotta admitted as she served Saverio the macaroni.

"Every Italian family in town is there when the truck arrives with the grapes, and they fight over the best of the lot." Chi Chi passed the hot pepper flakes to Saverio.

"And I always win." Mariano thumped the table.

"Dad has an eye," Chi Chi said proudly.

"And muscles," Lucille joked.

"Yes, I do." Mariano laughed.

"Anyhow, with those big muscles, Dad makes enough table wine for the year."

"And he makes vinegar and grappa, too," Lucille added.

"We waste nothing," Mariano said cheerfully. "Not a stem."

Lucille walked around the outside of the table with a basket of warm, crusty rolls, delivering one to each place setting. Barbara followed with a platter of grilled shrimp, wrapped around delicate stalks of asparagus. She carefully placed a sample on every plate next to the macaroni.

Isotta sat down at the head of the table opposite her husband. "I hope you like it," she said to Saverio.

"It looks delicious. I appreciate a home-cooked meal. Thank you for inviting me."

"We hope we're not taking you away from anything important."

"Not at all. I spend my days waiting for the sun to go down so I can go to work."

Mariano looked around the table. "Before we toast our guest, let us pray."

As the Donatellis and Saverio made the sign of the cross in unison, they blessed the meal and, when the prayer had concluded, blessed themselves once more. Saverio took his time blessing himself at the end of the prayer before placing his napkin on his lap.

"You take longer than the priest," Chi Chi said quietly to him.

Mariano raised his glass. "A toast to Saverio. May he sing long into every night, providing joy to audiences everywhere. *Cent'Anni.* Enjoy the rest of your stay in Sea Isle City!"

"Good wine, sir." Saverio sipped Mariano's vintage. The wine was hearty and woodsy, reminding him of his father's homemade wine.

Chi Chi passed their guest the gravy boat. He poured extra sauce on his macaroni and ate it with gusto. He was not skinny because he wanted to look good in photographs; he was hungry for homemade macaroni. Chi Chi felt pity for him. It was obvious that Saverio needed someone to take care of him. She looked at her mother, who observed the young man as he ate. The Donatelli women wondered if there was enough in the kitchen to fill him up.

"D Studio" housed in the family garage was a simple operation but Mariano had spared no expense on the recording equipment. It was clear he was in business to make a profit. The Donatelli sisters were gathered around the turntable. Saverio sat behind the console, next to Mariano, who served as the studio's sound engineer when he wasn't managing the act.

The cinder-block garage was painted beige, the series of small windows along the transom door were blocked with squares of plywood covered in black velvet. The concrete floor was swept clean, and although it had been many years since the old truck the family owned was parked inside, the faint scent of motor oil lingered in the air.

Saverio listened intently to his hosts' version of the standard *Oh Marie*. His hands were placed firmly on the console as he leaned forward with his eyes closed following the music. The Donatelli Sisters' recording, pressed into a 78 rpm vinyl record, was elegant. The package was Art Deco in design, black shellac with a silver label.

Mariano watched as the record revolved smoothly on the velvet wheel. The fine gold needle grazed the grooves, delivering a full-bodied sound through speakers rigged on a pipe he had hung from the ceiling. As the song played, Mariano adjusted the levels, gently turning the dials on the board, filling in the bass tone and modulating the treble.

In addition to the console, Mariano had built a soundproof recording booth. The simple structure, an enclosed room made of plywood with a padded door and a large glass window, took up half the space inside the garage.

The window of the booth faced the console, where Mariano had set up his two-reel taping system. Inside the booth was an upright piano, a ceiling microphone with an extension arm, and just enough space for a small combo to accompany the girls when they sang.

The Donatelli Sisters preferred to record in the fall; the booth could get very warm in the spring and hot in the summer months, and was too cold in the winter. But it would not have mattered to Chi Chi which season Saverio had chosen to show up. He was a professional singer, and it was rare that a front man for a traveling orchestra touring through was willing to visit the D Studio, much less lay down tracks for a song by an unknown writer credited as C. C. Donatelli.

Saverio turned to Mariano. "You made that record here? The vocals, instruments, levels, the mix, everything?"

"Right here," Mariano assured him. "I make the tapes here and run them in to Newark, to Magennis, where they press the vinyl for us."

"Pretty ambitious." Saverio seemed impressed.

"Everybody's got a recording studio in their garage now," said Mariano.

"Not like yours, Dad," said Chi Chi.

"I have pretty good microphones, and I figured out how to soundproof the booth."

"How did you do it?" Saverio was curious.

"I swept up the slag off the floor of the blouse mill and the cutting room. You know, all the strips of fabric and odd bits of thread that nobody wants—well, there's quite a bit of it each day. I'd gather it up, bring it home, and Isotta would stuff muslin bags she made out of old feed sacks with it. I took those bags and layered them between the interior wall and exterior wall—about six inches deep. That did the trick."

"You want to record something? For fun?" Chi Chi asked him. "A nice solo?"

"I don't have my charts."

"You don't need charts."

"You want me to sing *a cappella*?"

"I thought I'd accompany you on the piano. I wrote a song—"

"Here she goes," Lucille said, *sotto voce*, to her sister Barbara. "She's got him in her web."

"You can sight-read, can't you?" Chi Chi asked him.

"Yeah."

"So let's try it." Chi Chi handed Saverio the sheet music she had handwritten carefully on paper. "Just have fun." She pulled Saverio into the booth, closed the door behind them, and sat down at the piano.

"You can play?" he asked.

"I'm not sitting here because I look cute."

"But you do look cute."

"Beside the point. Here." Chi Chi opened the sheet music on the piano.

Saverio leaned in. "What is this?"

"It's a song."

"Has anybody recorded it?"

"No one. Yet."

"You wrote it?"

"We can't just sing standards."

"Why would you do that?" Saverio was amused. "I only make a living singing them."

Chi Chi played the tune on the piano. It had a swing feel. "What do you think? It's called *Mama's Rolling Pin*."

"A novelty."

"Humoresque," Chi Chi corrected him.

"Fancy," he replied.

"Of a stripe," she shot back. "The writer is in the booth, so be kind."

"There ain't no room in show biz for a sensitive artist."

She laughed. "I'll be the first."

"Nope. You'd be the second."

Outside the booth, Mariano listened as Saverio and Chi Chi bantered back and forth and teased one another. Barbara flipped through the pages of the *Bergen County Record*, while Lucille arranged the reel boxes on the shelf behind her father in alphabetical order.

"Dad, she's up to something," Lucille said.

"I'm keeping an eye on her. Nothing wrong with being ambitious."

"She's an opportunist," Barbara corrected him without looking up from the newspaper.

"She's smart," Mariano countered. "Nothing wrong with that, either. It's who you know."

"He's paying for his lunch," Lucille said dryly. "The hard way."

"I don't know about that," Mariano said.

Inside the booth, Chi Chi gently played the tune. "Okay, you be husband." She pointed to the sheet music.

"And you're wife?"

"Well, it would stand to reason."

"Don't get snippy," Saverio chided her. "Just play it, wouldja?"

Chi Chi rolled her fingers down the piano keys and cued Saverio.

Wife sang:

> He stays true or I beat him blue / With Mama's
> Rolling Pin

Husband sang:

I don't stray because she's mastered flambé / With her
Mama's Rolling Pin

"Okay, here's the chorus," Chi Chi explained.
"I got it," said Saverio.

Wife sang:

   I make dough

Husband sang:

   She makes dough

Wife sang:

   He makes dough

Together they sang:

   We make dough—with Mama's Rolling Pin

Wife sang:

   We got married, the church was nice

Husband sang:

   She wore a veil and a chunk of ice

Wife sang:

Preacher said are you out or are you in

Together they sang:

She said yes and I said yes—to Mama's Rolling Pin

Wife and husband sang together:

If you want your love to be true
Don't hesitate to follow our rule
Once you marry and become kin
Keep him on a short leash
With Mama's Rolling Pin!

Chi Chi spun around and looked out the window of the booth. "Dad? How was that?"

Before her father could answer, Saverio cut in. "Barbara? Lucille? We need you in here."

"But it's a duet," Chi Chi said.

"It will pack a bigger wallop if they harmonize on the chorus. Like you girls are ganging up on me. Musically speaking, I mean."

"Let's try it." Chi Chi shrugged.

Lucille and Barbara joined them inside the booth. Saverio instructed the girls where to come in during the song, and set the tempo with Chi Chi.

As the girls rehearsed and Saverio conducted their vocals, Mariano leaned back in his chair, put his hands on his head, and observed the process.

"We're ready to go, Mr. Donatelli," Saverio said. "Let's tape this one."

"Take one. *Mama's Rolling Pin*," Mariano said into the microphone at the console as he spun the tape reels into position and hit the dial.

As Saverio sang with the sisters inside the booth, Mariano marveled at the ease of the performance as he adjusted the levels on the console. As they stopped and started, refined and perfected their harmonies, the song emerged. They recorded the third, fourth, and fifth takes without stopping. Each version grew in personality, vocal heft, and eventually meaning.

Mariano was pleased. He chuckled with the kind of glee a prospector feels when he finds gold nuggets at the bottom of a tin pan, or the thrill an oilman knows when he recognizes the squish of black goo under his feet in a barren field before a geyser is about to blow, or the zeal of the scientist who combines two formulas in a beaker during an experiment and, surprising himself, creates a serum that becomes the cure.

Mariano could see the future, an endgame to their efforts. So what if the neighbors thought he was *stunod* when he took a perfectly decent garage and turned it into a recording studio? His wife didn't like the truck parked on the street but he told her to think big. Naysayers pummeled him: "What good could come of making records, anyhow?" Even his priest thought it was a scheme. He wished they could hear this track being cut! He had a hook now, a path to the prize: three pretty girl singers backing a handsome crooner on a song about love and marriage.

He could feel it: something in Mariano's bones told him that a song with humor in the midst of the Great Depression would be a balm, and if that song was also personal and specific to the immigrant experience—in this case Italian, but surely the Jewish, Polish, Greek, or Irish who populated the shore towns and cities a train ride away could relate to it, too, as long as the song's sentiment was true to their particular culture's traditional view, that tune would hit. If the song was also catchy, surely there would be a big audience for it.

There was no denying the sound. As the sisters' rich harmonies supported Saverio's strong lead vocals, Mariano imagined success. After all, it took only one song to launch a group from obscurity to fame. Through the window in the booth, anyone could see it. Engagement rings, Lucille's dream of secretarial school, and their union cards were no match for this magic. The Donatelli Sisters and that kid Saverio were on their way to the big time.

Saverio handed Lucille his empty soda bottle as Chi Chi held the door of the garage open for them.

"Would you like another one for the road?"

"No, thanks, Lucille. I have to get back to the hotel."

"Don't let Chi Chi work you over," she told him as she went to the backyard.

"She plays it sketchy," Barbara warned him as she followed Lucille.

"Ignore my sisters, they have absolutely no acumen for show business." Chi Chi ran ahead and opened the garden gate to the street.

"Are you going to open every door for me between here and the hotel?"

"You've been so generous. I'd drive you back in my dad's truck, but it's too risky. It breaks down all the time. We don't have a car."

"I don't have a car either. But if you had a car, what car would you want?"

"A Packard."

"Why?"

"Because everywhere you look, people drive Fords."

"That's the only reason?"

"That and I think a Packard is a work of art."

Saverio checked his pockets. "Here." He pulled out a small brown paper bag, opened it, and handed Chi Chi a scapular of the Blessed Mother on a silk cord.

"This is lovely. From your mom?"

"No, from me."

"How thoughtful."

"It's blessed. The nun was out of medals."

"You shop at the convent?"

"She was going door to door at the hotel."

"Encouraging good behavior, no doubt. Why'd you give me a present? I should be giving you one." She got up on her toes and kissed him on the cheek. "Thank you."

Saverio noticed Chi Chi's hair smelled like vanilla, fresh like a summer cake. "It's all I've got to give you. To remember this week. I bought my mom one, too."

"Of course you did. Nice Catholic boy, you have a couple more in that bag. You should spread them around."

Saverio laughed. "You caught me. I bought a few, but I didn't wipe out the nun's inventory."

Chi Chi laughed. "Of course not."

"My ma told me you saved a boy's life."

"Not at all." She shrugged. "The lifeguard showed up."

"Not what I heard. You went out and found him first. Take the credit," Saverio insisted.

"I'm a middle child. I don't like to."

"I'm an only child. I have to."

Chi Chi grinned. "I'm used to getting the blame, never the credit."

"I got both."

"Lucky you."

"Girls don't like to take credit."

"Whatever our mothers do, we do." Chi Chi put the scapular around her neck.

"Is it true of fathers and sons?"

"I don't know. My father only had daughters."

"I always wanted a sister or a brother."

"You wouldn't if you had them. They'd drive you crazy."

"I don't think so."

"What we imagine is always better than what we get," Chi Chi said.

"You're awful smart."

"Not really. Observant."

"You like my ma?"

"She's lovely. Not too many Venetians around, you know. My mom is Venetian too."

"No kidding." Saverio needed to get back to the hotel, but he didn't want to go.

"My father says you can never win an argument with a Venetian."

"He hasn't met my father."

"Where is he?"

"Michigan. He doesn't take vacations."

"Why not?"

"You'd have to ask him."

"You two don't talk?"

Saverio shrugged. "Not much."

"Let me guess. He doesn't like his son the crooner. He would rather his son have a traditional job."

"Sounds right."

"Can't you change his mind?"

"Nope."

"Do you want to?"

"It's not about what I want."

"I got it."

"I think you might." Saverio looked at Chi Chi, and then he checked his watch. "I wish we had more time."

"I talk too much."

"I like it."

Chi Chi didn't know what to say, and usually she knew exactly what to say.

Saverio folded his arms across his chest. "I go with a lot of girls."

"So?"

"I think you should know that."

"You want me to put it in the *Sea Isle Express*?"

"No, it's just for you to know."

"I don't judge you. So, you go with a lot of girls. All that means is that one girl that really mattered broke your heart."

Saverio wondered how Chi Chi knew, but he wouldn't admit the truth so he lied. "Nah."

"Whatever you say. Nobody wants to get hurt. Nobody chooses to get their heart broken. It just happens. But there's an upside. It keeps songwriters in business. And singers singing."

"What do you want?"

"What do you mean?"

"What do you want from life?"

Chi Chi breathed deeply, taking a moment to admit her deepest desire. "I want to sing."

"That's a job. I mean, for the rest of your life. You know, when you grow up and get serious."

"I want to sing and write songs."

"Girls don't do well in show business."

"Says who?" Chi Chi placed her hands on her hips.

"Says me."

"Forgive me, but how much can you observe about girls in business when you're on the make?"

"Not much." He laughed.

"So maybe a girl can be happy in show business. I think when you love what you do, that's happiness."

"But what about your home life?"

"I don't think about anything but singing," she admitted.

"You should."

"Because I'm a girl?"

"No, because it's not all there is, for anybody."

"How do you know?"

"Because I'm living it."

"I want to travel from city to city and sing in a different club every night and meet new audiences."

"You'd get tired of it."

"Never."

"When you're on the road, all you want to do is stay in one place. Have a home somewhere."

"Maybe if you could go home once in a while, you'd like the road more," Chi Chi suggested.

"Could be. But you wouldn't like the road for long."

"How do you know?"

"You come from a happy family. Why would you ever leave them?"

"Because I've already had that."

"So you want to try loneliness and misery for a while?"

"I have my own plans. I don't want what everybody else has. Never did. Never will."

"You don't think about your own house, windows, a little kitchen, a porch? A garden? What if you fall in love?"

"So what?"

"So when people fall in love they get married and make a home and have a family."

"Says who?"

"Says everybody—says the lyrics of every song ever written. You should know. You write them. They're always about love even when they're not about love," Saverio insisted.

"Maybe."

A thought occurred to Saverio. "I think this is an act."

"An act is when you go to the circus and a dog is riding a bicycle. This isn't an act," Chi Chi assured him.

"What if a fellow came along and changed your mind? Not the butcher or the tailor or the trucker, none of these Jersey jadrools, but someone else, and you wanted him more than show business?"

Chi Chi shook her head. "Not gonna happen. When I close my eyes, I don't see that. I see a band. I hear music. The boys in the box stand up in white ties and tails and they raise that brass up high and they blow and I don't want to be anywhere else in the world. I want to be there on the bandstand. I want to bring the song in—right there, in that moment, with my voice. What comes out of them and comes out of me is a creation. Sound. Music. Emotion. And there's no fella, no vista, no clime, no *thing*, not even a hulking emerald or ruby or diamond, and I mean that, set in the finest gold, that matters more to me than bringing the song in."

"But that's only good a couple hours a night." Saverio kicked a pebble across the sandy street. "The band plays so couples in love can come and dance."

"But it's a good living." Chi Chi said the word *living* as though it were sacred.

"It can be."

"It's the living I want to make. I love my family. But I don't want to make one. I just like making music."

"Okay, okay, I surrender."

"Good, because you can't convince me."

Saverio had to admit it: he liked this girl. She wasn't like the others he knew. She was direct—honest, and he could talk to her and forget the time. He didn't know what to make of that. When she talked about what she wanted her life to be like, she lit up, like something inside her was on fire. She was pretty, too. He wanted to kiss her, but he didn't know how to ask.

"I don't want you to kiss me," Chi Chi said.

"You don't?" Saverio wondered if she was a mind reader, a seer like the gypsy who followed the band, setting up a tent and a crystal ball, when they played county fairs.

"Nope. Save your pep. I have been sent to you because you need a true friend. You got girls lined up and down the boardwalk—the line's longer than the one for funnel cakes. I saw them. You have girls from Wildwood Crest to Brielle sashaying to get your attention. You don't need mine in that way."

"They all want something," Saverio admitted. "What do you want?" He put his hands in his pockets. "Besides my job?"

"I need a favor."

"Sure you do."

"It's not a big favor. I'd just like you to give our record to Rod Roccaraso and see if he thinks we got something. I can get it pressed before you leave town. Maybe he can play it, and figure something out. Will you do that for me?"

"Why should I?" Saverio teased.

"Because we're really good."

She looked so hopeful, so eager, that Saverio almost laughed. "Okay, Chi Chi."

"You'll pass it along? I'll have it ready for you tomorrow." Chi Chi clapped her hands. "Thank you! You're a prince!"

"Every Italian son is, you know."

"I know. But you're a good one." Chi Chi turned to walk back into the house.

"Hey, Chi Chi?"

"Yeah?"

"You're right about me."

She smiled at him before walking up the porch steps. When she got to the top, she turned. "Hey, Savvy?"

"Yeah?"

"There's nothing wrong with being a romantic figure."

"I didn't think there was."

"Then how come you act guilty?" Chi Chi went into the house and closed the screen door behind her.

Saverio stood on the sidewalk and surveyed the Donatellis' Cape Cod with its weathered gray shingles and freshly painted yellow trim, and wondered what it must be like to live inside. Mariano had laid the slabs of slate that formed the front walk, a hopscotch pattern in shades of blue, set in cement he had poured himself. Italians, given a choice, will always do their own stonework.

The matching patches of grass on either side of the walkway in the front yard were neatly mowed; the seagrass hedges that hemmed the porch ruffled in the breeze, as wind chimes, small white glass discs that resembled communion hosts, clinked a tune. It was a fine house for a good family.

Saverio heard their voices, carried outside through the screens. The sound of their conversation sailed over him like music. It was the kind of communication that can only be found deep within a home, where a family thrives, close and connected, where the members understand one another and speak their own particular language.

Saverio couldn't make out the words through the screen door and open windows, but when laughter pealed through the rooms, it sounded like bells, the kind the altar boy rang in church. A sacred sound. It was to him, anyway.

The late afternoon summer sky was speckled with lilac clouds as an egg-yolk sun slipped behind the Cronecker Hotel.

Saverio greeted his mother with a kiss on the cheek as she waited for him on the veranda. The last of the beach crowd walked home after another day on the sand. They carried their umbrellas on their shoulders like muskets and swung their empty lunch baskets as they listened to the last minutes of *Jimmy Arena and His SRO Orchestra* on their transistor radios out of WSOU in East Orange. The seamless wail of Jimmy's saxophone trailed off as they turned onto Seaforth Avenue.

Rosaria embraced her son. "I'm happy you could see me before the show."

"You look good, Mama. You got a little Jersey shore *bronzata*."

Rosaria looked at her arms. "I guess I did. Cousin Joozy is going to take me to the train."

"You'll be comfortable in the sleep car."

"Oh, I know. Thank you for making the arrangements. You're too good to me."

Saverio smiled at his mother. "Not possible."

"I love the Super Chief. Such interesting people. On the way here, I played cards with some ladies from Roseto, Pennsylvania. I find friends wherever I go."

Rosaria sat in a wicker rocker facing Ocean Drive. She wore her best beige linen suit and leather pumps. Her suitcase, hatbox, and purse were piled neatly next to the chair. "I've had a wonderful week."

"You came to every show."

"I wouldn't miss a note."

Saverio sat down on the bench across from her. "Why don't you stay longer?"

"Cousin would like that."

"So stay."

"Your father needs me."

"I'm sure he's getting along fine."

"He does all right. But he does better when I'm there to take care of things."

"Cook and clean."

"That's part of it. He's all alone there."

"Some people are better off alone."

"He's your father, Saverio. And he does his very best every day," she said pleasantly.

"He threw me out, Ma. What kind of father throws out his only son?"

"It was terrible. But men do things like that to make their sons strong. It's an old story you find in many books in the library. Fathers and sons have a rough time of it. But I assure you, he wants the best for you."

"Even if that were true, he's not nice to you."

"Not always."

"He does what's best for him. You deserve kindness every day, all day, and all night too."

"Thank you for that. But I can take care of myself."

"Your husband should take care of you."

"He does," Rosaria tried to assure her son.

"I've been thinking. I've been on the road for a few years now and I've saved up a few bucks. I'd like to send you to Treviso. Why don't you go home to Italy for a visit? Visit your cousins. See your aunts and uncles."

"I was so little when we left. I hardly remember it."

"You told me stories. You made it sound like some enchanted kingdom."

"It was. But I was a child, and children make up things when they leave a place, to hold on to it. I probably wouldn't recognize it now."

"You still write to your family?"

She nodded.

"You would be welcome there, and happy too. It would be good for you. You just said you make friends wherever you go."

"My place is with your father."

She said it so firmly that Saverio knew it was unlikely that he could change her mind. "I can't convince you, can I?"

"I made a vow to your father. Did you ever know me to break a promise?" She smiled.

"I'd forgive you this one."

"Don't be so hard on him. When you were born, he held you like delicate crystal. He was so afraid he'd drop you. He was so dear with you. You can't remember it, but I do."

"It would be comforting to remember nice moments. But I don't have any of those memories."

"It won't always be that way."

"I don't like leaving you there alone with him." He struggled to put into words what he was feeling. "I have anxiety about it."

"You shouldn't."

"Maybe the only way a son can leave his home is to forget it altogether."

"I hope not."

"I'm not welcome there. You know that."

"You can come home anytime."

"I wouldn't do that to you. He's an animal with me around."

"It's hard for him. He doesn't understand what you do. He thinks it's frivolous."

"He would. He loads a furnace with sand to make glass. And when it's lava, he breaks his back pouring it into the molds. And after that he has to cut it to form. He saw a man lose his hand once."

"I remember." Rosaria nodded.

"His job is dangerous, and it requires total concentration. He's been at it for over twenty years, and he must be numb inside and out from the rote work of it. He would say any man who wasn't aching and bleeding and breaking the bones in his back wasn't actually working. But Papa would be wrong. What I do isn't easy, and not everybody can do it."

"I know that."

"I don't really enjoy getting up in front of people."

"I thought maybe you'd grown accustomed to it by now."

"I haven't. I shake from nerves sometimes. And I get sick."

"Sick?" Rosaria leaned in, concerned.

"I get stage fright. Sometimes I vomit and sometimes I get feverish like I'm going to pass out."

"The stakes are high," Rosaria said. "It's competitive."

"Some of the boys drink to screw up the courage to get out there, and others smoke. There's all kind of vice to get your mind off the fear. To numb it. But I remember the line at the Rouge, and that gives me the guts to stick with it. I don't want to go back there. Not because I'm better than the work, but because I wasn't right for it."

"I tried to explain that to your father."

"Pop never got it. He thought it was so simple. On the line, all I had to do was my operation, and hand it off to the next guy without making a mistake. But it was so much more than that. I had to stay the same, to be consistent, without change, alteration, or deviation, every day, week after week."

"It's not for everyone."

"I saw men that reveled in the line. But it choked me, Ma. To this day, and it's been six years since I left, I still swing a wrench and bolt the door handle on the line in my dreams."

"Your father calls out to the men in his sleep."

"Sure he does. It becomes a permanent part of you. Entertaining an audience is the opposite, it's a thrill that comes and goes and lasts as long as the set. They come to you with high hopes, they want you to help them forget their troubles, forget their bills and the boss that won't cut them a break. Music is their reprieve. Dancing is their way of getting the girl, and sometimes, by God, they do!"

"I saw it happen right here," Rosaria said.

"It's the same in every town. Maybe we do help them get their minds off the things they don't have, and never will. They don't need to see a nervous Nellie up there."

"You seem at ease when you sing."

"I want to be. But most shows, when I don't think I'm good enough, or Mr. R. tells me I sound like a cheese grater, or the venue doesn't want to pay the band, it's not fun. There's no Henry Ford backing the operation."

"That's why your father worried."

"No, he worried because he's good at misery. He's not good at being happy—for you, for me, for anybody. He has the best wife in the world, and he doesn't appreciate you."

"He grew up so poor."

"So did you. And you know how to love."

"I've tried to teach him."

"Some people can't learn. You know, he's got one son. I even suited up and went to the plant, hoping that would prove once and for all that I was all right. But even that wasn't enough. If you want to know the truth, had he been proud of me, I'd still be on the line."

Rosaria snapped open her purse and removed a handkerchief. "Could you write him a note once in a while?" She dabbed her eyes with the handkerchief.

"For what?"

"To let him know you're okay."

"You tell him."

"It's not the same. Would you do that for me?"

Saverio sighed. "For you, I will. Is there anything you need?"

"Nothing."

"They don't make 'em like you anymore. Girls want a lot of things these days."

"Where do you find these girls?"

"Around."

"Around is not a good place to look," Rosaria said. "Stay away from *around*. A nice Italian girl who is *there* is what you need."

"You think so?"

"I don't want you to lose everything I taught you."

"Mama, I couldn't shake it if I tried."

At Magennis Records in Newark, four turntables with finished records spun at once. Saturdays were busy in the shop, as back-up singers, moonlighters, amateurs, and semiprofessionals came in to pick up their self-made records, to peddle them to pavilions, dance halls, and radio stations up and down the shore in hopes of being discovered.

"How many did you order, Dad?" asked Chi Chi.

"Six. We'll hit the big guys today."

"WRPR?"

"They're on my list. Mahwah."

"Yeah. They played the Mandarolla Sisters' record out of Free-hold. The Testa Sisters, out of North Providence, Rhode Island. Both those records charted. The Testas are still getting traction."

"How do you know?"

"*Music Hit Parade*. I check at the library. I wrote to every manager listed in the magazine."

"Any bites?"

"Just sent them."

"Bridges are important. Don't burn them. Build them. Cross them. Repair them."

"I want to give a record to Saverio."

"So give him one."

"The bus is leaving at four," Chi Chi said anxiously. "Can we make it?"

Mariano checked his watch. "Why not?"

The shopgirl placed *Mama's Rolling Pin* on a turntable. "Give it a listen while I run the register."

Chi Chi and Mariano leaned in and listened closely as their record played.

"It's good, Dad. Best we've done."

The shopgirl handed Mariano his change. "For whatever it's worth, the girls in the back all liked this one a lot."

Mariano left the windows rolled down on his 1926 Hudson truck, which at maximum speed did forty miles an hour. Chi Chi held the records on her lap. As they trundled down Route 81, most

every vehicle sped past them, including an old jalopy with a crank-
case and a rumble seat.

"I don't have a forwarding address for him." Chi Chi peered
ahead at the traffic on the road.

"You like this Saverio kid, don't you?"

"He's all right."

"Cheech, I can tell you like him."

"I'm not over the moon."

"Did I say love? I said like."

"He knows a lot of things I don't. He's a good pal."

"He likes you is what I'm trying to say."

"I feel sorry for him."

"Why's that?"

"He's a sad sack. Anyhow, I have other things on my mind. Like
getting air play with this record."

"You're gonna make it."

"I don't know, Dad. Sometimes I wonder."

"Stay true to your ear. You write a good song, and you can sing
as good as any of the girls out there. Believe in yourself. You know
what you are. You gotta have faith."

"What is faith?" Chi Chi waved a fly out of the truck window.

"Eight years with the Salesian nuns, and you don't know?"

"I guess I could give you their definition. What's yours?"

"Faith is courage. It's the unspoken pact you have with God
and your own soul that you will not stop until you are spending the time you've been given doing the thing you were born
to do."

"Where'd you hear that?"

"Made it up. *Coraggio*."

"Guts." Chi Chi chuckled to herself. The last time she heard
that word, Saverio Armandonada had told her she had it.

"That's right. Guts. You know what works."

"Do I?"

"Yes, you do. You only get one shot at this life. Take it."

"Dad, I'm the best buttonholer-looper in the specialty department at Jersey Miss."

"Nothing wrong with that. But you have other skills. God-given."

"Do you think I sing like a headliner?"

"Absolutely. But you're the one who has to believe it."

"I want it."

"That's important, too. You do well at whatever you tackle. Look at you over at the mill. But it's not enough to earn a paycheck and buy bonds, Cheech. That's not our idea of success. That's an American idea."

"But we're Americans, Dad."

"Yes, we are. But we're also Italian, which means the money isn't what matters to us. It is not the goal. That doesn't prove anything. A squirrel is good at storing nuts. He's still a squirrel and they're still nuts, no matter how many he hides, or how few. *Va bene?* Italians crave art like your boss craves his profits. Could you live a happy life working in the mill? Sure. You could do it. But then you'd be spending your life making someone else's dream come true, not your own."

"Making Mr. Alper rich."

"Be grateful for your job, but don't be a slave to it." Mariano pulled up to the bus stop at the pier in Sea Isle. "Risk is what makes you rich. Trying things. Reaching. Taking a chance. Those are the people who hear their own heartbeat."

A clump of girls in bathing suits and shorts dispersed from the platform. Chi Chi jumped out of the truck with the record.

"Hey, where's the Rod Roccaraso bus?"

"It left already," one of the girls answered over her shoulder, fanning herself with an autographed photo of the orchestra.

"What do you mean? It was supposed to leave at four."

"I dunno. Left at three." Another girl licking a custard cone shrugged and walked past her.

Chi Chi climbed back in the truck. "We missed it."

"You tried."

"If this buggy weren't so old, we could catch up with the bus on the turnpike and I could hand this off to him." Chi Chi spun Saverio's copy of the 78 on her finger and ruminated.

"We're not chasing the bus."

"This could be our last chance."

"Use your head, kid. We know his cousin. We'll get the record to Joozy. We got connections."

Every window on the *Rod Roccaraso Musical Express* bus was propped open. Hot air blew around inside, circulating nothing but heat. The musicians loosened their ties and relaxed in their seats, settling in for the long drive to Richmond, Virginia.

"I hope you are done once and for all with the local beach bunnies," Gladys sniffed as she opened a magazine and flipped through it.

"What are you talking about?"

"I have eyes, Saverio."

"Maybe you need glasses."

"Maybe you need to acquire some self-control."

"I want you to know I was true to you in Sea Isle City."

"Get you." Gladys closed the magazine. "For once, I actually believe you."

"It's the truth."

Gladys kissed him lightly on the cheek. "I suppose you're allowed to run with your tribe once in a while."

"Huh?"

"The guidos."

Saverio thought to call her on the jab. When he worked at River Rouge, *guido* was a slur, and surely Gladys knew it was one, meant it as one. But it was a long way to Virginia, and he didn't want to argue for five hundred miles. "Yep. Those are my people."

"At least they buy tickets to see us."

"Yes, they do. With their hard-earned lira." Saverio stretched his leg down the aisle of the bus and leaned back in the seat. He closed his eyes and shifted the brim of his fedora over them.

"Really? You're gonna sleep? You just woke up," Gladys whined.

"I'm tired, honey."

"You're always tired."

Saverio shifted in the seat, crossed his arms, and said nothing. He would have liked to tell Gladys that he was tired of her incessant nagging, but that would have just led to more of it. Besides, she could be nice to him, and she was a good roommate on the road. She looked after him, pressed his shirts and tuxedo like his mother might have done. Made sure he ate properly, too. And there were other comforts.

"I know you need your rest. That's why I sent you off to the beach. I know you like the sun. Swarthy people crave it."

"*Grazie.*"

"I was happy to stay behind and do the laundry. I pressed all your shirts. Starched the collars and cuffs of your shirts just like you like them."

"You're a doll."

"I'm your doll, baby." Gladys stroked his cheek with her hand. "I'm here to make your life easy."

"And you do." Saverio leaned over and kissed her on the lips before settling back in the seat once more. He closed his eyes as Gladys leaned over and tickled his ear with the tip of her nose.

"My ma wants to know when we're getting married," Gladys said tenderly. "I'd like to give her some notion of when."

Saverio sat up in the seat and pushed his hat back on his head. "I'm not ready for marriage."

"Could've fooled me."

"I'm not horsing around. I'm being honest. I am not ready."

"It was my understanding . . ." Tears welled in her blue eyes. She stopped the flow by blinking hard. "It is my understanding that we were to marry at some point on this tour. You promised me."

"When did I do that?"

She whispered, "You know."

"Gladys, you're very special, but a man says things sometimes."

She looked hurt. "You don't love me."

"I didn't say that."

"You either do or you don't."

"I have a deep affection for you."

"What does that mean?" Gladys raised her voice.

Saverio looked around the bus. Most of the musicians were asleep, and the rest were lethargic, draped on the seats like coats thrown over chairs at a party. The drummer and the trombone player were in the back of the bus with the sports section of the newspaper, folded small, as they ran numbers on bets they would place when the bus landed in Richmond.

"It means a kind of feeling," he whispered.

"I don't take care of you because I have affection for you, I take care of you because I love you. My mother is expecting me to come home with a husband because I told her I was coming home with one. Now, what are you going to do about it?"

Saverio wanted to be with Gladys, but not permanently, and not enough to offer her marriage. He thought about measuring his words, but he was simply too tired to negotiate. "Nothing," he answered.

"You have no intention of giving me a ring?"

"Not at this present juncture."

"A juncture is where train tracks cross a cow pasture. Who talks like that?"

"A man who isn't going to propose."

"You only think of yourself."

"That can be true."

"Can be? It is true. Ask me. I know."

"Gladys, can we discuss this later?"

"This is as good a time as any."

"We're on a bus with the band. It's a terrible time to talk about this."

"I have no secrets. I think you're tired of me. That's what it is. You're bored." She snapped her neck and looked out the window.

The New Jersey turnpike was nothing but a ribbon of gray asphalt, unspooling before them with no end in sight. The green rolling hills spilled away from the road on either side like ruffles on a skirt.

Saverio leaned toward her. "I'm sorry."

"Apology accepted."

"Thank you." Saverio slid down in the seat once more and closed his eyes.

"Honestly?"

Saverio opened his eyes. "What now?"

"We have not settled the matter of our pending nuptials."

"No nuptials are pending, Gladys."

"Can't you see how unhappy you're making me?" she whispered tersely. "You're humiliating me by withholding your proposal of marriage."

"Come on, baby," Saverio teased her. "I'm not ready for all this jazz."

Gladys didn't appreciate the humor. "You sound like a session drummer. That flippant kind of talk is beneath you. Remember who you're with, please." She smoothed her skirt. "You have got some crust."

Saverio ran his hands down the thighs of his pant legs and turned to face his girlfriend. "You don't even like Italians."

"I don't have to marry the entire country of Italy. I can marry one of you and cope."

"You called me a garlic eater in Albany," Saverio reminded her.

"I was pushed to the brink! You test my patience."

"Have I ever called you a name, or insulted you, or treated you poorly?"

"I gave myself to you," she whispered.

"I gave myself to you, too. The difference is, I don't want anything in exchange for it."

"There's no expectation of an exchange of any kind. It's a promise made, an intention rendered by one person in love with another, to honor that love with a vow of marriage," she explained.

"I don't recall doing any rendering."

"You're impossible." Gladys stuck out her chin. "I'll tell you what. I don't need this. I certainly don't need you."

Gladys was, from every angle, like one of those winsome girls who appeared in the lingerie advertisements in the fold-out of the social section in every Sunday newspaper from Chicago to Palm Beach. She was sultry and yet somehow virginal. No matter her mood, her beauty was undeniable. Her figure was in proportion, like any fine structure, built with deliberate curves that accentuated her clean lines. A white-hot blonde, her hair had just enough natural wave and the scent of rain.

Gladys bore the ice-blue eyes of the girls of the coldwater coun-tries of northern Europe, with the bone structure and resolve to go with them. She possessed an inner core of self-confidence that Saverio found intriguing, given that she was a girl singer who trav-eled with a pack of, let's face it, men who were often of sketchy character. Gladys never let her surroundings or the company she kept determine her self-worth or lessen her value. She could beguile, dazzle, and dismiss as she pulled on a white kid glove. Gladys Overby made men stop and stare at her in wonderment, like one would a blue jay in snow.

Saverio closed his eyes and breathed. The scent of her gardenia perfume was intoxicating. He didn't want to give her up. "Forgive me, please."

"Never, never, and I mean *never*, another apology will I accept from the likes of you," she said. "You say you're sorry like regular people say 'I'll have the pie.' I don't believe a word you say. Going forward, you won't make a sucker out of me. From now on, you're on your own, Mr. A."

She stood up, grabbing the back of the seat in front of her, and, her purse dangling from her wrist, climbed over him and out into the aisle of the moving bus. The driver looked up at the rearview mirror before steadying his eyes back on the highway.

Gladys straightened her skirt and her spine and walked to the back of the bus, taking an empty seat in front of the gamblers.

Saverio twisted around in his seat. He shook his head, but he knew not to go after her. The couple had made enough ugly scenes in front of the band, on the bus, backstage, and in more than a few hotel lobbies and hallways. He would have to fig-ure out how to get back in favor with her. It was swell having a partner on the road. Whenever he went out with the boys after the show, he never had a problem finding his hotel room in the middle of the night; he just followed the scent of Gladys's perfume to her door. Saverio would be giving up a lot on the road by breaking it off with her. Marriage might actually be a fine and practical idea.

Gladys settled into the window seat, placed her purse on the empty seat next to her, and fixed her gaze out the window. She was through with Saverio once and for all. She knew it for certain because she was not hysterical. She had shed enough tears over the emotionally distant Italian.

She was so confused! Weren't those people supposed to be hot-blooded? How had she fallen for the only Mediterranean since the lotharios of the House of Borgia who was a cold cookie? Just her luck. But she didn't have to take it, not one more minute, not one more city, not one more gig, not anymore.

Gladys Overby was a Minnesota girl. She knew when the fish weren't going to bite, when it was time to cut bait, pull in the rod, the reel, and the rig, row back to the shore, and call it a day. She had done her level best to snag this fellow, and he had no intention of swallowing the hook. Enough. She would move on. Her mother in Hibbing would have to understand.

Saverio again stretched his leg down the aisle, tugged the brim of his hat over his eyes, leaned back in the seat, and closed his eyes once more. Soon, he was asleep, like any regular Joe, who didn't know from trouble, like any man with a clear conscience. He did not stir until the bus turned into the circular driveway of the Jefferson Hotel in downtown Richmond. When the bus

driver shook him, he woke up. The bus was empty; all that remained was the faint scent of Gladys Overby's perfume, faded
gardenias.

"Are we here?" Saverio rubbed his eyes.

"You're here," the bus driver said. "Here's your bag and your
ukulele."

"Mandolin," Saverio said, taking them.

"That's right. Eye-talian boy, aren't you?"

"All my life," Saverio said as he got off the bus and walked to the
entrance of the hotel.

4

JULY 1938

Accelerando

(Push)

Chi Chi fixed the straw boater on her head as Mariano pulled into the parking lot of the WBAB radio station in Atlantic City. She flipped open her compact and powdered her nose quickly.

"We're going to make it, Cheech! This is a sign," her father assured her. "This is why you never give up. We may have missed the bus, but we're gonna make the golden chariot!"

Chi Chi jumped out of the truck and ran for the entrance door of the station. She pushed through the glass doors with high hopes and the freshly pressed 78 of *Mama's Rolling Pin* in her hand. She got on the line in front of the reception desk as her competition dropped off demo records into a basket outside the window. Chi Chi was about to place her record on the pile, but thought better of it. Instead, she poked her head through a small open window in the waiting area. "I'm here to see Mr. Gibbs."

"Put it in the basket." The receptionist, thin and wizened, was slumped over her typewriter like a melted candle, tapping the keys without looking up.

"It's not just any demo. It doesn't belong in the basket," Chi Chi said over the clatter of the keys. "See, I'm Chi Chi Donatelli of *The Donatelli Sisters*. I've got a new record by my sisters and Saverio Armandonada of the *Rod Roccaraso Orchestra*."

"You reciting the lunch menu at Sunny Italy?" the receptionist joked, spinning in her chair to face Chi Chi. "You here for the contest?"

"Yes. He said the deadline is five o'clock. It's ten till. This is my submission. It's special, and I'd like to speak with him, please." Chi Chi checked the nameplate on the desk. "Please, Miss Schlesinger."

"I'm not Miss Schlesinger. I'm Miss Peterson. I'm the weekend girl," the receptionist said wearily. "They don't make nameplates for weekend girls."

"Forgive me. And I forgive you for the crack about Sunny Italy. By the way, real Italians don't eat there. We go to the Vesuvio." Chi Chi looked at the clock over her desk. "May I please speak with Mr. Gibbs?"

"He's on the air."

"I'll wait." Chi Chi stuck her hand through the window with the record. "This has to be in his hands by five o'clock."

Miss Peterson took the record inside the studio. While Chi Chi waited for her to return, she scanned the wall of fame in the reception area. Some of the musical radio stars of renown who had visited the WBAB studio were featured in a series of framed photographs on the wall. She studied the glamorous photos of singers: Lisa Kiser wore a dramatic picture hat in black velvet; Valerie McCoy Kelly wore sunglasses and a courant houndstooth swing coat; and the incomparable Helma Jenkins dazzled in a faux diamond headband. They were the pinnacle of high style to a factory girl who was running around in the heat in a cotton sundress, her frizzy beach hair in a ponytail tucked under a boater. Chi Chi imagined her own image on the wall someday, and wondered what ensemble she would wear. She was certain it included a mink coat.

"Mr. Gibbs is not taking any more demos today." Miss Peterson handed the record back to Chi Chi.

"Why not?"

"He's up to his ears in vinyl. He can't listen to another homemade record. Those are his words."

"This isn't homemade. It was pressed in Newark at Magennis. Professionally."

"Look, kid. I'm going to give you a tip, which you can take or leave. You don't have a shot here. We only play name bands and the singers that front them."

"But Rod Roccaraso—"

"Is Rod Roccaraso. You can't sing with his sideman at a cookout, cut a single in a carnival booth, and expect air play here. We got sponsors. We stay on the air because they pay the bills. Even I get paid because of sponsors."

"What about the contest?"

"He's already made his decision."

"But that's not fair!"

"You're right. It's not fair. But this isn't a game of softball at Saint Mary's of Notre Dame, where the playing field is level and the nuns keep score. It's show business. And it's brutal. Better luck next time." Miss Peterson closed the window with a snap.

Chi Chi went outside and climbed back into the truck. "They

wouldn't take it. Gibbs made his decision before I walked in the door."

"Give it to me." Mariano took the record and went into the radio station.

In the waiting room, Mariano rapped on the receptionist's window. Miss Peterson slid it open with one hand while holding the receiver of the telephone with the other. She held up her hand before signing off on the call.

"I'm here to see Mr. Gibbs," Mariano said.

"Who shall I say wants to see him?"

"Mr. Mariano Donatelli."

"You're related to the kid in the hat," she said wearily.

"I'm her father."

"I just explained to your daughter that we are not accepting any further submissions for the contest." She reached up to close the window.

"I'm paying."

"One moment, sir." Miss Peterson left the glass window open and went inside the studio.

Mariano stood at the window, keeping his eye on the studio door. He caught his reflection in the mirror behind the secretary's desk, and was not pleased with the image he saw. The manager of the Donatelli Sisters was dressed to pour concrete, not conduct business on behalf of his clients or make deals with disc jockeys. He smoothed what was left of his hair with his hand and straightened the collar on his work shirt.

"Come in." Miss Peterson opened the door to the inner office.

Mariano followed her into the office outside the studio. Through a small glass window in the thick door that separated the studio from the office, he could see the renowned Mr. Gibbs, the disc jockey/host/radio announcer, his young male assistant, and a secretary as they broadcast live.

Mariano was taken aback by Gibbs's appearance. He was at least twenty years older than his photograph on the billboard on the boardwalk advertising his radio show. Mr. Gibbs wore thick eyeglasses; his dyed black hair was combed in a center part and slicked down with Brilliantine. His ensemble—a shirt, bow tie, vest, pocket watch, chain, and the sailor-leg trousers of the flapper era—dated him more than the pomade. The DJ advertised himself as the *Sultan of Swing*, but he was of another era, when the gramophone was hand-cranked.

The console, over which Gibbs had total control, was a complex force field of levers, buttons, and lights that twinkled, pulsed, and went dark as he touched them. Three felt-covered turntables twirled evenly on metal platforms.

Gibbs's assistant loaded the vinyl discs onto the turntables. He wore short white cotton gloves and delicately held each record by its edges before placing it on a turntable. The secretary logged the title and number by time code. When a song was finished, the assistant removed the record from the turntable, slipped it into a paper sleeve, and placed it onto a rack where it was cataloged.

Gibbs riffed on air with ease. His voice had a smooth, deep timbre as he introduced the band, singer, and interesting trivia about the artists. He operated a lever that placed the stylus and needle onto the grooves, thus controlling the show. As the song played through, Gibbs marked the next record in the queue. Behind the trio of turntables on a platform was a stack of 78 records so tall, it resembled a black top hat. Mariano was determined to get *Mama's Rolling Pin* on that stack and placed on the turntable by the kid in the white gloves.

There were hundreds of hours to fill on the radio; why not two minutes to feature the sensational *Donatelli Sisters*? Why not this song?

Mariano was surprised when Mr. Gibbs himself nodded at him from inside the studio. "He'll be out in a moment," Miss Peterson said as she breezed past him and returned to her desk.

Gibbs pushed the door to the studio open, grinning. "May I help you?" His teeth were even, square, and porcelain-white.

"Mr. Gibbs, we enjoy your show."

"Appreciate it. What can I do for you?"

"I want you to listen to this record. When you do, I think you'll feature it on your show. It's a hit."

"You have a nose for hits?"

Mariano puffed his chest a bit. "I think so."

"We have hundreds of records to play. We have more records than airtime to play them."

"I can appreciate such a dilemma. But we cut this record just for you. Just for your contest."

"I chose the winner already, so I'm afraid I can't be of help."

"You can pick whatever record you wish—it's your contest. But we played by the rules and we made it in time. Right under the bell, don't get me wrong, but we made it. The truth is, I don't really care about the contest."

Mariano had worked for the largest marble company in New Jersey since he was a young man; he knew all about legitimate business. The owners of shops and gas stations, the suppliers of all types of goods and services—they were the backbone of the local economy, even one suffering through the Great Depression. But Mariano was also aware that there was another way to do business and achieve results, which involved conducting deals on the side for additional compensation.

Under the table was a concept Mariano understood. It meant a worker could make money without reporting it, while the employer named his price when setting a wage. The worker could put a few extra dollars in his pocket, doing work no one else would take, or accept overtime for an enterprise that couldn't keep up output during regular hours, thus making the operation profitable faster, and without the encumbrance of rules or obligations to the worker. It was a way for the worker to advance, build up his personal savings, and add to his compensation without being taxed. It was also a way to cut in line, if you could not get a break any other way. In Mariano's mind, there were worse ways to get ahead.

Mariano handed Gibbs *Mama's Rolling Pin.* "I'd like you to play this song during Shore Hour—when you play the selections you chose for the Stars of Tomorrow. It's the last day of vacation week, and all of Sea Isle Beach will be listening."

"I don't have time to play it."

Mariano knew the powerful never scratched another's back unless their own itch was attended to first. He kept his gaze on Mr. Gibbs as he reached into his pocket and put money into the other man's hand. "Make the time."

"I'll see what I can do."

"You do that. *Mama's Rolling Pin.* Don't forget it." Mariano walked out of the studio.

Mr. Gibbs looked at the record, and then unfolded the bill in his hand. He went back into the studio.

The secretary looked up. "How much?"

"One dollar." Gibbs gave the money to the secretary.

"To play a record?" The secretary was mystified.

"It gets better. He requested Shore Hour."

"Somebody needs to tell the old man that he'd be better off

buying bologna with that buck," the assistant piped up. "At least he would spend it, and he wouldn't end up hungry."

"Poor soul," the secretary said under her breath.

"Mama's Rolling Pin. And he wasn't joking." Gibbs shook his head. He took the Donatelli Sisters' freshly pressed phonograph record and threw it under the console onto a pile with the rest of the 78s that had come in unsolicited over the transom.

He handed Mariano's dollar bill to the secretary. "For pencils."

The Jersey Miss factory, housed in a powder-blue saltbox on Landis Avenue, had a storefront entrance, with windows rolled open to let in the summer breeze on the street side.

The operation was nestled between the bakery and butcher shop, and across the street from St. Joseph Church. The devout attended daily mass before the first bell at the mill at 7:00 a.m., while others often made a quick visit later, stopping in to light a candle, offer an intention, and bless themselves with holy water before walking home.

Inside the old mill, the weathered floorboards buckled under the weight of the machines. Overhead a dense tangle of electrical wires hung like circus ropes from the ceiling. Additional rooms had been built onto the back, railroad style. From the front of the factory, you could see clear through to the finishing department.

The factory produced women's and children's blouses. Neat rows of sewing machines, with their sleek black enamel cases and brass bobbin and needles, filled the main room, separated by a single main aisle.

The pattern pieces arrived in bundles, tied with string, delivered in rolling bins, from the cutting room located down the street. At the sound of the start bell, the bundles were promptly untied by the runners and the pieces dispersed row by row, operation by operation, down the line to the seamstresses in the main room.

As a seamstress completed her task on the garment, she passed it to the next operator, until the assembled blouse made it back into the bin. The blouses were bundled in counts of twelve, and wheeled into the next room, where operators who mastered the specialty machines added buttonholes, bound welting and loops, embroidery, and branded stenciling. Labels were stitched into the collars. The final stop was the finishing department, where the pressers ironed the finished garments, and placed them on spin racks while a small team of finishers lifted them off the racks, folded the garments, and pinned size and sales tags to the sleeves according to the buyer's specifications.

At the end of the line, the runners stacked the empty bins and rolled them back up the street to the cutting room to be refilled. The process was repeated until a shipment was complete.

The blouses, either bagged on hangers for immediate display or folded in boxes, were carried to the sliding door, counted, and loaded onto a Freightliner. The truck drove the shipments into New York City during the night, in just under two hours, to be dispersed to middlemen in the garment center on Thirty-Fourth Street.

The machine operators assembled the garments expertly; repetition had made them masters of their machines. The Donatelli girls began working during the summers when they turned thirteen. After high school, they went into the factory life full time. Once Isotta raised her daughters, she followed them into the mill.

Returning to work in the heat was a particular sacrifice. The ladies longed for the ease of their vacation week as they stood on the line to punch their timecards. Chi Chi tied her hair back with a bandana and followed Rita as they took their seats at their machines, adjusted the work lights, and gently pumped the foot pedals. Chi Chi was pleased that the machinist had greased the gears. At the sound of the forelady's whistle, the operators flipped the power switches. The machines hummed in unison like the run of scales before a song.

The factory roared in full operation as the air clouded with a haze created from a combination of the fine dust from the electricity that juiced the machines and the fibers from the fabric. By lunch break the air would be thick with it, as thread and fabric were snipped, sewn, and hemmed through each station until the bundled garments were wheeled into finishing at the end of the line.

The women made sailor blouses, white cotton with blue-and-white-striped ties, attached underneath a Peter Pan collar. It was an over-the-head style with a single button loop at the neck. The collar lay flat in a placket. The demand had been high for this style as the child star Shirley Temple had been seen wearing one, causing a fashion frenzy.

Rita's machine had a thread jam. She flipped the bobbin on the base, snipped the knot, threaded it, snapped the closure, and picked up the first garment that lay on her feeder shelf.

Chi Chi swiftly attached the fabric loop in a half-moon motion on the blouse. The needle pulsed up and down evenly, the stitches disappeared into the cotton. Chi Chi pulled the blouse from under the machine and snipped the thread before passing it off to the collar setter.

As Chi Chi looped blouse after blouse, she aimed for accuracy and speed. She took some interest in the design, noting color combinations and feel of the fabric, but never lingering long enough to stop what she was doing and examine the garment in full. By mid-morning, her mind began to wander, and she created costumes in her mind's eye to get her through the long workday. She dreamed up ensembles for her sisters and their act, or men's novelty shirts for the orchestra that would back them for special numbers in a nightclub, engaging her imagination as best she could in a place that did not require it. The drone of the machines became a musical baseline for her theatrical ideas. She pictured herself onstage in a costume she had made, in a sketch she had written, leading into a song she had composed. Ambition was her constant companion as she looped the sailor blouses.

"Faster, Rita!" the forelady barked. "Pick up the pace, Chi Chi!"

Chi Chi nodded without looking up, moving her fingers deftly as the forelady moved ahead to the next row, barking an order to the collar setter.

"*Strega*," Rita said under her breath.

Chi Chi laughed as she attached a loop. A shadow fell across her machine, and she looked up. Her sister Barbara was standing over her. "What's the matter?"

"Don't panic."

"What is it?"

"Ma just left the mill."

Chi Chi stood and looked down the line at her mother's station. Another operator had already filled in, taking her mother's seat, keeping the work flow uninterrupted.

"Did she get sick?"

"No, it's Pop. Mrs. Acocella came to get her. He's at the hospital."

"I'll go." Chi Chi reached under the machine to get her purse.

"Ma will handle it," Barbara insisted.

"What happened?"

"He got some chest pains. She's with him now."

"But I want to go."

"So do I. But we can't. You have to stay. We all have to stay. Understand?"

Chi Chi sat back down at her chair. Two blouses had already landed on her feeder tray in the short time she and Barbara had been speaking. Barbara would find the same at her station, if not more. Barbara didn't have to say it; Chi Chi already knew. The family could only spare one Donatelli woman to look after their father. They did not have the luxury of sitting at his bedside and tending to him for their peace of mind, or his. The family needed the income. The best use of his daughters was not at St. Joseph's Hospital, but on the machines at Jersey Miss.

Saverio finished his set in the ballroom of the Jefferson Hotel in Richmond, Virginia, with a musical tip of the hat to the ladies of the South with a rendition of *Ain't She Sweet*, which the Roccaraso orchestra had knocked off from the song-styling of the great Jimmie Lunceford. Luckily the folks in the crowd had not heard the spectacular Negro band live, but Saverio had. He figured his vocals on the tune were, at best, an homage, because he knew they fell short in comparison to the original.

The dance floor was filled with fancy couples. Women moved in the blue light in ruffled gowns of stiff pastel faille, while their partners dazzled in white tie. The ballroom around the dance floor and the gardens beyond had the look of a magical forest in some ritzy romantic land, where the scents of freesia and lilies waft through French doors, and lights do not illuminate but shimmer and blink like jewels in the dark. Candles floating in crystal bowls staccatoed the small marble tabletops, while the orange tips of cigarettes punctured the air, and the occasional flash of the flame from a silver lighter flared and quickly was extinguished, swallowed by the blue.

Saverio loosened his tie as he pushed through the black velvet curtains behind the orchestra box, on his way to the greenroom the hotel provided for the band for their breaks.

The hallway between the kitchen, greenroom, and ballroom was narrow and crowded. Waiters angled past, juggling silver trays of delicate hors d'oeuvres. Nobody knew how to make a slice of cucumber and a ruffle of pimiento cheese look more artful than the chefs in the South. His fellow musicians filed out on their way to take a smoke. Saverio reached into his pocket for his handkerchief to dab the perspiration from his forehead when Gladys emerged from the elevator in a pale green chiffon evening gown. She nodded as she squeezed past him.

"Honey," Saverio called softly after her.

She turned. "Hello."

"Are you ever going to talk to me again?"

"No. If I didn't have a contract to sing with you, I wouldn't sing with you either."

"C'mon, you're making a melodrama out of this. We were happy."

"You made your choice."

"I miss you."

"I don't care." Gladys walked down the hallway and into her dressing room. The door snapped shut behind her.

"You wailed on that last song." Sammy Prezza caught up with Saverio.

"I didn't come close to the real deal. But thank you."

"Don't sell yourself short. I remember that kid who had them weeping in that church in Detroit a few years back. You took that *Holy Night* apart as I remember it."

"I had a broken heart then, too. Maybe it's you, Sam. Maybe you bring me bad luck."

Sammy chuckled. "Could be. Or you're just getting yours. Men go down one of three ways. It's either women, booze, or dope. When you choose women as your vice, you end up broke, but you look good until the end."

"And that right there is the good news, boys," Saverio said.

Sammy lowered his voice. "There's a fellow who wants to talk to you tonight. You heard of Paul Godfrey?"

"Out of St. Louis?"

Sammy nodded. "They just lost their singer. He sent a scout. Wants to make you an offer."

Saverio looked at the door Gladys had slammed shut. He didn't want to make any career moves based on a girl, but there were worse reasons to shake things up. The tight hallway was crowded, the ceiling was low, and the doors were closed on both sides. He could hardly breathe. If Saverio were looking for signs, he had plenty. The world felt like it was closing in. Maybe it was time to leave the only band he had ever known.

"Said to meet him at the bar afterward."

"What's his name?"

"He'll find you."

Sammy Prezza made his way back to the band box while Saverio pushed through to the greenroom. A few guys sat around having a smoke, in the windowless room, but it was the South, so there was a touch of civility: a silver tea service with small crystal bowls containing slices of lemon, shards of fresh ginger, and a compote of honey were set out for the band.

Saverio was preparing a cup when he held the honey compote up to the light. A tiny silver spoon hung from a loop on the cap. Inside the glass, thick golden honey swirled around the small tower of gold.

"You're supposed to eat that comb," the trombonist said from his seat on the couch. "I've got kin in North Carolina. That honey's got properties."

"What sort of properties?"

"Medicinal."

"How so?" Saverio asked.

"Well, there are a variety of things honey can do. For singers, you want to take that ginger and lemon and some of that honeycomb right there and you want to mash them together on a spoon. Make a paste with it. And you want to rest that paste on the back of your throat awhile without swallowing it. That will heal up any vocal cord you got a problem with. If you got a cut, no matter how small, or deep, you put some of that honey on it—and you wrap it—it will heal that wound. My grandmother, her mother before her, and my own momma washed their faces with honey and made a mask of the comb to ward off wrinkles. None of them had a line on their faces, so do what you will with that information. And of course, for anybody who blows a horn, honey on the lips gives your career longevity. I happen to know that because I use the cure myself."

"Good to know."

"I thought you'd think so." The trombonist smiled. He had a wide smile and full cheeks. "Go ahead, mash it up. No time like now to heal."

The horn player went back to his conversation. Saverio made the potion as instructed and then placed the mash at the back of his throat. He closed his eyes. The lemon made his sinuses burn, but the ginger cleared them, and the honey, as promised, soothed his throat.

The conductor called them back to the stage. Saverio kept the mixture on the back of his throat as long as he could, until the conductor counted the band down to begin. Gladys took her place downstage right in front of her microphone stand. Maybe it was the horn player's suggestion, or voodoo, or something else entirely, but there was something to the honeycomb. Saverio looked at Gladys, and she was no longer his girl, or the girl he wanted back; she was just another pretty girl in a green dress. It was time to move on. It was time to heal.

Isotta sat by her husband's bed in St. Joseph's Hospital in the general ward. She held his hand as Barbara, Lucille, and Chi Chi burst into the room and scanned the rows of occupied beds for their father.

Lucille spotted their mother in the sea of patients, and led the others to her. Isotta nodded at her daughters to indicate that their father was asleep, and to be quiet. Barbara was relieved to see her father rest. Lucille clapped her hands together joyfully. Chi Chi burst into tears.

"Why are you crying?" Lucille whispered. "He made it."

Chi Chi went around her sisters and knelt next to her father's bed. She took his other hand into her own.

"What did the doctor say?" Barbara asked her mother.

"He had a scare."

"What kind?" Chi Chi said.

"His heart," Isotta explained. "He had a bad pain and he couldn't breathe. So he walked to the neighbor's and asked her for a ride to the hospital."

"He couldn't drive?" Lucille asked.

Isotta nodded that he couldn't. Lucille looked at Barbara, concerned.

"Is he going to be all right?" Chi Chi asked her mother.

"Yes, I think so."

"Why doesn't he have a room?"

"They are all filled," Isotta said.

Barbara shot Chi Chi a look.

"How long has he been asleep?"

"A few hours."

"Is he going to wake up soon?"

"Lucille, will you stop asking questions?" Barbara said tersely.

"I want to know what is going on."

"You have eyes, don't you?" Barbara shot back.

"I'm not a doctor!" Lucille snapped.

"Stop it!" Chi Chi said. "This is not the time." The moment Chi Chi said the word *time*, the second it hung in the air, she regretted it. Her mother's face fell. "Sorry, Ma."

"Sorry," Barbara and Lucille echoed.

"Girls, I don't know a lot more than I've told you. There's one doctor on this floor, and he makes the rounds in the morning."

Chi Chi looked around the crowded ward helplessly. She thought of her father and what he would do if it was her mother in the bed. She believed Mariano wouldn't be complacent, he would do something. He would fight for a good doctor, better care, and a nurse. Chi Chi's mind raced. "Did you ask to see Sister Margaret?" she asked her mother.

"I didn't."

"Ma, she runs this place. She was our principal at Saint Joe's. We have connections." Chi Chi stood up and dried her tears. "I'll be right back." She left the ward and went out into the hallway. Nuns dressed in their black and white habits moved in and out of the nurses station looking like dominoes.

"Hello, Sisters," Chi Chi said cheerfully, "I'm a proud graduate of Saint Joseph's School, class of 1928. I'd love to say hello to Sister Margaret."

The busy nuns ignored her, except for the receptionist, who was overwhelmed with paperwork. She looked up at Chi Chi through her thick glasses. "She's at supper."

"Thank you, Sister . . ." Chi Chi squinted at her nametag. "Bernadette. Where do you good servants of our Lord take your meals?"

"Third floor."

Chi Chi thanked her and raced to the stairwell, bolted up three flights of stairs two steps at a time. When she began to make a mental list of all the times her parents had supported the church and convent, her work shoe caught on a step and she stumbled. Her tickets from the mill, which indicated extra work she had done, fell out of her apron and scattered over the second-floor landing. For a moment, she thought to leave them there, but she knew it meant a dollar added to her paycheck in piecework. Chi Chi got down on her hands and knees and gathered them up, stuffing them back into her apron pocket. She vowed not to tempt fate with a tit-for-tat list for the Holy Roman Church. It would remain a one-sided argument.

She sprinted up the final flight of stairs, pushed through the door, and found the nurses station and more nuns. Thinking of her father, she found the oldest nun at the desk, the nun who would most likely be friends with the old nun downstairs. "Sister Bernadette sent me up to you."

"Yes?" The nun looked at Chi Chi.

"She sent me up to see Sister Margaret, who is taking her meal. It's important that I speak with her. Sister Margaret is a dear friend of our family. The family of Mariano Donatelli."

The nun's eyes narrowed suspiciously.

Chi Chi thought fast. "My father Mariano built the stone wall at your convent in Sea Isle. It was his pleasure. Hauled the stones and donated the supplies and his labor. I won't take much of her time."

The nun frowned and left the station. Chi Chi felt a sense of doom. What if Sister Margaret did not remember her father or the family? They might throw her father out of the hospital altogether. Chi Chi believed if she did not get her father out of the public ward, he did not stand a chance.

"Chiara Donatelli?"

"Sister Margaret?" Chi Chi turned around to see the nun, whom she had not seen since she was a girl. She threw her arms around her. "I need your help."

"What's the matter?" the nun asked.

"My father is downstairs in the public ward. He had a heart attack. It doesn't look good. He needs a doctor. I didn't want to bother you but we're out of ideas."

"You, Chiara? Out of ideas? I'll never forget when you wrote the Sisters a song on our jubilee. You were how old? Ten?"

"Eleven. It wasn't a great song, Sister. Now I wish it would've been better."

"It was a great song. It made Mother Superior cry." She patted Chi Chi's arm. "Don't worry. I'll take care of your father."

"Thank you, Sister. I know it's a lot to ask, and he's not more important than anyone else . . ." Chi Chi could not finish her thought. Instead she burst into tears.

"None of that," Sister Margaret said, all business. "There's no need to explain. If he were my father, I'd ask, too."

Chi Chi nodded, trying to control herself as she watched Sister Margaret order two of the orderlies to have Mariano moved to a room, and directed one of the nuns to ask the cardiologist to attend to him immediately. Chi Chi flew down the stairs to tell her mother and sisters the news.

Saverio stood at the bar at the Jefferson Hotel and ordered a Manhattan, even though he only drank on occasion. It was a fine cocktail to impress, and one of the few that did not make him sick when he sipped it.

He felt a hand on his shoulder. "Saverio? Lew Lewis."

Lew scooted up onto the bar stool. Short-legged and built like a beer keg, he was around fifty years old and pickled in Aqua Velva cologne. "Some show tonight. I wish I could make a play for that tomato you sing with—what's her name, Gertie?"

"Gladys. Miss Gladys Overby. She's a fine young woman, sir."

"Sure, sure, as fine as they come."

"She is. Truly. Can I buy you a drink?"

"Martini. Straight up. Olives," Lew said to the bartender. "So, let's get to it."

"Appreciate it. I've had a long night." Saverio folded the paper napkin into a triangle.

"Understood. I'm here to make you an offer to join the Paul Godfrey Orchestra."

"What are you thinking?"

"You'll start at eighty-five dollars a week—that's ten dollars more a week than you're getting now. We're giving you three weeks off a year. And we're going to do some recording. Paul gives you one cent on every three sales of a seventy-eight, worldwide net."

"I'm listening."

"December first through January eighth of every year we're in residence in Chicago at the Drake. They do a little ice show on the floor—it's kitschy but it pays and they pack them in. We can give you a tour schedule as we get it. Here's the contract."

Saverio scanned the one-page agreement Lew Lewis handed him.

"Take your time. Read it. Take it to your lawyer. Whatever." Lew looked around the bar at no one and nothing in particular.

"Fine, fine," Saverio mumbled as he read it.

"And there's one other matter to discuss."

"Yes?"

"Your name. It's a honker."

"Too long?"

"Too everything. Nobody can say it. Nobody can spell it. And the problem with that is eventually no one will want to. So it's got to go. You got any ideas for a name?"

"Could I just be Saverio?"

"Sounds like a decorator. You need a name that says who you are, but with fewer vowels."

"But I'm Italian, and I don't want to be anything but Italian."

"You couldn't be if you tried. So go for an Italian name. How about Joey? Can't do Paul, of course. Michael? Augie? Too close to Artie. All right, none of them fit. How about Tony?"

"Tony's all right. I like Anthony better," Saverio admitted.

"Anthony is too long. Okay, so Tony. Last name?"

"I like Armandonada."

"Too long, kid. Arman. Tony Arman."

"Doesn't sound right."

"Tony Arma. Take off the *n*. The *n* makes it sound off. Tony Arma. Now that's Italian. I like it. Short. To the point. Like a blade. Sharp."

"Tony Arma." Saverio said the name aloud.

"I'll make a note in the contract."

"Just like that, I'm Tony Arma?"

"Just like that. I love it." Lew Lewis cackled. "I can see it on a marquee. Very, very pithy, and if I do say so myself, it's sexy. Tony Arma. I can see the girls from Nesquehoning to Naperville chanting your name. 'I want to be in the arms of Tony Arma.' Get it? In the arms of Arma! I'm a genius. I know women. They'll be swoonin', all right. And indeed!"

Saverio signed the contract to join the Paul Godfrey Orchestra and initialed the amendments that changed his name, which Lew Lewis scribbled into the blank space on the boilerplate document marked "Addendum." Even if Saverio would have shown it to a lawyer, he would have overruled any legal advice and agreed to the terms. He was ready to leave Rod Roccaraso, the sooner the better, and that night suited him just fine. He was done with the Roccaraso tour, the bus, the boys, and especially Gladys Overby, who was over him. It was time to leave the past behind like the hat he had forgotten at the Birdsall Club in Kansas City. It was time to replace what didn't work any longer. Saverio, now Tony, wanted a new audience, a new suit, and new friends to go with his new name.

The Paul Godfrey Orchestra was by reputation elegant, but it also had exciting new arenas for growth—more theatrical shows, with dance, comedy, and sketches. It was all new, and Tony Arma was eager for reinvention.

"Cheech!" Lucille met her sister in the ward.

"You did it. Sister Margaret got Dad a room. Just like that. A great room. He's awake, he's sipping broth, and he's waiting for the doctor."

Chi Chi followed Lucille up the stairwell. Giddy with relief, she threw the entrance door to the fourth floor open.

As soon as they stepped into the hallway, they knew that their father had fallen into a vat of Roman Catholic luck, Salesian style. The nuns moved methodically in and out of the rooms; the only sound was the brush of their long skirts on the linoleum floor. The cool ocean breezes blew through the open doors on either end of the hall, ruffling the sheers like angel wings.

Barbara leaned against the wall outside their father's room. "How did you do it?"

"It turns out we have connections. Evidently my jubilee song for the Salesians was one for the ages."

"It didn't dawn on Mama to ask for help," said Lucille.

"She just sat there all day and didn't think, *My husband needs a decent doctor*?" Chi Chi asked.

"She's in shock. Not exactly, but close. She's really scared and doesn't know what to do," Barbara said.

"She doesn't have the luxury of being scared. Dad needs her. She has to be strong and stand up for him. We all do." Chi Chi led her sisters into their father's room, and whistled. "Dad, you're in the Ritz," she said as the girls gathered around their father.

Mariano's color was poor, but he was upbeat, which reassured the family. "Yes I am."

"This is what you get for making the good Sisters a stone wall," Barbara said as she embraced her dad.

"No good deed goes unrewarded," Lucille reminded him.

"Yeah, something like that." Mariano smiled. "Now if I can just get the Sisters to pray your song onto the airwaves."

"You're not supposed to think about work right now," Isotta chided.

"Why not? It makes me happy. The possibilities."

Chi Chi shot Barbara a look.

"Think of the possibilities of a vacation for you and Mama," Barbara said.

"You need a vacation, Iso?" Mariano asked her.

"I have everything I need."

"So do I. I got the shore. The backyard. The garage. What else do I need?"

"A few tests," said the nun from the doorway.

"I'm all yours, Sister," Mariano said cheerfully.

Chi Chi was asleep in the chair under the window in her father's room when he returned from the last round of tests around midnight. She woke up, groggy, as two nuns and an orderly wheeled him into the room on a metal gurney that creaked like the floorboards on a rusted-out battleship.

"How'd he do?" Chi Chi asked.

"Your father is strong," one of the nuns said.

"Because I'm built like a cement mixer." He patted his ample stomach. "Reserves."

Chi Chi watched, amazed, as the nuns half his size lifted her father with two bedsheets from the gurney and positioned him in the bed with ease.

"You're all set, Mr. Donatelli," one of the nuns said.

"We'll be in to check on you on the hour," the other reminded him.

"Thank you, dear Sisters," said Mariano gratefully. "Good night."

Chi Chi rubbed her eyes. "I sent Ma and the girls home."

"Good girl. Your mother was tired."

"How do you feel, really?"

Mariano lowered his voice. "I heard them talking. All those doctors downstairs. I have a bad heart. Bad valves. It sounded like they were talking about our old Hudson. They checked everything. Heart, lungs, brain. Blood. What else? Oh yes, muscles. But it doesn't matter. When you have a lousy ticker, you're out of luck."

"That's not true. You can stop eating sweets. There's medicine. And you can slow down."

"I can't sit around all day, you know that."

"You can and you will. You're going to get better."

"You think so, Cheech?"

"Sure."

"How do you know?"

"Your color is good."

"You're lying."

"No, it's fine."

"I thought I would live to be a hundred. My great-grandfather lived to one hundred and three. He lived in the Dolomites. Ate figs and berries. Snorted snuff every morning. Climbed the mountain every day. Like a goat. Nobody could keep up with him. He

could've been an Olympian. Buried three wives. And back then"—
Mariano sliced the air with his hand—"that was a feat. A feat."

"You're going to come out of this better than ever, Dad."

"I like your positive attitude. I wish I had it. I'm making a mess
of everything. Barbara is excited about her wedding. And this situation with me just craps all over it. A girl needs her father on her
wedding day. It's proper."

"You're going to walk her down the aisle."

"How do you know?"

"I'm a believer," Chi Chi said softly.

"That's good. Put your faith in God. But right now, I need to put
my faith in you. You're my daughter, but Cheech, you're also my
friend. Funny how this went. Your mother kept having girls, and
I kept praying, 'One son, Jesu. Jesu, could you send me one son?'
And now, if I had one, I'd send him back. I got just what I needed
and more than I deserved."

"You deserved the best."

"Now listen to me. Because there are some things you need to
know. I want you to make sure Lucille goes to secretarial school."

"I will."

"And don't let Barbara push you around."

"She will no matter what I say."

"But don't let it get in," Mariano insisted, tapping his head.

"I will try."

"Your mother will surprise you. She'll make a life again."

"You're her true love, Dad."

"So she says. I know she was mine."

"Dad, I don't think you're dying."

"You didn't hear what I heard."

"Maybe they were talking about the guy in four-nineteen."

"Nice try, kid."

"You're going to live a long life."

"Forty-one isn't so bad." He rested against the pillow. "I saw my girls grow up. Many men get less."

"I don't know if I've thanked you enough for everything you've done for me. Building the studio. Recording the songs. Trying to get them on the radio. I know it was a sacrifice."

"It was nothing but a pleasure."

"It was everything to me. You know my sisters think we're nuts. They think the Donatelli Sisters is some game we made up to pass the time."

"It's not in their veins, Cheech."

"You knew all along that it's my life to write songs and perform them."

"And you got the goods."

"They don't believe it."

"But it's all right to be the crazy ones. We have each other." Mariano chuckled. "Now, maybe I give way too much advice, and it could be said I never took any that was given to me. Maybe that's part of giving it in the first place."

"You got advice for me?"

"I do. They're thoughts I have when I'm driving you around places, but I don't let go of them; they've stuck with me, so it must mean I'm supposed to share them with you."

"I'm listening."

Mariano nodded. "I hope you'll always live near the ocean. No matter what happened to us, your mother and I had the shore. They say that salt water can heal, and it does, and that the rays of the sun can strengthen your bones—no doubt that's true—and that the sand makes you slow down and savor your steps. If you close your eyes and listen, the sound of the ocean is the most beautiful music ever written. The tempo of the surf as the tide rolls in matches your breath, the sound of the waves as they crash over the rocks sound like the brushes on a snare. It's like the opening riff to a great piece of jazz. Sometimes I'm standing out there and I hear the blend and I think Ethel Waters is going to rise out of the surf and start wailing. The ocean is God's orchestra. I will miss it."

"Okay, let's say you're right, and they were talking about you downstairs. Could you forget what they said?" Chi Chi sat down on the bed next to her father. "Could you stay for me?"

"You don't need me anymore, kid."

"But I do."

"Listen to me, because time doesn't owe anybody a favor. Whatever happens, don't give up your music. You fight for it like it's your baby, your country, and your savior. Nobody will tell you this, but work is your salvation. Even when it's bad, it provides for a life. I figured that one out when I lost my job. It's not called losing your job for nothing—you do, in fact, wind up lost. Work gives you something to do but it also grows you, even when you're old. I'm sad to leave my family behind, but that studio, it was all new, I was learning, I was just getting started. There's so much coming that I won't see, that I won't be a part of, and how I wish I were young and had a strong heart and the opportunity to get in on it. But here's the beauty part: you do."

"It won't be any fun without you."

"Yes, it will. You know how peevish I got when Gibbs didn't play your song during Shore Hour? Well, I thought about him later, with his shoe-polish hair, and I felt for the guy. He's just trying to hold on like everybody else. He wants the old days back because he thought they were better, but they weren't. He was just young then, so they seemed better because he had verve. Along the way, he didn't learn much, except to hold on to his fear and hang on to his turf. His voice reaches thousands up and down the shore, he can play a record and it becomes a hit, but he isn't listening and he doesn't see it."

"See what?"

"The voices of this century will rise from the factories, from the working people. They won't come from the nightclubs of Europe like they did when I was a kid. Enough with the kings and the queens with their fancy crowns! The message will come from some kid from a slum who has seen it all and who will know how to sing it because he feels something. Gibbs should've taken one look at me and said to himself, 'This fat guy with the oil stains on his pants from fixing his truck that keeps breaking down, this guy knows something I don't.' Because, if he thought that, he would've been right. Look to the audience who needs the inspiration for your inspiration. They know. Trust me, they *know*."

Chi Chi wanted to talk, but her father had fallen asleep. Soon he was snoring. Quietly she rose from the bed and went to the window to close it. Before she did, she leaned out and looked at the ocean, lit by a three-quarter moon so bright that for a moment Chi Chi thought a regatta of sailing ships was coming toward Sea Isle Beach to claim it, their oil lamps lighting the prows. But it was just the moon shining on the water.

She closed the window to shut out the damp air and went to turn off the lamp next to her father's bed. But before she flipped the switch, she straightened the blanket over him. She looked at his face. He had stopped snoring. His color was off. She moved to the other side of the bed, thinking it was the light. In a panic, she placed her head on her father's chest. She heard a faint tap. She placed her fingers on his neck, but could barely detect a pulse. She ran into the hallway and screamed for help.

Saverio woke up in the Richmond Squire Inn, a few blocks from the Jefferson Hotel, in a cold sweat. He flipped on the light on the nightstand. It took him a moment to remember where he was, which city, what day of the month and year it was, and what he had been dreaming when he woke up.

Next to the door was his suitcase; the dress bag holding his tuxedo hung on the back of it. His sports jacket, trousers, socks, undergarments, shoes, and hat were laid out neatly, ready to wear. Everything was as he had left it the night before. He began to shake. He did not like to be alone.

He tapped the last cigarette out of the pack on the nightstand before swinging his legs over the side of the bed, grabbing a match, and lighting it. He went to the window, lifting the sash as high as it would go. It had to be a hundred degrees outside; a gauzy coral haze of humidity hung over the city. Saverio took a long, smooth drag off the cigarette, trying to calm his nerves. The sun was rising, a smear of shimmering pink beyond Monument Avenue. The hotel was quiet, as were the streets outside. The Rod Roccaraso Orchestra bus had pulled out at 3:00 a.m. without him.

The change settled over Saverio, and he was determined to embrace it. There was just one problem, one stinging regret.

Saverio had agreed in haste to change his name. He didn't want to change it, and didn't like it—it sounded phony. Tony Arma sounded like a guy running numbers in South Philly, or a middleman in the garment district hawking thread in New York City. He wasn't even sure Tony Arma sounded like a crooner, though it was a name that fit on a marquee. So did *Bozo*, he thought, or *Betty Boop*. It also fit in a newspaper ad, in the fine print where the singers were listed, which made it all the worse.

Saverio remembered when his father told him that show business wouldn't stop until it took everything away from him, and now it had. Show business had taken away Saverio's name and handed something back to him anew, as though his lineage, history, and identity weren't his in the first place.

Who was he now? According to the contract he signed, he belonged to the Paul Godfrey Orchestra, but outside of that, what was he besides another expendable singer, replaceable in any city, like a flat tire on the tour bus? He was just working another line, he figured, but this time he held a microphone, and not Henry Ford's wrench.

After Mariano Donatelli's funeral mass at St. Joseph Church, the family home was filled with mourners from as far away as Albany and as close as next door. Barbara made sure they food trays were refilled. Lucille cleared dishes, busing them back to the kitchen to be washed for the next round of guests stopping in to express their sympathy. There was plenty of food to serve; every surface in the kitchen was stacked with trays of manicotti, tiramisu, rolls, cold-cut platters, salads, pastries, and cookies prepared by family and neighbors.

There was a lot of chatter about fate. Chi Chi overheard plenty as she refilled glasses and placed food on the tables. The Donatelli girls and their mother were always gracious hosts. The mourners would leave Mariano and Isotta's home having had a delicious meal and homemade wine. They reminisced about the Fourth of July, and how, only days before, they had gathered under the same sun in the same garden to celebrate. Chi Chi caught fragments of their lamentations. "Mariano looked *robusto*," one friend said. "Remember how he hoisted a keg," another said. "He was shooting off fireworks for the kids." Others chimed in, "He was so vibrant. So young. Too young."

Chi Chi learned the definition of *young* that day. If people said that you were too young on the day you died, that meant you were still young. She would never look at forty-one as old again. Chi Chi went into the kitchen. She wrapped a moppeen around the handle of the espresso maker on the stove and filled tiny cups with the brew. Peering out the kitchen window, she observed her mother as she sat at the table under the umbrella, surrounded by her friends. They were trying to make her laugh. Chi Chi watched Isotta politely play along as she listened to humorous stories about her funny, warm, exuberant husband, but her daughter knew that particular kind of joy was lost on her mother that day. It would be a long time before her mother would laugh again.

Chi Chi lifted the tray and checked in with her sisters in the living room. She handed off the tray of espresso cups to Lucille, who took the cue and began serving them to the guests.

"You girls should open a restaurant," Mrs. Brennan from church commented.

"I'm too fast on the typewriter," Lucille countered.

Chi Chi slipped out the front door and down the walk. She needed to be alone, if just for a few minutes. She wanted to think about what to do going forward, which she had not done in the days since her father had died.

She had intended to walk down to the beach, but instead she found herself walking in the other direction, to the garage. She found the key under the mat outside the door and unlocked it.

White light came through the windows in separate beams, landing in rectangular pools on the concrete floor. The place reeked of fresh paint; inspired by Saverio's visit, Mariano had just given the studio a fresh coat. Chi Chi was certain her father had not intended to die. He had plans to advertise, and to record other artists besides his daughters. That was her father's way—he thought big, without limitation, and made plans for the future. Mariano lived in hope, if only his daughters could be like him, in this moment.

Everything on the console was as her father had left it. His handwritten notes, in block print, had key codes and times listed for the last song they had worked on together. Chi Chi hadn't finished it, but was planning to on the day Mariano went to the hospital. *Haven't We Met* was a ballad, Chi Chi's first attempt at one. Her father teased her that she was listening to too much Sarah Vaughan on the radio. She remembered telling her father that there was no such thing as listening to too much Sarah Vaughan.

Chi Chi picked up her father's pencil. He had chewed the eraser tip. She looked at his teeth marks, remembering his front teeth, which were a bit larger than the rest. She remembered he'd once joked, "My front teeth are as big as my feet." Now that he was gone, everything he touched was a relic, a sacred object to treasure, proof that he had lived and had thought about things and pondered how best to do his work. She put the pencil in her apron pocket. Who would she talk to about music now? Who would make notes when she was recording a song?

She pushed open the door of the recording booth, flipped on the light, and sat down on the piano bench, facing away from the keys. She found herself turning toward the keyboard and rested her fingers on the cool white ivory, but she could not play. She rested her hands in her lap. It was odd. Usually, the booth was warm in summer; on this day, it was cool, like a tomb.

Barbara pushed the door of the recording shed open. "Cheech?" She presented a cup of coffee to her sister.

"No, thank you."

"Drink it," Barbara ordered, holding the cup out until Chi Chi took it.

Chi Chi sipped the coffee. "What are we going to do without Dad?"

Barbara sat down next to Chi Chi on the piano bench. "We'll figure it out."

This was what Chi Chi loved about her older sister, and also what she hated about her. She had an answer for everything. "I didn't see this coming, did you?"

Barbara shook her head.

"How is Mama holding up?"

"Cheech, it's not good."

"They've been married since they were eighteen."

"I'm talking about her circumstances. This house."

"What's wrong with the house?"

"There's debt."

"They owned it outright, free and clear. Don't you remember? He told us that three years ago."

"That was before he took out a mortgage to build this studio."

"What are you talking about?" Chi Chi got a sick feeling in her stomach.

"He did all the labor," Barbara said impatiently, "but there were costs, the wood, glass, the supplies. All this equipment—it's expensive, and he couldn't afford it. So he borrowed against the house to buy it."

Barbara's tone forced Chi Chi onto the defensive. "He had plans to record all kinds of acts in here."

"But he didn't."

"He didn't live long enough. Besides, he was putting all his efforts into our act." Chi Chi thought about how many times her father had driven them to a talent contest, or dropped everything to take them to a radio station for an open-mic audition, or how many hours a day he had spent with her when she was writing a song, and more in the studio as he recorded it over and over again, playing it back until they were satisfied. "He worked hard."

"The act wasn't going anywhere."

"It could have, in time. We talked about it. We were building a business that would last. A business in music."

Barbara looked at her sister wearily. "I know how badly you wanted it. But it was not to be."

"It doesn't happen overnight. It takes time. You have to give it time."

"Most of the time it never happens."

Chi Chi wasn't going to argue with her pragmatic sister. Barbara's droll sense of humor was funny onstage, but in life, it was exhausting. There was little room for failure in her world, and none for whimsy. She looked at life practically, with a set of rules that outlined how things should work.

Chi Chi sipped the hot, black coffee. "What's the freight on the mortgage?"

"Dad exchanged the value of our home for the cost of this studio. Charlie is already trying to unload the contents of the studio."

"Whoa. Without asking me?"

"You're too attached. And we don't have time. It's not going well. Charlie can only get pennies on the dollar for the stuff. Dad overpaid for the console, the microphones, the amplifier. Even the radio stations don't want the turntable."

"I was with him when he bought this equipment. Dad went into the city to the best places."

"And got took."

"Dad wasn't a sucker."

"He was trying to make you happy. He spent his last dollar trying to make your dream come true."

"Our dream."

"Yes, we all enjoyed singing, but you and Dad had bigger ideas."

"What's wrong with that?"

"Nothing, if you can afford it."

"We're all working."

"Dad lost his job because he was taking off too much time to wheel and deal in music on your behalf. I'm not telling you this to hurt you. It's the truth. He got caught up in it. He thought *Mama's Rolling Pin* was a hit. He really did. He took Ma's grocery money last week and went around paying disc jockeys to play the song on the radio."

"No, he didn't. We dropped off the records. No money changed hands."

"Not that you saw. But he paid them. Charlie found out when he called to sell the equipment. The first guy let it slip, and from there, Charlie acted like he was going to pay to play your record, and they spilled."

Chi Chi put her head in her hands.

"And if we want to save the house for Ma, and it's unlikely we can, we have to pool all our savings. Charlie will go down to the bank and renegotiate the mortgage."

"He will not! I'm his daughter."

"The bank responds to men. Let him handle it."

Tears stung Chi Chi's eyes, but she quickly wiped them away. She had to show strength, not emotion.

Barbara was moved by her sister's pain. "I am so sorry to tell you all this. You tried. Dad tried. But we weren't good enough."

"The audience decides who is good enough."

"Cheech, we don't have an audience."

"You have to build one."

Barbara refused to argue. "You should know what we're putting on the table to save the house. I have saved one hundred and eighty-two dollars. Lucille has one hundred and fifteen. Ma has two hundred and four dollars squirreled away. I don't know what you have—"

"Of course I will help," Chi Chi cut in. She knew not to offer hard numbers to Barbara, who would hold her to them. "What do we owe?"

"We owe around six thousand dollars."

"But the house is only worth two thousand dollars, and that's if you could find a buyer. What's the rate on the mortgage?"

"Eight percent."

"That's a terrible deal!" Chi Chi couldn't believe it. "My bank offers a mortgage at three."

"They saw Dad coming. That's why I want Charlie to go in and try to reason with them and get the number down. They will try and foreclose, they always do. And they have some cause. Dad has been late with his payment a few times. Including last month."

Chi Chi remembered her father trying to talk to her about the finances, but she was too busy writing songs. How she wished she had paid attention.

"He didn't even tell Mama," Barbara went on. "She never had an inkling. His own wife! He was his sweet, happy-go-lucky self until the end. And we loved him, and we'd do anything for him. And he'd do anything for us. But, make no mistake, our paychecks from the mill kept this all afloat."

Chi Chi found it hard to speak. Her sister was outlining the future, and it was grim. There would be no music career; it would be the hard slog at the mill for all of them, just to keep a roof over their heads. As surely as it was in her grasp, Chi Chi had to let go of the dream Mariano and she had imagined together.

"Listen to me, Chi Chi. We need to keep our heads down and work hard. We'll work at the mill as we have been, do our piece-work and make as much extra money as we can, and concentrate on keeping our home. We will all have to make sacrifices. I'll marry Charlie in the sacristy after Labor Day—no big wedding, no fancy gown."

"But you dreamed of your wedding day."

"They were just dreams. Charlie will move in after we're married, and we'll live here and we'll pay rent." She sighed. "We would have paid it somewhere else anyway."

"That's between you and Mom. But Charlie is not to go to the bank. He's not in the family. I know Mr. Polly, the bank manager, personally."

"How do you know him?"

"Through Dad."

"But you didn't know about the mortgage?"

"No. But I do now, and I'll talk to him about it. Give me a chance to take care of this."

"It's a bad idea."

"Barbara, I will fight you on this."

"I need to talk to Mom."

"I will fight her, too," Chi Chi said calmly.

Barbara stepped back.

"I will take care of this." Chi Chi walked to the door and held it open for her sister. "If this is the end of the studio, I want to be the one to close it."

Chi Chi punched her time card in the vestibule of Jersey Miss, slid her wide-brimmed straw hat onto her head, and ran up the street to the New Jersey National Savings & Loan to beat its three-o'clock closing. She took the steps two at a time to the entrance of the stately red-brick building, flung the door open, and stepped inside with nineteen minutes to spare.

Her work shoes squeaked on the polished marble floor, so she walked on her toes instead. No matter how many customers came into the branch for service, the volume never went above a whisper. Besides the bank, this kind of silence and reverence could only be found in church or at the public library.

She made her way to the manager's desk, an ornate mahogany rectangle covered in a sheet of thick glass set behind an arch of wrought-iron scrollwork. She used to find the opulent setting reassuring; now it intimidated her.

"Miss Donatelli?"

Mr. Polly had a friendly smile and white hair. He waited until Chi Chi had taken a seat across from him before he sat behind the big desk. "I'm sorry to hear about your father."

"We're all devastated, as you can imagine." Chi Chi pulled a handkerchief from her pocket. "My mother is now a widow, and we're all alone in the world."

"What can I do to help?"

Chi Chi leaned forward. "The first order of business? I want to renegotiate the bum mortgage you saddled my father with. Mr. Polly, were you serious, sir? Eight percent?"

"He had debts he wanted to clean up. We bundled them."

"You bundled and buried him. It's wrong. I'm not implying what you did is illegal in any way. It's your bank, and you can charge twenty percent, and if a customer wants the loan, and is willing to pay it, and you make the deal—that's good business for you. But my father was in a desperate state of mind."

Mr. Polly opened the file. "Your father requested a balloon mortgage. He was convinced that a business he was working on would take off sooner rather than later. He bet the family home, his best asset, on it."

"But he died, and we can't continue in this fashion. The house is worth two thousand. He owes six thousand."

"Six thousand fifty dollars and seventy-two cents."

"Understood, sir. My father had been paying on this loan for a year, which means you've already made close to five hundred dollars in interest on it. I'd like to cancel the current mortgage and renegotiate it. I'm willing to put down half of the value of the home as collateral—in cash. And I want to renegotiate the debt at two percent, a figure my mother, my sisters, and I can manage."

"The house isn't enough collateral," Mr. Polly said calmly.

"I'm offering my government bonds. Today, at the current rate, they are worth one thousand one hundred seventy-seven dollars and forty-three cents. I hold them here at your bank. I have cash on hand totaling two hundred dollars, which I would like to add to the pot. That's more than half the value of the house, and it's a full cash backup. I think, under the circumstances, it's an excellent deal."

"I'm sorry, we have to hold you to the original mortgage rate."

Chi Chi leaned forward. "Mr. Polly, I'm going to ask you to reconsider one more time. See, I work down the street at Jersey Miss, and I think you know most of those young ladies don't trust the bank with their money. How would you like it spread all over the mill—and all over town—that you gouged a woman the entire town of Sea Isle respects, on a loan you have already made a generous return on? I don't think it looks good for the bank. I don't think it looks good for you. Perhaps you need to talk to your regional manager and see what he can do for me. In fact, I'd like that, sir."

Mr. Polly looked startled. "One moment, Miss Donatelli." He stood up, went into the interior office, and closed the door.

Chi Chi was sweating so profusely, she felt it run down her back underneath her work blouse. If Mr. Polly didn't take the offer, she had no backup plan. Her mother would lose the house. Even with the girls working, the loan would suffocate them.

Mr. Polly returned and sat down at the desk. "Miss Donatelli, the bank is willing to adjust the mortgage rate to two-point-five percent, but we'll need an additional one hundred dollars in cash. So, the government bonds worth one thousand one hundred seventy-seven dollars and forty-three cents, plus three hundred dollars cash, and the loan at two-point-five percent, for a monthly payment of sixty-two dollars and fifty cents until the loan is paid in full."

Chi Chi did a quick calculation in her head. "Excuse me, Mr. Polly, but my math tells me the payment should be forty-one dollars and fifty cents per month. I'm paying off fifteen hundred dollars of it today."

"Late fees and a renegotiating fee brought the monthly payment up."

Chi Chi bowed her head and buried her face in her handkerchief. She wept. "We can't afford it. Please, sir, please, can you waive the late fees and the renegotiation fee? Please? I guess I could try and pass a hat at the mill, but I don't think it would set well."

Mr. Polly excused himself again. Chi Chi kept her face in the hanky until she heard the door snap behind him. The handkerchief was dry. There were no tears; Chi Chi was furious. When she heard the door creak open, she put her face back into the handkerchief.

"Miss Donatelli?"

"Yes, sir?"

"You have a deal. Forty-one dollars and fifty cents is your monthly payment, with late fees and renegotiation waived."

Once Chi Chi was outside the bank, she scanned the pages of the mortgage before carefully folding it and returning it to the envelope and into her purse. She turned up the street to walk home, but found herself breaking into a run to share the good news with her mother and sisters.

The coral sun slipped below the horizon. Dusk followed in shades of teal that streaked the sky in the last of the light as Chi Chi walked briskly along the water's edge alone.

Her mother had taken the news of the mortgage renegotiation appreciatively, but she did not comprehend the scope of what Chi

Chi had accomplished. Barbara was pleased, but remained anxious about how their family would survive. Lucille was glad that her sister had managed to save a portion of the money she'd set aside for secretarial school; she'd been convinced that all was lost. But the truth was, none of the Donatelli women were satisfied. This victory did not make up for the loss of Mariano, or for their disappointment in him. It was true that he had been a good husband and father. It was also true that he had disappointed them with his secret business schemes. Only Chi Chi understood his motives, and only she could forgive him in full for being a dreamer and wanting more.

As she made her way back to the family home, she thought about her father, his hopes for the family, the record studio, and the sister act. He had worked diligently on Chi Chi's behalf. After the funeral and burial, she remembered her father as her friend, as the only person in her life who truly understood her and rooted for her. She could not imagine the world without him, but here it was, and it was every bit as awful as she had imagined it might be. Sitting alone on the front porch, she began to cry. She was left to stay behind and live without his laugh, wisdom, and dreams. Her mourning had begun.

Through the screen door, Chi Chi could hear her mother and sisters in the kitchen. Instead of going inside the house, she went to the studio. She pulled the key out from under the mat and let herself in.

Chi Chi marveled at her father's handiwork. Mariano had done a splendid job turning a cinder-block garage into a professional operation. It was his idea to build the studio within the garage, thus ensuring as close to perfect sound as was possible. Every detail had been researched. He was particular when choosing the materials for construction and meticulous in the execution of the building of the structure by the labor of his own hands, as was his way, the old-world way, in the Italian style. Eventually—and soon—his small shrine to music, an art form he revered, would be disassembled and sold for scrap.

How quickly everything they had worked for was gone.

Plenty of widows along the shore found ways to raise additional income. Some rented space to fishermen who stored their crabbing baskets, rowboats, oars, and gear in their empty garages; others rented to men who needed a place to park their work vehicles. And now Isotta, with the help of her daughters, would have to find a new purpose for their garage. Rental fees were determined by a garage's size and location. So close to the water, the Donatelli women might do all right.

It was the end of the D Studio; there was no fighting to save it. Chi Chi was outnumbered. However, when it came to her father's dream of having a hit record, she didn't need her sisters' support or approval to proceed on her own. A hit record made in his memory would be Chi Chi's mission. She would write the song and find the best artist to record it to take it to the top of the *Hit Parade*.

No scrap collector, mortgage lender, or skeptical relative would stand in her way.

5

1939–1940

Volante

(Flight)

Chi Chi Donatelli took the twenty-block walk from the Thirty-Third Street train station in midtown Manhattan to the Musicale nightclub and dance hall on West Fifty-Second Street at a clip. Overhead, the pink morning sky was dense with low white clouds. The tops of the skyscrapers poked through them, looking like sticks holding tufts of cotton candy. New Yorkers gripped their hats and buttoned their coats as the first cold winds of autumn whipped around corners and blew through the streets below.

Chi Chi walked on Ninth Avenue past tenements dusted with

soot set among shady storefronts whose vendors rolled out half-empty bins with meager offerings of dry goods. One old man sold secondhand scarves and belts, while two shifty brothers hawked sewing supplies: fabric remnants and spools of thread in odd colors, castoffs pinched from the sample salesmen in the garment district. The merchandise was on final sale, a fitting swan song to the last gasp of the Depression. Everything was about to change, or at least it felt that way to Chi Chi.

The confident Jersey girl crossed the wide avenue and walked past a passel of city workers working around an open manhole. Their wolf whistles were lost in the cacophony of car horns, the clang of the train cars, and the howl of distant sirens. Chi Chi heard none of it. Her mind was elsewhere; she had come to the city for business.

As Chi Chi turned the corner onto Fifty-Second Street, her heart sank. It appeared as if any girl who thought she could carry a tune in the tristate area had come to try to win a spot to sing with the Paul Godfrey Orchestra. As a rule, Chi Chi didn't enter these types of contests, but this one was irresistible: the winner got a guaranteed six-month contract to tour with the name band. Chi Chi needed the break. An opportunity like this was not likely to knock on her door in Sea Isle City.

Aspiring professional girl singers who longed to front the big bands stood patiently in their best hats, gloves, and coats in a line that unspooled around the block in one long ribbon. They carried folders filled with sheet music, like the one Chi Chi had tucked under her arm. She took her place at the back of the line and surveyed the street. Jazz Alley was lined with cabarets and clubs that featured singers and musicians from her favorite bands. She was thrilled at the thought of the talent she admired walking these streets and playing these venues, passing under the red canopies and marquees lit by purple neon.

Up the block, Chi Chi observed a petite blond dynamo around her age talking to the contestants. The young woman wove in and out of the line, accepting their paperwork. Once in a while she stopped, pulled a young woman from the line, and sent her directly inside the club.

"What's going on?" Chi Chi asked the young lady in front of her. "Do you know?"

"You go to the front if you have your paperwork. You got yours?"

Chi Chi fished her application out of the folder. "I do."

"That was using your bean. I don't. I thought I could get the paperwork here."

A girl in a velvet cloche overheard them talking and turned around. "Don't worry. You can fill out an application inside."

"We won't get inside that club until lunch," said the girl who hadn't planned ahead.

As Chi Chi waited, she went over her audition song in her mind. From time to time, she checked her wristwatch. It was almost 9:30 a.m. when the energetic blonde finally approached her.

"Paperwork?"

Chi Chi smiled warmly and gave her the application she had obtained from an insert in the previous Sunday's *Newark Star-Ledger*.

The woman looked it over. "Nice penmanship. Palmer method. Convent training?"

"Absolutely. The nuns of Saint Joseph."

"Come with me. I'm Miss Bowman. You can call me Lee."

Lee Bowman was young, but she was in charge, which made her seem more experienced and sophisticated than the hopefuls on the line. Lee had a cherubic face, blue eyes, and golden hair that was cropped under her chin and set in marcel waves, but her outfit was all business. She wore a navy blue suit, matching pumps, and a sleek wool fedora with a navy grosgrain bow.

"Are you convent trained too?" Chi Chi asked her. She practically had to run to keep up with Lee, who moved in double time.

"Yes, but I am the only girl who would admit that in a ten-block radius. This is Times Square. There's not a lot of piety in the area. If I were you, I wouldn't pause, linger, or look, because if you do, they will. Avoid the *they*s. Keep moving, and you'll stay out of trouble."

"I want to win the contest."

"Uh-huh." Lee surveyed the line as they walked.

"I sing."

"So do the two hundred other bathing beauties on this line. What else do you do?"

"I write songs."

"Better."

"I also play the piano."

"How well?"

"Very. Since I was five years old."

"Better still. Could you play with the band? Accompany rehearsals, if needed? Mr. Godfrey doesn't like women in the orchestra, only at the microphone, but he's not averse to using us behind the scenes to put the show together. Do you think you could sit in with the boys?"

"I think so."

Lee leaned in, her blue eyes steely. "Say *yes*, sister."

"Yes," Chi Chi said definitively.

Lee pushed open the stage door, passing the security guard and another line of young ladies waiting to audition in the hallway inside. Chi Chi followed her backstage. The work lights formed gold circles on the black floor. The pair skipped over thick cables until they found a spot where they could hide and observe the audition process in the club.

"This is how we're going to do this," Lee whispered. "I'm gonna get you in at the top. You'll do your song, whatever you planned on singing—and I hope it's not *Brother, Can You Spare a Dime?* because I'll pay the next girl a quarter myself not to sing it. I will have already flagged your application on the stack. It will be in the hands of the conductor—he's the shrimpy dyspeptic guy in the brown tie—before you've sung for Paul Godfrey. Mr. Godfrey's the looker in the hat."

"Got it."

"I happen to know they're in desperate need of a rehearsal pianist. Mr. Godfrey also wants new material, and if your songs are any good . . . well, you see how I'm thinking." Lee squinted and looked out into the theater.

"You'd do this for me?"

"The nuns of Saint Joseph got me out of an iron lung when I was six years old. Dire asthma. They cured me." Lee shrugged. "I owe them. Consider this an indulgence paid for a blessing given."

"I appreciate it."

"Besides, it's my last day on this job, and I want to get paid. I want to deliver exactly what they're looking for."

"How do you know if I'm any good?"

Lee looked at Chi Chi. "That's the easy part. I just follow my gut."

"Miss Donatelli?"

"Here," Chi Chi called out from the back of the theater as she joined the conductor, Mr. Godfrey, and his secretary at the edge of the orchestra pit.

"Have you got charts?" the secretary asked.

"Yes, ma'am." Chi Chi handed her charts to the secretary, who took them to the pianist onstage.

"What have you got for us today?" the conductor asked, looking

Chi Chi up and down as though he were measuring her for a girdle. Mr. Godfrey gave Chi Chi a quick once-over, too.

"It's a song I wrote."

The conductor and Mr. Godfrey looked as if they'd just heard they had consumed tainted clams at Howard Johnson's on West Forty-Sixth Street.

"I can do a standard if you wish," Chi Chi said diplomatically, "but I write a lot of songs, and I figured you might like to hear one."

"Okay, let's hear it."

"Or I could sing *Brother, Can You Spare a Dime?*" Chi Chi joked.

"No." The conductor chuckled and looked at Godfrey, who smiled.

Chi Chi climbed the steps to the stage and pulled a mason jar three-quarters full of jelly beans out of her purse. She placed her purse on the piano.

"It's uptempo. Lively," she said softly to the rehearsal pianist, who looked to be around seventy-five years old or so, and as if he hadn't felt lively since the invention of the cotton gin. "I'll count us down . . . and one, two, three, and four . . ." Chi Chi tapped her foot.

He began to play her song. The tempo was off. Chi Chi walked around to the back of the piano and whispered in the pianist's ear while she shook the jar of jelly beans expertly, making a sound like maracas producing a soft-shoe beat. She cued the pianist once more. The smooth rhythm seemed to grab the attention of every person in the theater, including the contestants and the men who would judge them.

"This is a little tune called *Jelly Bean Beach*," Chi Chi said as she shook the candy in the jar and strutted back and forth, working the downstage lip of the stage like an experienced performer.

The pianist nodded, catching on fast. He tickled the overture on the keys and followed Chi Chi as she ramped up her intro. She winked at him. Now they understood one another, which made them a team, which made her job easier.

Chi Chi faced the audience and vamped, "If you've been to the Jersey shore, or any shore, really, Maine to Florida, or cruised that spicy strip along the Gulf of Mexico, or even sashayed along at the pier on the Hudson River overlooking the garbage barge . . . you'll know what I'm singing about. This is about a summer day when the beach is so crowded, the hot dog man runs out of mustard, the girls run out of coconut oil, and the strong man runs out of cornball lines to pick up your pretty sister. In other words, it might as well rain."

Chi Chi sang:

> Jelly Bean Beach, down the shore
> The kids take a dip and the boys are bores
> Girls, roll up your clamdiggers and take a clue
> You won't find love here, you'll just wind up blue
>
> You can't see the sand, it's packed with folks
> Jelly Bean Beach, they've run out of Coke
> The ocean is wide and the water's warm
> But nobody wants to go in, they'd rather swarm—
>
> On Jelly Bean Beach, down the shore
> The girls take a dip and the boys are bores
> Will they ever grow up and take a clue?
> I want to find love here, don't wanna be blue

Chi Chi finished her audition with an attenuated shake of the jar. The pianist sat back on the bench and nodded his approval.

Chi Chi thanked him and took the steps down to the club. The conductor stood up as she passed.

"That was cute. It's going to be a long day—maybe stick around."

"I can do that."

"Give Miss Bowman the details."

Chi Chi glanced at Paul Godfrey, who looked over some charts. "Thank you, Mr. Godfrey."

Godfrey nodded without looking up. Chi Chi left through the back of the club theater.

"Could I handle that kind of pep?" Godfrey said softly.

"There's something charming about it," the conductor admitted. "If you're wrangling cheetah cubs."

Chi Chi went outside the club, where the line had been replenished with a new crop of singing ingénues waiting to audition for Paul Godfrey. One girl was prettier than the one before, and if they sang as beautifully as they looked, her audition would soon be forgotten. As Chi Chi stood and watched the young ladies file by, she got an up-close look at her long-term prospects in the music business.

Lee Bowman was halfway down the block, collecting more applications. Chi Chi reached into her purse and shook a few jelly beans into her hand. At first she thought she shouldn't eat her percussion section, in case she got a callback. But she was feeling more famished than hopeful about her prospects, so she proceeded to eat them daintily, one by one.

There was not a park in Times Square or a bench outside the club, at least none that Chi Chi could find by looking. She wondered as she checked her watch: When the conductor asked her to stick around, where exactly had he meant for her to stick? She walked to the corner and looked up and down Eighth Avenue, hoping to find a place she could loiter until Mr. Godfrey made his decision, when she heard screams coming from the stage door outside the *Musicale*.

The girls had abandoned their spots on line and had clustered around someone at the stage door. Chi Chi followed the sound, scanning the line as though it were a long fuse and she was searching for the point of ignition. She had moved in behind the crowd to see what the hoopla was about when she spotted the object of their affection. She recognized the shape of his head, the line of the nose, and the cut of the jaw, and when she got close enough, she would know the hands.

Saverio Armandonada was surrounded by fans who pawed and petted him as though he were a new kitten. He raised his arms and hands to shield his face as he moved through them. She found herself joining in, pushing through the throng to get to him, not only because she knew him but because she was relieved to see a familiar face.

"Tony! Tony!" the girls chanted.

"Back on the line, ladies," Lee said firmly from behind her.

"I know that fellow. He's an old friend."

"Come with me." Lee pulled Chi Chi around the gaggle of fans and back into the club through the work door.

Saverio lunged into the dark theater through the stage door. The security guard snapped the door behind him, keeping the girls outside.

The guard grinned. "You're popular."

Saverio smoothed his hair. "I'd like to be a little less popular."

"You say that until you ain't," the guard retorted.

Chi Chi moved into the light. "Saverio?"

Saverio squinted. "Cheech, is that you? Long time!" He embraced her.

"When did you become a Tony?"

"When I left Roccaraso. What do you think? Does it suit me?"

"Not bad."

"You mean it?"

"Tony works," Chi Chi said supportively. "It's Italian."

"Right. And Arma? They shortened my last name."

"Lopped it right off, huh. So your name has to fit on a marquee?"

"Or a pack of matches," Tony joked. "What are you doing here?"

"I auditioned for the band this morning. I was going to sing *Stormy Weather*, but I walked into the hurricane instead and sang *Jelly Bean Beach*."

"So you finished the song. No *Mama's Rolling Pin*?"

"It will never be performed in public without you. What are you doing here?"

"I sing with the band now."

Chi Chi smiled. "What are the odds?"

"How's your family? Your mom and dad?"

Chi Chi's smile fell away. "My mother is okay, but my father passed away. It was sudden."

"I'm so sorry. I didn't know. Wonderful man."

The secretary emerged from the club. When she saw Tony, her face softened. She was around thirty, and had a look of desire in her eye. "Mr. Arma? Mr. Godfrey is waiting for you."

"I'm on my way, Mary Rose."

"I have to go. Stick around, will you?" Tony gave Chi Chi a quick kiss on the cheek and left.

"You really know Tony Arma," Lee said, joining Chi Chi.

"I wouldn't say I knew someone if I didn't."

"You're still so pure, so honest." Lee sighed. "But not for long."

Chi Chi grinned. "I think I can stay honest."

"It's going to go late with these auditions." Lee handed Chi Chi a card. "I arranged for a room at the Longacre Hotel for you."

"Thanks, Lee, but I can't afford it."

"You're not paying. Mr. Godfrey holds the rooms. He told you to stick, so you get a room."

"I don't know."

"It's on the up-and-up. No hanky-panky. You're on the short list. Give this card to the front desk at the hotel. If Mr. Godfrey wants to see you again, I'll call the hotel, and you can come right back. But go over, get your room settled, and put your feet up."

"I can do that. Thank you. But what about you?"

Lee swatted her fanny. "This won't see a chair until after supper."

Chi Chi tucked the card into her purse and thought of her father. He had spoken often of angels, blessings, and mystical connections. Perhaps, knowing his daughter was in need of one, he had sent Lee Bowman to her. And what about Tony Arma? She'd figured it would be years before she ever saw him again. Maybe a life and a career of consequence was all about luck and timing, being in the right place for a contest, all that jazz. Chi Chi was beginning to feel the flutters of potential regarding the opportunities that lay ahead for her in music. Besides, she had that little something extra Mariano Donatelli had encouraged his daughter to cultivate: connections.

Chi Chi peered out the lone window in room 317 of the Longacre Hotel for Women. The brick wall of the next building, about a foot away from her window, held a wide metal vent. It was so close she could open the window and touch it. She looked up through the tunnel between the buildings until she could see a small pocket of gray sky.

Chi Chi had removed her shoes and hung her suit jacket on a hanger on the hook on the back of the door. Her hat rested on the small end table by the bed. The cubicle room held a twin bed, chair, and table. She sat down on the straight-backed chair and propped her feet up on the bed.

There was no art on the walls and no mirror, but to Chi Chi, this spartan room was just right; it served as the holding cell to her dazzling future. She checked her wristwatch when she heard a knock at the door. She got up and went to the door, peered out the peephole.

"Cavatelli?" an older woman in a housecoat whose head was covered in pink curlers said gruffly through the door. "You got a call."

Chi Chi grabbed her key and went outside. The woman motioned to the public phone on the wall at the end of the hallway. The receiver dangled from its cord, swaying back and forth.

"Don't yak long. I have a callback," the woman said before the door to her room snapped shut behind her.

Chi Chi broke into a run with the certainty of a woman who knew for sure she'd gotten the job. She was breathless when she answered the phone.

"Chi Chi, it's Tony."

She had to think. *Tony?* "Oh, Saverio. Hi."

"You sound disappointed."

"Not at all. I was waiting to hear from Lee."

"No word on that yet. There's still a few more singers for Paul and the team to audition."

"I'll bet. It's like they took the five boroughs, turned them upside down and shook out every twenty-one-year-old girl, and sent her in to audition for the band. I haven't got a chance. Do I?"

"It's not that hopeless."

"You're not a girl, so you wouldn't know."

"How about I take you out to get your mind off things?"

Chi Chi looked down the long hallway. The thought of sitting in the room all night depressed her. "Sure. That would be great."

"I'll pick you up in an hour."

Chi Chi brushed her hair in the reflection of the window glass. She dabbed on some lipstick, straightened the blouse underneath her suit jacket, and lined up the seams on her stockings. She checked her wristwatch again. She was surprised to feel her heart racing. She inhaled deep breaths and exhaled slowly as she did whenever her nerves got the best of her.

Chi Chi took the steps down from the third floor to the lobby. Saverio sat in one of the two Windsor chairs facing the check-in desk. His coat was unbuttoned, his custom Homburg rested on his lap, and his hands gripped the arms of the chair as he watched the comings and goings of the hotel guests with interest.

"Tony," Chi Chi said as she approached him. "That's going to be odd for a while. May I still call you Saverio?"

"How about you always call me Saverio?"

Chi Chi took Tony's arm in the street. The air was crisp and cold; the scents of tobacco smoke, wood-burning fires, and the perfume of fancy women as they swirled through the air. Three autumn leaves fell from the spindly chestnut tree in front of Manhattan's Downbeat Club on West Fifty-Second Street as Chi Chi and Tony approached the entrance. The chalkboard on the sidewalk announced the sold-out appearance of trumpeter Sy Oliver, in New York City for an exclusive week-long engagement.

Chi Chi leaned in and read a review from the *New York Herald*

Tribune that had been pinned in the glass box next to the stairs that led down into the club:

> Sy Oliver is the unspoken heir to the great Jimmie Lunceford, performing and arranging jazz standards for orchestras across the country and around the world with a keen sense of history coupled with a hip, forward-thinking style that packs venues wherever he appears.

Tony led her to a small café table near the stage.

"This close?" Chi Chi said enthusiastically.

"You'll see Mr. Oliver blow his trumpet to high heaven." Tony turned and ordered their drinks.

"Where do you live?" Chi Chi asked him.

"On the road."

"You don't have an apartment somewhere?"

"No need."

"Where do you go when you have a week off?"

Tony smiled. "I find a place."

There was always a new Gladys Overby for the Tony Armas of the big-band circuit. He didn't need a permanent address when he had temporary digs. Chi Chi understood his meaning. "Oh. Okay." She turned, noticed Lee Bowman at the back of the club, and waved her over. Lee wove through the patrons seated at the café tables to join them.

"What's the verdict?" Tony asked.

"I'm not sure I want to know," Chi Chi said. "But tell me."

"Don't lose heart," Lee began.

"There's the wind-up for rejection," Chi Chi said to Tony.

"It might be if you believe that the Paul Godfrey Orchestra is the only band in the world," Lee said.

"I didn't get it." Chi Chi put her head on the table.

"No, you didn't," Lee said. "It went to a nice girl from Illinois with golden hair."

"They're always from Illinois, and they're always blond," Chi Chi cracked. "Just like corn."

"That's funny." Lee laughed. "Save it for the act."

"What act? I didn't get the gig."

"When you're done here, I want you kids to meet me at the Automat on the corner of Forty-Third and Ninth. We'll have a bite, and I've got an opportunity to float by you. Right now, I have to get Miss Illinois acclimated to the tour."

Chi Chi put her face in her hands as Lee left. "I should dye my hair."

"It wouldn't suit you," Tony said.

"How do you know?"

"I'm one of the few men who is not color-blind, and I know a good palette from a bad one. You'd be a terrible blonde."

"I'm listening." Chi Chi sat back and folded her arms. "Make a decent argument, because I'm thinking about Helen Forrest and Marie Hillman Smith and Dinah Shore and Martha Tilton and Nita Leftwich, and there's a new girl out of Kentucky named Rosemary Clooney. A lot of gold hair in that lineup."

"With your black hair and brown eyes, you're every bit as lovely as a blonde with blue eyes or a redhead with green eyes."

"Unless they're hiring blondes and redheads, and you're a brunette."

"I'm not talking about jobs. I'm talking aesthetics."

Chi Chi took a sip of her Manhattan. "You spend an awful lot of time studying women."

"And matching socks for the boys in the band who can't do it for themselves."

"So it's a job when you look at women and compare them against one another in the light, like paint chips?"

"Is it your job to call me on it?"

"The way you are with women?"

"I'm not talking about socks."

"Women line up like you're the guy handing out candy canes on Christmas morning and they're addicted to peppermint."

"It will pass."

"Not anytime soon. But what do I know about show business? I thought I was all right. I did my best this morning."

"They were looking for a girl who can look pretty and sing the standards."

"I could do that too."

"You would've been bored stiff with that gig. How many times can you begin the beguine before you want to kill the beguine and throw it off a cliff?"

"As many times as Mr. Godfrey asks me," Chi Chi assured him.

The lights dimmed in the club, until the only flickers that remained in the dark came from the sputtering firefly tips of the patrons' cigarettes. The musicians filed onto the stage in the blackout. Soon a glint of gold sparkled on the cabaret stage as a light pulled on slowly to reveal the polished brass horn belonging to Sy Oliver. He lifted the trumpet to his lips reverently and blew a note so sweet, the patrons began to whoop and holler with such ferocity, they practically drowned out the glorious sound of his horn.

Sy was stylish, manicured, and genteel. He had an au courant pencil-thin mustache and bronze skin. His custom suit, cut from rich chocolate-brown Savile Row wool, was piped with delicate silver thread that gave it the patina of brushstrokes on a Renaissance painting.

The musicians, a quartet of Sy's favorite sidemen, fired up their instruments—a cello, saxophone, drums, and piano—and with one tip of the maestro's finger, the Cotton Club's finest artisans tore into *Uptown Blues*, rattling the joint until the folks at the tables were compelled to stand and move, despite the cramped space. The club was small, but the sound was big, and Chi Chi wondered if the walls could contain the sound. Chi Chi heard Sy Oliver's trumpet as a revelry. After all, he and his fellow black artists had invented swing, and now everyone wanted in, including the Italian girl from the shore. Even though Paul Godfrey hadn't hired her, she believed she belonged in their world. This was the right time, and the music would never be better. She let the music shore up her soul and ignite her determination anew.

Chi Chi took Tony's arm as they walked from the club to the Automat to meet Lee Bowman. "That was like church," she marveled.

"You're right. It was inspirational."

"Thank you for taking me to the show."

"You're a nice date, Chi Chi."

"Well, you would know. You've certainly practiced."

"Is that a dig?"

"Not at all. I appreciate wisdom and experience in all aspects of life. I'd probably know more about the world if I had a brother." Chi Chi gave him a playful nudge. "You could be my brother. Of course, if you were, it's obvious I got the better nose."

"If this is what it's like to have a sister, you can keep it," he teased, holding the door of the Automat open for Chi Chi.

Lee waved them over to her table. "How was the show?"

"Superb." Chi Chi removed her gloves and coat and sat down next to Lee.

"I wish I could quit and follow Sy Oliver around the country," Tony admitted, taking a seat.

"Sy isn't hiring any Italian boys."

"And I've got a contract with Paul Godfrey anyway."

"Well, Tony, I want to talk to you about that. He wants to let you out of it," Lee said gently.

"He's canceling my contract?" Tony was surprised. "The crust."

"Mr. Godfrey's putting a theatrical show together. No more solo 'stand and sing.' He's going from dance band to show band. Says there are too many dance bands out there, and he had to pull in front somehow. Maybe some burlesque."

"You're serious." Tony sat back in his chair. "Usually acts try to break out of Minsky's, they don't fall back in."

"Yeah, well, now they're joining them. It's called the fast buck. In the meantime, as of ten a.m. Monday morning, I have officially left the Godfrey organization and joined another."

"Did you leave in solidarity, Lee?" Tony joked. "Let me be the first to thank you."

"You'll be glad I did. My new job is a doozy. I'm an agent with the William Morris Agency in the music department, which means I'm looking for clients to book, and I'd like to sign you two."

"Sign *us*?" Chi Chi was confused.

"Sign you. Tony gave me *Mama's Rolling Pin*, and I think it's a hit. It's funny, but it's a great tune, too. It could sell. Now, one song isn't going to cut it. You have to come up with an act."

"What kind of an act?" Chi Chi asked.

"Are you two friends who like each other, are you a couple pretending to be romantic who bicker, or are you cousins who put on a show together? Figure out what you want to be. I'll do the rest."

"No offense. I like to sing solo," said Tony.

"And you can. You remain a solo act, Tony, but there's something extra to sell with a boy-girl duo and routine. Everybody wants pairs. They're booking them in clubs, and the bands want in on the action. They don't care about the configuration either. Two men comics who can sing. Two women playing singing sisters. A man and a woman, a married couple singing about their life together. I don't know. You two come up with it. You can pose as brother and sister, for all I care. Chi Chi can write songs and play, and you can sing them. Or write them together. You're always complaining about the material, Tony, how you don't get offered good songs—so get together and create the material yourselves and see where they go. I will put your songs in the right hands. Like I did with *Rolling Pin*."

"What do you mean?" Chi Chi's eyes widened.

"I canvassed the radio stations. Somebody is bound to play it."

"You don't even care about the Godfrey gig, do you?" Tony wondered.

"Not really. I can get you more money with a hit record behind you."

"It's always about the record."

"Afraid so. It turns out the ladies you sing with do better without you, Tony—which tells us something. You need an act. And it's wise to put together what they're looking for. Sell what they want to buy."

"I think Lee is saying you need me." Chi Chi patted Saverio's hand.

"That's what you heard in all that chatter?"

"Not forever," Lee said, "and you two don't have to get married, professionally speaking, either. But Tony, you have to get over this hump. And I saw the solution—and it came in a jar of jelly beans."

"I saw the future too," Chi Chi said. "The girls were all over Tony outside the club today." Chi Chi turned to him. "You have a fan base already."

"Godfrey knows it, too," Lee said, "but he's more concerned about the survival of his band than his lead singer's popularity. He thinks bobby-soxers are a passing fad."

"They might be," Tony admitted. "What happens when those girls grow up?"

"They get married," Chi Chi offered.

"And on the other side," said Lee, "waiting for them, with a great act, is a man-and-woman team who sing together about home, babies, domestic bliss, and rolling pins. You'll beat the crowd to the top of the charts if you listen to me. If you don't, they'll drop you for the next handsome crooner to come out of the auto plants of Ohio."

"Detroit."

"There too. Look, you get off course when you try to fit in. It's the great conundrum of show business. You want to appeal to everyone, but the truth is, you should aim to be yourself, and cross your fingers. When you try to fit a mold, you'll have to shape yourself to circumstances, and you whittle parts of yourself away to accommodate whatever is popular in the moment. In the process of whittling, sometimes you cut off some of the best parts of yourself, the most original edges and angles—for example: the trill in a phrase that says 'Tony Arma.' You know, the low hum you do at the end of a ballad that sounds like an afterthought. Or the one word sung in Italian that tells everybody within the sound of your voice on that radio transmitter that you're from the Boot—and they're also from the Boot, so you belong to them, and by God they'll buy every vinyl you cut because you're one of them."

"Our people are loyal," Chi Chi agreed.

"No cutting the coat to fit the other guy," said Lee. "Tailor it to *you*, and emphasize the stuff that makes you who you are and different from the crowd. Trying to appeal is death to the artist. Sing what you sing the way you sing it. And sing it the way you sang in your mama's kitchen. Whatever you two do together, make it about them, the people who buy the records and listen to the radio and show up to see you."

"The people who need a reprieve." Tony lit a cigarette.

"If you can make people remember a moment that mattered

to them, if the music reminds them of when they were happy, you will sell records. Tony, if you can plant a fellow in his shoes the moment he first got a girl to kiss him, you got a hit. And if you're smart, you will sing one about Mama, and you will be a star. Guaranteed. Mama is always the queen of everybody's heart, and she has a built-in holiday every May that needs a theme song. Think about it."

"Give them what they want," Tony said softly.

"But give it to them in the way only you can deliver it. If you pump out a Bing Crosby imitation, they'll be talking about Bing, and how the original can never be topped; they won't be talking about Tony Arma and his new sound. Is this making sense?"

Tony and Chi Chi nodded.

"My job is to find the right band and tour for you whereby you can work on your act and Tony can sing the big solos. I like this new band." Lee handed Tony a tear sheet. "They want to widen out their show with some comedy and strong soloists. They're already on the road. The word is, they are tearing up the tour."

"Hmm. SRO Orchestra. That's wishful thinking."

"Wishing made this one so. They are doing big business," confirmed Lee.

JIMMY ARENA AND THE SRO ORCHESTRA
Minneapolis/St. Paul/Duluth/Chisholm/Hibbing:
confirmed—Valentini Supper Club
Elkhart/South Bend/Gary: confirmed—Morris Inn, Civic
Center confirmed
Gurnee/Chicago proper/Milwaukee: confirmed—The Drake,
Pfister
Champaign/Urbana/Indianapolis TBA
Youngstown/Cleveland/Pittsburgh/Dayton: confirmed—Jungle
Room, Lake Club confirmed, The Shoreby Club

Lexington/Louisville/Bristol, VA/Knoxville, TN TBA
Nashville TBA
Florence/Birmingham/Mobile TBA
Naples/Sarasota/Miami/Boca Raton/Palm Beach:
confirmed—Fontainebleau
Allentown/Easton/Stroudsburg: confirmed—Mount Airy
Lodge, Saylor's Lake Pavilion confirmed
Stamford/New Haven/Long Island, NY: confirmed—Marine
Theater Jones Beach

Chi Chi studied the list of cities. "They're in St. Paul, Minnesota, now. Sheesh."

"You'll have to run to catch the train. It's already moving," Lee said. "But you can do it."

"I'll give it some thought," said Tony.

"You do that. I'm starving. All that career advice took a piece out of me. Who wants pie?"

"I've got it." Tony stood.

"Chi Chi, let's get the coffee."

Lee and Chi Chi walked to the coffee station, Lee's heels tapping in rhythmic clicks as she walked across the linoleum.

"Are you wearing tap shoes?" Chi Chi asked.

"Just the taps. I put them on all my shoes."

"Are you a tap dancer?"

"Who isn't, in this line of work? The truth is, I put taps on my shoes so people hear me coming. When I come into a club they hear the clicks, and it's suddenly silent night. When you're petite like me, you have to find a way to let them know you've arrived so you can be ferocious. How else can I make tough deals and make sure to get the band paid? As long as the club owners fear me, I get the purse. They don't fear me if they can't hear me. The day they don't hear me coming, the bank envelope will be empty. That's the day I take up knitting and head for my grandma's screen porch in Susquehanna, Pennsylvania. I will be, as they say in the trade papers, irrelevant."

Carrying three cups of coffee, they joined Tony at the table.

"Do you know anybody with a recording studio who might want to buy some recording equipment?" Chi Chi asked Lee.

"What do you have?"

"The entire kit that goes in a studio. The console. Speakers. Tape-recording machine. Microphones."

"I have a friend on Forty-Eighth Street who deals in second-hand."

"Would you ask him if he's interested in some used equipment in excellent condition?"

"Are you selling off your dad's studio?" asked Tony.

"Yeah. Are you interested in any of it?"

"Nope. Staying loose. But maybe someday I'll have my own studio in a house by the ocean." He smiled.

"I can offer you a good deal now," Chi Chi promised.

"Rule number one in business. You can't force a sale, Chi Chi," Lee said.

Chi Chi sipped her coffee. "Too pushy?"

Tony shook his head. "One day in the city, and she's already a noodge."

"Don't worry about me, I'm just getting started," Chi Chi assured them.

Chi Chi laid out every article of clothing she owned on the twin bed in the bedroom she shared with her sister Lucille.

"Do you have enough dressy dresses?" Lucille asked as she studied the list of cities for the tour. "It looks like one show a night."

"I'll wear the same gowns in different cities and I'll follow Mama's rule. Never eat in a fancy dress. Treat it like a costume. I won't even sweat. That should help."

"We can sew and send you some new things on the road."

"Thanks, and no offense, but I'm a better seamstress. I'll be sewing all day and singing at night."

"Take this, then." Lucille presented her sister with five yards of sumptuous emerald-green silk taffeta, folded and tucked neatly into a triangle shape.

"No, that's yours. You were saving it for good. You keep it."

"I'm not going anywhere special anytime soon. Use it." Lucille placed the fabric on Chi Chi's bed.

Chi Chi loaded the trunk with her undergarments, in separate pressed-cotton drawstring bags embroidered with her initials. She owned two nightgowns, light cotton for summer and flannel for winter. She folded her blouses with the technique she had mastered in the finishing department at the mill: Arm fold, arm fold, one sheet of tissue paper, and fold over once. Add one layer of tissue between the blouses. Upon arrival, one shake and hang. Chi Chi could wear the blouse straight from the suitcase without having to iron it again.

Barbara carried a basket of foodstuffs and the *Farmer's Almanac* into the bedroom. "I packed everything nice and tight, and wrapped it double so no leaks."

"Thanks. I'm like a zoo animal. I need to eat on schedule."

Barbara sat on the bed and scanned the pages of the *Almanac*. "They say snow in October in Indiana."

"Pack your boots," Lucille advised.

"I don't have room."

"Make room—you've got a blizzard when you get to Minnesota."

"You're just trying to keep me here, aren't you?" Chi Chi crammed her snow boots into the trunk.

Barbara shrugged. "You hate the snow."

"I'll learn to like it. Every tour stop isn't Miami."

"Looks like you're on the sleet and ice tour, sis."

"Until the very end." Chi Chi pointed out the southern swing on her schedule.

"Everybody ends up in Florida in the end," Barbara joked.

Isotta stood in the doorway with a box.

"What have you got there, Ma?" Chi Chi asked.

"Just put it in the trunk," her mother said.

Before she did, Chi Chi opened the box. She lifted out a formal evening wrap made of dove-gray silk charmeuse, delicately embroidered in silver thread. Hand-knotted rosettes of velvet trimmed the creation. "Ma, it's gorgeous!"

"You can wear it with your black faille gown, and you'll look like Lady Astor. My cousin Francesca sent it from Treviso."

"It's so elegant." Chi Chi kissed her mother. "Thank you."

Isotta sat on the edge of Lucille's bed as Chi Chi snapped the trunk closed. She placed her hatbox and purse on top of the trunk.

"They said two pieces of luggage. We did it." Chi Chi stood back proudly before sitting down. "Well, that's it. That's everything I own." She looked around the room. "Except . . ." Chi Chi went to her desk and lifted her manual typewriter into its case. She snapped the hard shell closed and placed it with her trunk by the door.

"That makes three items," Lucille observed.

"It will be fine. It's my instrument. One fella's trombone is my typewriter."

The Donatelli women sat in silence. It was the first time they had taken a break since Chi Chi began to pack that morning. The only sound was the rustle of the pages of the *Farmer's Almanac* as Barbara turned the pages, consumed with weather predictions for the winter of 1939 into the spring of 1940.

"Mrs. Calza?" Charlie hollered from the bottom of the stairs.

"Have you gotten used to that yet?" Chi Chi asked Barbara.

"Nope." Barbara smiled. "That was the 'I'm hungry, what's for supper?' call." She stood and went to the doorway. "I'll be right down, hon."

"Being married is a lot like working for the WPA. You learn to read the signs," Chi Chi said.

Barbara laughed. "Because like the WPA, you've signed on for the duration. You'll find out someday for yourself." She pulled an envelope from the back of the *Farmer's Almanac* and handed it to her sister. "For you."

Chi Chi looked down at the thick envelope before she opened it. Inside was a greeting card.

No matter where you go, you'll always have a place with us here. Safe travels and take our best wishes with you!

The interior sleeve was covered with the signatures of the roster of her coworkers at Jersey Miss Fashions. It was stuffed with cash.

"But they only do this when a girl gets married," Chi Chi said quietly.

"They know how much your music means to you," Lucille said.

"They wanted to buy you something, but didn't know what you'd need, so they said to get whatever you need with the money. Rita pulled the whole thing together."

Chi Chi cried. She wiped the tears with her sleeve. She had worked hard at the mill, but so did every operator on every machine. She was moved that they were so generous with her, giving her money she knew they needed themselves.

As she tucked the envelope into her purse, she remembered lunch breaks on the church steps across from the mill, where she'd shared her dreams of leaving the factory. She worked on song lyrics on their breaks and would read them to the girls. For many years, her coworkers were her only audience. She was sad to leave behind the best group of women she had ever known. They had come up together, and as it had gone with her mother's generation, these would have been the friendships that sustained Chi Chi throughout her life, no matter what lay ahead. Typically, the girls would marry, and their factory friends would help with the wedding. Once there were children, the ladies would help one another with childcare, school, and sacraments. Whether there were costumes to sew, cakes to bake, parties to throw, sympathy dinners to organize, or money to raise for the local school and church, the women locked arms and put in the hours to make the world beautiful for their families. And, they did it after a forty-hour work week in the mill. The solidarity of the line, which fostered the loyalty among the machine operators, was the great bonus of the factory life.

"I'll write to every girl," Chi Chi promised.

"They'll want to know your every move," her mother assured her.

"So, what would you like to do on your last night in Sea Isle City?" Barbara asked.

"It's too cold to ride the roller coaster," Lucille joked.

"We made you dinner." Isotta put her arms around Chi Chi.

"What did you make?"

"Your favorite. Bracciole in gravy. Ravioli."

"Leave your bags," Barbara said. "Charlie will bring them down in the morning."

Her mother and sisters left her alone to review her baggage. Chi Chi sat on the bed and went through her notes a final time, making certain that she had packed everything she needed for the tour. Satisfied that she was prepared for life on the road, she ran a brush through her hair and slipped into her loafers before going down to the kitchen for dinner.

As she skipped down the steps, the first floor of the house was in total darkness. "Ma, I think the fuse blew," Chi Chi hollered. "Get the flashlight, will you?"

The lights blazed on, and from every corner of the house, a roar of "Surprise!" rang out from the crowd that had gathered.

From the kitchen to the living room, the Donatelli home was filled with the women from Jersey Miss Fashions. Rita placed a sash on Chi Chi that read *Buona Fortuna* in gold glitter as her coworkers surrounded her.

Chi Chi embraced each operator, committed their place on their machine in the mill to memory. She had spent eight years of her life working with these ladies. They had been with her through plenty, and she had been there for them.

Rita sat to her left on the buttonholer; the Vechiarelli sisters were in pressing; the Pipino sisters, in shipping; the Watkins sisters, in accounting, and in the office, the beloved Lavinia Spadoni handed out the pink checks in the blue envelopes on payday. Mrs. Spadoni was too pretty to be Santa Claus, but she might as well have been, as much joy as she brought to the working girls every other Friday.

One by one, these fine women, her beloved friends, celebrated Chi Chi's good fortune, happier for her than they would be for themselves, than the singer-songwriter was for herself on the eve of her big break. The fifty-eight women who surrounded her that night believed she could not fail. That conviction made Chi Chi want to succeed all the more for them, as proof of the faith they had in her.

Jersey Miss had been Chi Chi's life; the time she spent there had defined her. The girls assured her that if the music business didn't work out, they would welcome her back and never mention the swing era; they would even ditch their transistor radios in solidarity and never listen to Harry James, Tommy Dorsey, or Benny Goodman again. Whatever it took, they wanted her to understand that she always had a place beside them in the mill, no questions asked.

That night Chi Chi had a feeling that the love of her friends, their pride in her accomplishments, and their admiration of her courage in taking a risk, would get her through whatever challenges lay ahead. No one was thinking about what might go wrong that night; they were too busy anticipating Chi Chi's success. Their belief in her lifted their friend off the line and into a new life, giving Chi Chi the push she needed to take flight on the wings of her musical dreams.

Chi Chi was dressed and ready to go the next morning, plenty early to catch the 4:00 a.m. train that would take her into New York City. She would transfer to the train for Chicago at Pennsylvania Station, and then take another train to South Bend, Indiana, where she would meet up with the tour.

As she made the rounds through the dark house, she reminded herself that home as she knew it would remain; she would only have to picture it when she needed courage. She kissed her sister Lucille goodbye as she slept in her bed, went into her mother's room and did the same, leaving an envelope of cash on her dresser, and finally into Barbara and Charlie's room, where she embraced her sister and thanked her before leaving the only home she had ever known.

Charlie had already loaded Chi Chi's typewriter, trunk, and hatbox into his roadster. She grabbed her purse off the kitchen counter and went outside. The sky was still dark; she shivered as she walked down the front path, inhaling the scent of the sea a final time as the sand crunched under her dress shoes. The sand from Sea Isle Beach was forever underfoot, an essential element of their lives. No matter how many times a day Isotta swept, sand managed to creep back onto the walk and porch and inside the house. Sand had been as much a part of her life growing up as macaroni had been, and now, she would miss it.

Chi Chi stopped at the gate. She said a silent Hail Mary and invoked Mariano in heaven to look over the house that only one year before had almost been lost. The thought of her mother and sisters safe in her father's house comforted her. She could focus on the work ahead, knowing that they were secure.

For Chi Chi to make records and perform on tour with a name band had been as much her father's goal as it was her own. Mariano had not had the good fortune to live long enough to see her take this step, but that did not matter now. He had believed in her, and the confidence he had instilled in her would remain with her wherever the tour would take her.

Charlie started the engine. "Cheech, we should get going."

She nodded and closed the gate behind her without looking back. Chi Chi Donatelli had to leave home to become the person she was meant to be because the world had something to offer her that the people who loved her the most did not.

As Charlie and Chi Chi drove off, the sun rose in a fan of gold and magenta light that pushed through the woolly gray clouds. Only the garage where her father had built the recording studio with high hopes fell into shadow because Chi Chi had taken the music with her.

Jimmy Arena sat at the piano inside the Syburg rehearsal hall in South Bend, Indiana, plunking keys on the piano while making notes on his charts. The youngest of the new crop of big band-leaders, he was looking to shake up the scene with a new format.

Jimmy liked an eclectic show: long orchestral interludes of swing, peppered with comedy sketches, singing sister acts, and dance routines. As he squinted at the charts, he leaned back in the chair, balancing on the back legs and lifting his feet off the ground, suspending himself in the chair like a trained seal on a circus lift. The maestro wore horn-rimmed glasses. His thick brown hair was slicked back neatly, and there were leather patches on the elbows of his corduroy sports jacket. He came off as a quirky professor with a secret, a good-looking philosopher who also blew a mean saxophone.

Chi Chi stood in the doorway, nervous as the new kid in the portal of the classroom on the first day of school. She searched the room for the only familiar face she knew. Saverio Armandonada—Tony Arma, she reminded herself—who himself had joined the band a few days earlier as the new lead singer. Lee had sent him out ahead to rehearse the music he would perform as the front man. Chi Chi was hired to be the centerpiece of the novelty portion of the show, so Lee had arranged for her to arrive later.

Chi Chi couldn't find Tony anywhere in the room, even though the boys in the orchestra were on a break. A few of the musicians were taking a smoke; some tuned their instruments, others updated their charts, and a couple chatted up the pretty dancers who were working on a routine.

When the stage manager called the band back into rehearsal, Chi Chi made her way through the crowd and introduced herself to him.

"Dancer? Singer? What?" he barked impatiently as he motioned for the band and the dancers to move quickly back into their positions.

"Singer. Songwriter. I'm doing the novelty songs and routine with Tony Arma."

"Go to rehearsal room A, down the hall."

Chi Chi went outside and exhaled. She walked down the hallway and peered into each rehearsal studio through the window in the doors. She stopped to stare when she saw a row of tall, strapping, muscular young men attempting ballet on the barre. Chi Chi was mesmerized as they attempted deep pliés. They were not very good, which made them hilarious.

"May I help you?" a man said gruffly from behind her.

"I'm looking for room A."

"This ain't it."

"Who are the ballerinas?"

"That's the offensive line of the Notre Dame football team. The coach thought they needed grace."

"Are they getting it?"

"I'll let you know."

Chi Chi continued down the hallway until she found room A. She knocked on the door. She was both relieved and happy when Tony opened it.

"Welcome to the road, Cheech. How was your trip?"

"Long." She removed her hat and surveyed the room. "But I liked the train."

"Too bad. It's a bus from now on."

"I can handle it."

"You got the charts? Jimmy wants *Mama's Rolling Pin* in the show by Elkhart. We have twenty-four hours to make it work."

Chi Chi sat down at the piano, opened her binder, and unfolded the music. She warmed up on the piano. "Let's sing it through a few times, and then we'll get it on its feet. Okay?"

"Can do." Tony stood behind her.

Chi Chi played the piano and Tony sang when the stage manager burst in. "We just lost the Rutledge Sisters. Evidently Cynthia threw a telephone at Jayne at the Morris Inn, and she quit the tour."

"Better than a rolling pin," Tony said, not looking up from the charts.

"How about a novelty all-male ballet?" Chi Chi offered.

"What? Where am I gonna get that?" The stage manager looked at Tony. "Who is this kid?" He looked at Chi Chi. "Are you loony or what?"

"I just saw something funny. A bunch of guys who can't do ballet attempting it. Listen. The band plays something like this—" Chi Chi played a classical riff, which she spun into swing. "That's just an idea for the music. You take a few guys from the orchestra and you do the ballet with them—they're terrible, but they can swing. It's a funny segue into something, or you can expand it. I mean, I can. If Mr. Arena likes it."

"I'll take it to Jimmy," the stage manager said on his way out.

"Where were we?" Chi Chi asked Tony.

"At the corner of the rich and famous," he joked.

"Just sing, Tony."

"I'm serious." He leaned over her shoulder to read the charts. Her hair had the clean scent of vanilla and peppermint. "You calling me Tony now?"

"Isn't that what it says on the marquee?"

"Yes, but we're old friends."

"I just got here. Don't flirt with me, Italian boy. My clothes are wrinkled and I'm hungry. I don't feel rich or famous. I want to try not to get fired."

"Look." Tony handed Chi Chi a telegram. "MRP 67 on HP. WABC played it 7 times in one day. LB."

"When did this happen?"

"When you were on the train."

Chi Chi put her head down.

"You're not praying, are you?"

"What's it to you?"

"You prayed to get here. You got here. You can stop praying."

"I wish my dad were here."

"Oh, I get it."

"Are you going to write to your mother and father?"

Tony took a seat next to Chi Chi on the piano bench. "Why don't we make a deal? I don't ask you about your private business, and you don't ask me about mine."

"That's a dumb idea. We know each other's families."

"I meant to say, beyond pleasantries."

"Why?" Chi Chi asked.

"I don't want to talk about them."

"Who's going to share your joy, Saverio?" Chi Chi asked as she unfolded the charts and placed them on the music stand. "I mean, Tony."

Before he had a chance to reply, the Arena Dancers entered. The trio of young professional women were lovely, leggy, and game. "Toot sent us down here, something about a routine," the lead, Shirley, said.

"Give me a sec, girls. I may need you to *share my joy*," Tony said pointedly to Chi Chi, who ignored him.

Shirley frowned. "Is that the new dance out of South Bend? Odd name. *Share My Joy*."

"Better than *The Deer Tick Slide* out of Duluth." Ruby shrugged. "What are the steps?"

Chi Chi left the window open in her hotel room as she worked. The Lora Lodge in Elkhart, Indiana, was spare but clean. A fresh breeze ruffled the paper piano on the table and flipped the pages of her composition book. Chi Chi decided it was time to roll up the piano and put it aside with her composition book. She was hungry, and it had been a long day.

Before the Donatellis inherited their upright piano from Isotta's cousin, Chi Chi had taken lessons at Kathleen Sweeney's house on a Steinway baby grand. But when she returned home she couldn't practice because the Donatellis did not own a piano. Mariano made his little girl a regulation keyboard using butcher paper and black paint. Chi Chi learned to hear the musical notes in her head as she played the paper piano. Years later, when Chi Chi began writing songs, and could compose them using the upright, she often chose to write them using the paper keyboard anyway because she didn't want to make noise and disturb her family.

Chi Chi had never cooked anything on a hot plate but she was determined to try. She decided to attempt spaghetti. This tour would last a few months, and the thought of going that long without macaroni was inconceivable to her.

The front desk loaned her a pot, a couple of utensils, and a serving plate. Barbara's basket of supplies was filled with essentials from their family cupboard: packages of dried macaroni, a bottle of olive oil, home-canned tomato sauce, jars of banana peppers in vinegar, and small vials of spices; a brick of aged Parmesan cheese; a bulb of fresh garlic; a small jug of wine; a tin of cookies, and another filled with oil pretzels, which would stand in for bread when none was available; along with a bag of ground coffee. Barbara had promised to replenish the basket and mail ahead when supplies ran low.

Chi Chi boiled water in the pot until it was rolling, added the macaroni, and stirred it, cooked it through al dente. She strained it as best she could using a slotted spoon and the lid of the pot.

She put the spaghetti back in the pot and onto the burner for a few moments to burn off any moisture. She poured the steaming pasta into a bowl and covered it. She minced one of the cloves of garlic and glazed it in the pan with olive oil. As the fresh garlic danced in the pan, the scent made her think of home. She poured some of the tomato sauce over the mixture and cooked it until it bubbled. She removed the sauce from the burner. She was blending the sauce over the pasta when there was a knock at the door.

"Just a second," Chi Chi called out before going to the door. Leaving the chain on the door, she peered outside.

"Hey, it's me, I want you to meet someone," Tony said.

Chi Chi dried her hands on the moppeen she had packed and took off the chain.

Tony brought a glamorous young woman into Chi Chi's room. "This is Delilah Entwistle. She's our girl singer." Delilah had soft brown hair, gray eyes, and pale skin with a golden patina. She wore a day dress of lilac silk with a gold belt. Chi Chi liked her style instantly.

"Where are you from?" Chi Chi asked her.

"A sweet place called Dorset in England. It's on the sea." Delilah had a lovely accent.

"Me too! I come from a shore town. In New Jersey."

"How do they live here?" Delilah wondered. "There's no sea in Indiana."

"But they have lakes," Tony offered.

"You and your lakes," Chi Chi joked, giving him the brush-off. "Tony will try and sell you on the Great Lakes. I'll decide how great they are when I lay eyes on them. Are you kids hungry?"

"Starving," Tony admitted.

"I'm famished," Delilah said.

"Go get your plates. I made enough."

"Are you sure?" Delilah asked. "We don't want to impose."

"No imposition whatsoever. I'd love the company."

"It does smell like home," Tony admitted.

Delilah clapped her hands together. "This is so much fun."

A couple of boys from the brass section of the orchestra stuck their heads in the door. "Who's cooking?"

"Who do you think?" Chi Chi joked.

"Do you have enough?" Tony asked her.

"There's always enough." Chi Chi laughed. "And I can make more."

"Go get your plates, boys," Tony told them.

The word spread in the Lora Lodge that there were good eats and a party in room 202. Soon, the room filled with anyone who was looking for a little camaraderie and a home-cooked meal.

"Look, Chi Chi," Delilah said when she came back with some plates. "Dessert." She placed a tin of Scottish shortbread on the table. The dancers from the act showed up with a loaf of French bread and butter, Tony fetched a bottle of wine from his room, while Kal the trombonist offered a jar of pickled zucchini and a jar of marinated mushrooms to add to the feast.

Chi Chi cooked more spaghetti. Every strand was eaten hungrily. As she cooked, she met Mort Luck out of Milwaukee, who played several horns; Bobby on trumpet; and Bill on cello; along with the dancers, Shirley, Bess, and Ruby. A few more boys who played keyboards, drums, and vibes joined them after dinner.

"And I thought I was going to be lonely." Chi Chi laughed as she washed the spaghetti pot in the small sink.

"Oh no, you'll love this crew. They're a good bunch," Ruby, the petite dancer, assured her.

"Jimmy will work us to death, but so what?" Shirley, a striking blonde, added.

Chi Chi felt a part of things, when she had wondered if she ever would. She looked around her hotel room. The SRO band was having fun. In the corner, by the window, Tony and Delilah had their heads together, talking.

"Those two." Ruby nodded. "Already an item."

"No kidding." Chi Chi was not surprised. "Tony Arma is a genuine Latin lover. By way of Michigan."

"They got 'em everywhere," Shirley added dryly. "But somebody needs to warn the teacup."

"She'll be all right," Ruby commented. "This ain't her first duet."

At the far end of the room Mort shouted, "Hey kids! They just said your names on the radio. Tony and Chi Chi . . . *When the Saints Go Marchin' In*?"

"*Mama's Rolling Pin!*" Chi Chi corrected him.

"What do you want from me? The signal's weak out of Chicago." Mort moved around the room with the radio, using the antenna like a diviner uses a stick to seek a hidden spring. Finally the radio signal came in steady and strong.

The band shifted in the room and gathered around the transistor radio to listen to Tony and Chi Chi's single. Delilah and Tony joined the group around the radio. Chi Chi looked at Tony and nodded, partner to partner. The room was quiet except for the song, which hummed and crackled out of the small radio with as much force as the mechanism would allow. The musicians closed their eyes, leaned forward, and concentrated on the music. The dancers let the uptempo rhythm move through their lithe bodies, as their toes tapped, knees bent, and fingers snapped silently, until the disc jockey broke the spell.

"And that was *Mama's Rolling Pin*, a tune that's traveled up and down the Eastern Seaboard and is now making its way across the Great Lakes and Midwest. It's got charm and swing. That's Tony and Kee Kee."

"Chi Chi," Ruby grumbled.

"That hit novelty," the DJ was saying, "is finding traction on the

Hit Parade charts at number sixty-seven out of the D Studios in Sea Isle City, New Jersey."

Chi Chi hoped her father had heard the announcement, wherever he might be.

Tony had his arm around Delilah's waist. He put his other arm around Chi Chi's shoulder. "We did it, Cheech. It sounded pretty good."

"Yeah, it did," Chi Chi agreed with him politely. But in truth, she was not pleased. As the song played over the airwaves, all she heard were flaws. There were so many things she would do differently with the song, now that she had tested it on the road. She hoped the record was good enough to lead to the next opportunity, but this was show business. Chi Chi knew better than to expect anything more to come her way. And if by chance it did, she knew it was all about luck, and she did not mean Mort Luck of the SRO Orchestra, she meant the mother of all luck: fate.

Chi Chi checked the clock. It was 4:30 a.m., and she couldn't sleep. Instead of fighting it, she leaned over and turned on the bedside lamp. This was her sign that a song was about to be born. So she put on the coffee, rolled out her paper keyboard, and set out her composition book. She pulled on her robe and tightened the belt.

She cracked open the window. She was surprised to find fresh snow on the sash. It was thick, like the Ivory soap flakes she had packed to wash her clothes. It turned out that Barbara's *Almanac* was correct. She'd have to write to her sister and tell her the prognostications were correct. Chi Chi pulled the bottle of cream in from the ledge and shook it. She poured some into the cup.

The scent of fresh coffee filled the room. No matter where she was in the world, the aroma of coffee made it home. Chi Chi

poured the steaming brew over the cream, and stirred it. She unwrapped the heel of French bread she had saved from the night
before, and set it out on a plate. She placed a napkin on her lap,
buttered the heel of the bread, and dunked it into the hot coffee
and cream.

Here in Elkhart, Indiana, in an old boardinghouse, in a clean,
plain room with a window and nothing more than a hot plate,
bed, chair, and table to make it home and with nothing more than
a simple breakfast to sustain her, Chi Chi felt blissful. She was
the happiest she had ever been in her life. She had hours of work
ahead. She would spend the day engaged in the creative enterprise of writing a song, hopefully a good one. All she needed was a
pencil and paper. The rest would come from within her, from her
imagination, which had regenerated overnight as she slept. Now
she was wide awake and ready to create anew. The silent hours
before sunrise, when the rest of the world is asleep, are God's gift
to writers.

Out of Chi Chi's window, Elkhart, carved out of the flat fields
of northern Indiana, had a haunting beauty. There was a thin crust
of white on the ground, an expanse of blue revealing a rickrack
pattern of old roads. Tiny daggers of diamonds floated from the
sky, violet in the morning light, as purple as the robe of a queen. It
gave her an idea, and she began to write.

> Poor Delilah
> Does she know?
> The tins are empty and the funds are low
> Poor Delilah, so long on the road
> Met many a frog, once kissed a toad

Chi Chi plucked out the notes on her butcher-paper piano.
She pulled the pencil from behind her ear and made notes in the
composition book. She shoved the pencil back behind her ear and

played the notes on the silent piano again. She softly sang the chorus *a cappella* as she invented it, discovered the words as she went.

A queen knows she's a queen
Whether or not she marries a king
And if she settles her whole life long
Forsaking home, family, fun, well, everything
It's her time to waste, life to squander and

Chi Chi fluttered her hands over the keys until the words came.

It is her right to mope

The songwriter raised her hands in victory before placing them back on the silent keys. She sang:

because life is what it is when you love . . .
A . . . Big . . . Dope.

Chi Chi read back over the lyrics, and realized what she had written.

She erased the name *Delilah* and replaced it with *Mariah*.

6

1941–1942

Dolcemente

(Sweetly)

Chi Chi picked up the *Chicago Tribune* at the front desk of the Drake Hotel. She opened it and flipped through the pages until she found the review of their engagement at Danny Galloway Presents, a new nightclub on the lake.

> Jimmy Arena and his SRO Orchestra swung into Chicago on the strings of a cello and rode the "L" on the power of the best brass section since Guy Lombardo toured through in the spring. Notables: The delectable Delilah Entwistle. Comedy sketch with woodwind ballet with specialty singer Chee Chee was noteworthy.

Chi Chi laughed at the quartet of *e*'s in her name (no journalist ever spelled her name correctly, it seemed) and tore out the page to send home to Lucille, who would add it to the stack of clippings she had compiled from reviews around the country. When her sister found the time, she would paste them into a scrapbook already fat with reviews from every outpost with a band box between the Jersey shore and Phoenix.

Jimmy Arena and his SRO Orchestra had extended the first tour from the fall of 1939 four times. What began as a three-month commitment had turned into a rolling tour with no end in sight. The band thrived on the steady bookings. When a trumpeter fell out, another fell in, and so it went throughout the orchestra to percussion, from brass to strings through the woodwinds. However, even with replacements and the infusion of new energy, time on the road was taking its toll on the regulars.

Chi Chi dug into the experience of living and performing on the road, using the time to write as many songs as she could, and when she was not writing or performing, she sewed. "Don't send me food," she had written to Barbara earlier that year. "Send taffeta!"

Chi Chi folded the newspaper. She was headed to the elevator bank at the far end of the lobby when the doors peeled open and Delilah Entwistle stepped off the lift. Wearing a cinnamon-brown velvet hat and a matching coat, a purse dangling from her wrist, Delilah looked straight ahead as she pulled on her gloves in a state of agitation. A bellman followed, pushing a cart loaded with her luggage.

"Where are you going, Delilah?" Chi Chi asked.

"East. As far east as the train will go without dropping into the Atlantic."

"You're leaving the band?"

"I cannot stay."

"What happened?"

"Ask Mr. Arma."

"What did he do?"

"What doesn't he do, with every shopgirl, waitress, and bobby-soxer he meets?"

"I'm sorry." Chi Chi felt she had to apologize for Tony. After all, he was the other half of their act.

"It's too bad. I liked this band. I liked you."

"You sing like an English lark, a dream. I feel awful about this. Is there anything I can do? Do you want the charts for your songs?"

"Keep them. I'll never sing *Mariah* again. Even though it's a lovely song." Delilah began to walk away but turned back. "The songs you write?"

"Yes?"

"Try writing one for the brokenhearted. You peddle joy, but it's not real."

Chi Chi watched as Delilah left through the hotel's revolving door. The doorman flagged down a cab on Michigan Avenue. He and the bellman put Delilah's luggage in the trunk and helped her into the car. The driver snapped the trunk closed before sliding into the front seat and pulling out into traffic.

Chi Chi was furious. Delilah's sudden departure meant another girl singer to break in, new songs to write, and older songs to rearrange to fit the new singer's voice and range, all because Tony could not resist the ladies who could not resist him. She had avoided addressing it for a year, but now she was forced to have a conversation with her *paisano*. Someone had to. It was time for Tony Arma to grow up.

There was a soft rap at Chi Chi's hotel room door.

"Come in," Chi Chi called out as she stirred soup in a pan on the hot plate.

"You busy?" Tony stuck his head around the door.

"Yeah, I'm busy writing another opener, because Delilah quit the tour." Chi Chi speared a pickle from the jar and put it on the plate next to the ham and butter sandwich she had made. "Nice going, Valentino."

Tony closed the door behind him. "She overreacted."

"That's your story?" Chi Chi handed him a napkin and motioned for him to sit down.

"It's the truth." He sat and put the napkin on his lap.

"It's always somebody else's fault, isn't it?"

"You're not on my side?"

"Not anymore."

She handed Tony the plate with the sandwich and pickle.

"This is your dinner."

"I'm not hungry. You eat. You need your strength. Evidently." She snapped the cap off a cold root beer with a bottle opener and set it on the table.

"You're being awful mean to me," he said as he sipped the root beer.

"You're being awful stupid."

"That hurts."

"Is it getting into that thick head of yours?" Chi Chi ladled tomato bisque soup into two mugs. She tore a French baguette in two, handed half to Tony, and placed the soup on the table between them.

"Okay, I'm an idiot," Tony admitted.

"Go on." Chi Chi sipped her soup.

"Instead of telling a girl it's over, I show her."

"I'm fairly sure Delilah would have preferred an honest conversation, instead of having the message delivered by a kick line of random girls telling her they'd been with her boyfriend behind her back. Whatever you did, she woke up humiliated this morning."

"I feel bad about that."

"Do you?" Chi Chi looked at him.

"Don't look at me with those eyes."

"They're the only eyes I got."

"Delilah wanted to get married."

"She fell in love with you."

"That's what she said."

"So you can't blame her."

"I guess not. But I wasn't in love with her."

"There's an obvious solution to your problem."

Tony leaned forward, eager for a solution. "There is?"

"Don't behave like you're in love when you're not."

He smiled. "That would make everything so simple."

"Wouldn't it? But it would leave half the women who buy tickets to our show bereft. Good thing that bus we're on has wheels."

"I'm not a hound," Tony said defensively. "There are those eyes again. You make it sound like there's something wrong with me."

"I'm sure there's a universe or a planet or a continent or a country or a city or a town or a corner booth in some diner somewhere where the likes of you and the way you behave is considered acceptable. But it ain't Chicago."

"If you'd listen to me for a second, you might be able to help me. I need it." Tony leaned back in the chair. "There *is* something wrong with me."

"What is it?"

"I don't feel anything," he said quietly.

"Nothing?"

"Nothing at all."

Chi Chi put down her soup, went to the settee, and sat down next to Tony. "It won't always be this way."

"How do you know?"

"Life on the road isn't for everyone. It's not for you. You aren't happy."

"I don't think about happiness."

"Looks to me like you spend an awful lot of time pursuing it."

"Where else do you find it, if not in someone else?"

"You have to know what you want. And don't say it's a pretty girl. That's not enough. You may have it all wrong. You might need to walk into happiness, like it's a joint, and once you're inside, you own it. Think of happiness like an actual place, like a scene in a play. You know where the door is, where the chairs are, you placed the window and the table. There's a bowl of roses on the table, and the sun's coming in the window. Once you enter it, you understand it because you built it in your imagination, in your soul. If you try this, you might realize you need a home someplace with trees and a yard and a nice wife taking care of you in order to be happy. Maybe if you're settled in this place you've dreamed of, and you have everything you need to make yourself feel secure, you'll stop chasing strangers to find it. Because when you go with a girl to find happiness and expect her to provide it to you, that will never bring you happiness. You have to decide what it is before you seek it."

There was a knock at the door. "Come in," Chi Chi hollered.

"Are you cooking?" Mort Luck, the dapper saxophone and piccolo player out of Milwaukee, sniffed the air. "Yes, you are cooking." His black hair was slicked back with pomade, his bow tie hung in two wide ribbons against his starched white dress shirt collar. "The hallway has the aroma of a first course being served."

"We ate the soup," Chi Chi said apologetically.

"Here, take the rest of my sandwich." Tony handed it to him.

Mort sat down and took a bite. "Delish."

Tony stood and pulled on his dinner jacket.

"Before you go, I need a favor." Chi Chi turned to Tony.

"Don't do it, big Tony. Don't do it. It's a trap," Mort teased. "*Before you go* are three words that can start a war or force a man to buy the wrong hat."

Chi Chi ignored him. "My friend Rita is getting married in Sea Isle next month, and I was wondering if you could go with me."

"All the way to New Jersey?" Mort made a face.

"I didn't ask *you* to take me all the way from Milwaukee, Mort."

"Couldn't oblige you anyway, sweetie. Betty's waiting for me while we're on our break. And she's a tasty morsel."

"I'll be in New York," Tony said.

"Not too far from the shore," Chi Chi said hopefully.

"Don't you have a fella?" Mort asked Chi Chi.

"She has so many suitors, she can't choose," Tony said, rekindling the old joke.

"I can see how that might be the case," Mort said. "Chi Chi, any fella in the orchestra would drive six or seven blocks to take you to that wedding."

"Gee, thanks."

"My point is: you can do better than this schlub."

"Hey, I gave you my sandwich," Tony reminded him.

"That doesn't make me faithful," Mort said. "Just full."

"Sponger."

"I wouldn't ask if I had another idea," Chi Chi explained. "All the guys I know are signing up for the service. The cousin I usually dance with—Nicky Palermo, he's from Hazlet—got married, and his wife, Dianna, will not allow him to dance with any girl under the age of seventy-two. So I lost my Lindy partner."

"*Tradge-eek.*" Mort rolled his eyes at Tony. "Please take this kid to the wedding before she regales us with another fascinating story about her relatives in Sea Foam."

"Get out of my room, Mort." Chi Chi pointed to the door.

"Bye-bye, Chi Chi. Thank you for the ham." Mort waved on his way out.

"I'm sorry. I can't take you to the wedding." Tony placed the dish in the sink. "I promised Irv Raible I'd sing at his new club downtown."

"My mother will be so disappointed."

"Those are the words a man most wants to hear." Tony draped the moppeen over the sink.

"Well, she will be. I told her I was going to ask you."

"What about you?"

"What about me?"

"Are you disappointed I can't make it?"

"Sure. It would be fun."

"Why would it be fun?"

"It's an Italian wedding. You're Italian. You know. It's the most fun you can have anywhere. At least, I think so. But don't give it another thought." Chi Chi smiled.

"I'll see you over at the club. Lock this door behind me, will you?"

Chi Chi locked the door. She washed the dishes in the efficiency sink and placed them on the rack to dry. She checked her nails. The red lacquer looked pretty good despite having had her hands in water.

Chicago was an important town. Chi Chi knew Jimmy Arena would ask her to take Delilah's solos in the show that night, so she would be sure to wear her best chiffon. She'd have to press it and steam the ruffles on the hem. The dress was blah unless there was movement in the fabric. Besides, that night the dress mattered.

The band would need a boost. There was always a ripple effect when Tony Arma broke a girl's heart and it had an effect on everyone but the man himself.

The pavilion on the boardwalk at Sea Isle City was packed to the rafters on Valentine's Day 1942 as the newly married Mr. and Mrs. David Osella entered through the saloon doors and under a handheld canopy of bouquets created by the twelve bridesmaids, composed of the girls from the specialty department of Jersey Miss. Only Chi Chi, her maid of honor, was employed elsewhere.

The town had turned out for the football wedding.

Everything had gone according to tradition. After the nuptial high mass at St. Joseph's that Saturday morning, the wedding party took the official photographs on the church steps. This took time, as both the Milnicki/Millix side and the Osellas had big families. However, it gave the guests the opportunity to stop at the Millix home to see the wedding gifts on display in the family dining room before the reception. Rita's cousins served coffee and cookies as the guests walked through and surveyed the bounty of spiderweb doilies, handmade lace-trimmed sheets, place mats, embroidered tablecloths, monogrammed napkins, a sturdy set of kitchen pots and pans, a Lenox china tea service, Lady Carlyle china, Wedgwood silverware, nine place settings, including one given by the girls at Jersey Miss, a four-slice electric toaster, a mixer, an Electrolux vacuum cleaner, and a framed congratulatory wedding blessing from Pope Pius X. The couple had everything they needed to start their life together, and set a proper table for Sunday dinner.

"Ham or roast beef?" the boys stationed next to baskets asked guests as they passed. The sandwiches had been made fresh and wrapped the night before. The baskets were loaded; the groom's nephews were assigned the chore of dispersing the sandwiches by tossing them to the guests, which is how football weddings found their name.

At the reception, a buffet of cold Italian salads, charcuterie, and fruit salad was prepared and served by the ladies of the church sodality. Set on each table around the dance floor was a centerpiece, a cookie tray, Italian and Polish delicacies made by the ladies in the Milnicki and Osella families.

Phil Costa and the Something Special Big Band, from Bethpage, Long Island, played as the guests filled their plates and claimed their seats. There were kegs of birch beer for the kids, and real beer for the adults. Jugs of homemade wine were set on every table. The wedding cake, a seven-layer masterpiece of white cake frosted in white buttercream icing, was topped with a miniature bride in a lace gown and a groom dressed in an army uniform, in anticipation of David's pending hitch, set to commence the week after the couple's brief honeymoon in New York City.

Chi Chi peeled back the cellophane wrapping on a centerpiece and stole a coconut cookie as Barbara and Lucille joined her.

"Just like the old days, stealing cookies," Lucille said, poaching a cookie for herself.

"How long can you stay?" Barbara asked.

"I have a week off."

"That's all?"

"I'm lucky I got that, Lucille."

"We just haven't seen much of you. You've been out every night with Jim."

"Can you blame her?" Barbara took a bite of a coconut cookie.

"He's got it bad for you, Cheech. He never goes for a girl seriously, and he goes for you. The girls at the mill had a pool with odds about who he'd marry. We never split the pot."

"He's interesting. He went to college and he knows a lot about business. We have a lot in common."

"Don't forget your sisters. That's all I'm saying. We'd like to spend time with you too." Lucille swigged her birch beer. "They may be playing you on the radio, but remember where you came from."

"I will. I still owe you twelve bucks for the taffeta." Chi Chi went for another cookie.

"I hope you can come home when the baby's born," Barbara said.

"What baby?"

"Not mine." Lucille put her hands in the air.

"You're having a baby?" Chi Chi said in delight as she threw her arms around her sister. "When did you find out?"

"I went to the doctor last week." Barbara grinned.

"Congratulations!" Chi Chi handed her the cookie. "Eat!"

The drummer in the band hit the snares to announce the first dance. Phil Costa leaned into the microphone: "I'd like to invite the bride and groom to the dance floor for the first dance. Mr. and Mrs. Osella, your future awaits."

The crowd cheered as Rita and David joined one another on the dance floor. After a moment, Charlie led Barbara to the dance floor. Lucille's boyfriend, Frank Communale, beckoned her to join him from the far side of the dance floor.

"May I have this dance, Chiara?"

Jim LaMarca was definitely the best-looking man on the Jersey shore between Atlantic City and Brielle. Tall, slim with thick, wavy, dark brown hair, he was what the girls at the mill called dreamy. He extended his hand to Chi Chi.

"You may, Jim."

He looked at her and brushed some cookie crumbs off her upper lip.

"I hit the cookie tray early," Chi Chi explained.

"I see that." Jim smiled.

"You can't get the frosted coconut ones just anywhere."

"I know. They're only for special occasions," Jim said as he kissed her. "They're my favorite too." He took Chi Chi in his arms and spun her effortlessly across the dance floor.

Isotta watched as her daughters danced with the young men in their lives, as memories of Mariano washed over her.

"It's got to be tough," Cousin Joozy said behind her. "Here you lost your husband so young, and now your girls are starting their own lives."

"I'm happy for them."

"What mother wouldn't be? But it doesn't erase your pain." Joozy sipped her wine and dipped a cookie from the tray on the table into the wine before taking a bite. A few drops of wine trickled onto her dress like droplets of blood. The fitted gold-sequined chemise with exaggerated sheer, short puffy sleeves grabbed the light.

"I do miss Mariano," Isotta said.

"A fine man. And your girls aren't doing too badly either. Charlie Calza, associate's degree from business school. Frank Communale, sells doors and windows—who the hell doesn't need those? And your Chi Chi? So creative and talented. And she's about to bring in the net big time with the biggest fish of all: that Jim LaMarca. He is the ungettable get, you know. A six-footer, at least. Look at that face. Chiseled out of marble and set in brass like the doorknocker at First National. Polite too. Did you know he graduated from Rutgers with a degree in business? He didn't need school, he's going to work for his father with the trucks. I heard he volunteered for the Air Force."

"My goodness, Joozy, you know everything about him."

"Know the terrain, Isotta. When you know the terrain, the ride goes smoothly. You don't hit the potholes. I understand Chi Chi has seen Jim every night since she's been home."

"Just about."

"You may have a LaMarca in your future."

On the dance floor, the band had switched it up from a waltz to a Lindy. As Jim and Chi Chi made the transition, Chi Chi leaned in. "It would be so much easier to leave for California if you were a lousy dancer."

Jim laughed. "Is that all you'll miss about me?"

Chi Chi took his hand and pulled him off the dance floor. "I hear there's a list of your attributes that all the ladies covet. Did you know there's a pool on who you'll marry over at the mill? They even have money on the Vechiarelli girls. One of them is set to take you before you go overseas."

"They're beautiful girls."

"Gina's got the biggest crush on you."

"Duly noted."

"A tall Italian boy is as rare as a handsome pope."

"But good looks are wasted on a pope," Jim joked.

Jim poured Chi Chi a glass of wine and then one for himself. She found a table near the entrance to the boardwalk.

"Do you plan on being on the road for a long time?" Jim asked.

"How long are you going to be in the Air Force?"

"Three years."

"I'll stick with the band for three more years. I'd like to eventually write songs for big singers and orchestras. I don't mind the travel now, but I might not like it as much someday."

"When you get married and have a family?"

Chi Chi thought for a moment. "You never know what life holds."

"No, you don't," Jim agreed. "It's important to stay open."

"Yes, it is."

"You have a talent, and you have to use it. You'll probably write songs and sing them for the rest of your life."

"I hope so."

"It isn't like what I do, or what most people do. We find jobs to make a living, or we work in the family business. What you do is . . ." He searched for the right word. "A calling."

"I guess, but I look at it like it's practical. Somebody has to write songs that amuse, you know, the kind that get sung at weddings."

"Like *Mama's Rolling Pin*."

"Yep."

"But even that song, in its fashion, is all about family. We come from people who live life around the kitchen table. It's all about that." Jim took her hand.

"Why didn't we go together before I left?" Chi Chi asked.

"We went out a few times."

"I liked you."

"And I liked you." He laughed. "But there's something about the times now."

"Because of the war?"

"Or because we're older, and the things we want change."

"What do you want?" Chi Chi asked him.

"The order changes every day." He smiled. "We need to lick the Germans, for starters. My mother is worried about her family in Italy. It's bad there."

"So we win the war and you come home. Then what?"

"My father expects me to go into his business, and I could do that or I could do something else. I like real estate."

"Me too! I have my eye on a property in New York City. I think it would be a wise investment. I like government bonds as a rule, but I want to expand my portfolio."

"I don't know about New York City. I think it will become less residential as the years go by."

"Maybe. But people always need a place to stay in the city. Musicians travel through, and I could rent the place out to them. I want to buy a classic six. Two bedrooms. Two bathrooms."

"You've made up your mind."

"I have to think about the future. At Jersey Miss, it's mostly women working in the mill. On payday, the girls would cash their checks and either give the money to their husbands if they were married or their parents if they still lived at home; others put it in the bank, and a few stuck the money under their mattresses, but nobody ever talked about what they should do with it or about the future. I never heard a woman talk about interest rates or stocks or bonds. And we should be. Look at what happened to my mom. Men die, and often they're young. Women end up alone, and we aren't prepared for it. The only difference, to me, between men and women is the purse. When we do control it, it's a secret. We have a cookie jar or a bank account on the side. As if being responsible with the money you earned is shameful! I think it's cuckoo. I'm on the road with a bunch of men and I have to hold my own writing the songs, getting them into the show, performing them, recording them, fighting for them. And since I have the time, I use it to study the men. It's not ambition or talent that gives men the edge over women, it's the money. So my philosophy is: ladies, get control of the money, and you'll have control over your lives."

"You just summed up a degree in business school, Chiara."

Chi Chi stood and extended her hand. "Come on, big Jim. I have to burn up these cookies."

On the dance floor, Chi Chi leaned against Jim's chest. His

hand in hers felt just right, and as he held her close, she felt at ease. His neck had the scent of sandalwood, which she found delicious. Whenever he dropped her off from a date, she found herself missing him and wishing they had more time. Chi Chi hadn't planned on falling in love, but she figured that's why they called it falling; it wasn't something she could control. And even if she could, she didn't want to. She closed her eyes and savored the moment when a peal of screams echoed through the hall, followed by a small stampede toward the pavilion's entrance door. The dance floor emptied out as couples left to see what the hoopla was all about.

"What's happening?" Chi Chi asked Jim. "Are they rolling out the cake already?"

A cluster of guests moved from the entrance into the hall; at the center of the group was Tony Arma, wearing a tuxedo, his bow tie loosened, clearly enjoying the attention. A hush fell over the crowd as the group pushed him up the steps of the band box to the stage and into the spotlight where the lead singer ceded his microphone to the better known crooner. A few of the Osella nieces, bobby-soxers, ran forward and squealed, "Tony! We love you on the radio, Tony!" as he consulted with the conductor.

"Ladies and gentlemen," the conductor announced. "We have a surprise for you tonight. All the way from New York City, Mr. Tony Arma."

The crowd whistled and applauded.

Tony came up to the microphone and leaned into it. "I want to wish my good friend Rita Milnicki, now Mrs. David Osella, my very best. David, you got a beautiful, bright girl who will make you so happy, you won't know what to do with it. Congratulations and God bless. I'd like to sing for you tonight, but I need a little help up here from a local girl. Chi Chi Donatelli, will you please join me?"

"I'm gonna kill him," Chi Chi whispered to Jim.

"Go ahead. You'll be great."

The crowd full of her friends and family applauded and whistled as Chi Chi made her way through the crowd, her blue taffeta gown rustling behind her. Tony helped her up the steps to the stage.

"You're kidding, right? I thought you had a gig," she said through a clenched smile.

"You know the song," he said.

The cellist handed Tony a mandolin. Tony plucked a few notes as the crowd settled down to listen. Tony began to strum an elegant tune as the pavilion fell into silence.

"This is for Mr. and Mrs. Osella," Tony said into the microphone.

Chi Chi closed her eyes, recognizing the tune of *When I Grow Too Old to Dream*, a popular hit by Oscar Hammerstein II and Sigmund Romberg. Most of the guests knew it, too, and applauded in approval.

Chi Chi had never sung this particular song with Tony, but every other girl singer from the start had, including the recently departed Delilah Entwistle, who, in Chi Chi's opinion, had sung it best of all.

As Tony sang, Chi Chi took the part of the girl singer and came in on key. Soon the band behind them folded in; the piano, cello, and percussion created a sweet sound that filled the pavilion with the feeling of a lullaby in a music box, melodic and tender.

Tony and Chi Chi's voices meshed like threads of gold and silver, different qualities for sure, but both rich, each with a timbre and tone that complemented the other. Tony's mandolin was simple but it reminded the older Italians in the room of the days before they emigrated. The music brought them home to their villages, high in the rocky hills of southern Italy, or deep in the green fields of the Veneto, or along the sapphire-blue shores of the Mediterranean Sea. The guests cheered as they finished the song.

Tony instructed the conductor to underline their patter with a soft brush of the snare drum. Then Tony gave Chi Chi the cue. "That dress of yours makes a lot of noise," Tony said.

She looked at him, irritated. *"Gown.* When it hits the floor, it's a gown. Higher up, it's a dress."

"Forgive me."

"You're such a *gavone,*" she admonished him, pinching her fingers together. The crowd went wild. "All the girls you've been with, and not one ever explained the difference?" Chi Chi looked out into the crowd. "Sorry, Monsignor."

Tony ignored her. "I want to tell you something."

Chi Chi held her ear. "I can't hear you over the gown."

"I didn't come all the way from New York City to have you give me a lesson in dress design."

"Then why did you come all this way?"

"Well, Chi Chi, there's a little tune that climbed the *Hit Parade* chart, written by a young lady from this very beach."

"Who would that be, Tony?"

"That would be you." Tony shielded his eyes as he too peered into the audience. "Where are Barbara and Lucille?"

The girls from the mill pushed them forward.

"Come on up," Chi Chi implored her sisters. "Ladies and gentlemen, without any rehearsal or what they call *further adieu* in France, I present my family, the Donatelli Sisters."

"With Tony Arma," Tony added.

The crowd roared.

Tony conducted the band into an uptempo version of *Mama's Rolling Pin.* The guests filled the floor. During the musical interlude, Tony put his arm around Chi Chi and turned upstage.

"They know the song," he said.

"It's a hometown thing."

"Explain Bristol, Virginia. It was huge there, too."

Tony and Chi Chi returned to the microphones to bring the song in. The quartet ended the song live as they had on the record, with a melodic four-part harmony that blew big. The crowd cheered as they took a bow.

Keeping the momentum going, the band segued into a lively polka. The pavilion came alive once more with the exuberance of the traditional Polish dance. Chi Chi, Lucille, Barbara, and Tony slipped off the stage and joined the Italians at their table.

"That was beautiful, Tony," Isotta said. "Chi Chi, *bella!*"

Jim kissed Chi Chi lightly on the lips. "That was swell."

"Thanks. Tony, this is Jim LaMarca," Chi Chi introduced them.

Jim shook Tony's hand. "Nice to meet you."

"I didn't know we made 'em this tall," Tony joked.

"Well, now you know," Jim said politely.

"May I have this dance, Mrs. Donatelli?" Tony extended his hand to Isotta.

"Of course." She smiled and took Tony's hand and followed him to the dance floor.

"Look at that," Lucille commented as they watched their mother dance for the first time since their father had died. "He's so smooth."

"If you only knew," Chi Chi said as she took Jim's arm and headed back to the dance floor.

Chi Chi moved through the tables at the reception with Jim, greeting the guests as if it were her own wedding. She left him with the Osella boys to enjoy a cigar.

Tony was kept busy as he danced with every woman at the reception. It turned out he had more than a few fans in attendance, and even when they weren't, he was polite and obliged the ladies who were widows or had already sent their husbands off to war and were in need of a dance partner.

Chi Chi poured herself a birch beer.

"Can you pour me one too, Cheech?" Tony said from behind her, mopping his forehead with his handkerchief.

"I should take you outside and hose you down." She handed him her cup of birch beer and poured herself another.

"I'm dying out there. I need reinforcements. The women of this town are dance deprived."

"Tonight, you are the most popular guy in town."

"Only because there's a war on."

"Nah. It's you. Your savoir faire is built in like a rumble seat."

"I try to be a nice guy."

"You are a nice guy."

"Then why did you let me have it in Chicago?"

"You deserved it."

"Fair enough. But give me some credit. I'm working off my penance tonight."

"How are things going in New York?"

"I'm lonely. But you're not."

Chi Chi watched Jim LaMarca laugh with the Osella brothers across the dance floor. "He's a doll, isn't he?"

"Whatever you say."

"What's the matter? You jealous? You shouldn't be. I figured you were fed up with me by now." Chi Chi offered Tony a slice of pizza with *alige*. He ate it hungrily. She offered him a napkin.

"You're the best friend I have, Cheech. I know that girls don't want to hear that—somehow the word *friend* is reserved for the ladies you laugh with at the mill. But for a man, it's a word that carries the highest esteem, it comes with the deepest respect."

Chi Chi put her hand on Tony's forehead. "Nope, no fever. You're not dying."

"Cut it out. I'm serious." Tony got a funny look on his face.

"What's with the look?"

"You're a little thick sometimes," Tony said quietly.

"Isn't everybody?"

"Sure, but you're only thick when it comes to being a woman."

"What's that supposed to mean?"

"I'm flirting with you, and you act like I'm fooling around."

"Isn't that what flirting is?"

"Chi Chi, I took what you said to heart. About Delilah. About what I did to her."

"You ran around on her."

"It was more complicated than that."

"*Complicated* is a fancy word you hide behind, when in fact it was simple. You told Delilah you loved her, then you made love to other girls while you were loving Delilah. So who made it complicated?"

"Now you're my priest."

"I don't want to be your priest. Go see a priest if you need a priest. Monsignor Nibbio is at Table Four."

"The fellas in the band wonder why you don't have a boyfriend. I guess I can tell them about Stretch over there."

"You tell them nothing. No, you tell them this: that I am there to work. To do a job. To get paid. To get better at the job. To get better pay on the next job. And so on."

"Take a breath, wouldja?"

"Ever notice it's the girls who pack up and leave the band when the love affairs go south? Every contract a woman signs should come with a rider: 'Don't fall for him, sister. When it ends, and it will, you'll lose your heart and your job.' The man? He stays on the tour like nothing happened. Gets a raise and climbs ever higher. You tell the boys that I will never be some man's *nothing happened*."

"I can do that."

"I'm twenty-four years old. I don't want to fritter away my time playing footsie with a drummer. Or a horn player. Or a crooner, for that matter."

"Nobody said you should."

"Then why are they asking? They're like a bunch of washerwomen. That's disparaging washerwomen in laundry rooms everywhere, by the way. They should demand an apology."

"The boys like to talk."

"Ugh."

"They think you like me."

Chi Chi got angry. "They think because we work together, there's some monkey business going on?"

"I don't know. I guess."

"You guess *what*? A girl and a fella can't be in a room with a paper piano and come out with a song, there has to be more to it?"

"That's what they think."

"I hope you straightened them out."

"Of course I did."

"It's the height of unprofessionalism to assume a man and a woman can't work together without getting involved. I wonder where they get that idea? Oh, that's right. You."

"Why are you rankled?" Tony said calmly.

"Because you don't listen."

"Then listen to this: I signed up."

"You did what?"

"I signed up."

"For the service?"

"The priesthood wouldn't take me." He shrugged. "I want to do my bit, and pull my weight. It's time I got off this hamster wheel and did something with my life that matters."

"You joined the Army." Chi Chi was impressed.

"Nope. The Navy. You used to say, there's something about the ocean. And I think you're right. I think the answers are out there." Tony whispered in her ear, "I think I need the ocean."

"Chiara?" Jim placed his hands on Chi Chi's shoulders.

"You call her Chiara? Fancy."

"It's a lovely name." Jim smiled.

"Of course it is," Tony said as he picked the crumbs off Jim's lapel. Chi Chi looked up at Jim. "Tony just told me he joined the Navy."

"Is that right?" Jim extended his hand. "I'm in the Air Force."

"I think we can win this thing, don't you?"

"We have to."

"True. Or the world as we know it will no longer exist. Tell me, Jim, what do you do for a living?"

"My family is in the trucking business."

"Where do your trucks go? California? Texas?"

"No, we stay on the East Coast. New York, Pennsylvania. Connecticut."

"Nice areas. Sung in the Poconos. Fine hotels up there in the woods. Mount Airy Lodge."

"Very fine."

Cousin Joozy barreled through a group and joined them. She had freshly powdered her face and reapplied her blood-orange lipstick, the combination of which gave her portraiture the effect of a gouache, dry yet bright. "Saverio, you've danced with every lady at the wedding except for me."

"My pleasure, Cousin Joozy. Excuse me, Chiara. Jim."

Tony led Joozy to the dance floor. The Sea Isle Garden Club gathered around them. As a member, Joozy shared her cousin as they embarked on a kind of group dance, where every member took a spin with the crooner.

Chi Chi followed Jim to the dance floor. He took her in his

arms. Soon, they were sailing around the pavilion, moving with the beat, in that moment outrunning time, or it surely felt like it.

Jim draped Chi Chi's taffeta stole around her shoulders as they stepped out into the night air. The last revelers from the wedding reception were getting into their cars. The ladies juggled napkins filled with slices of wedding cake; others carried flower arrangements from the dais, while others held bundles of cookies in doilies, the final remnants of the cookie trays for snacking on the ride home.

A small group of ladies had gathered outside Tony Arma's town car for hire, which would take him back to New York City. The black four-door Buick was waxed like a patent leather shoe. It shimmered under the streetlights as though it were wet. Tony had one arm propped on the open car door and one foot inside the car. His homburg was tilted slyly over his left eye as he regaled the ladies with one final story about life on the road. He rolled his bow tie into a coil, placed it in his pocket, and undid the top button of his dress shirt.

Chi Chi and Jim stopped on their way to Jim's car. "Good night, Tony," she called out.

"Good night, Cheech. I mean Chiara," Tony said. "Nice to meet you, Don."

Chi Chi was about to correct him when Jim stopped her. "Not important," he said quietly.

Jim walked Chi Chi up the front porch steps of her home. A moth danced around the porch light in figure eights.

"Thank you for another wonderful night." Chi Chi looked up at Jim.

"It was fun."

"I hope so."

"You couldn't tell?"

Chi Chi slipped her arm through his. "It was a little awkward with Tony."

"He's a little awkward, Chiara."

"I think he was intimidated by you."

"Why? He'd have no reason to be—unless, of course, he was interested in you."

"We're just friends. We work together."

"I think he wants something more."

"I'm not interested."

"Are you sure?"

"I feel sorry for him."

Jim took Chi Chi's hand as they sat down on the glider on the porch. "That's a dangerous thing. When you feel sorry for a man, it puts him in charge. He knows you have a soft spot for him, so you'll let him get away with things he shouldn't."

"He's my friend, not my boyfriend. He's always got a woman in his life."

"But they don't last."

"No, but that's because he doesn't commit to them."

"Be careful. You're the smartest girl I know. Don't let him make a fool out of you."

"I won't."

"If this were a different time, and I had something to offer you right now, I would. But I don't. I'm going into the service, and I don't know what's going to happen. I see lots of my friends rushing into marriage, but that's not something I want to do to a woman I would profess to love. I wouldn't do that to you."

"I appreciate that."

"I think that's wrong. If it's right, it will be there on the other side of all this." Jim stood and lifted Chi Chi to stand next to him. He kissed her. "Chiara is your name, and it's really who you are. Chi Chi is the name of a spice, something you add at the end. To me, you're the everything."

Chi Chi entered the William Morris Talent Agency office building on Sixth Avenue in New York City through the revolving door. She took the elevator up to the sixth floor, hoping that by the time the doors opened onto the pale green waiting area with the beige couch and walnut coffee table, she would have made her decision, or maybe her agent could make it for her.

The secretary ushered Chi Chi into Lee Bowman's office, a small but tasteful space with a window. Glossy black-and-white photos of every act she represented made a bold Art Deco collage behind her. Chi Chi took a seat and removed her gloves.

"You look like Venus, Chi Chi. The touring didn't wizen you a bit. You're fresh as a poppy."

"You look good too, Lee. Making the deals agrees with you."

"It actually gets my blood pumping." Lee slid an envelope across the desk. "Here's the check for the sale of the equipment from your father's studio. I did the best I could."

Chi Chi opened the envelope. The check was made out to her for $1,273.44.

"I can't believe it, Lee."

"Not enough?"

"No, it's plenty. I didn't think you'd be able to get anything for it."

"My guy sold it to a studio on Long Island. It took forever. But he came through. Sometimes I actually like the music business. Men can be decent."

"This will really help my mom."

"Now, about you," Lee said. "Jimmy took your resignation hard, but he understood. He couldn't just plug in another Italian singer from the rust belt to stand in for Tony and keep your duet thing going with substitutes."

"I'm glad he understood."

"I have something I think you'll go for. I know how you hate the cold and the snow."

"I hate it. So I guess I will love the humidity of Florida."

"No, no humidity. There's an orchestra that works the West Coast line. I hear they're swell. She pays. Have you heard of her?" Lee showed Chi Chi the offer, headed *"Vickie Fleming and the Forty Carats—All Girls—Sirens Swing!"*

"All girls?"

"It's not for everyone. Though there are some fine bands out there. Ethel Smith. The International Sweethearts of Rhythm. Good girls. Great music. "

"Tell me about Vickie."

"She's a professor of music. Daughter of a librarian. Has that knowledge of music across all genres. She said you could write new material and perform it. Will let you keep a recording schedule too. She's open. And she's already booked through the new year. Look at this lineup of cities. And she's adding in as she goes."

San Francisco—Hotel Stanford
Portland—The Ashby
Seattle—The Corning
Los Angeles—The Hollywood Canteen
Carmel-by-the-Sea—The Stardust Club
San Diego—Little Millie's on the Beach, Villa Marquis
Santa Barbara—The Corner Club

"I could take this gig, or I could take a few months off and help my sister with her baby that's due before Christmas."

"You know what I say about babies?" Lee leaned in. "They're really wonderful when they're thirty."

"I've got my eye on a baby of my own, Lee." Chi Chi pulled a newspaper clipping from her purse and gave it to Lee. "Can you come with me? It'll take fifteen minutes of your time."

Lee scanned the clipping. "Sure. These boys owe me a lunch hour." She reached under her desk for her purse.

Chi Chi and Lee arrived at East Fifty-Fifth Street and Second Avenue on foot. A construction site fenced off at street level revealed a red-brick building, twenty stories high, nearing completion. A crane lifted bricks on a scaffold onto the roof of the building. The silver ropes of the pulleys swung against the blue sky like marionette strings. Stonemasons suspended on platforms installed the bricks onto the exterior walls of the upper floors. Construction workers poured the walkways on the ground level, raking wet concrete from the trough of a cement mixer into frames that formed the entrance.

"May I buy you lunch?" Chi Chi stopped at a hot-sweet-potato cart on the corner. The earthy aroma of maple and wood fire was enticing. The vendor loaded strips of kindling from the open mesh carrier on the side of the cart into the square aluminum oven as the smokestack blew gray puffs into the air. He wrapped two potatoes from the warming pan for Chi Chi. She handed one to Lee, before paying the vendor thirty cents.

"So, this is the building." Lee squinted at the work in progress.

"I want to buy a piece of real estate."

"Why buy when you can rent? It's cheaper."

"I want to own. And I want you to negotiate the deal for me."

"Be your straw man?"

"Yep. I have a funny idea about this place. An instinct," Chi Chi explained. "I'm on the road, and I've met a lot of musicians who need a place to stay here in the city when they come through. If I have an apartment, I can offer it as a short-term rental, and eventually, it will pay for itself. When the time comes, if I choose to, I can use it too. Or, even better, sell it at a profit."

Lee looked over the clipping of the sales offering on the new building. The Melody on East Fifty-Fifth Street and Second Avenue promised to be an apartment residence like none other, according to the offer: an oasis in the city with modern appliances, rooftop garden, and laundry service. The units were being sold in advance of the completion of construction.

"I believe in signs. The Melody." Chi Chi looked up at the building, drinking in the potential of the place.

"Do you want the efficiency or the one-bedroom?"

"I want the classic six."

"You aim high. Though you are making bank on *Mama's Rolling Pin*," Lee reasoned. "It's being sung at every wedding on the East Coast."

"At least the ones held in garages." Chi Chi laughed.

"I don't think those royalties are going to stop anytime soon," Lee said. "Okay, I'll go and see what I can do."

"No higher than fifteen hundred dollars," Chi Chi said. "The efficiency is three fifty. The one bedroom is five fifty. The math doesn't make sense if they go for twenty-five hundred for the classic six." Lee watched Chi Chi take out a pencil and scratch out figures in a small notebook with a pencil. Lee had never met a musician who was as savvy in business as she was at art until she met Chi Chi.

"Make sure you go for a corner on the front of the building," Chi Chi said. "That way, I get east/west sun."

"You've done your homework, I'll say that."

"I trust my gut, Lee. There are days when I think it's all I've got."

California had an orange sun, wide eggshell beaches, a foamy, wild blue ocean with a silver surf, towering palm trees, and, to Chi Chi's delight, buttery avocadoes, lemon trees, sweet strawberries, and fat purple grapes for the picking. She hiked hills that were green and lush in November while her sisters were back east shoveling snow. Spikes of birds-of-paradise and thick bougainvillea vines drenched with hot pink and purple blossoms flourished among thickets of beach roses in winter. Technicolor wasn't an explosion of color confined to the motion-picture screens in Hollywood, it could also be found in every garden on the West Coast.

The only problem with California, as far as Chi Chi could tell, was that she occasionally forgot what month it was because, in the perennial warmth, it always felt like June. She was guilty about taking a job in such plush surroundings, when most of the men she knew were fighting in the war, but it made her feel better when she saw how many bond drives the band would sponsor on their tour. Everyone was doing their bit.

The Saint Rita Boardinghouse in Ojai, California, was base camp for the all-girl orchestra, and enough of a convent that it gave some of the ladies of Vickie Fleming and the Forty Carats the heebie-jeebies. The complex was isolated, but that was beneficial. Chi Chi could write and rehearse with no distractions. She began the most creative period of her life in California composing music, writing lyrics, and testing her leadership skills as a musical director for the all-female orchestra.

Expectations were low when it came to accommodations for the traveling band. The girls were used to cheap motels, renting rooms that smelled like canned corn with mattresses that were so lumpy they needed to go a few rounds with Gene Tunney before they were suitable for slumber. But the convent accommodations were safe and clean. Room and board included the option of morning prayers and vespers, which most of the ladies politely declined. It turned out that Miss Fleming wasn't interested in saving souls either; she wanted to save money, and the nuns offered the cheapest accommodations around—as she put it, the best deal, "for a song."

The Forty Carats weren't exactly forty instruments strong as advertised. That number included everyone in the band: musicians, singers, dancers, and even the bus driver. When Chi Chi signed her contract, she found a letter in her welcome packet:

RULES OF THE ALL GIRL TRAVELING BAND
If you dated him, I won't.
If you married him, I won't.
If two girls in the band like the same fella, flip a coin.

Chi Chi took one look at the rules and turned them into an anthem that the ladies performed as the finale in the first show under Chi Chi's direction. She added one line to the rules before setting them to music:

And if any fella hurts a sister, he's gonna boin (burn).

A week after she'd been in Ojai, Chi Chi picked up her mail in the lobby, including a letter and a package from home. She crossed her fingers there would be a jar of her mother's homemade tomato sauce in the box. Before she opened it, she tore into a letter, from "T. Arma."

NOVEMBER 1, 1942

> *Dear Cheech,*
> *You would not believe all this. It is not what I imagined. I pray a lot, which will please you. I have been thinking a lot. There's nothing but ocean out here. I do a lot of thinking.*
> > *Love, Saverio*

> *P.S. Are you pen pals with that tall drink of water out of Newark?*

NOVEMBER 5, 1942

> *Dear Saverio,*
> *Your letters don't say much, so I read between the lines. You're praying, so maybe that takes up all your time and leaves very little for writing. That's fine. I've never been in the US Navy so I have no idea what you are enduring, and it must be very difficult. I read the papers and go to the library when I can; not as often as I like. Right now I'm at a convent rehearsing with an all-girl orchestra. The conductor is a character. Her name is Vickie Fleming. She has red hair and she could be forty or eighty. I can't tell. She keeps her youthful glow by washing her face with a pumice stone. That's right. A rock. It peels off the top layer of the skin, revealing, I don't know, skin that is so*

translucent, the texture of the skin on her face looks like the underside of a frog. I don't believe looking glowy and youthful is worth it, though she says that when I am her age, I'll rub anything on my face to erase the years. But a rock? Come on, sister! That's something else she says all the time. Sister this and Sister that, and we're in a convent. She makes us so crazy, a few of us are actually considering taking the veil.

Miss you. Love, Cheech

P.S. Jim LaMarca is a good fella, and almost as good a dancer as you.

NOVEMBER 12, 1942

Dear Cheech,
I read your last letter to the boys, who say it's better than a Hope and Crosby picture. That's how hard they laughed. Send more funny stories. We need them.

Love, Saverio

P.S. The P.S. made me sick.

NOVEMBER 17, 1942 (AFTER THE SHOW)

Dear Saverio,
Your soul searching and deep thoughts as you serve Uncle Sam are astonishing. Hope and Crosby? At least tell the boys how much I resemble Dorothy Lamour. Anyhow, here's

another one. Vickie booked us in a club in San Diego. We
got there and set up and rehearsed. The joint was sold out.
We arrived to play and the owner was about to let in the
patrons and said, "Ladies, off with your clothes." June said,
"Whatever do you mean, sir?" And he said, "You're the
all-girl revue I booked, aren't you?" June said, "Yes," and he
said, "Well, then, off with the costumes." And June said, "I'll
call the cops." And he said, "I'll show him the paperwork
and he'll put you in the slammer for breach of contract."
Well, there was a switcheroo. We were supposed to be at a
club in San Obispo, I think that's how you spell it, and the
other group went there—well, the California State Kiwanis
Club got an eyeful and they didn't get to hear my new song.
Inspired by you, old friend. By the way. I don't think they
missed a note of my song. The alternative was much more
satisfying evidently.

Love, Cheech

P.S. Whenever you're sick, lie down with a cool compress.

NOVEMBER 22, 1942

Dear Cheech,
Send the song.

Love, Saverio

P.S. If I do that, the guys on this tub will pound me like cheap
hamburger.

Chi Chi stood at the console of Maccio Recording Studios in Santa Monica with her arms folded. She looked critically down at the chart she had written, erasing a phrase of the song, adding a rest into the bridge. Through the glass window, Sheila, Annie, Christine, and Deborah slipped headphones over their ears and leaned into the microphone to test the sound levels.

"You going in?" the engineer asked.

"Yep. We'll take it from the top again."

Chi Chi joined the girls in the sound booth and took a seat at the piano.

Everything about this particular day in the studio reminded her of her father. She could not shake her feelings of sadness. It was like that: sometimes waves of grief would swallow her when she least expected it. Usually, she hovered over the blues as if observing herself floating over old memories, but on days she needed her father's counsel, she was reminded how much she missed him.

"Here we go, girls. Let's nail this chorus." Chi Chi put on her headset, adjusted her microphone, and played the tune on the piano. The quartet sang in a velvety four-part harmony:

Dream boy, Dream
Dream boy, Dream
She's waiting on the shore, boy
Dream boy, Dream.

The women bowed their heads to listen as the engineer played the song back. Christine, the tall brunette, looked at the floor and tried not to cry. Deborah chewed a fingernail trying to distract herself, while Annie fished her handkerchief out of her purse.

"You okay?" Sheila asked. "Because I'm a first-class mess." She wiped her tears on her sleeve. "Cripes almighty. I hate ballads."

Christine had a brother fighting in Burma, Deborah's husband was in Italy, Sheila's father was on a sub, while Annie's boyfriend was in training in Georgia. The song had too much meaning for them.

"There's a glitch after the first phrase." Chi Chi rubbed her eyes. "Let's fix it."

Tony was working in the brake room on the submarine, adjusting levels of safety bolts. He swung his wrench around the bolts, locking them into place. The motion reminded him of his time on the line at the River Rouge plant.

"You got a letter, Arma."

"Thanks." Tony took the package. He sat down and opened it.

Happy Thanksgiving

NOVEMBER 26, 1942

> *Dear Saverio,*
> *I hope they have a turntable on that tub. Yours in FDR,*
> > *Love, Cheech*

Tony made his way through the caverns of the submarine, holding the 78 record with care. He climbed a short ladder into the teletype room, using his free hand. Barney Gilley, a private out of Big Stone Gap, Virginia, was sending out code. Tony waited.

"You think you can play this for me, Barn?" Tony asked.

"Don't see why not."

Barney flipped a turntable down from a shelf. He handed the headphones to Tony, who slipped them on.

Barney carefully placed the 78 onto the turntable. He dropped the needle.

Tony closed his eyes and listened.

From the look on Tony's face, Barney wanted to hear the song, too. He plugged in his earpiece and listened along.

> Nothing but ocean/Thoughts of you
> Nothing but ocean/Brother I'm blue
> I long for her eyes and lips and the scent of her hair
> But all we got is this tub and cold sea air
>
> Dream boy, Dream
> Dream boy, Dream
> She's waiting on the shore, boy
> Dream boy, Dream.
>
> Nothing to eat/Nothing to say
> Nothing but the radio/Dance the night away
> I write him a letter to show him I care
> So far away on that tub in the cold sea air
>
> Dream boy, Dream
> Dream boy, Dream
> She's waiting on the shore, boy
> Dream boy, Dream

Tony lifted one side of the headset. "Again?"

"Yes sir." Barney dropped the needle. "That there is a fine tune."

Tony and Barney closed their eyes and listened to the song again.

DECEMBER 5, 1942

> *Dear Cheech,*
> *The song is perfect. Made me want to sing again. I'm in San*
> *Diego Christmas week. Can you come and see me? That's*
> *not a request. An order.*
>
> > *Love, Saverio*

DECEMBER 12, 1942

> *Dear Saverio,*
> *The number at the hotel where we're staying is SAN-7866.*
> *It's the Villa Marquis. Yes, would love to see you, old*
> *friend.*
>
> > *Love, Cheech*
>
> *P.S. You up to doing some crooning? A few of the girls and I are*
> *doing a gig at the Hollywood Canteen. We can do the old stuff.*
> *The boys would love it. And so would the girls.*

Tony opened Chi Chi's letter in his bunk. He read it once, folded and placed it back in the envelope, and set it aside. He put his hands behind his head and stared up at the gray metal ceiling, a shell of tin embroidered with a row of nailheads.

He picked up the envelope, took out the letter, and read it again. *Old friend.* Tony mulled it over. Chi Chi's description of him did not sound promising. Maybe she was serious about that LaMarca character. Maybe he was going to be handed his hat at the Hollywood Canteen. Maybe the boy she was dreaming about wasn't him. After all, the ocean was full of the fine men of the US Navy. That would be a fine *how do you do* after all this war stuff. That would just be Tony Arma's luck.

7

CHRISTMAS 1942

Crescendo

(Loud)

Chi Chi burrowed down under the covers of her bed in her room at the Villa Marquis Hotel. She had left the windows wide open to catch the fresh ocean breezes off the San Diego coast because the scent of the salt water reminded her of home. She was dreaming of Sea Isle when she was aroused from a deep sleep by a persistent knock at the door.

Vickie Fleming stood before her wearing a purple satin robe, slippers, a hairnet, and a face slathered with cold cream that had another hour of wear to go before it would completely dissolve into her skin. "You have a phone call from the East Coast. I'd like to kill whoever it is on the other end." Vickie turned and shuffled back down the hall to her room. "If there wasn't a war on, I'd kill you, too," she said before she slammed the door to her room shut.

"Sorry, Miss Fleming," Chi Chi said on her way to the phone.

"I'm sorry I'm calling so early," Lee began.

"This better be good." Chi Chi could barely open her eyes.

"Doesn't get any better than this. Dinah Shore wants to record *Dream Boy, Dream*."

"You mean it?"

"She wants an exclusive. You want me to negotiate a bigger apartment on Fifty-Fifth Street? I think you can go for the one with the wrap-around terrace."

"Stick with the classic six. I can't believe this. Dinah Shore!"

"I told you that song was a hit. I told you! You're up there with the big boys, Chi Chi."

Chi Chi hung up the phone and went back to her room. She slid back into bed and under the covers. The alarm clock said 3:48 a.m. as her head sank into the pillow. She couldn't wait to tell Tony— she would write to him that afternoon. As she closed her eyes, she let the melody play through her mind, but now it wasn't simply a sweet tune written for a pal and his mates on a submarine or a ballad snuck onto a song list on any show night—it had something songwriters hope for: *Dream Boy, Dream* had potential to be a hit song in the hands of an incomparable recording artist. Chi Chi could not believe her good fortune.

The long line of servicemen and -women outside the Hollywood Canteen was wrapped around Cahuenga Boulevard. They were treated to supportive toots of car horns as they waited, and to the occasional rogue young lady who showed her appreciation as she jumped out of a vehicle, kissed a soldier, and would just as quickly get back into her car to drive off into the night.

As the doors of the Canteen opened, the brave were greeted by Hollywood starlet Linda Darnell, the brunette bombshell. She looked lovely in a red silk cocktail dress and matching hat. The flashbulb pops lit up the night.

Chi Chi gathered the quartet in a corner of the kitchen and went over the show order.

"We'll open with *Jelly Bean Beach*. Who's got the jelly beans?"

Christine rattled the jars.

"I gave the band the charts, and I told them to give us a good eight minutes of dance time. So we'll work it like this. Each of us will fan out and pick a serviceman. Take him out on the floor for a spin. When the song gets to the second chorus, return him to his seat, come back to the stage, and we'll wind it up with some patter. The MC said he'll get Linda Darnell to pick a grunt from the audience to dance with; once she does, they'll lower the lights, and we'll go into *Dream Boy, Dream*."

"Any sign of Tony?" Sheila asked. "And when is Margaret Whiting getting here?"

"He didn't write back, so we can't count on him." Chi Chi bit her lip. "We'll do our material and punt to Margaret Whiting. She said she'd show up around nine thirty."

"In the meantime, we could do our send-up of the Boswell Sisters and the Andrews Sisters if nobody shows up to relieve us," Annie offered.

"If we need to stretch, that's a great idea."

The emcee, Corky Lister, poked his head into the kitchen. "Girls, you're on. If you sing as good as you look, we got gravy."

Chi Chi and the girls followed him to the stage.

Corky moved into the spotlight on a drum roll. "Servicemen and -women, please welcome, fresh from their West Coast tour,

with their all-girl orchestra . . ." Wolf whistles from the men made
the introduction impossible to hear. Corky raised his voice. "The
four with finesse . . . please welcome the Vickie Fleming Quartet!"

Chi Chi led the group to the microphone. As they sang *Jelly
Bean Beach,* the dance floor filled with couples. The crowd at the
bar cheered when Chi Chi and the girls kept the beat with jars of
jelly beans; for a moment, it felt like the old days at the pavilion in
Sea Isle City when there was nothing but fun to be had on a Saturday night. They were old enough to remember their summers
before the war, and young enough to hope those carefree days
would be theirs once more.

As the ladies finished their song, Margaret Whiting climbed
the steps to the stage. She shook out her curls from under her hat,
shoving the blond waves out of her eyes. "You girls go take a smoke,
I'll do a couple of songs. Come back in fifteen, twenty tops."

Tony Arma entered the Canteen unnoticed through the stage
door. He stood against the wall, taking in the scene. He removed
the cap worn with his uniform and tucked it under his arm.

The band wasn't half bad. Margaret Whiting was performing
an encore. He liked her a lot. She had a full, honey tone to her
voice, and was a fresh song stylist. He watched as she captivated
the crowd. She looked like she was having fun. He missed singing
in clubs more than he thought he would. Living on the road, moving through the world by bus and living in lousy hotels had made
him numb in many ways about a life in show business, but he had
never tired of the music. The music was always a joy. Tony missed
the audience. They appreciated the songs, too; the music meant
something to them.

The Canteen was packed, surely violating safety codes. But what was a safety code when the lot of them took their lives into their own hands in fighter planes, subs, and fields? There was barely enough room to move, much less dance. Volunteer waitresses shuttled trays of drinks over their heads, navigating through the crowd like the munitions experts who dusted enemy territory for grenades. Dinner was served buffet style by pretty contract players from the studios, who slung the turkey and mashed potatoes onto plates like the best lunch ladies from their school cafeterias back home. Chi Chi wore a form-fitting bias-cut satin gown of shell pink that was shiny like a candy wrapper. "What a shape!" Tony overheard a fellow say, and he would have called him on it, but the man outranked him.

When the orchestra blew into the instrumental, Chi Chi came off the stage, and enchanted a four-star general when she invited him to dance. The kid that Tony had met on the beach who became a workhorse for the band was now something else altogether. She was no longer just a novelty act, she had the looks and confidence of a lead singer, and was glamorous enough to get out in front and hold the attention of the audience. The war had changed plenty, even those who stayed behind.

Chi Chi delivered the general back to his table as the girls made the segue into *Dream Boy, Dream*. Chi Chi joined the girls onstage as Linda Darnell walked to the center of the dance floor and, choosing a fresh-scrubbed middy, wrapped her arms around his neck, rested her head on his shoulder, and made every dream he'd ever had about a beautiful woman in his arms come true. The young man would have a story to tell someday when he made it home to North Carolina.

Tony snuck around the outside wall of the room and made his way to the stage. He was in uniform, so no one took notice as he climbed up onto the stage. Chi Chi was looking over the crowd when Tony came up behind her and put his arms around her.

Chi Chi turned to face him. "Savvy!" She gave him a hug. "You made it."

"That's some dress." He slid his hands down her back.

She reached behind and took his hands from her waist. "You've been on that sub too long."

"Tell me about it." He kissed her on the nose. "We got a show to do."

"You mean it?"

"How are you gonna stretch this night? You already blew through Margaret Whiting."

"She'll come back and do a few more songs."

"Not if she's at the Copa."

"She left?" Chi Chi was annoyed.

"What are you going to do?"

"I don't know, I can have the band play another dance number."

"They're sweating like animals out there. They need to sit. The general's been pulling a plow all night. He's danced with every gal in the joint. You're no good without me, Cheech."

"Do you have an idea?"

"What's the show order?" Tony leaned against the piano.

Chi Chi looked through her notes. "We can do some banter."

"Which banter?" Tony pulled her close and studied the notes over her shoulder.

Chi Chi wriggled free. "The pound-sand material. Which I may have to use on you for real. Loosen your grip there. What's gotten into you? You're fresh."

"I miss you." Tony buried his face in her neck.

"We are here to entertain the troops."

"I am the troops."

"One troop. See this room? They're all in need of entertainment."

"Who's going to take care of me?"

"Why don't you worry about that after the show?"

"Why don't you give me something to live for?"

Christine, Sheila, Deborah, and Annie climbed up the stairs and joined them onstage. They reached into their evening bags for their compacts.

"I can't dance with another soldier. I have no feeling in my right foot," Sheila complained.

"Girls, say hello to Tony Arma."

"Oh, this is big Tony." Sheila looked him up and down. "Heard a lot about you."

"You have?" Tony was amused.

"Sheila is a real card. Don't believe a word she says."

"Yep. Chi Chi told us about the time you two were doing your show in Youngstown at the Jungle Room and Chi Chi changed costumes, forgot to zip up her dress in a quick change, and you did it for her."

"I remember." Tony grinned.

"Chi Chi said it was half awkward and half romantic."

"Is that what she said, Sheila?"

"Scout's honor. And I made it to cadet level."

"I bet you did," Tony said, without taking his eyes off of Chi Chi. Corky Lister charged up the steps. "Okay, kids, the band is wrapping up the number. You're on."

"Are we doing backup, Chi Chi?" Annie asked.

"What are we doing?" Christine asked, fanning herself. "Add syrup and you could put me on pancakes."

"Yes, yes. Backup." She was flustered. "Tony, over there." She pointed to the center microphone.

"What have you got?" Corky hissed from the side of the stage.

"Introduce Tony Arma," Chi Chi instructed.

"Is he here?"

Tony pointed to himself. "Yeah. The skinny guy in the Navy getup."

"Sorry, Mr. Arma. I didn't recognize you without the hair."

Corky took the microphone to the center of the dance floor as the couples drifted back to their seats. "Ladies and gentlemen, a big treat tonight. All the way from the Pacific theater, that's right, we got him, you love him, the Cosmopolitan Neapolitan, Tony Arma!"

The crowd cheered. Tony took Chi Chi by the hand and stood before the microphone onstage. He cued the drummer, who underscored his patter. "How about this beautiful Italian girl?"

The wolf whistles were earsplitting.

"I found her on a beach in Sea Isle, New Jersey, folks. True story. She did my nails."

"I did not." Chi Chi played along.

"Yes, you did. You were sitting on a moppeen."

"It was a blanket."

"You were under a canopy."

"It was an umbrella."

"I asked you to lunch."

Chi Chi feigned disinterest. "I told you I was busy."

"I didn't believe you."

"I told you to pound sand."

"There was a lot of it. A lotta sand. And I had no place to go. I was a ninety-eight-pound weakling, and there was nobody to take me in. So I followed this one home. *Madone!* She made me macaroni. We had some homemade wine. And when it came time for dessert, I asked for cannolis—you know, I like cannolis. And so she went to the drawer in the kitchen."

"That's where we keep the cannolis." Chi Chi rolled her eyes, deadpan.

"Not really. That's where she keeps the rolling pin."

"Mama's Rolling Pin," Chi Chi corrected him. "It's a kitchen tool."

"And it was a hit on the *Hit Parade* charts. Back us up, ladies."

Christine, Annie, Deborah, and Sheila gathered around a second microphone and harmonized the opening riff.

"Let's go, boys!" Tony pointed to the band.

The band exploded with a horn-heavy, vivacious rendition of *Mama's Rolling Pin.* Chi Chi and Tony sang their parts, but they were tickled by the odd blast of the brass in the band. It wasn't quite right in tone—it had a loose, shaky quality to it, and when the trumpet player blew the quivering notes, it made them laugh. They did their best to restrain themselves, but the strange sting gave them a case of the church giggles. The harder they tried not to laugh, the more they broke up. Soon it didn't matter, as the joy spread from the girls, through the band, and out into the audience.

Tony jumped off the stage and dared Chi Chi to jump into his arms. She looked perturbed, and then hesitant, and finally resigned as the crowd goaded her to jump. Tony caught her in midair, like a bunch of flowers. He spun her around, put her down on the floor, and faked a bad back.

Chi Chi motioned for the girls to join her on the floor. Tony and the girls formed a line and mimed the rolling-pin dance. Soon, Linda Darnell joined them, and the patrons filled the dance floor, making like rolling pins. The band kept the song going as the crowd was having a marvelous time. They were lost in the music, having forgotten their troubles and the world outside.

As the band eased into another song, Tony swept Chi Chi into his arms.

"What is the matter with you?" she asked.

"We have a hit."

"You're acting crazy."

"How do you want me to act?"

"I don't know, that's up to you."

"Tell me what you want me to be, and I'll deliver the goods."

"Just be yourself."

"This is myself. And those letters I write to you. That's me too. How about you?"

"That's me in those letters."

"I thought you got a little romantic with me. Maybe you thought I would get blown up and you'd never see me again, so you got a little cheeky."

"I did not," Chi Chi lied.

"I don't think you'd let Monsignor Nibbio read them."

"Probably not."

"So I'm right. Sheila said you talked about me. Do you talk about me a lot?"

"Hardly ever."

"I don't believe you." Tony held her tightly. "You smell good. It's been too long."

"Are you drunk?"

He laughed. "No."

"You're acting crazy."

"Forgive me. I thought maybe." Tony pulled away to a respectful distance as they danced.

Chi Chi moved closer to him and rested her head on his shoulder. "Sav?"

"Yeah?"

"You know how I'd always know where you were on the road and you wondered how I knew? Like when I was playing the piano and my back was to the door and you'd come in and you'd say, How'd you know it was me?"

"Yeah."

"It's your neck. You have a particular scent. Cedar and lemon and leather."

Chi Chi had given this some thought, which meant she had given him some thought. He still couldn't read her though. He had no idea what she was thinking, or where this was going. For all he knew in this moment, she had no romantic interest in him whatsoever. The letters she sent had been funny, entertaining. They weren't mushy or covered in lipstick kisses or spritzed with cologne like the letters the other fellas received from girls back home. Chi Chi's letters were written to help him get his mind off things, to ease his burden a little and make him laugh. That kind of a letter is written by a pal and nothing more.

Chi Chi stopped moving to the music.

"Did I step on your feet?" Tony asked.

Chi Chi shook her head that he hadn't. She took his face gently into her hands. She kissed his cheek, his nose, and his lips softly. If her kisses had been words, they would have been whispers. She rested her cheek against his for a few moments until Tony pulled her closer still, and this time, he kissed her.

Tony hoped he'd stay in that kiss with Chi Chi forever until the lousy trumpet player hit a bum note. They laughed, they couldn't help it, though they held on to one another. It was just their luck to have the spell broken, when all they had ever done was try to make that same kind of magic for lovers in every club, dance hall, and lodge on the circuit. Tony was leery that the piker blowing brass had ruined the moment. Was it a sign? But he needn't have worried, because it was too late to ruin anything. Tony had Chi Chi's heart. He knew.

Chi Chi folded up the musical charts as the band packed up their instruments. Tony took pictures with the servicemen, but he kept an eye on Chi Chi.

"Chi Chi, we have to go," Sheila reminded her. "The driver has to have the car back by two."

"I'm on my way." Chi Chi wrapped the shawl her mother had given her around herself. She picked up her purse.

"Hey, where are you going?" Tony followed her to the door.

"I have to get back."

"No, you don't."

"The driver has to get the car back."

"I didn't come all this way to sing and dance. I came all this way to see you. I'll take you home."

"You don't have to."

"Hey, what's going on here?" Tony said quietly.

"I have to get back."

"And I said I'll take you. Cheech, everything changed tonight. Give the girls your stuff. I'm in the Packard out front."

Tony waited outside the Canteen on the street. It was late, and the air had turned cold as it does in Los Angeles after midnight in December. *It might as well be Vermont*, Tony thought, as he put the collar of his trench coat up against the breeze. He took the last drag off his cigarette as Chi Chi gave the charts to Sheila. The girls had a conversation. Sheila looked over at Tony and the Packard, then back at Chi Chi. Tony made a praying-hands gesture to Sheila that only she could see. It worked. Chi Chi came across the street and joined him.

"Where'd you get this buggy?" Chi Chi asked Tony as he held the door and she climbed into the Packard.

"I wish it were mine," he said through the passenger window.

"I do too."

Tony came around and jumped into the driver's seat. "It's a loaner." He started the car.

"You must know some ritzy people."

"You only need to know one." Tony smiled. "Is it necessary for you to sit all the way over there? It's like I'm in California and you're in Ohio."

"I like Ohio."

"I think you'd like California better."

Chi Chi scooted closer to him. "What is going on here?"

"Nothing."

"Something happened to you on that submarine."

"Something happened to you on that dance floor."

"I got an excuse. I got carried away," she said as she spun the beads on her pearl bracelet.

"You asked me and I'm going to tell you. A lot happened on the sub. I read your letters."

"I was trying to cheer you up."

"You did. And I came to rely on them. I needed to hear from you. I waited for the mail. When a new one arrived, I'd go back and read all the previous letters in order. It was like I was starving and you had the only food that could possibly fill me up."

"It's not like I'm Dorothy Parker."

"You're better because you're talking to me."

"I'm sure you get lots of letters from lots of girls."

"Not any I want to read."

"But you get them."

"You know, I have pals who talk about their lives before the war. And they talk about the world as though it were perfect, as if they were happy and fulfilled and then this war came along and ruined it."

"How do you feel about that?"

"I hate the war. It's an awful thing, maybe the worst situation a person could find himself in. But sometimes I think my life didn't begin until I got on that submarine. I don't know how to explain it."

"Try."

"I never had a chance to think like I do in the Navy. It's not like there's more time. I just use it more wisely. How about you?"

"Everything changed, and everybody. I never had anxiety before the war, and now I worry about everything." Her voice broke.

"Are you crying?" Tony asked. "Because if you are, I want to pull over and get a good look. I've never seen you cry. Ever."

Chi Chi fished her handkerchief out of her purse. "I'm not going to cry so keep driving."

"You sure?"

"I just don't want anything bad to happen to you." She dabbed her eyes.

"I don't want anything bad to happen to me either."

"Okay."

"But it's not up to me."

"I know. Are you hungry? I'm really hungry."

"You're the only girl I know that could eat Thanksgiving dinner between sets and after a show."

"What do you want from me? I'm Italian."

"I don't think any place is open."

"Let's find a place and sit outside until they open for breakfast."

"Do you mean it?"

"When does the Packard turn back into a pumpkin?"

"Noon tomorrow."

"So we have time."

Chi Chi placed her head on Tony's shoulder, as he put his arm around her. The highway unspooled before them like a gray velvet ribbon. Tony Arma almost felt too grateful to pray. He had a girl to love that he could talk to, a true friend. He had a full tank

of gas in a car he had coveted since he was a boy. He had everything but time, but if he had that, he would be pressing his luck.

The moon hung over the Pacific Ocean under a filmy cloud like a veil
of chiffon as Chi Chi and Tony walked along the beach in San Diego.

"Do you remember when you were a kid, and two days seemed
like a hundred years?" Tony asked her.

"Sure."

"How long did the past forty-eight hours seem to you?"

"Like ten minutes."

"Five, to me. That's how long it took you to eat that stack of
pancakes."

"I won't apologize." Chi Chi kissed his hand.

"How's your family? Your mom and sisters?"

"Barbara and Charlie are good. Baby Nancy is teething. Worse
than a puppy, my sister says. My mother is busy, having fun with
the baby. Lucille is serious about the Communale boy."

"Good for her. So the Donatelli girls are all settled. Except for one."

"I'm holding my own. Writing songs. Touring. Forty dollars a
week, room and board included. In show business, that's settled!"

Tony picked up a seashell. He gave it to her.

She held the pink seashell in her hand and looked up at him.
"Thanks, Saverio."

"It's just a shell."

"But it's beautiful, and you gave it to me."

"Only you and my mother call me Saverio anymore."

"I kind of like that. I remember you when."

"Tony is a made-up character."

"He's just fine. But Saverio is the kid who couldn't fit on a marquee. It's important to remember when you couldn't fit."

Chi Chi and Tony walked along the edge of the water. "Why don't we get married, Cheech?"

"You're crazy," she said softly.

"What kind of an answer is that?"

"Let's *not* get married. It's an answer."

"I'm hurt."

"You'll get over it," she assured him.

"How would you know?"

"You're not thinking straight."

"I've given this a lot of thought."

"You've been submerged for months. Thoughts are different underwater."

"I'm sincere."

"It's the war. Perfectly intelligent men and decent, smart women are getting hitched for no other reason than that they truly believe the world is going to blow up, and they don't want to be alone when it happens."

"You paint one bleak picture."

"It gets worse. Think ahead. The war ends. The soldier comes home, he walks through the front door, and the wife that he married in a whirlwind twister of panic stands there, and they both think, *What did we do?*"

"I had no idea you were such a romantic."

"One of us has to be realistic."

"Are you sure you wrote all those love songs?"

"Most of the songs don't last, and neither do the love affairs. We've been very smart to remain friends."

"I don't want to be friends. I want to be your husband. I've never asked anyone else to marry me."

"Maybe you should have because I'm not right for you."

"How can you say that?"

"Because you are not right for me."

"How do you figure?"

"You go with too many girls."

"They didn't mean anything to me."

Chi Chi considered this. "You know, when you talk like that, it's worse. You sound like you're using those ladies."

"Maybe they're using me."

"That doesn't make your part in it honorable in the least."

"You're such an angel."

"Don't drag me into your melodrama. Whenever you do—and by the way, you have—I have to provide the brokenhearted girls you've spurned with a shoulder and a handkerchief. You know how many Irish lace hankies I've given up for your cause? A few. And an embroidered one. It said 'Bless You' in cross-stitch. One of my favorites."

"I'll buy you another one."

"That's not the point. Some things in life can't be replaced."

"Like what?"

"Like a woman's dignity."

"I will always treat you with respect. Haven't I always?"

"You have."

"So count on it."

Chi Chi was unswayed.

"You're in love with someone else, aren't you?" Tony said. "With Dick LaMarca."

"Jim. And no, I'm not."

"So what is it?"

"I believe in a proper engagement period."

"But there's a war on."

"Doesn't matter. Time gives a girl time to think. Rumination prevents many a heartache."

"Don't you already know what you feel? Haven't you ruminated enough?"

"If I had, I wouldn't need a proper engagement period."

"You haven't been thinking about me in the same way that I've been thinking about you."

"I don't know, Sav."

"I misread the signs."

"I wasn't ever going to get married. And I've been asked plenty."

"You're making this worse."

"I've been asked, but why wouldn't I be? Do you think you're the only one of us who has a little savoir faire? I'm a workhorse in a world of show ponies. But I've got pretty good features. You don't see pins like these on every girl coming and going. I'm a lot of fun, but I'm serious when it's called for. And an Italian boy is at an advantage because he has an Italian mother, so he knows he will have a good life with someone like me, so there's very little risk in it—for you. For my part, marrying you would be nothing but risk."

"I haven't kept anything from you," Tony said. "You know everything. You've been my confidante."

"No wonder I'm exhausted."

"Do you love me?"

Chi Chi thought about it. "What I know, I understand, and so I can love. But there is a lot about you I don't know."

"That's the part we learn as the years go by."

"Maybe. But you disappear."

"You know exactly where I am. I'm a midshipman in the US Navy."

"I don't mean your geographical location. I mean you. You fall out of the moment. I saw it when you came to lunch for the first time in our backyard."

"The day you were wearing a white two-piece swimsuit," Tony recalled, whistling. "Okay, I whistled so you'd laugh."

"I remember macaroni al fresco," Chi Chi said. "We were all jab-
bering at the table, and you were engaged in the conversation, and
in an instant, you were gone. You looked off into the distance and
disappeared. It's happened other times too. In a group, or sometimes when it was just the two of us. I used to think that you were
done with a particular topic, but then I realized it was something
else. It doesn't happen when you're working onstage. Only in life."

"So you won't marry me because I daydream?"

"No. I'm not going to marry you because . . . You don't understand what commitment is. Marriage is about love, sure. But it's
about courage too. You're over there in that submarine, and you're
scared. You know the worst could happen at any moment—so
your proposal is a little about your fear of things ending, and coming home once the war is over, and being alone. There's nothing
like living with a bunch of men to sell a fellow on how great living
with one woman could be. But I listened to my father, see, and he
had one really good idea, and I've lived by it."

"And what is it?"

"My dad said, 'You must decide what is sacred to you. It's different for every person. And, once you have the answer, you have
to live in service to it. If you don't, your life will be meaningless.' "

"That's not a difficult question for me. It's you. You are sacred
to me. You're the only woman I want to marry. And if you say no,
I will never marry anyone else."

Chi Chi looked at Saverio. He was so thin, his belt was on the
last notch and it was loose. He was so skinny, the blue-green veins
on his forehead stuck out like roads drawn on a map. The Navy
had shaved his head, so the bountiful curls he'd once had were
gone. But without his hair, she could really see him. She could
almost see into his mind, through to the very essence of him. She
felt a deep sympathy for him, that she had only felt for her father.

"Knock it off, Cheech. I'm not taking no for an answer. This is nuts! Make the deal. You get your engagement period, no matter how long you need. I'm shipping out, and you have your tour, and when I come home, you can take more time if you need it. Take twenty years, I don't care. Big wedding, small. I don't care. If you wait twenty years, that first tier of cousins will be dead, so you're looking at small. No pavilion, you can squeeze the family into your backyard. Whatever you want, as long as you're at the end of the aisle with a yes when the time comes."

Chi Chi's head spun. "I'm listening."

"I believe that knowing you, in all your facets, will take time. We need more time. But I don't need time to know that I love you above all others, and that the thought of living my life without you fills me with a kind of despair I can't describe. You can't live your life alone or with any other man because I can't live without you. You're my family."

Family was the essence of Chi Chi Donatelli. The power of *family* unlocked her ambition, determination, and sense of self. It would always be the thing she held sacred. Mariano's support of her talent had been so deeply intertwined with her own belief about her abilities that they were inseparable in her mind and heart. Family meant she was never alone, even on the road. Family meant that there was an impenetrable wall between her and trouble. Family meant that same wall could contain joy within it that only those she trusted and with whom she shared a history could know. So, if she became family to Tony, marriage was a sacrament she could enter without hesitation if she believed he felt the same.

"Take your time: I'd give you to the end of it if I could." Tony meant it.

"Okay, Sav. Okay, okay, okay."

"You mean it?"

"Yes."

"This isn't surrender, you're not just giving in, you really want to get married?"

"Yes, I'll marry you."

Tony reached into his pocket for a ring box. He knelt before her on the sand and opened it. A platinum ring, with a diamond pavé heart, rested in the fold of the midnight-blue velvet. The heart glittered, catching a glint of pink light from the moon.

"If it's too flashy, I can take it back."

Chi Chi's eyes narrowed. "Hand it over."

"Italian girls." Saverio sighed as he stood and placed the ring on her finger.

"It's the most exquisite ring I've ever seen." Chi Chi whispered the lyric *A little gold and a diamond bright* as she threw her arms around him and kissed him.

Saverio finished the line: *Will make you mine in a gown of white.*

"Good lyric," Chi Chi said.

"Novelty song," he teased.

"*Humoresque*," she corrected him.

Tony held her; the scent of her skin was like the first day of summer. "Are you going to do that for the rest of my life?" he wanted to know. "Correct me?"

"Only when you're wrong." She kissed his hands. "Sav?"

"Yeah?"

"Are you going to be true?"

"Only always."

Chi Chi sat up in the driver's seat of the Packard steering carefully as she drove slowly down the streets of San Diego.

"I can't be late."

She squinted. "I might need glasses."

"Now you tell me?"

"Pipe down. We're almost there," she said.

"We'll make it to the base, but how are you getting back to that convent?"

The car lurched. "Like a kangaroo. I'll drop the car and Sheila sent our driver to pick me up. I'll be just fine."

The headlights flashed on the sign on the chain-link fence of the Naval Repair Base, San Diego.

"We made it." Chi Chi pumped the brakes until the car bucked to a final stop. She put it in park and turned off the car. "Still want a Packard?"

"She hummed along nicely until she didn't. I think those brake linings might be stripped," Tony guessed.

"I'll tell the guys at the garage when I drop it off." Chi Chi turned to Tony and lifted a gold chain with a medal from around her neck. She unhooked it and placed it around Tony's neck, clicking the clasp shut. "This is a miraculous medal. It's been blessed. No harm will come to you as long as you wear it."

"No harm will come to me as long as you love me."

Chi Chi kissed her fiancé tenderly. "When will you come home?"

"My next furlough should be in eight months. After that, who knows?"

"Unless the war ends."

Tony smiled. "Say a prayer on that one."

"Do you know where they're sending you?"

"The bottom of the ocean looks the same wherever you go."

"What's it like?"

"Working on a sub is like the line at the Rouge. I try not to think too much. But when I do, I think about you."

"And I'll be thinking of you." Chi Chi looked down at her hand. "This is the most beautiful ring I've ever seen. Thank you."

"It suits you."

"It's too much."

"So are you."

Tony kissed Chi Chi goodbye. It had been a few months since he had kissed any girl, and he had almost forgotten how essential kissing was to living. It was breathing for him, better nourishment than food for sure. After years of knowing Chi Chi, he had become an expert on her lips from afar: watching them when she spoke, observing her as she bit them when she wrote a song, or intrigued at how she could swipe them expertly with red lipstick backstage without a mirror, and stay within the lines. "Savvy, are my lips even?" she'd ask before they went out onstage. Occasionally he'd fix the line on the cupid's bow with his thumb. At the time, he'd thought nothing of it, but now he was going to marry her and someday his children would have those lips and her smile.

"I'm going to buy some thank-you notes tomorrow," Chi Chi said.

He was used to her pronouncements, so he played along. "What for?"

"Gonna send them to all those girls you kissed on your way to me. Gonna thank them for getting the kinks out."

"Look around, Cheech."

Chi Chi looked through the windshield of the Packard. Wives and girlfriends were saying goodbye to their midshipmen. The couples speckled the road like tumbleweed. There were lots of them. They came from the corners, alleyways, and streets, out of cars, off buses and trains, and emerged from the shadows near the base, as the sun rose. Just like Tony and Chi Chi, they were squeezing every second out of their goodbyes.

"There's nothing to be sad about," Chi Chi said. "You'll be home in no time, and by then I'll have planned our wedding, and the war will be over."

"Do you know President Roosevelt?"

"Nope. Don't need to meet the man because I have faith in you."

Tony kissed her one last time before getting out of the car. The door creaked loudly when he opened it, its rusted hinges in need of oil. They laughed when everyone within the sound of the creaking stopped kissing and turned to see what could possibly be making that awful sound.

"Before you go—"

Tony leaned in the window. "Yeah?"

"Out of all the girls in the world, I'm curious. Why me?"

"Out of all the fellas in the world, why me?"

"Because you're a good man."

"You're the best person I've ever known, Cheech. That's why."

Chi Chi watched her fiancé follow the men onto the base. He turned around a final time and waved to her before entering the barracks. He kissed the medal and tucked it into his shirt before going inside.

Once he was out of sight, Chi Chi sat in the car and shivered. She had never been so afraid.

Inside the base, Tony got in line to pick up his uniform. He also had a choice of a book, a deck of cards, or a pack of stationery with stamps provided by the Navy Wives Clubs of America as an amenity. Tony chose the stationery.

Tony would write a long letter to his mother about Chi Chi.

She would certainly remember the girl from Sea Isle. His mother had liked her. He would have to explain his feelings, something he didn't do very often, but tonight he felt it was important to tell his mother what was in his heart. He would explain that he wanted to marry Chi Chi Donatelli because she understood him.

Tony wanted a certain happiness to look forward to after the war. He did not know how to battle the grim thoughts in his head without something and someone to look forward to. He could not wait for his salvation; he had to be sure of it now. Sometimes, when he couldn't sleep on the sub, he'd imagine his children, a family of his own, but having one seemed impossible; he often felt forgotten and lost, idling inside the ship beneath the surface of the ocean.

Tony would also write to Chi Chi. He wanted to explain the difference between being truly loved by her and having been amused by other girls, to feel less lonely. It had turned out that sex, even when it was satisfying, was a short-term fix for a long-term ache. For most of his life, that had worked out fine for him, but now, when faced with hard truths, he required deeper meaning to his actions. He didn't know if this change of heart had to do with a fear of death or a fear of ending up like the old singers who tour until they can no longer hear the band and take comfort wherever ladies are willing. Tony observed that misery and was determined to avoid it.

He would try and find the words to tell Chi Chi that the moment he could finally make love to her would be the happiest of his life. Chi Chi was the only woman who had ever taken the time to get to know him. What an odd thing to admit, when he had known so many women. Chi Chi hadn't rejected him when he did something stupid or didn't measure up; it wasn't a painful lesson in shame every time he was human. Her capacity for forgiveness was equal to her ability to love.

And that is why Chi Chi Donatelli got the glittering heart.

DECEMBER 23, 1942

San Diego, California

Dear Mr. and Mrs. Armandonada,
I hope this letter finds you both in the best of health.

It is with great joy that I write this letter to you. Your
son, Saverio, has asked me to marry him. I have accepted
his proposal of marriage. As you know, he is presently
in service to the United States Navy as a midshipman
operating in the Pacific theater of operations. We have had
a chance to see one another, as I have a position with an
orchestra in California for the duration.

Mrs. Armandonada, I remember meeting you at my
parents' home with your cousin Joozy. You were a lovely
lady, and I have often thought of you since. I look forward
to meeting you, Mr. Armandonada. Knowing that you
raised such a wonderful son, he must have the world's best
father. I wish you both a very Merry Christmas.

With affection,
Chi Chi Donatelli

Chi Chi

Saverio's fiancée

P.S. I sent him back to the USS Nevada *with a miraculous medal*
blessed by Father Krause of the Church of Loreto to keep him
safe.

8

1943–1944

Marziale

(Regimental)

Lieutenant Tony Arma felt pressure in his ears as he gave the first command to fill the ballast tanks on the USS *Nevada* with salt water. He heard the clang of the cages as they opened, followed by the soft whirl of the propellers as they slowed to a stop. His ears were as effective an indicator of the timing of the submarine's descent as any of the gauges he monitored in the control room. He had come to rely on his five senses, as well as the data and intelligence, in the same way his commanding officers engaged sonar to navigate the sub through the dense black tangle above the ocean floor.

The repeat chain of command echoed through the main hull, the engines cutting from a dull hum to complete silence as the sub plummeted into the deep. It was a routine drill, the third one on that day. Tony studied the pressure gauges on the utility wall, recorded the numbers on the ship's log, when the overhead lights flickered and went out. Typically, the safety electrics fired within seconds of a blackout; Tony gripped the hatch ladder and held on, waited for the lights to return, and listened for a command. He heard the interior clangs of doors being latched within the main hull. Standard procedure: not a cause for concern. There was no callout. The lights on the board returned. Tony exhaled a sigh of relief as the numbers blazed brightly and the gauge needles began to whirl. When no further command was issued, the lieutenant kept his eyes on the numbers before him and waited.

The submarine rocked gently, followed by a rolling sensation. Tony was certain this motion was not caused by the crawl pattern that had been determined earlier by the chief officer on the boat. The COB had outlined a drill earlier that day, but it had not included review of any safety maneuvers during operations that included ballast weights.

Tony heard the sound of rapid footsteps overhead, followed by the snap of the hatch that led to the conning tower. The COB must have called for the operations team to join him from the main hull, Tony reasoned. He heard the hatch snap shut and seal. He heard the soft pads of their steps as they climbed within the tower.

Tony wiped sweat off his forehead and away from his eyes. The heat in the main hull was suddenly tropical, making him perspire so heavily, he could not see. The fans in the electrics and operations went out with the lights but had not resumed. A submarine, essentially a steel box encased in iron, was a hot oven; without fans and air flow, the temperature rose quickly.

Tony pulled his flashlight from his belt and examined the numbers on the grid; they pulsed oddly, and were difficult to read. He heard the sound of more footsteps overhead when the sub dove forward in the bubble, tilting down to the ocean floor. He dropped the flashlight.

The force of the move spun Tony around as he gripped the ladder, throwing his back flat against the control panel. As the ship righted itself, he fell to his knees and groped on the floor for the flashlight. Luckily, it rolled toward him. He grabbed it, flashed the light around the control room, checking for hazard flashers or distress signals. There were none. He thought to try and move up to the tower to join the other men. Instead, he followed the steps he learned in his training. He went over the board, checked his handwritten notes by the beam of the flashlight, and awaited command.

He turned to peer down the tunnel.

Frightened at what he saw, his heart began to race. A lone figure joined him in the doorway, eerily ghostlike and oddly still. Tony shone the flashlight on his pal Barney, who appeared pale in the pin light, with an expression of terror on his face.

"They've got us," Barney said softly. "I saw it on the satellite feed."

A deafening crash rocked the submarine from side to side. The sound of steel as it rips open and tears away from itself led to the deep rumble of iron as it buckles against a fireball of heat. These sounds were followed by a series of seismic shakes, which felt as though the ocean floor were opening up and swallowing the ship. When the jolts subsided, a wild rush of seawater poured into the outer hull. The rush of the flood hit the electrics. The panel went out, the emergency systems sputtered, crackled, and hummed, wired by a weak generator, plunging the submarine into complete darkness, except for the flicker of the emergency lights that lit the exits.

An earsplitting explosion erupted from the heart of the sub

and rocked the ship. The force of an enemy torpedo blew the two men out of the open doorway and sent them careening down the main aisle of the hull, into a pitch-black abyss.

Chi Chi curled up next to her mother on the sofa in the living room of the Sea Isle house. Barbara worked on the sewing machine nearby, as baby Nancy crawled inside her playpen.

"You want to get married here?"

Chi Chi couldn't help but notice that Barbara passed judgment on any decision she made, great or small. "I want a traditional shore wedding," she said. "A football wedding. Live band. Sandwiches. Dance all night. Cookie trays. A genuine Italian *festa.*"

"What does Tony say?"

"Whatever I want."

"That's what they all say at first. Everything is perfect until you disagree with him." Barbara bit off the dangling thread with her teeth. She checked the seam on the curtain she sewed. "The moment you marry the man, what he says goes."

"Every marriage is different."

"Sure." Barbara lined up the seam and pushed the fabric through under the bobbin. "So is every dish of macaroni, and in the end, it's still macaroni."

"I should reach out to the Armandonadas and offer them a room here for the wedding," Isotta said.

"Where will we put them? We're packed in over here. Joozy has room. Of course, that means you have to invite the Fierabraccio crew."

"True." Their mother thought about it.

"I'd rather have them at Joozy's. Savvy doesn't get along with his father," Chi Chi admitted.

"They'll work it out by the wedding, no?" her mother asked.

"Tony won't discuss it."

"He comes from one of those Italian families that does the deep freeze."

"Like the Fierabraccios?"

"Yes. Like them." Barbara flipped the switch on the sewing machine. "They don't speak to one another when they get angry. It goes to the grave."

"His mother is very nice. How bad can his father be? She puts up with him."

"You'll soon find out," Isotta said as she picked up her granddaughter. "I want you to go and see the priest as soon as possible."

"If he's going to marry you, make it a high mass in the morning," Barbara said. "Father Rosalia hits the sauce by noon."

"White or red?" Chi Chi joked.

"Rye."

The phone rang. Chi Chi answered it, then listened. "I'm Chiara Donatelli."

"She must have won a ham," Barbara said. "I put her baptismal name on the ticket in the church raffle."

Chi Chi hung up the phone. She gripped the back of the chair.

"Who was that?" Barbara asked.

"Tony's submarine was hit. He's missing." Chi Chi grabbed her coat and headed for the door.

Barbara got up to follow Chi Chi out, but Isotta stopped her. "Let her go."

Chi Chi trembled, pulling her coat closely around her, and looked down at her hand. The engagement ring did not sparkle as there was very little light. She tried not to take that as a sign.

It probably meant nothing; the sun was buried deep behind the thick November clouds. She pulled on her gloves as she took the path to the beach.

Tangled vines laced with seaweed covered the bluffs. Beyond them, the shore was deserted as far as Chi Chi could see. She walked along the water's edge, where the gray expanse of the sea mirrored the grim sky.

The waves of the Atlantic rippled gently in white folds. She imagined the wild surf of the Pacific Ocean she had seen on news-reels, and felt the distance between them. There was nothing she could do for Tony; she felt useless.

Chi Chi tried to conjure a world without him. She should have prepared for this moment—her friends with boys in the war had advised her to cope with reality by facing it—but she hadn't prepared for the worst. Chi Chi examined her conscience with the kind of desperation known only to those driven to bargain with God.

I will give up everything to have him come back to me.

Her *everything* was her ambition, which was also her sin. She had fed her artistic dreams with craft, cunning, and a single-minded determination, to the exclusion of romantic love, deep friendship, and the creation of a family of her own, which made her selfish. She wore Tony Arma's ring, but she knew it repre-sented the promise of a career partnership as much as it did the preamble to a holy sacrament. The self-recrimination had once been resolve. The only women who survived in the business of the big bands attached themselves as a romantic partner to the most important man in the orchestra, or made like a mother and served him as a secretary. Chi Chi's plan was to invent her own life. But now, the test arrived.

I never wanted to marry, and now it has been taken from me because I did not value it and I did not love him enough. The work was always more important; it was always the goal. If Tony hadn't become part of the fabric of my dream, I would not be engaged to him.

We would travel the world, write songs, sing them, and make 78s, one after the other. The records would stack like pizelles, high hats of them, hundreds of them. Hits, hits, and more hits. The songs would be born in the night, rehearsed in the day, and put in the show with a full orchestra behind them the next evening. The routine of our lives would be to create new music, and revel in the process. It would be our version of the factory life, but instead of making blouses and assembling cars, we would write about the desires and dreams of the people who worked the line, and I would set the words to music. We found the threads of the stories in our families, the table around which we gathered, and the love that bound us together like the binding of a book.

But I got greedy.

Women who want too much are punished for their ambition with a lifetime of loneliness while a man who aims for success is rewarded for it. Only war asks him to offer his life in exchange for the lives of others. A woman is expected to give up everything for the privilege of loving one man.

She folded her hands, bowed her head, and closed her eyes.

I offer everything—my career, my ambition, my future—in exchange for his life.

Chi Chi heard Barbara call her name from the bluffs. Barbara waved to her with both arms crossing over her head, the SOS signal her parents had taught them to use on the beach. She must have news. Barbara shimmied down the bluffs as Chi Chi broke into a run.

"They got him! They found Tony!" Barbara shouted.

"The Japs?"

"No, no, the hospital. He's in the Naval Hospital in San Diego."

"How is he? What did they say? Tell me everything!" Chi Chi grabbed her sister by the lapels of her coat.

"I pried as much information as I could out of the nurse. We know he's alive, and he's had surgery."

"He made it. He made it!" Chi Chi let the news sink in. "I have to go." Chi Chi locked arms with Barbara and began to walk back home. "I have to make this right."

Lee Bowman wore her best cranberry wool suit on the Super Chief from Chicago to Los Angeles. She had packed lightly, as she was in a rush, but she knew from her time on the road representing bands that packing was about extra blouses, stockings, and under-garments, not about an array of heavy skirts, jackets, and dresses. She had brought one hat, which she wore on the train, a fetching Tyrolean trilby in salmon pink with a cranberry grosgrain ribbon.

Chi Chi sat across from Lee in her best outfit, a gray bouclé silk suit with a long jacket and matching straight skirt. Her hat, a black felt Italian fedora, rested on her lap. Her dark hair hung in waves loosely around her shoulders.

"I want you to let Vickie Fleming know I'm not coming back," Chi Chi said.

"It's a little soon to make a decision, don't you think?"

"I'm not in a state of mind to tour right now."

"Are you worried about how Tony will be when we get there?"

"I get more anxious as we get closer."

"Me too," Lee admitted.

"My cousin from Long Island lost his leg in France," Chi Chi said. "He's learning how to walk again."

"Don't let your mind go to that place."

"You know what I think about?"

"What's that?"

"What I can possibly say, or do, for him to make this better."

"You can't make it better." Lee sighed. "No one can."

"But that's my role in his life."

"You'll have to pick a new one, because being an angel is an impossible gig. Even I wouldn't let you sign on for that job at a ten percent commission."

"Whatever condition he is in, however awful it is, and whatever it means about the future, I accept it. I'll take care of him. We'll get married and he'll come home with me."

"You're made of the good stuff, Chi Chi. He's lucky because I've seen every kind of show business wife. There aren't many who would sign on for that life sight unseen."

"I am."

"And what if he's fine?"

"I owe God."

"We all do."

"I made a few bargains."

"Oh, those." Lee looked out the window.

"You have to help me try and be a traditional wife."

"You can be whatever you want to be. There are wives who stay home and take care of everything, and don't want to hear about the road. Just bring home the purse, honey, and I'll keep a log on the fire and a hot meal in the oven for you. Others take care of the home and children too, and they make it to a show here and there, come backstage afterward, and stand on the fringes of the room like fans, not knowing what to say. Think about it, that's her husband up there, and she doesn't say anything."

"It's a club, Lee. I know all about it because I'm in it. If you're not in the band, you're an outsider. Of course the wives feel out of step."

"The wife doesn't say anything because she doesn't feel she has the right. It's his world, and she knows she has no place in it.

Occasionally, a girl comes along like you who has dreams as big as the men."

"What happens to them?"

"The smart women never stop working."

"Is this your agent way to keep me on the tour?"

"No. But you have to do something. You have momentum." Lee reached into her purse. *Billboard* hasn't forgotten about you and Tony. Look at this."

Of all the duos around, Tony & Chi Chi brought musicality and comedy to the charts before the war. Their ethnic material, fire-crackers in the kitchen sink, chili powder in the marinara, is explosive and we can't wait to see what they cook up after victory is secured. Donatelli, for her part, is a first-rate songwriter. *Dream Boy, Dream* as styled and sung by Dinah Shore is an instant classic, a song that will stand the test of time as it defines it, note by glorious note.

"I tried for years to get a line in that magazine for you, and finally they're taking notice."

"I don't want to quit, Lee."

"You may not have the option. If he can't work, you'll have to support him."

"I'll take care of us financially too. I don't mind. No matter what shape he is in, I'll get him well, and I'll keep writing."

"Good. Because Dinah wants more songs from you. As fast as you can write them."

The Naval Hospital in San Diego had taken over a warehouse by the shipyard and put up a temporary hospital unit to treat American servicemen and -women injured in battles in the Pacific theater. The nuns of the Poor Servants of God from Ireland ran the nursing staff expertly.

Lee and Chi Chi looked at one another as they walked through the impromptu facility. Rooms for patients were areas of the floor cordoned off with white burlap curtains, hung with grommets on a system of poles that covered an area the size of a football field. It reminded her of the public ward where her father had been a patient in New Jersey, except that in this enormous room, there appeared to be more nuns tending the wounded than patients in the beds.

Chi Chi took Lee's arm as they searched for Tony's bed. It was a daunting task. They had been at it for half an hour, walking up and down the rows. The sections were constantly changing, which made squaring the numbers difficult. Lee would peek behind the curtains. She had the stomach for it, and could have been a nurse. Chi Chi was the opposite. It debilitated her to see all of the injuries and take in the suffering. She felt weak in her legs, and was worried they would not hold.

"You can do this," Lee assured her.

Chi Chi kept her eyes on the cards pinned outside the curtains, holding the names of the wounded. "There it is," she exclaimed. "He's in section 1028."

Lee grabbed her hand. "I'll wait out here. Remember, no matter what, be cheerful. Lift his spirits."

Chi Chi took a moment. She feared what she would find behind the curtain. The Navy had given her almost no information on Tony's health. She imagined the worst, and steeled herself to accept that their life together going forward might very well be different from what she had imagined. She vowed that no matter what condition she found her fiancé in, she would take care of him for the rest of his life.

Chi Chi opened the curtain and stepped inside. Tony was sitting up in the bed. His nose was bandaged, over a splint. His dark brown hair was in need of a cut, as new curls were fighting for a comeback. He was reading the paper, but dropped it when he saw her.

Chi Chi ran to him. "What happened to you?" she asked as she put her arms around him and held him close.

"We got hit." Tony kissed her tenderly. "You want to know the good news?"

"Sure." Chi Chi squeezed onto the bed with him.

"We didn't lose one man. It's a miracle. The torpedo hit the tub in such a way that it ripped the outer shell, but did not penetrate the hull. The second blast was all noise; the torpedo skimmed past us, but on its way ripped the ballast cage which sounded like the end of the world. But, all fifty-five of us made it out. But, I'm a mess. I got this"—he pointed to his face—"and a bad case of claustrophobia."

"After months on that tub?"

"It came on the night of the blast. Hit me like a wave. Right before the first one. I began to sweat. I thought I had a fever. I was scared, sure, who wasn't? But this came from feeling enclosed. When I go back on the ship, I guess I'll find out for sure."

She held his face. "What happened here?"

"I broke my nose on impact and passed out. They found my buddy Barney and me a few hours later. Somehow, we wound up in the aft, at the opposite end of the sub. We have no idea how we got there. They think the second shell blast threw us down the hallway."

"How's your friend?"

"Barney got the worst of it. He got beat up pretty good. They took him to a hospital in Los Angeles. Two broken legs. Broken hip."

"Who did your nose?"

"They set it here."

"Oh, Sav."

"You know, lots of the boy singers are getting nose jobs." He grinned. "Well, the Italian ones, anyway."

"You didn't need one."

"You're being kind. Lee thought I needed one, but then she dropped the subject. I told her I would never do it."

"She's here!" Chi Chi remembered. "She's right outside. Lee?" Chi Chi called for her.

Lee peeked in through the curtain. "Tony, how are you?"

"How do I look?" He pointed to his bandaged face. "I did this all for you. I'll be pretty now."

"My novenas paid off."

"And at no cost to me. Uncle Sam paid for it."

"You got a hit." Lee pulled *Billboard* magazine out of her purse and gave it to Tony. "You're on the charts with *Mama's Rolling Pin*. How about some elation?"

Tony folded his hands. "Lee, I'm reserving my joy for the end of the war. Pray we get out of this thing, will you?"

"I will," Lee assured him. "In no time, you'll be back on the boards with a new act and a top-tier orchestra and a brand-new nose."

"It might be worse under here."

"I doubt that."

"What a supportive agent we got here." Tony looked at Chi Chi. They laughed.

"Your face is your fortune. Well, part of it, anyhow. And that schnozzola of yours takes up about a third of it. So when they take off those bandages, and we're looking at a nose that resembles an artichoke, if Dr. Plaster Splint of the United States Navy made a mess of it, I know a fine surgeon in Scranton, Pennsylvania, who can give you the Tyrone Power special."

"Oh, you do?" Tony's surgeon, Captain Desloges, stood behind Lee. "Lieutenant, are you thinking of getting your nose reset?" he teased.

"No, sir. That's just my agent talking."

"Why don't we take a look first and see if you need that hatchet job in Scranton?"

"Forgive me, Doctor." Lee was embarrassed.

"That's Captain Desloges to you."

The captain lifted the bandages off of Tony's nose. There was some swelling, and a bit of bruising on his cheeks.

"It's a fine nose. Straight. I'd call this one the Robert Taylor." Chi Chi gazed at the artistry. "Thank you, Doctor."

"Better than Tyrone Power," Lee raved.

"Would somebody give me a mirror?"

Chi Chi handed Tony a compact mirror from her purse. He looked at his new nose. "Not bad, Captain. Not bad at all. Thank you."

Tony Arma's new nose was a sleeker version of the original. It had a straight bridge, the bulbous tip was gone, and appeared streamlined and sculpted to fit the rest of his face.

A nurse entered and applied two small ice packs to the sides of Tony's new nose. Chi Chi took over the chore as she left to tend to other patients.

"I don't think you need any adjustment. Cancel your ticket to Scranton," Dr. Desloges said before leaving.

"It's not like I could go to Scranton even if I wanted to." Tony reached over to the aluminum nightstand on wheels. He handed Chi Chi the open envelope. "I have my orders."

Chi Chi read the letter. "Another six-month hitch." She gave the letter to Lee.

"You take care of that new nose, Tony. There's a place in Holly-wood for that mug."

Tony laughed. "You think so?"

"She's already working on it."

"The first order of business is not the movies when I'm out of this. It's getting married. Right, Cheech?"

"I'm all yours, Sav." And now more than ever, Chi Chi meant it.

Chi Chi got off the M-3 bus at Park Avenue and checked her watch. She was right on time. She soon reached the corner of East Fifty-Fifth Street and Second Avenue, where she gazed up at the newly finished apartment building which lived up to the architectural rendering on the offering. The Melody had instant and impressive curb appeal. The modern building stood out against the older high-rises on the avenue, with its cranberry brick facade, gleaming windows with high-gloss black sashes, and an entrance awning in bold stripes of evergreen and white that led to the gleaming marble foyer. The singer-songwriter was well pleased with her first real estate investment.

Claire Giannamore waved at Chi Chi from under the canopy. "Miss Donatelli!" The trim, elegant fifty-year-old, an interior designer from the B. Altman department store, worked with Chi Chi long distance to decorate the apartment as she toured the West Coast. "I can't wait to show you the place."

"Your sketches were stunning. And I could use some beauty right now," Chi Chi admitted as they rode the elevator to the tenth floor. "Sometimes I think this war will never end."

"It will," Claire promised. "And when it does, look out. The world as we knew it will have changed."

"Hasn't it already?"

"You have no idea. I visit showrooms around the country. Dallas. San Francisco. New Orleans. With international clients.

When our boys finish off Hitler, and our boys will, there will be an explosion of new business. There's rebuilding to do. It's going to be good for everybody, from the farmer to the furrier to you and me. People want to be happy again. To dance, dine, dress up."

"And decorate," Chi Chi added.

"Of course. But you, young lady, are the wise one. You got in early, and you got a deal. I hope you like what I've done." Claire gave Chi Chi the key to her apartment. "Ten C, madame. C for Chiara."

Chi Chi looked down at the gold key in her white-gloved hand.

"What are you waiting for?" Claire asked.

"I'm only going to feel this once." Chi Chi placed her hand on the door. "Everything I have since I began writing songs and went on the road is in this apartment. It's more than an investment to me."

"I hope you think it's a worthy prize for all your hard work."

Chi Chi turned the key in the lock, opened the door into her newly decorated classic six. She stepped into a foyer papered in a vivid pattern of deep-green elephant leaves on a lavender background. A simple crystal bobeche chandelier hung from the ceiling, throwing prisms of light onto the white marble floor veined in gold.

The living room was a respite of calm with soft lilac walls, elegant Georgian furniture covered in emerald-green velvet, and a jewel-toned crewel work rug underfoot. An upright piano painted in white lacquer, with a table and chair positioned nearby for writing, was set in the living room alcove. Chi Chi stopped and tinkled the keys on the piano before she walked into the all-white kitchen.

In the dining room, Claire had installed bright yellow silk draperies, a mahogany table and chairs, against walls painted a deep magenta. She followed Claire to the bedrooms down the hallway, which Claire had artfully lined with bookshelves.

The master bedroom was a cocoon, decorated simply in a

peaceful neutral of palest pink. The guest bedroom was decorated in gray. The bathrooms were outfitted in white marble, with a single wall mirrored floor to ceiling. Both were papered in bold prints, the master bath with fig leaves, and ferns in the guest bath, carrying the motif from the foyer through the entire apartment.

"I put the best-quality materials I could find into your home. The fabrics should outlast you. Let the Schumacher velvets wear, and as they do, they will develop a patina. Let the Scalamandre silks change their luster as the sun moves through and night comes."

Chi Chi turned around full circle taking it in. "Claire, thank you! It's exactly what I wanted. The apartment has a personality."

"It's all yours. Have you told your fiancé?"

"I will when he comes home."

"Do you think he'll like it?"

"He'll have to." Chi Chi sat down on the comfortable sofa and looked out the window onto Second Avenue below. There was something soothing about the busy street. She could be a part of city life, and yet could retreat to the oasis Claire had created for her.

Chi Chi had considered Tony's comfort in the design of the apartment, but she had not asked him to help her purchase the property or contribute to the decorating costs. Lee believed Chi Chi had invested alone because it was necessary for Chi Chi to own it outright, in case something happened to Tony. But that had nothing to do with Chi Chi's decision; she had another line of thinking entirely.

Chiara Donatelli was not going to rely on anyone to take care of her. She had her own accounts, portfolio, and real estate investments. She had created the Studio D Company to purchase the apartment, knowing the obstacles to doing so in her own name would be formidable, though the legal restrictions on women owning real estate and bank accounts had been loosened for the duration of the war. She took full advantage of the lenient laws.

Chi Chi took ownership of her intellectual material as seriously as she did real estate. She alone held the copyrights on all of her songs and kept them separate from her investments. A portfolio of stocks and bonds was kept at the Banker's Trust Company and another at the Chase Manhattan Bank in New York City. She also kept an account in Sea Isle City, and had a joint account with her mother at the same bank. The amount of cash in these accounts might ebb when the withdrawals needed to flow, but for a show business professional, Chi Chi made saving a priority.

Chi Chi had learned more than songwriting, arranging, and showmanship in nightclubs as she toured professionally; she had also become a keen observer of financial matters, production, box office, and their abuses. She consoled her fellow songwriters when their royalties melted away like ice in the hands of greedy managers. Entertainers who did not have a financial plan often frittered away their income on vice, gambling, irresponsible relatives, and fair-weather friends. Chi Chi observed Monday mania. Typically, a performer was hit with a financial emergency from a close friend or family member on a Monday after a four-show weekend. The borrower knew the performer was flush with cash from a weekend of work and would go in for the kill. Entertainers, who loved their work so much they insisted they would do it for free, often lost their money because of that philosophy.

Chi Chi had seen enough and heard enough on the road from her own fiancé. She knew that finances were not his strong suit. Once married, she knew the family budget, bookkeeping, taxes, and savings would fall on her.

Tony was in the conning tower of the USS *California* near Honolulu, sending signals to the new Pearl Harbor control tower, when a private delivered his personal mail on the desk. The return address read "Barney Gilley. BSG, Va." Tony removed the note and a small square of tissue paper:

SAINT VALENTINE'S DAY 1944

> *Tony My Friend,*
>
> *I trust this finds you happy and healthy. How is your nose? One of the perks of my brief desk job for Uncle Sam in San Diego before they awarded me an honorable discharge was the autopsy of the contents of the USS Nevada. They are presently in the process of melting the old girl down. Your pal Edsel Ford transported her in pieces by rail to Dearborn, Michigan. Evidently the steel the Japs ripped to shreds was worth something after all. You might end up driving the old tub someday when they make cars out of it. The irony! Uncle Sam wastes not. God bless the USA!*
>
> *Before the ship was dispatched, she was stripped of all contents. The nubs who performed the duties must have had eagle eyes, because they found this in the navigation room. The original gold chain is gone—sorry about that, buddy—but here's the amulet. I don't know what you Catholics call these things, but your Baptist friend is returning it to its rightful owner.*
>
>
>
> *Sincerely yours,*
> *Barney Gilley, Colonel US*
> *Navy Retired*
>
>

P.S. I opened a jewelry store. Come see us sometime! The enclosed new gold chain is my gift to you.

Tony unwrapped the tissue paper carefully. The miraculous medal that Chi Chi had given him the night of their engagement had found its way back to him. It was worse for the wear, for sure, but it was safely in his hands once more, having protected him, just as Chi Chi promised. As he clasped the medal on the sparkling new chain around his neck, he made the sign of the cross, hoping next time the Blessed Lady would keep him out of trouble.

Chi Chi plucked out a tune on the piano in Studio B at WJZ Radio. She sang the jingle softly to herself as she looked up at the box of Duz soap powder set on the top of the piano.

The most popular jingle writer on the staff sat back on the piano bench and frowned at the keys. She missed writing about life, and found it challenging to write about soap. She rooted around in her purse for an apple. When she found the Granny Smith, she stood and walked to the window. She looked out and polished the apple on the pilgrim collar of her blouse until it shone.

The traffic was jammed on West Forty-Second Street as rain poured down in silver daggers over midtown Manhattan. The showers were so heavy, the street gutters filled, becoming rushing gray streams that pedestrians leapt over like deer. Chi Chi didn't mind the rain; it was as much a sign of spring as the budding treetops in Bryant Park, whipping to and fro in the sky in waves of soft green.

"Hey, you got that jingle ready for Mr. King?" Ann Mumm Mara sifted through the notes in the bins. "I didn't mean to scare you."

Chi Chi took a last bite of her apple. "I was lost in thought."

"Anything to do with Duz detergent because I don't see anything new here, Chi Chi." Ann was a stunning Irish girl with blond hair and blue eyes, a looker in a sweater-and-skirt set in pastel yellow and pink, the colors of saltwater taffy. Ann may have been dressed like candy, but she ran the jingle department like a general. As manager, she had yet to miss a broadcast deadline.

"I've got it, Ann. Never fear. I'm gonna sing it for you. I call it *Duz You Love Him?*"

Chi Chi's hands floated over the piano keys. She began to play. She sang:

> Duz you love him
> If you do
> Wash his shirts in Duz detergent
> And he'll love you too
>
> HARMONY, LIKE CHIMES: Duz, duz, duz!
>
> Duz 'cause you do
> Duz 'cause you must
> Duz 'cause you love him
> So in duz you trust

"It's funny. He'll like it. I need the lyric sheet," Ann said in her direct fashion.

"How do you know he'll go for it?"

"Mr. King gave up rejecting good jingles for Lent."

"No kidding. Maybe he'll bonus me for this one."

"Not likely. He gave up raises for Lent too."

"How about I give up this job for Lent?"

Ann sat down next to Chi Chi on the piano bench. "You can't. You're the best writer in the stable. I'll get you a raise, if that will keep you. It won't be much, but it'll be something."

"It's not the money."

"What is it? What can I do?"

"I don't feel in control of my life."

"What do you mean?"

"I never wanted to marry."

"Why not?"

"It didn't seem like a good deal."

Ann laughed. "In a lot of ways, it isn't."

"Why do we do it?"

"Don't you want a family?"

"I guess."

"It's a sacrament. It's a good thing to aim for a state of grace, don't you think?" Ann reassured her.

"Of course."

"Every woman has doubts, Chi Chi. And we don't know the world without a war in it. It makes everything feel tenuous. We're on hold, really. The boys are gone, and we're here working, holding down the fort. Such a funny expression, because it's about war too. We're in one, even though we don't call it that. We're fighting for our future and we have no idea what it will look like. That's all you're feeling. It's not about your fiancé. It's about the unknown, the uncertainty of it all. It's about everything else."

"You think so?"

"Love can do a lot, but it can't stop bad things from happening. It can't make a war end faster. And it can't keep you from being afraid. Do you love him?"

"I do."

"That's all you got. You have to find a way for it to be enough." Ann slid Chi Chi's song off the music holder and into the folder she held. "You know what my mom would say? She'd advise you to go and see a priest."

"That's what every mother says."

"That's why there will always be mothers." Ann stood to go. "And priests."

Even though Chi Chi spent weeknights in New York City at her apartment in the Melody, the moment she could steal away after work on Friday afternoons, she hopped the train for Sea Isle City. The shore rejuvenated her, and by the time she returned to town on Monday morning, she was ready to face the advertisers at WJZ and write songs about beef Stroganoff in a can and long-lasting lightbulbs.

"When are you heading back into the city?" the priest asked.

"I'll take the seven-o'clock train tonight." Chi Chi sat in the straight-backed chair facing the pastor's desk in the parish office as Father John Rausch perused dates on the official church calendar at St. Joseph's.

Father Rausch was in residence as their summer priest. He was a substitute out of the Philadelphia diocese whenever their full-time clergy went on their annual vacations and retreats. The Donatellis had an affinity for him because he often invited his sister Marian, a talented coloratura, along to sing the masses. The sister act liked the brother-and-sister act.

"Looks like 1945 is filling up fast. Father Shaughnessy left a note that the church was available for two weddings on any Saturday in November. That gives us plenty of time for the banns of marriage in the church bulletin."

"Pencil us in on the first two Saturdays," Chi Chi said. "I'll write to Tony to choose one or the other."

"When is he done with his hitch?" Father asked.

"Whenever the Navy says he is."

"Maybe I should wait on the calendar." He closed it. "Your regular pastor is better at this anyway. I'd rather talk shop. Have you heard the new Ella Fitzgerald?"

"How is it?"

"Her aim is true." Father Rausch stood and went to the credenza. He flipped open the top of the hi-fi and dropped a needle on a record. The honeyed tones of the great singer poured out of the speaker. She was joined by a quartet who harmonized with her in tones as luscious as satin. "Those are the Delta Rhythm Boys doing backup."

Chi Chi closed her eyes and listened. When the song was over, she nodded in approval.

"When do you go back on the road?"

"I'm not going back, Father."

"Are you going to sing locally?"

"I don't think so."

"If you don't mind me asking, why not?"

"I'm getting married."

"God doesn't take away your talent when he gives you a husband."

"If that's the case, he needs to change the world, and men with it."

"You've done very well, Chi Chi. What are you struggling with?"

"I made a deal with God. If he brought Tony home, I'd give up the road."

"That was dumb."

"Thanks, Father."

"I'm teasing you. We all make bargains with God in desperation. He doesn't hold us to them. If he did, I'd be fly fishing in Montana right now."

"It's not so simple."

"You and Tony have a family business. It's no different from the LaMarcas' trucking company or the Faiccos' butcher shop or the Casellas' restaurant. You happen to write and sing songs together. Why would you break up a business that worked?"

It snowed in New York City the morning Chi Chi left for Chicago to make the transfer for the train to Los Angeles. A telegram had arrived from Tony with news of an unexpected three-day holiday furlough in San Diego, followed by the delivery of a round-trip train ticket to visit him. It had been the longest period of time they had been apart since they had become engaged to be married.

As the train crossed into Pennsylvania, Chi Chi remembered the last time she had taken this route to see Tony. The snow made dizzy patterns in the sky over the fields as it fell, covering frozen drifts that resembled slabs of white marble striated with gray as they sped past. She searched through her purse for a pen and a piece of paper. When she could not find paper, she pulled out the envelope holding her return tickets and itinerary. She wrote on the back of it:

Winter is coming and you are far from me
It's colder here without you, and I'm sad as can be

She looked down at the couplet she had written. She sat back in her seat. What was the matter with her, anyway? Why was she so blue, she wondered, when she was on her way to see Tony?

She wrote:

Winter is coming, and while you're far from me
It feels like summer because you'll soon be free
This train makes tracks as it speeds across the miles
It won't get me there fast enough, into your arms to
see you smile
Winter is coming, and the world is bleak
But my love is eternal, my heart is yours to keep

Tony waited on the platform as Chi Chi's train pulled into the station in Los Angeles. When Chi Chi looked out the window and spotted him wearing his immaculate, white naval uniform, all doubts about their future together left her, just as they had on show nights when they took the backstage walk from the dressing room through the wings and onto the stage, before the spotlight hit them. There was something about the very presence of the man that reassured her.

Chi Chi moved through the main aisle of the train car, following the other passengers to the exit as a porter lined up their luggage in a neat row on the platform below. She maneuvered past passengers scrambling for their luggage, grabbed her suitcase, and looked back to the spot where she had seen Tony from the train, but he was gone. For a split second, she wondered if she had really seen him. She turned to go inside the station when she was scooped up in a man's arms by her waist.

Tony had broken through the crowd and claimed her. He lifted her off the ground and kissed her. She dropped her suitcase as he held her close.

"I knew you two would get together back in Elkhart, Indiana," Mort Luck announced as he stood back on the platform. "It was the canned bisque."

"Mort!" Chi Chi shrieked as she let go of Tony and embraced their old friend. "What are you doing here?"

"I'm on my honeymoon," he announced.

"*We're* on our honeymoon. I'm Betty, Mort's wife." Betty was a girl who could easily win any beauty contest she entered, a butter blonde with an unforgettable shape and dazzling aquamarine eyes. "Mrs. Luck."

"Doesn't that sound official?" Mort said proudly.

"They saw me on the platform," Tony explained to Chi Chi. "That's why I was late."

"A vision in white," Mort said of his old pal.

"You liked your shirts bleached and starched too, as I remember, Morty."

"You remember correctly, Lieutenant. And let me tell you, this little lady can wield a steam iron like Satchmo moves his horn. We got married in Chicago. Betty's mother sent a trunk on the Super Chief. It's filled with ring bologna and rugelach."

"If we're lucky," Betty joked.

"Why California for the honeymoon?" Tony wanted to know.

"Let me guess," Chi Chi offered. "Louis B. Mayer himself wants to sign Betty."

Betty laughed. "Even if he did, I'm not biting."

"My wife has bigger plans. She's going to be busy building a family. She's going to turn out the front line of the football team for the University of Wisconsin–Madison. If she starts today, we'll have, I don't know, eight, ten sons, and they'll be playing by the '62 season."

"Because you're such a jock." Tony shook his head in disbelief.

"No, because *she* is. I married a girl who could letter in every winter sport there is. And she can sing too."

"I'm done with all that," Betty said without regret.

"So am I, folks." Mort kissed his new bride on the cheek. "Betty was singing with a band and I was blowing noise in a combo in Chicago, the summer before I signed with Arena, and she was on her way to buy a hat, and I know a thing or two about hats so I tagged along. And now look. She got a little straw number by Mr. John, and I got her."

"I don't get it," Chi Chi said. "You're a great musician, Mort."

"I'll still play around the campfire. Listen to this. We're out of the circus. My uncle offered me a job in his lumber business. I'm going to take it. We're going home to Milwaukee and have some fun the old-fashioned way. You know. Sleigh rides. Snowshoeing. Taffy pulls."

"All right, Mort, but if I ever need a sax player . . ." Tony warned.

"I'll give you the numbers of three of the best fellas I know."

"You're not fooling around."

"Not with music, anyway." He pulled Betty close.

"You got it all figured out."

"I don't know about that, brother. But I do know that life is simple. Keep it that way. Here's the number at our hotel if you kids want to have dinner."

Tony opened the draperies in Chi Chi's hotel room. "Okay, you're all set. I'll pick you up in the morning."

Tony turned to go, but Chi Chi reeled him back into the room. She kissed his cheek, his neck, and his ear tenderly. "I want you to stay," she whispered.

"We're not married," he whispered back.

Chi Chi stood back and put her hands on her hips. "I don't care."

"I do."

"Now you're pious?"

"I want a fresh start with you."

"Maybe this is my fresh start," Chi Chi said impatiently. "Tonight. With the man I love. I wear your ring, Sav. Remember this?" She waved her hand and the diamond heart.

"Our life begins when the priest marries us."

"Have you become religious?"

"I don't know anybody who has fought in a war who isn't."

Chi Chi sat down on the edge of the bed. "This is horrible."

"I'm not rejecting you."

"What do you call it?"

"I want to stay."

"Such enthusiasm."

Tony laughed. "Do this for me. I want this to be right."

"It couldn't be more right. I'm like a California orange that didn't get picked. You know them. You drive by the groves and you can smell them from the highway because they're so ripe, if they don't get picked that morning, they'll spoil. That's me. I'm getting gamey as I wait. As time passes, I'm getting heavier, the branch almost can't hold me. It bends lower and lower. It's about to snap, and one day I'm so ripe, I hit the ground and explode."

"That's funny, Cheech."

"It's a riot."

"I want to do right by you. Will you give me that privilege?"

"How is this good for you?"

"I'm not proud of the way I lived. I've had time to think."

"Away from the distraction of women."

"Yes. And I thought about the kind of man I was and the kind of man I want to be. I was never faithful to any girl, Cheech. Not one. Only you. I stopped fooling around and started taking things seriously when you took me on. I want to be a good husband."

"I won't follow you around," she vowed.

"You won't have to follow me. There won't be any need. I'll be your shadow. See, I want you to have all the things you were raised with—your traditions. I want you to have that football wedding and the band and you in a veil and, after the nuptial mass, the parade through your mother's living room where the gifts are displayed like a sale table in Gimbels. You think that stuff doesn't matter until it's taken away from you. I know what it's like to be cut loose. I ended up like flotsam, the seaweed that gets tangled up on the periscope and you can't see out."

"I don't care about that stuff anymore," Chi Chi said.

"You've waited this long."

"I'll be almost thirty years old when you finish your time. Thirty. How much more do we have to sacrifice for this war? My mother had all three of us before she was twenty-five. I've missed out on years of happiness. I'm already late for everything."

"And this is the girl who never wanted to marry. Is this because of the attack on the sub?"

"It's not about the fear of losing you. It's about the fear of never living. Time does not belong to us. You say wait, and I say you don't know if you'll be there on the other side of waiting. Rules feel like they belong to another time. A time when people were safe and knew they'd see each other in the morning."

"I'll tell you what. I want you to think about it overnight. And if you still want to get married without the hoopla back in Jersey, we'll marry here in the morning. There's a chaplain on standby on the base. I know him and he's a good fella and he'll marry us. But if the Italian girl in you wins out and you decide you must have the cookie trays, *la boost*, and your cousin Joozy to perform her tap-dance routine to *Toot Toot Tootsie*, then we wait. But whatever we do, you'll be my wife when we spend the night together."

Chi Chi walked him to the door. "All right, okay, I understand. You have a deal, Lieutenant." She extended her hand. When he took it, instead of a handshake, she pulled him close and kissed him.

Tony pushed through the door of his barracks. He undressed, careful to hang his uniform so it wouldn't wrinkle. He sat down to write his mother a letter. Instead, he wrote:

A girl I can talk to
Is one I'll take home
I'll marry her soon so
We'll never be alone
A girl I can talk to
Brings nothing but joy
Because a girl I can talk to
Is everything to this boy.

When Tony worked with Chi Chi, he had never written a lyric. He would make suggestions about word changes, but that was the extent of his writing ability. But having written a verse to a song proved something to him, an idea he had been kicking around for years. The girl he was to marry would make him a better man in every way. The love would be so deep, he could be faithful. Her talent would cut such a swath, it would inspire his own originality. Chi Chi was his match.

Tony lay down on the cot. The truth was, he didn't want to wait either.

The next morning Tony knocked on Chi Chi's hotel room door. She opened it wearing a yellow chiffon dress and matching hat. She carried a bunch of daisies.

He was amazed at the sight of her. "You look like somebody chipped off a piece of the sun."

"It's a lot of yellow." Chi Chi waved the daisies. "The lady at the front desk gave them to me. Stole them from the dining room."

"So you made up your mind."

"Yes. I want to get married this morning."

"I'll call the chaplain."

"You don't have to. I called a priest."

"That will take weeks," Tony said.

"No, I explained the situation. And besides, I had the paper-work from Saint Joseph's with me for you to sign, and that was good enough for him. Plus, he's the biggest Dinah Shore fan this side of Memphis. *Dream Boy, Dream* is his favorite song of the year."

"Do you mean to tell me that my future rests in the hands of Dinah Shore?"

"What's the difference? There's a war on. We have to take whatever we can get. We're collecting tinfoil, my silk stockings have more runs than Joe DiMaggio, and evidently Dinah Shore has more sway with the Holy Roman Church than its lifetime members."

"What about your family?"

"They'll be happy. You know, with my dad gone, it doesn't much matter to me to have a big wedding. If he can't be there to walk me down the aisle, I don't need anything fancy. Barbara felt that way and I do, too."

"Hey, kids." Mort pushed the hotel door open. "May we come in?"

"Good morning, young lovers." Betty smiled. She wore a cornflower-blue silk dress and carried a basket of pink tuberoses.

Tony looked at Chi Chi. "Our witnesses?"

Chi Chi blushed.

"How could you?" Tony asked her, before he turned to Mort. "Sorry to interrupt your honeymoon."

"Anything for the cause of true love."

"There's only one snag," Chi Chi said.

"We're Jewish." Mort shrugged. "But evidently, with the war on, the priest is playing loosey-goosey with the rules."

"One of my grandmothers is a Christian Scientist," Betty of-fered, "if that's helpful."

"Hon, that's like a teaspoon of salt water out of the Pacific

Ocean," Mort said. "No matter how your grandmother digressed from the House of David, at the end of the day, we're Jews."

"The word *Christian* has to help," Betty insisted.

"Father Quadrello said it was fine. Mort and Betty are proxies for whoever we were going to choose, and I figured we would choose Barbara and Charlie, just to push this thing through, so I did, and Father spoke to them on the phone."

Mort checked his watch. "We should get going. Father Quadrangle isn't going to wait all day."

"It's *Quadrello*," Betty corrected him. "No horsing around, Mort. We don't want to annoy the priest. These kids want to get married. I would hate for you to be the obstacle."

"Watch your tone, Mrs. Luck. I don't want to get the rep that I'm henpecked."

"Too late for that, my friend." Tony patted his pal on the back as they departed for the chapel.

Chi Chi and Tony stood before Father Quadrello in the sacristy. Betty and Mort stood behind them, as the priest recited the vows. He spoke the prayers in Latin, which threw Mort. Betty shot her husband a look, warning him to behave himself.

The sacristy was a small, sacred room that held the lingering scents of incense and roses. The sun shone brightly through a stained-glass triptych depicting Saint Ann, Saint Margaret, and Saint Elizabeth, bathing the room in coral light. The polished white marble baptismal font stood empty, but it reminded the couple that they would someday have children now that they were a family.

Betty's basket of tuberoses had been placed at the foot of the statue of the Blessed Mother. Tony had purchased two gold bands from a peddler the chaplain knew. Tony's ring was too tight, and Chi Chi's was too loose, but they could be sized and engraved later. It would be the first of many adjustments they would have to make, the priest reminded them.

As Father proclaimed them married, both man and wife were convinced that their love would last a lifetime, and when they kissed, Tony and Chi Chi would have bet eternity on it, too. They craved the security of a partnership, knowing that they understood one another. They believed marriage was the foundation upon which they could build their lives, family, and the music. As they stood before the priest, their witnesses, and God, both Tony and Chi Chi vowed to give one another strength to face whatever fate might bring. Love, they believed, would take care of the rest.

The cove on Malibu Beach had majestic rock walls on three sides, several stories high, which formed a grotto that enclosed a field of white sand where the teal-blue waves of the wild Pacific lapped the shore, hitting the rock wall like a shower of emeralds. Inside the cove, the rock formations resembled drips of candle wax, with folds of silver and gray stone made smooth over time.

Tony helped Chi Chi climb down the rocky path to the secluded beach. They walked hand in hand to the water's edge.

Chi Chi was struck by the serenity of the place. "This is where mermaids come to pray," she said as she embraced her husband.

"Are you happy you married me?"

"That depends."

"On what exactly?"

"If you're happy."

He kissed her. "I might be better than happy."

"I should wear yellow more often."

"It wasn't the dress, Cheech. Though you were beautiful. You *are* beautiful. I'm better than happy because finally I have peace— the kind that comes from knowing where you belong in the world. And I can tell you, I finally know where I belong on November fourteenth, 1944."

"You had better never forget our anniversary."

"I won't. This day is the first day in my twenty-seven years on earth that I've felt at home. And it's all because of you."

"I haven't hung a curtain or made you a dish of macaroni yet."

"I know you can cook. You're the only girl I know who travels with her own wheel of Parm."

Chi Chi's feet sank deep into the sand. She loved when the tide came in, and the foam fringe of the water rolled in and receded, but her feet remained fixed. With each pull of the tide, her feet would sink deeper into the cool sand.

There was no one on the beach but Mr. and Mrs. Arma. For a girl born and raised by the ocean, her husband had given her what she most required, the longing, restless roil of the sea, the pull of the tides, and the familiar carpet of sand. She was grateful because she didn't have to ask for it, Tony knew.

For her husband, the California coast was a dreamscape. He had imagined a place where it rarely rained, never snowed, and the sun stayed close to the earth even in winter. Their childhood dreams merged like the sand and sea.

Tony spread a blanket on the beach and reached for her. Soon their years of curiosity about one other turned to kisses, and their bodies came together, as naturally as the blend of their voices. As Tony cradled her body in his hands, it was as though she floated above the ground as his embrace held her close to the earth. Tony could see the reflection of the clouds in her eyes as the chiffon folds moved overhead.

He imagined his past, tinged with regret and shame, wash

away beneath them as he held her close. If anyone on earth had the power to change Tony, it was Chi Chi. He wanted to start over again, to baptize himself anew, and to claim what was sacred. He was not certain he was worthy of it, but this was the closest he had come to deserving the best life had to offer.

For Chi Chi, love presented her with her highest dream, and a pang of sadness as she let go. It had been right to wait for this moment, but it came with regret. She knew her husband, which made it natural to give herself to him. But having waited to do so for so long filled her with sadness. Somehow, even with all the joy she found in this moment, it was not enough. This would be the first day of many that she would find it impossible to trust her feelings.

Time was wily when it came to Tony and Chi Chi. It seemed not to unfold, but rather to race or evaporate. Whenever they had come close to happiness in the past, something or someone— forces beyond their control—had pulled them apart. There was no pretending they had a guarantee of years of togetherness ahead. She knew better. She had seen the worst happen to her own parents.

Tony had no doubts about his new wife. He knew her people, and understood her moral code. Her pledge of fidelity to him was eternal.

Chi Chi thought his lips tasted sweet on their wedding day, but there was a hint of salt water, too, like tears.

9

⚜

1944–1950

Diminuendo

(Soft)

DECEMBER 25, 1944

Dear Mrs. Armandonada,
Since I'm all alone without you on this Christmas Day,
my Cheech, I hauled out the big surname, because it's
yours too now, by state seal and stamp, and you might as
well claim it. I hope my gift arrived safely and that you
liked it. You're easy to shop for, honey. It has to sparkle.
Because you do. I thought it would be easier to be married
and come back to this work, but it's worse. I just want to
be home with you. And I can't wait to see what you have
cooked up for us. You said you were going to surprise me.
The memories of our nights together sustain me through the
tedium here. The end of a war is like the end of anything
that once was an enterprise of detail and scope. As it shuts
down, the pieces fall away and all that remains are the

broken bits—can't fix them and they can't be resold. Melted
down for scrap—maybe. We are all sad, somber because
we're full of regret for lost time and our fallen brothers. And
men, when they feel helpless in the face of forces bigger than
they are, often refuse to forgive but instead engage in a lot
of chest beating.

I love you, my dearest wife.
Savvy

Chi Chi straightened the tasteful diamond drop pendant around her neck that Tony had sent her for Christmas and smoothed the collar on her white blouse. She leaned into the mirror in the ladies' room at WJZ and checked her teeth in the mirror before leaving.

"Come on, you don't want to miss her!" Ann Mumm Mara waited for Chi Chi in the hallway.

"We don't know if she's even going to sing the song," Chi Chi said as they rushed down the hall.

"But if she does, can you imagine? And it's going national!"

Ann broke into a run when they turned the corner to the recording studio.

Chi Chi stopped when she spotted the singer inside the glass box, looking like a corsage of yellow dahlias.

Dinah Shore stood before the microphone inside the studio wearing her blond hair in a sleek chignon. Her skin was luminous despite the dim lighting. The chanteuse was already hard at work, her hands buried in the pockets of her skirt, a gold velvet dirndl nipped tightly at the waist with a knot of fabric. She wore a white blouse with the starched collar up. A glistening choker of pink pearls caught the reading light on the music stand.

"She's a knockout," Ann said. "You must say hello."

"We shouldn't disturb her."

"You wrote a hit song for her. Now is not the moment for humility." Ann pushed open the door of the studio and motioned for Chi Chi to follow. *Come on*, Ann gestured with the cock of her head. "Excuse me, Miss Shore. I'd like to introduce you to Chiara Donatelli. She is the songwriter who wrote *Dream Boy, Dream.*"

Dinah smiled. "I'm crazy about your song, Chiara."

Chi Chi was certain she had never seen a more beautiful smile or whiter teeth. "My song is crazy about you, too."

"I thought I'd open with it tonight. I'll dedicate it to our troops. I figure it would sell a lot of war bonds. Don't you think?"

Chi Chi nodded. She was perspiring and felt woozy. Ann noticed. So did Dinah. The engineer looked concerned.

"Can I get you a glass of water?" Dinah asked her. "Maybe you should sit down."

"I'm okay."

"She's parched." Ann poured Chi Chi a glass of water and handed it to her. "She's having a baby."

"Congratulations! What wonderful news!"

"I think so."

"What does your husband do?"

"My husband is a singer. Tony Arma. Right now, he's in the Navy. He's serving in the Pacific theater."

"When's your baby due?"

"In the summer."

"That's just lovely."

"Miss Shore, we're counting down to go live," the engineer reminded her.

"Good luck, Miss Shore." Ann grabbed Chi Chi and pulled her out of the studio.

"Thank you!" Chi Chi hollered before the door snapped shut.

Rosaria fiddled with the station dial to pick up the affiliate of WJZ out of Detroit broadcasting the *Dinah Shore Show*. She was more likely to get better reception after nine in the evening. "Papa! *Andiamo!* Come and listen, will you?"

Rosaria heard the kitchen chair scrape against the floor followed by her husband's footsteps as he made his way into the living room. He took a seat on the sofa as the announcer introduced Dinah Shore.

"I am going to sing a song tonight I simply adore. It's called *Dream Boy, Dream.* And I'd like to share some happy news at a time where there isn't much of it. The songwriter Chiara Donatelli is expecting a baby with her husband, the singer Tony Arma. He's serving in the US Navy. I'm sure they would appreciate it if you would purchase war bonds for the child in your life. I know I will. In the meantime, why don't we all do a little dreaming?"

As Dinah sang, Rosaria looked at her husband. "We're going to be grandparents!"

"*Va bene.*" Leone stood.

"That's it? *Va bene?* Leone. It's time to heal this nonsense."

Leone left the room and went up the stairs.

"Did Dinah Shore just tell the world I'm expecting?" Chi Chi looked up at the speakers in the hallway at WJZ.

"She did."

"Tony doesn't know yet. I just mailed the letter."

"Well, who better to tell a man he's going to be a father than Dinah Shore?"

"Oh I don't know. The mother of his child?"

"Maybe he's listening to the *Rosemary Clooney Show*," Ann reasoned. "There's always Western Union."

The white sun blazed in the tangerine sky over the hills of California as Tony lit a sunrise cigarette on the deck of the USS *Carolina*. He wondered how Chi Chi was feeling. Tony leaned over the railing on the deck. He had grown to love California. He couldn't get enough of Catalina Island, the vineyards and the mountains to the north, the snow showers on Lake Arrowhead, and the nightlife in Hollywood. How could he ever convince his Jersey girl to leave the east behind and come west?

"Lieutenant Arma?" The ensign handed Tony a telegram.

"Congrats Papa," it read. "Twin girls: Rosaria 5.1, Isotta 4.9. Mama overjoyed."

He wasn't one for remembering dates, but July 7 held particular significance for the Arma family. It was almost seven years to the day he had met Chi Chi Donatelli; as a card player (a better one since he joined the Navy), the number 7 mattered and was the difference between winning the pot and going home empty-handed. Tears stung his eyes at his good fortune. He was a father. *Gemelli!* The old Italians believed the birth of twins was good luck. He felt grateful and so much more as he raced to the hatch to go below and call his wife, the mother of his children.

In late autumn, the fallow farm fields of Michigan looked like sheets of old tin. The fall leaves were long gone from the trees, leaving behind gray branches that reached up to the sky like spindly fingers. The corn had been harvested, and the hay gathered; all that was left were the barren hills waiting for snow.

Chi Chi, her mother, and the twins were settled comfortably on the train from Philadelphia to Detroit, the first and last stop on the grandparents tour. As the train trundled through the countryside, the babies slept, while their mother took a few minutes to think. The scenery flipped past like pages in a scrapbook of her days on the road with the bands. Train stations, bus stops, and road signs reminded her of places she had been, and the venues she had played. She hadn't found the time to miss her old life in much detail when the conductor announced the Evergreen Park stop in Detroit.

"There she is. I remember her, Ma." Chi Chi waved to her mother-in-law from the window as the train pulled into the station.

"It wasn't that long ago, was it?"

"Seven years. People change."

"Not that fast. Well, babies do. The time flies. You'll see," Isotta promised her.

"I just want them to stay babies long enough for their father to see them."

"Chi Chi, I thought you were crazy to take these babies halfway across the country, but they were good. They practically slept the whole way."

"The motion of the train was perfect, lulled them right to sleep."

Isotta gathered up baby Rosie and followed Chi Chi, who carried baby Sunny down the aisle. The porter stacked their bags on the platform before helping them off the train.

Rosaria ran to meet them. "Oh, they're beauties. Rosaria is like a rosebud, and look at Isotta . . . she's . . ."

"Always cross," Chi Chi whispered. "But she looks like Hedy Lamarr, so let her have a temper. She'll do just fine in this world."

Leone Armandonada lingered by the station entrance. Chi Chi had expected a tall man, perhaps because he loomed so large in her husband's life, but instead she observed an older Italian man, broad-shouldered and built square and sturdy like a pushcart.

"Is that my father-in-law?"

"Yes, that's him," Rosaria said.

"Come on, girls, time to meet Nonno."

"Signore Armandonada, please call me Chi Chi."

"*Buon giorno*, Chiara." He bowed his head quickly and held his hat.

Chi Chi was surprised by the formality. "Or call me Chiara. This is my mother, Mrs. Donatelli. And I would like to introduce you to your granddaughters, Rosaria and Isotta. We call them Rosie and Sunny. But you can call them Rosaria and Isotta, of course."

Leone leaned down and looked at the babies. One, then the other. They looked up at their grandfather and burst into tears.

"I'm sorry."

"Leone, you scared them," his wife chided him. "What did you do?"

"No, no, it wasn't you, Signore. They're hungry," Chi Chi insisted.

Isotta shot her daughter a look as they followed Leone and Rosaria to their car. Leone held the door as Chi Chi got into the back seat with one baby, followed by her mother with the other.

"Signore Armandonada?" Chi Chi asked.

"*Si?*"

"*Grazie*," Chi Chi said before he closed the door behind them. "I guess he wants me to call him Mr. Armandonada," Chi Chi whispered to her mother.

"So, this is Saverio's favorite dessert?" Chi Chi asked her mother-in-law. "*Ciambella*, right?"

"This is it. He couldn't wait for summer. I used to take him cherry picking, and then we would come home and I would make this fresh for him. But now I can the cherries, so I can make *ciambella* all year. I'll send you home with a crate."

"First, the cherries. Three pints, pitted and sliced in half."

Chi Chi spooned them out of the mason jar.

Rosaria continued, "Put them on the stove with a cup of sugar and the juice of one lemon, and let them slow-cook, until they're a little soupy. While you're doing that, I'm making the dough for the biscuits. That's what we call them. Some people call it a cake, others a doughnut. You will take three cups of flour, one cup of sugar, two eggs, and one egg yolk, and a tablespoon of baking powder. Now sift all of that together. You're going to add a teaspoon of vanilla, and then you'll take two sticks of cold butter and cut it up in chunks and add it to the sifted ingredients. Zest a lemon, and throw it in there."

Chi Chi put her hands in the mixing bowl and blended the ingredients. "How am I doing?"

"Keep going. Mix it, but not too smooth." Rosaria removed a baking pan from the cupboard and greased it with butter. "Now we take the dough and make a ring. We call it a wedding ring."

Chi Chi formed the ring on the pan. Rosaria made a few adjustments to her daughter-in-law's handiwork.

"Sorry. I'm not too good at this."

"You'll learn. Now bake it at three hundred and twenty-five for twenty minutes, until it's golden."

Leone entered the kitchen from the back porch, carrying a large brown paper bag filled with artichokes. He placed it on the table.

"I guess I'm making artichokes for dinner."

"I know how to make them," Chi Chi offered.

"That's all right, I can make them." Rosaria smiled.

"Let Chiara cook," Leone said.

"I can do it, Mama," Chi Chi said. "Go take a rest. I'll have Nonno help me."

Rosaria laughed.

"What's so funny?" Leone asked.

"You in the kitchen." Rosaria removed her apron and went up-stairs. "Cooking."

"Did I get you in trouble, Nonno?" Chi Chi asked.

"No."

Chi Chi sifted through the bag of artichokes, choosing the most firm to prepare. Leone sat at the table and watched her. Chi Chi and her family had been visiting for close to a week, and never once had her father-in-law initiated a conversation or asked her a single question.

"What do you think of your granddaughters?" she asked Leone as she brought the artichokes to the sink.

"Bella, bella."

"I hope you will come and visit us in New Jersey sometime."

"I have to work."

"I understand. But maybe sometime, when you're not working." Chi Chi cleaned the artichokes, cutting off the long stems. "Saverio is coming home soon. He's touring again."

"You call him Saverio?"

"When I met him, that was his name."

"It is my father's name."

"It's a strong name. I love it."

"When did he become Tony?"

"A bandleader named him."

Leone grimaced. "It's stupid."

"Actually, people remember it." Chi Chi was careful not to sound too defensive. She lined the artichokes in a baking pan, adding about an inch of water at the bottom. She placed them in the oven to steam them.

"People are sheep. They remember what is easy, not what is important."

"That can be true," she said diplomatically.

"It is true. I am ashamed that my son gave up his name."

Chi Chi wiped her hands on her apron and sat down with Leone. "That must have been difficult for you."

"He can do as he pleases."

"It happens in show business. Our Italian names are difficult to say and to spell."

"Frank Sinatra didn't change his name. He said no. He has the name he was born with. He is proud of his family. His region. His origins. Not my son."

"But he is proud of his family, and he is proud to be Italian. That's all he sings. It's who he is."

"If he were proud of his name, he wouldn't be a singer."

"Why do you believe that?"

Leone shrugged. "Look at the world of show business. Gamblers. Gangsters. Riffraff. Speakeasies. Dens of crime. Those are not people of honor or places that people of honor choose to go."

"I don't know about that, Signore. Your son has sung for plenty of cardinals." Chi Chi stood to gather the ingredients to make the stuffing for the artichokes. "Maybe if you talked to him about it."

"He doesn't talk to me."

"Why?"

"This is my house. I built it with my own hands. And I live inside these walls a certain way. And I expect my son to live the way I brought him up."

"He's a fine man, Papa. He works hard and he has good morals. He's a man of fine character. He isn't any of the things you assume about show business; he is his own man."

"If he was his own man, he would have kept his own name." Leone got up from the table and went outside. Chi Chi watched him as he walked down the path to the garden. Her father-in-law was a man of another time. Chi Chi was compelled to find a way to bring him into the moment—for his son, and for their new family.

ALL HALLOWS' EVE, 1945

Dearest Husband,
Mom and I took the train to Detroit. Your mother and
father met us at the train station. We stayed with them
for a week. Your mother made ciambella (good news, she
taught me how to make it for you!). She was a natural with
the twins. Between my mother and yours, I actually got a
lot of rest.

Your father was very kind to me. He was sweet with the
girls. I know that this is a source of pain for you, and I don't
know what happened, except for the big trouble when you
were only sixteen, but he wasn't an ogre. He was fine. He
spoke of you a lot. They have your records and clippings
and photographs of you. For the sake of our girls, who only
have one grandfather, I would like us to make the peace.
With peace in the world coming, we need it in our family. I
love you with all my heart and want you to have happiness
in all corners of your life.

Your wife

Tony was furious that Chi Chi had taken the babies to see his father before Tony had seen his children first. He couldn't believe that she had not asked his permission or sought his opinion.

He lifted the photographs of his daughters out of the envelope and placed them in his wallet before he tore up Chi Chi's letter.

Tony ordered a beer at the Anchor, a bar near the pier in San Diego where the servicemen went on weekends. He leaned on the bar when he caught the scent of a familiar perfume—gardenias, he remembered. He turned around. A woman around twenty-five, with long dark hair, stood holding a drink.

"I'm sorry," she said. "I thought you were my date."

"Where is he?"

"He's late."

"He's a dope." Tony took a swig of his beer.

She smiled. "You think so?"

"Leaving you alone was a bad idea."

The woman smiled and slipped onto the bar stool next to Tony. She lifted his left hand off the bar. "Ugh. You're married."

"I'm Tony."

"Joan."

"Nice to meet you, Joan." Tony paid his bar tab and stood.

"Where are you going?"

"Staying out of trouble."

"Harder to do than finding it." She turned away from him on the bar stool.

Tony moved toward the door when a record dropped in the jukebox. The stale air, heavy with smoke and the stench of spilled beer, was cut with the sound of Jimmy Dorsey's *Blue Champagne*. The song was an open invitation to Tony. He was incapable of leaving the bar until the song played through. He walked back to the bar, put his arm around the waist of the brunette, and lifted her off the bar stool to dance with him.

As they swayed to the music, he pulled her close, and put his hand through her hair. The scent of her filled him up and sent him down the long road of what might be as she pressed against him. Her dress was made of silk or satin, one of those fabrics that felt like skin. Tony ran his hands up and down her back. She responded to his touch by nuzzling into his neck. She whispered something in his ear, but he was imagining the song, the actual notes, inside the charts, marking them in time. He saw himself onstage, singing in front of a big band.

Tony felt her hands slip under his windbreaker jacket. She kissed his ear and grazed his cheek with her lips.

He pulled away from her, running his hands down her arms until he was holding her hands. He returned her hands to her, as if they had gotten loose and were out to do damage. The waltz was far from over, but he was done.

Tony walked out of the bar and into the street. The night air in San Diego had turned cool. He shivered as he began to walk back to the base, and quickened his pace. He couldn't get back to the barracks fast enough. His hitch was up in a matter of weeks, the papers had been signed, he had his ticket home. Tony would be going home to his wife. He would see his babies for the first time. He had not even met them, and he had almost made a mistake that would affect them. The thought of it sickened him. He was so angry with Chi Chi he could not get past it. It would be too easy to hurt her.

Tony felt pressure in his chest. He felt feverish. He stopped, leaned against a building, and tried to steady his breathing by taking in big gulps of air. He closed his eyes for a moment to settle his nerves. The pressure subsided. He knew he wasn't having a heart attack. When he opened his eyes, he remembered this feeling. He'd had it on the submarine. It was claustrophobia. The walls were closing in.

Chi Chi wasn't the only war bride who stood outside Penn Station to greet her soldier boy home from the war. Thousands of women crowded the streets in midtown Manhattan, waiting for trains. Many had brought their families. Chi Chi saw young mothers cradling infants and others corralling children. As the snow came down, Chi Chi found refuge under a tent selling Christmas trees on the street corner. She had so much to say to Tony, and she wanted to hear everything about how his service had ended. She had barely written any letters since the twins were born. She was nervous. She reached into her pocket and checked her face in her compact mirror. Eventually, Tony emerged from the station carrying his duffel. She threaded through the crowd and into his arms.

"Welcome home!"

"Did you come alone?"

"The babies are at the shore at Mom's."

"What are we waiting for? Let's go."

Tony and Chi Chi climbed aboard a bus to take them down the Jersey line. Tony was quiet on the ride, but the bus was full, and it was unlikely that he would share much in a crowd. Chi Chi laced her arm through his and counted the minutes until they were home and he could meet his daughters.

Chi Chi put her hand in his and placed her head on his shoulder. She didn't expect much from her husband based upon all she had read and heard from other wives of servicemen. The women who welcomed home husbands from the war had to be patient as the men made the adjustment from the war front to home. Tony was distant and that was to be expected. Chi Chi reached up and kissed him on the cheek, even though he had fallen asleep on the crowded bus.

Chi Chi, Barbara, and Lucille had decorated the Donatelli family home with white lights in the front trees and along the porch, and placed small paper American flags in the wreath on the front door. Inside the house, they had put up a large blue spruce tree and decorated it with shimmering ornaments for the twins' first

Christmas. Isotta and the girls had put out a buffet, and the place was full of their family and friends. The Donatellis were back to their prewar parties.

The guests cheered when Tony entered the house. Wild applause and the pops of champagne corks greeted him, but he heard none of it. "Where are my girls?" he shouted over the din.

Barbara carried Rosie to him. Lucille brought Sunny. Tony looked at his babies, almost six months old, back and forth, one to the other, delighted, taking them in, the details of their features, their smiles. In moments, he was juggling both of his daughters in his arms. "Aren't they beautiful?" he said.

Chi Chi fished her handkerchief out of her pocket. "They've gotten so big. I wish you could have seen them when they were tiny."

"They're mine," he said. "My girls."

He kissed each baby and held them close.

"You always know your father and you never forget him," Chi Chi said as she fussed with Sunny's dress.

Tony stiffened. "You putting the knife in?" he said under his breath.

"No, honey, not at all. I'm talking about you. Not your father. You." Chi Chi had a pained expression on her face.

"That's why you took my kids to see him before I had a chance to see them?" Tony took his daughters and went upstairs. The party that was prepared for him, in his honor, would go on without him.

Chi Chi was devastated, but she did not let on. She was certain Tony was tired. After all, he had been traveling for days to get home.

"What's his problem?" Barbara asked Chi Chi quietly.

"Don't start, Barb."

"It's always his show, Cheech. He doesn't think about what this has been like for you."

Chi Chi rinsed the last pot and placed it on the drying rack. "Ma, go to bed."

"Are you sure?" The arthritis in her hands was acting up, and her joints ached. She kissed Chi Chi good night, untied her apron, and went to her new room.

Chi Chi had added a small apartment onto the back of the homestead for her mother, so she would not have to go up and down stairs. Barbara and her family were settled down the block; Lucille and Frank lived close by in Ocean City, where they were close enough to run over when they were needed. It was all part of a surprise for Tony. Chi Chi planned to unveil the Manhattan apartment, their pied-à-terre in the city, and convince Tony that the girls needed fresh air and the ocean, too, and that the family could commute between the two. Lee was cooking up a come-back nightclub engagement for Tony in Manhattan. Chi Chi had worked hard to make Tony's transition from the Navy back into show business as seamless as possible.

Chi Chi climbed the steps, turning off the lights as she went. Tony's duffel was in the hallway. She picked it up and brought it to the master bedroom. The bed was as she had left it that morning. She had decorated a small, fresh Christmas tree on the bureau for Tony with trinkets from their past.

Chi Chi went down the hall to the nursery and pushed the door open. The babies were asleep in their cribs, as their father slept on the floor next to them. He had taken a stack of cloth diapers out of the bureau and used them as a pillow. She checked on the babies, who slumbered peacefully. Her mother had agreed to take the early-morning feeding for her, so she and Tony might sleep in. It didn't matter now. Chi Chi knelt next to her husband

and gently woke him by embracing him. "You're home, Savvy."

His eyes opened.

"I know you're angry with me," she said. "We can talk about it tomorrow. Tonight, you should sleep in your own bed. The babies are fine. Come with me."

Tony was going to put up a fight, but he was exhausted. He followed Chi Chi down the hall to the master bedroom, sat on the edge of the bed, and untied his shoes. Chi Chi knelt and took over. She removed his shoes and socks, unbuttoned his shirt and slid it off his arms, and unfastened his belt. As he lay back on the bed, she removed his trousers.

Chi Chi shifted the bedspread as Tony climbed under the covers. He sank into the soft warmth of the bed. He had missed the silky sheets and soft pillows, the scent of vanilla and roses and his wife, but he wasn't about to admit it. His anger was deep. The walls around him had grown tall and impenetrable, layers of vines on an ancient palazzo overgrown by neglect and anchored by time.

"Do you need anything?" she asked as she tucked the blanket around him.

"Nice," he said. Soon her husband was sleeping. This was not the Christmas reunion she had planned. Tony could hold a grudge, and nothing, it seemed, could end it, not even his babies, not even Christmas.

Tony stood in the foyer of 10C of the Melody and let out a low, appreciative whistle.

"This is what you did with the royalties for *Dream*?"

"And the addition in Sea Isle."

"That much?" he asked as he walked through the apartment. "This is sensational, Cheech."

"I figured we'd always have it. We have business here."

"It's smart. So smart." Tony opened cabinets and looked under the sink in the kitchen. "Fine craftsmanship."

"We used the best materials. I don't want to do this again."

"It doesn't look like you'll have to, hon."

Chi Chi grinned. Tony had not called her an endearment in the weeks he had been home. Chi Chi let him have his black mood. Slowly, she was breaking through, making progress by not pushing him. "This is all about comfort. You do a show at a nightclub, and you don't have to take a train home. You just come to the apartment and relax."

Tony sat down in the living room and lit a cigarette. "You doing any writing here?"

Chi Chi moved an ashtray near him. "I haven't yet."

"You got the setup. The piano. Looks like you have a desk there."

"I had that table made from Dad's console in the old garage."

"No kidding."

"Yep. I hope it has some magic in it."

"You blocked?" Tony asked.

"I think I'm just exhausted." She looked at her hands. "That's the first time you've asked me anything about myself since you got home. Two words: 'You blocked.' "

"That's not true."

"Okay, Sav."

"You don't believe me."

"I don't recall you asking about me."

"I'm trying to get back into things. You look good. You figured everything out. The babies are fine. What do you need me for? Compliments?"

Chi Chi tried to hold her temper. "I need you to be my partner."

"Oh. Well, a partner *partners*. Am I right about that? If you want a man who just nods and agrees with you, that's not me. But that's the way you treat me. You make all the decisions and you expect me to applaud like that toy monkey the girls have, the one that clangs the cymbals and clacks his teeth when you tap his head."

"I tried to make things nice because I knew you had been through so much in the Navy. I didn't do these things to exclude you. I did all these things to make your life easier."

"You could've written to me about the apartment."

Chi Chi thought about it. She owned the copyright to the song, so it was her money. But they were married, and she knew that all the money she earned was in fact *their* money now. He had turned over all his accounts to her. There were no secrets on his side, so why had she kept this one from him? She had not told him about the apartment purchase because she did not think she had to ask his permission.

Instead of the truth, she said, "I wanted to surprise you. I made the wrong choice. I really am trying to make you happy. I'm sorry."

Low clouds covered Manhattan like a dingy flannel canopy on the blustery January morning. Chi Chi looked out the windows from the sofa as her husband put out his cigarette. He got up from his chair and sat next to her on the couch. "I've never been married."

"Me either."

"Do you think you can tell me things now that I'm home? Not everything. Just the big things."

"I didn't do all of this to upset you. I want you to be proud of me."

"I'm always proud of you. You're a good mother, Cheech."

"But a lousy wife?"

"I wouldn't say that. I've only had one, and she's been all right."

"You're not going to trade her in?"

"Why would I do that?" Tony put his arms around her and pulled her close. Tony kissed Chi Chi, and soon their problems fell away, or seemed to, as they forgot about them long enough to remember what they meant to one another. He lifted his wife off the sofa, carried her to their bedroom, and placed her gently on their bed. She loosened his tie as he undid the buttons down the back of her dress.

"I like this room, Cheech."

"I was worried about the color," she said as she kissed him. "Too girly?"

"Nah. It's like being inside a seashell."

She pulled him onto the white velvet coverlet. "I never thought of that."

"It's always about the ocean with you," Tony said as streaks of pink sun glimmered through the haze. "Even when you don't think it is."

Lee Bowman pushed through the posh glass doors that led to the reception area of the William Morris Agency and greeted Tony with a hug. "You look good, soldier."

"That's all behind me. Time to get me back on the boards."

Tony followed Lee to the conference room. A team of agents stood when Tony entered. He shook the hands of seven men, all dressed in navy blue wool suits, white dress shirts with French cuffs, and black silk ties. "Was there a sale at Hiram's on East Fifth Street?"

"Why do you ask?" said the eldest agent.

"You're all wearing the same suit. I've seen enough uniforms in my lifetime."

The agent cracked a slight smile. "We'll work on that."

"I'm Henry Reisch," the youngest of the men said, "and I head your talent team here at the agency." Henry was polished, and looked as though he had just graduated from college. He had a wide smile and impish brown eyes.

"You head my team? I didn't know I had a team."

"You do now, and we hope you'll be pleased with the plan we've come up with on your behalf. Your primary agent is Miss Bowman, that doesn't change. But we've got ideas for you."

Lee nodded. "We feel that we can extend the borders of your talent. You're a marvelous singer who has extensive touring chops, but we'd like to see you take it up a notch and do an extended tour through South America, parts of Europe, and major US cities. We'd like this tour to wind up in Hollywood, because we think you have a future in the movies."

"You do?" Tony was surprised.

"Absolutely, sir. The movie musical is the profit center of the major studios these days. They need singers with chart hits. They need you," Henry assured him.

"And you're photogenic," Lee added.

"How long a tour are we looking at?" Tony asked.

"We believe this tour could take, if we do it properly, three years."

Tony sat back in the chair.

"It's daunting to contemplate, but here's what we know," Henry said. "Record sales are fed by personal appearances. If we shore up your fan base in Argentina, Peru, Venezuela, all of South America—book you in the big rooms of the posh hotels—and we arrange a record deal in Spanish, you are suddenly in the top five percent of international sales with the big boys. South America will fuel sales in Europe. And so it will go. When you come back home, we get you cast in a movie, and that fan base supports the movie, and an entire new avenue of potential opens up for you."

Tony lit a cigarette. "What's the purse like on these gigs?"

"We get you top dollar, Tony. Expenses paid. First-class accommodations. The works. A *Billboard* ranking goes a long way in foreign territories. And the deeper into the calendar we can book you, the longer your commitment, the better the tour. And the more you make."

"I like this."

Henry glanced at Lee.

"The team was concerned you might want the option of staying in New York."

"New York isn't going anywhere," Tony said. "I can always come home. Book the tour, Henry."

Lee was surprised. Tony sat back and lit a cigarette. Making his own decision without consulting Chi Chi evened the score between them, but he was not thinking about that; he was elated to be wanted on a new continent.

Chi Chi sat on the steps of the back porch in Sea Isle sorting through a pouch of mail that had arrived from William Morris. Tony's South American tour had come together quickly, and by March he was already on the road.

She flipped through a clip file of reviews from the tour. The articles were written in Spanish, but the photographs needed no byline. Tony, in a bespoke tuxedo, holding a glass of prosecco in one hand and a cigarette in the other, stood on an Art Deco stage set surrounded by gorgeous showgirls, with marabou plumes on their heads and less below the neck. The costumes were downright scanty.

The phone rang, and Chi Chi went into the kitchen to answer it.

"Thanks for the clippings, Lee. I especially appreciate the ones with Tony and the show ponies."

"Are you talking about Rio? Oh, it's Carnevale or some such thing. You have to ignore it."

"I don't think my husband can."

"Don't worry about him. Where's he going to find a girl as marvelous as you?"

"Evidently he has his pick on the stage of the Candelora in São Paolo."

"Let's get your mind off all of that, shall we?" Lee coaxed her.

"I'd like that. What do you got?"

"There's a lovely new young singer named Diahann Carroll who is looking for a ballad. She wants a real heartbreaker for her run at the Latin Quarter. She wants to record it, too. Has a spot for it on her debut album."

"You called the right girl."

"I always do."

"Let me see what I can whip up. And I promise not to mention my three-year-old twins who got into Mommy's cold cream and fingerpainted the living room walls."

"Save that for the novelty number."

"Already have the title. *Mommy's Nervous Condition Made Her Commence Drinkin'*." Chi Chi hung up the phone. The twins were napping, and her mother had gone to the store, so she had time to write.

Tony had been on the road on and off for almost three years since the war. His life had resumed at full throttle, but hers bore little resemblance to what came before she married. This is precisely what unnerved her. Everything had changed for her, from her sleep patterns, to where she lived, to the size of her waist. The prevalent attitude was that she should be grateful to be Tony's wife and the mother to his children. Day by day, little by

little, she was losing the woman she was before she met Tony
Arma.

Chi Chi reached up behind the spice rack and retrieved her
notebook and pen. She opened it and flipped through neatly
printed lyrics from four years earlier. She sighed, mourning the
loss of her fine penmanship. These days even her handwriting had
been sacrificed, once she became a homemaker.

She wrote:

> Love you but I'm alone
> Love you kids are grown
> Who are we when the house is empty
> Who am I when my heart is empty
> If you stay, please do
> If you go, I haven't been a fool
> It's never easy, so Mama said
> It's sorrow, pain, and struggle
> It's there in all the books I read
> But if you stay, please do
> If you go, you're a fool

Chi Chi practically broke into a run as she jumped out of the cab
at Fifth Avenue and Eighth Street. She was late. Rosie and Sunny
had a fifth birthday party to attend in Sea Isle with their cousin
Nancy. Barbara was late picking them up which made Chi Chi late
for the train into the city.

Chi Chi was also cross because she had hoped to get her hair
done that morning, but she had run out of time. When didn't she
these days? So she set her hair herself, but in a rush, she put it up
wet. It was humid outside and her thick curls hadn't dried prop-

erly. She wanted to look good for Tony. She gave up and pulled it back into a ponytail.

Chi Chi slipped into the Decca Recording Studio on East Eighth Street in Greenwich Village. She saw Tony through the glass partition, singing *Gravy, Gravy, Gravy,* a new song she had written for him.

The jazz combo that accompanied him were swinging. She put her head down and listened as the musicians played the chorus. The engineer called for Tony to sing it again all the way through. Tony turned around when the song was done and saw Chi Chi in the control room.

He motioned for her to join him inside and kissed her on the cheek. "What do you think?"

"I think you can juice up that chorus. Hello, boys," she greeted the musicians. "How about this: when you get to the first trio of *Gravy, Gravy, Gravy,* Tony sings it solo, on the reprise, the band joins in, harmonize if you can find it. If you can't, don't harmonize—just a high-energy, fun feel to the song."

Tony looked at the band. "Let's try it."

Chi Chi took her place in the control room.

"You know your stuff, sis," the engineer said, stroking his measly goatee.

"I should. I wrote it."

Tony sang the song through. When they got to the chorus, they followed Chi Chi's prompt. Chi Chi bowed her head once more and listened. "That works."

"You sit in with me anytime," the engineer said. "You got any other ideas?"

"You need the wail of the sax in this song. That clarinet in there isn't going to cut it. It's getting lost."

"Vito plays the sax, too."

"Tell him to take it out of the case and blow."

Chi Chi hit the button on the console to talk to her husband inside. "Tony, this song needs a couple of layers. We're going to take out the clarinet and put in the sax. I want you and the boys to give it that street corner feeling again, but this time, Tony, you hold *Gravy* at the bridge, as long and high as you can. Mimic the sax and let it come under you as you sing and rip it. Got it?"

"I got it." Tony put out his cigarette.

"Let's take it from the top." Chi Chi folded her arms across her chest and bowed her head to listen.

Tony watched his wife through the glass. This was exactly why he needed her in his life: when it came to his work, she never settled for less than perfection.

Chi Chi leaned back and put her feet on Lee Bowman's desk to make her laugh. "This is what top-ten *Billboard* songwriters do—we move in when we make the gravy. Can you believe it? Another hit."

"I've got the follow-up," Lee said. "Babies, Babies, Babies."

"Not a bad idea."

"Tony should be here any minute." Lee checked the clock. "You give him the news."

"He loves to hear it from you. It sounds more official."

"What do you have today? Make him take you out for a nice lunch."

"We have an appointment. At Samson's."

"Oh, that. Get that done."

"That's why I'm here."

Lee's intercom buzzed. "Mr. Arma is in the lobby."

"I'll see you later." Chi Chi grabbed her purse, pulled on her gloves, and took the stairs to the lobby.

Tony was pacing when she emerged from the door. "Let's go, hon." He grabbed Chi Chi's hand as he hailed a cab. "Are we late?"

"We're just fine. Tony? Do you ever notice since we had the girls, we are never on time?"

"Yeah, I noticed."

"Why is that?"

"I don't know. More to do?"

"Or maybe we don't want to go."

"Could be." Tony sounded preoccupied.

"You okay?"

"I'm not sure about this."

"So we cancel."

"Nah. I can't. I gotta do it. Henry says it's imperative."

Chi Chi and Tony got out of the cab at 537 Fifth Avenue, whose entrance was recessed between the grand entrances of two larger stores.

"Hard to find," Tony said as he followed Chi Chi inside.

"Discreet," Chi Chi commented as they got into the elevator. "Third floor."

Tony pressed the button.

When they got off the elevator, they stepped onto a polished terrazzo floor. A stately walnut door in front of them bore a small brass plaque: "Samson's of Fifth Avenue." Inside the suite, a receptionist greeted them in the waiting area, decorated in somber tones of charcoal gray, brown, and mauve.

"This reminds me of the bank where we got our mortgage," Chi Chi whispered.

After a short wait the receptionist called them to wait in a private room. Tony and Chi Chi took their seats at a polished cherrywood conference table and matching chairs. Two large books were set on the table. Paintings depicting hunting scenes in colonial Virginia hung on the paneled walls.

An older man with short white hair and a mustache, wearing a bow tie and a doctor's jacket, joined them. "I'm Sy Warmflash, and I'm your hair consultant. How can I be of service?"

"It's pretty simple, Sy," Tony said. "I'm thinning out, and I need a piece."

Sy stood. "Do you mind if I take a look?"

"By all means."

Warmflash looked closely at Tony's head and scalp, examining the balding patterns, the thinning and premature grays. He stood back to get a sense of the proportion of his head to his body. He pulled out several index cards and made some notes on them. He sat down and faced his client.

"Here's how it's going to go, Mr. Arma. You'll recede at the front until the age of fifty-two. The balding at the crown will spread quickly, and most of the hair at the top will be gone by forty. You're how old?"

"Thirty-three."

"Amend that. Crown will be gone closer to thirty-eight."

"What's the process, sir?" Chi Chi asked.

"We choose a style. For your husband, I would recommend side part, loose wave, to blend in with the curls around the collar. I do a nice blend. His hair is fine in texture, but he has a lot of it. We choose a lace. I measure his head. I do a form of his head. Ever had a hat made?"

"Yes."

"It's similar. So as you age, as you gray out, and eventually go white—yes, this is a toupee—we have your head measurements. They never change. I buy excellent quality human hair from Greece, Italy. Lately, I like Polish hair, but they tend to have a thick, straight quality to the hair, at least what is offered me. I like to give you the hair in its natural state."

"How do you put a toupee on?"

"Adhesive. If you can paste a photo of yourself with hair in a scrapbook, you can place a toupee on your head. Don't worry about that at all. If you knew how many Hollywood stars came in that door, you'd plotz. I like to say it's only hair, but as long as it's only hair, why don't we make the best hair we can for the best result we can? You want to look good, I want to look good, who can blame us? Am I right?"

Chi Chi drew the drapes in room 903 of the Waldorf Astoria Hotel. She had bathed, put on her lipstick, and brushed her hair. The hotel robe was soft against her skin.

As she untied the robe and let it drop to the floor, she studied her body in the mirror. Even though her waist had gotten thicker after the twins, she still had a nice shape and her legs were holding up just fine.

She slipped into a new peignoir set, an eggshell chiffon nightgown and robe. Chi Chi was trying to be alluring, to get Tony's attention. As she waited for him to arrive, she straightened up the room, hanging her husband's clothes in the closet. She put the Samson's toupee contract in her purse.

Tony burst into the room. "I got it, Cheech. I got it." He picked her up and twirled her around. "I got the movie. I'm singing in it, too. And they said if the studio likes it, I'm getting second song."

"Honey, that's great."

"We start in a week."

"The girls just started school."

"So we move them."

"Do you think?" Chi Chi asked

"Why not? You loved California."

"I did. And you know what? Wherever you are, we want to be.

And this will be so much better than the road. You can make records and do a concert here and there. No more living out of a suitcase."

Tony glanced at Chi Chi's peignoir. "Are you expecting company?"

"You got here before William Holden."

"Lucky me." Tony kissed her. "You like William Holden?"

"Just trying to make you jealous."

"Why's that?"

"So you remember me."

"I couldn't forget you."

"That's when trouble starts, Savvy. When you forget me." Chi Chi kissed him.

"Remind me, what are we doing here?"

"A little change."

"But we have our place. We could walk there, for cripe sakes."

Chi Chi was frustrated that her husband was breaking the spell. She had planned this getaway, and he was throwing ice cubes all over it. Finally, she gave up. "It was free, Savvy."

"I'm in enough hotel rooms."

"But I'm not."

Tony looked at his wife, and understood: she needed a change. "Come here." He held her. "Forgive me. Sometimes I'm a dolt."

He reached down and turned off the bedside lamp. Chi Chi unbuttoned his shirt. As their lips met, they smiled inside their kiss. "I know what you're thinking," Tony said.

"That every time we kiss we start all over again?"

"Every kiss is a chance to fall in love again."

"I like it. That's a song."

"Write it in the morning. We're busy tonight."

Tony lifted his wife onto the bed. The stars over New York City pushed through the blue night sky like pearls as Tony and Chi Chi started all over again.

Isotta brought a platter of sliced apples and cheese to her grand-daughters. As the girls reached for them, Chi Chi gave them a look. "What do you say, girls?"

"Thank you, Nonna!"

The girls made room for their grandmother on the couch. "This is so exciting."

"My dad is going to be on television!" Sunny hollered.

"My dad, too!" Rosie screamed.

"No more screaming, we want to hear Daddy sing."

"We get to stay up until nine o'clock!" Sunny bragged.

"As soon as Daddy sings, it's straight to bed."

Tony came on the small television screen. The striped tie he wore vibrated in black and white as he sang *Gravy*. Chi Chi would never have approved that tie.

"Daddy looks funny."

"Why is his hair so poofy?"

Chi Chi peered at the set. "Is it?"

"They must have used pomade," Sunny said with the authority of youth. "They used too much. It looks teased."

"It's not teased," her sister said.

"Tomorrow at school, Monique Gibson for sure will tell us that Daddy teased his hair."

"Tell Monique that's impossible, there isn't enough to back-comb. Okay, off to bed. Brush your teeth."

"Mama, Rosie skips the toothpaste."

"It burns my mouth."

"You have to use it, or your teeth will get black spots." Chi Chi reminded them.

"I will supervise," their grandmother said.

As soon as the girls and Isotta were upstairs, Chi Chi dialed Tony at the studio. "You were spectacular, honey."

"You think so?"

"It was tight. Perfect."

"They gave me attitude about the shirt and tie," he said.

"Tell them to put you through wardrobe next time if they're concerned."

"I will."

"I miss you, Sav," she said hopefully.

"I miss you, too."

Chi Chi wondered how much. "I've got news," she said softly.

"Let me guess. You bought some more of that General Electric stock?"

"I'm expecting again."

Whatever Tony thought she was going to say, it wasn't that. "Are you sure?"

"I went to the doctor today, and yes, it's for sure."

Tony laughed. "I should've left a bigger tip at the Waldorf."

"Are you happy?"

"Thrilled. If you want a hundred babies, I'd be happy a hundred times over."

"Sav, I can't take being apart anymore. With a baby on the way, well—I can't do this alone any longer."

"It's hard for me, too."

"I know. You're missing too much."

"With all that's happening with television and the movies, I think we should move you all out here to California."

"Oh, Sav."

"It won't be forever. And you like California. Remember? This is where our story began."

"I do love the sun."

"So, should I look for a house?"

"I suppose so."

A few minutes later, they hung up. Chi Chi stared at the phone. She had a funny feeling. More and more, she found herself agreeing with everything her husband wanted to do to avoid an argument. Discussions, it seemed, were not about sharing points of view but listening to Tony and doing his bidding. Maybe she was wise to avoid conflict because he needed a place in his life where he was loved and supported without criticism. Or perhaps she was holding on to what they had together because she knew that if she let go, even for a moment, the life she had built for their family would float away, out of her grasp forever, like the kites her girls flew at the shore. That's how she saw her marriage of late. It had become a flimsy harlequin diamond of rice paper held aloft by a wily wind and tethered to the ground by her will and a tenuous grip on a thin string that would not hold, no matter how tightly she held on.

10

THE CALIFORNIA YEARS

Pizzicato

(Pluck the strings)

Tony turned into the circular driveway of 1001 Hummingbird Lane in Toluca Lake, and parked at the entrance of the inviting Georgian-style home.

"What do you think, girls?" Tony turned the car off. "That includes you, Mama."

"It's a knockout." Chi Chi lifted her sunglasses to take in the new home. It was painted a soft white, a lovely contrast against the licorice shutters and the blue sky.

"It's all yours. You're not the only one in this family who knows a prime real estate deal."

"Never said I was the only one, Sav." Chi Chi opened the front door of the car and swung her legs out. She looked down at her feet. "My feet look like I bought new shoes and forgot to take them out of the boxes. I'm wearing the boxes." She shook her head in disbelief. She had put on more weight with this pregnancy than she had with the twins, and she was only in the second trimester.

Sunny piggybacked on her father while Rosie took a ride on his hip as they walked to the front door. He threw it open and dropped the girls in the foyer.

"Does it have a swimming pool?" Sunny wanted to know.

"Monique Gibson said every house in California has a swimming pool."

"You'll have to go and see." Tony pointed to the back of the house.

The girls scampered off.

"Be careful!" he shouted.

Chi Chi walked in behind him and turned around, spellbound. There was a double-sided staircase to the second floor, a full living room to the left, and a full music room to the right, both with walls of windows with a view of nothing but green. Light danced on the highly polished, knotty pine floors.

"What do you think, hon?"

"It's a beauty." She kissed her husband. "We'd better follow the monsters."

Chi Chi and Tony walked through the house to the bright, sunlit kitchen, done in tasteful black and white, through the door to the patio. The trellis walls of the veranda were drenched in hot yellow, pink, and purple bougainvillea in full bloom. In the center of the patio was a two-tiered fountain of three hand-carved cherubs holding urns that poured water into the basin.

"Is this what Italy looks like?" Chi Chi asked.

"It does. But this is all yours."

Beyond the patio was a swimming pool shaped like a lake hemmed by artful natural rock formations. The girls were already climbing on them. A series of fully grown palm trees swayed along the property line.

"A genuine oasis, don't you think? You won't miss the winter." Tony put his arms around Chi Chi. "How did I do?"

"We can make a home here."

"That's all that matters. I want my girls to be happy."

Chi Chi watched Rosie and Sunny scoot down the rocks and run to the lawn. The scent of lemons filled the air. There were lemons trees growing tall in terra-cotta pots under the grape arbor. She plucked a ripe lemon off of a tree. "I think I'm going to love California."

Chi Chi hung the last ornaments on the Christmas tree in the den of the Toluca Lake house. The miniature baby grand piano ornament had glitter on the keys, a gift from her mother when Chi Chi was a girl. She turned the room lights off and turned on the Christmas tree lit with red, blue, and green Roma lights. It was a beauty, a tall, fragrant blue spruce from Northern California, decorated with glass ornaments from New Jersey and festooned with strands of silver tinsel. The lights and the colors reminded her of Christmas back home in Sea Isle.

Chi Chi was homesick; she missed her sisters and mother. She remembered the mill. When a girl on the line was expecting, the women rallied around her with advice and support. She was certain her pregnancy was fueling her longing for home. She consoled herself with the knowledge that she would soon be too busy to be blue.

In a few weeks, the baby would arrive. The idea of having it alone, without Tony there, made her anxious. He had been cast in a film and had spent the last few months on location in Nevada. He had not seen the Toluca Lake house with furniture, rugs, or the draperies hung. She had sewn the kitchen curtains herself. Chi Chi had kept busy with the girls and her chores, but the ache of her loneliness for her husband and the life she used to know only became worse as the holidays approached. She felt uncertain about the future, stuck in time, as if she were underwater, in a vast ocean, near enough to the surface to see daylight but tangled in a morass of seaweed, unable to break loose and swim for the shore.

The key turned in the lock of the front door. Tony pushed through, carrying Christmas gifts tied with ribbons. He wore an Italian-cut suit in navy silk wool, a white shirt, and a sky blue necktie. His Borsalino tipped forward. He looked more handsome than he ever had before, like one of those suave movie stars in *Modern Screens*. Chi Chi burst into tears.

Tony went to her. "What's the matter, honey?"

"I missed you, that's all," she said as she hugged him.

"You need your family around you at Christmas. I bet you miss your sisters and your mother this time of year."

"I've never been away from them at Christmas. Even when I was with the band. I always found a way to get home."

"I remember a Christmas when you insisted that the bus drop you in Pittsburgh. We had just played the Jungle Inn in Youngstown. You were determined to catch a bus to the Port Authority, to get you home in time for midnight mass."

"And I made it. It was a miracle."

"Cheech, sometimes home has to come to you."

"Surprise!" The front door burst open. As if in a dream, but it surely wasn't, it was wonderfully real, Chi Chi's mother and sisters ran to her and embraced her. Charlie and Frank followed with the children, Nancy, Michael, and Chiara. When Rosie and Sunny heard the children, they ran down the steps to join their cousins. Tony scooped up the twins and kissed them.

"Maybe we shouldn't have surprised a lady who's expecting," Barbara joked, taking in the size of her sister.

Chi Chi looked at Tony, who gave her a wink. In that moment, all the months of loneliness were forgotten. She could see that Tony missed their old life, too, and their family as much as she did. How did he know? Tony Arma always found a way to give her exactly what she needed.

"It's almost Tony time!" Lucille shouted from the living room. "Steve Allen says he's up next!"

Chi Chi, Barbara, and Isotta joined the family in the living room.

"There is Daddy!" Sunny exclaimed as the studio audience applauded as the *Tonight Show* band played her father onto the stage to take the center microphone.

Barbara squinted at the television set. "What's in his hair?"

"Pomade," Sunny replied. "They like it poofy on the television set."

Tony sang:

> Love me, he said
> Love me, she said
> Love, they agreed, is the reason they wed
> But does love pay the bills?
> Does it butter the bread?
> Does love stop the fear
> That fills you with dread?
> When he doesn't come home and you're alone in your bed

She's true through and through
Better not to wed unless he's true too
And if you got that, the world is yours
Your heart will be safe, your soul it soars
And everything else is
Gravy, Gravy, Gravy
Gravy, Gravy, Gravy

Barbara cleared the dishes, Lucille washed them, and their mother dried them. Chi Chi sat with her swollen feet propped on the kitchen stool. "I bet if we add up all the time we spend setting tables, clearing, and washing dishes," she said, "it would come to half our natural lifetimes."

"What else do we have to do, ladies?" Isotta said cheerfully. "Our family needs to eat. The table is the center of the home, and that means cooking, cleaning up, and dishes to do."

"Three meals a day until we're dead," Lucille sighed.

"A career in suds," Barbara joked.

"I like to think I have a career in songwriting," Chi Chi said wistfully.

"You do!" Barbara placed a stack of dessert plates on the counter. "Or you did and you will again."

"That gravy song is a hit," Lucille said as she ran more hot water into the sink.

"Number ninety-six on *Billboard*," Chi Chi said proudly. "It will go up after the *Allen Show*."

"Is Saverio home much?" Barbara asked.

"Not really."

"That's rough," Lucille commented. "Have you made any friends out here?"

"There hasn't been time."

Barbara sat with Chi Chi at the table. "Tony's going to be on the road all the time, why not move back home and live in New Jersey, near us?"

"When he got the movie contract, he didn't think he'd be on location so much. He figured he'd be working at the studios in town and be home at night for dinner. As these things go, it hasn't worked out that way. It's like when he's on the road, except he's off in one place instead of one town a night. Truthfully, not much has changed, except that we moved out here."

"We're worried about you. You're out here alone. And for what? You used to have a career, too. That was your song tonight on national television. Steve Allen could've said something."

"I thought so, too," Lucille admitted. "I didn't want to say anything, but Tony could have said you wrote it. You never get any credit."

Chi Chi did not want to argue with her sisters. "Let's go outside," she said. "Perpetually I'm overheated like Cousin Joozy's Cadillac."

The Donatelli women joined their husbands outside on the veranda.

"This is living, Lucille," Frank said, as he puffed on a cigar.

"Don't get used to it, Mr. Fancy. When we get home, you have snow to shovel."

The phone tucked under the veranda rang, and Chi Chi answered it.

"Look at that," Charlie marveled. "They have a telephone outside."

Tony laughed. "Because it doesn't rain. I could even leave you outside all night, and you'd be fine."

"Hon, it's your mother," Chi Chi said quietly.

Tony took the phone and had a conversation with his mother

as his in-laws relaxed by the pool. Chi Chi poured nightcaps for the family as Tony joined them.

"Is everything all right?" Chi Chi asked.

"My mother wishes you all a Merry Christmas," Tony said.

"Merry Christmas, Detroit!" Charlie toasted the Armandonadas.

Chi Chi crawled into bed next to her husband. He lay on his back, his eyes wide open.

"What did your mother say?"

"My father is very sick. It's bad, and I need to go home. Or I won't see him again."

"Oh, Sav."

"I want you to go with me."

Chi Chi looked down at her stomach. "Look at me. I can't travel. I could go after the baby is born. You go. It will be fine."

"It will be too late."

"Then you have to go alone. You can do it. You can face him."

Tony rolled over to sleep. Chi Chi lay awake, imagining a satisfying visit for Saverio and Leone. They would mend their broken relationship. Leone would tell his son he was proud of him. Their long feud would end in peace, a graceful ending to a long war.

When Tony Arma got off the airplane at the Detroit International Airport, he felt ill. He had not returned to his childhood home since he left it, as Saverio Armandonada. He had not seen his father since Christmas Eve 1932, though when he called his mother and Leone picked up the phone, his father had inquired about his son's health. There had been signs of a change of heart on Leone's part over the years.

Lee Bowman had arranged for a car service to take him from the airport to his parents' home and back to the airport again in time to get him on a plane to New York for a television appearance. *Gravy* was on a slow and steady burn up the charts so the record label insisted he feed the sales with appearances on television and concert performances.

"Mama." Tony embraced his mother on the porch. Rosaria was exhausted. It could not be easy to care for a stubborn man who had never taken a sick day in his life. Tony looked around. The exterior could have used a fresh coat of paint, the only sign to the outside world that indicated Leone Armandonada was ill. Little else had changed.

As Rosaria invited him inside, Tony stepped through the front door and closed his eyes. The scent of the fragrant gravy on the stove simmering with bundles of *Bracciole* rolled with basil in a sauce of crushed tomatoes, sweet butter, and garlic brought him back to his childhood.

Leone sat in a chair in the living room, his legs wrapped tightly in a blanket. Tony was struck by how thin his father had become, and how, like his mother, he had aged. This indicated something about his own life, and the passage of time, but for now, he felt nostalgic for all they had lost and what might have been had they been able to heal their feud.

"I will be in the kitchen," Rosaria said as she went.

"Papa." Tony extended his hand. "How are you feeling?"

Leone took his son's hand. His father's grip, once so solid, was weak. Empathy for his father's situation surged through Tony, for the loss of Leone's good health and vigor. Illness had taken away his father's best attributes, while time had diminished his strength. Where was the man who could lift his grown son with one arm off a platform onto a flatbed truck, as though he were as light as a sack of zeppole? He was dying, the wayward son observed.

Tony sat down next to his father. "Mama says you haven't been well."

"I'm sick." Leone's voice was hoarse. Gone, too, was the deep voice that could instruct a team in the glassworks at the Rouge plant or destroy his son's enthusiasm.

Tony looked at his father's hands. They seemed small now. "What does the doctor say?"

"Cancer."

"I'm sorry."

Leone looked away. "Why did you come?"

"Mama asked me. And I wanted to come."

Leone cocked an eyebrow and looked at his son, taking him in from his alligator shoes to the top of his head. He squinted at Tony's full head of hair but said nothing. His mother joined them.

"Papa, I think we should be kind to one another. It's time."

"You do not honor your father."

"Come on, Pop," Tony said gently.

"Why do you disrespect me and change your name?"

"That's show business. It's just a stage name."

"Frank Sinatra didn't change his name. He does not hide behind another man's name."

"Okay." Tony shook his head. He looked at his mother.

"And I don't like what I read. You run around with women. You have nice wife and children, and you run around."

"Don't believe . . ." Tony began.

"It's in the papers. They say you chase women. Starlings."

"Starlets," Tony corrected him.

"You're a married man. You don't belong in the nightclub."

"I work in nightclubs, Pop."

"You stay in your house and take care of your wife and children."

"I take care of my family."

"There is more to being a man than paying the bills. You live one life in music halls and another life at home. It will catch up with you. You can't have everything, Saverio. You can't have the girlfriend and the wife because one of them will demand fidelity. That's when you have a problem. You may have a problem now for all I know. I did not raise my son to be an infidel. You lie to your wife with your body. That's no good." Leone pointed at his son. "You're no damned good."

Tony had heard enough. He could have fought back, but as it had been before he left home, he was not a worthy or equal adversary for Leone. His father had the Ten Commandments on his side. Besides, the son did not possess his father's judgmental nature, and therefore was incapable of a strong defense. "Okay, Pop. I should go."

He motioned for his mother to join him in the kitchen. "It was a mistake to come. I upset him."

"He'll be happy you came."

"I can't take it. He hasn't changed."

"Your father is a complicated man. You're young. You can bend."

"How about I don't want to? How about I want a father who loves me the way I am and not the way he wants me to be? You know, Ma, you made your choice, and you live with it. You shouldn't have to take care of him, but you do. You can always come and live with us. Chi Chi and I would love to have you."

"I can't leave him."

"I won't keep asking you to find the courage to stand up for yourself."

Tony Arma kissed his mother. "Are you going to say goodbye to him?"

Tony did not answer her. Instead, he left his family home through the kitchen door, taking the path on the side of the house to the street, like the man who puts the coal in the furnace, or the plumber who checks the pipes, or the neighborhood kid who waits for his tip after shoveling snow. Tony left his father's house for the last time.

"I called the hotel in Lake Tahoe to track Tony down to tell him about the new baby," Lee explained.

"Thanks." Chi Chi lay back on the pillow at Cedar Hospital in Los Angeles. Out the window of her sunlit room, the sky was filled with tufts of gray clouds, odd for the dry January days in California. It looked like rain.

"You know how you always say babies bring you luck?" Lee said into the phone.

Chi Chi held her son close. "Yes, they do."

"Well, *Gravy* is now number eleven on the *Billboard* charts. Congratulations, my friend! As soon as I reach Tony, I'll get him home to you."

Chi Chi's baby gripped her index finger tightly. This baby was so different from the twins, at least in his response to her emotions. While she was pregnant, if she was upset, he would gently kick her, as if to remind his mother that she was not alone. Now that he was out in the world, her son held on to her to let her know that he was aware that she needed him. Tony would be happy with the news, but it also meant he would feel the pressure to provide for the new addition. He would hit the circuit in earnest to make bank while he could.

After she put down the phone, Chi Chi looked down at the baby in her arms. "You have a big job, little one. You have to bring us together. Are you up for it?" Chi Chi looked down at her infant son, a pink bundle in a powder-blue blanket. He was his father in every way: the full lips, black eyelashes, and curly hair. "Maybe your curls will stay. No Samson's of Fifth Avenue for you."

Without opening his eyes, the infant reached his hand out of the bunting, opened his fist, and wiggled his five fingers, just as a pianist stretches his hands before playing. "So that's why you're here. You're going to make music. All right, little man, Mama will teach you everything you need to know."

Chi Chi tucked her newborn baby's hand under the blanket. Her son was safe, warm, and loved, the three essential gifts a mother bestows upon her child at birth, and vows to provide the rest of his life, no matter the sacrifice.

Chi Chi took it upon herself to bestow a fourth gift on that January day, without consulting her husband. The hospital would not wait, and besides, the new mother wanted to surprise her husband. Chi Chi named their son Leone Mariano Armandonada in the Italian tradition, the firstborn son named for the paternal grandfather of the baby. Chi Chi was certain that Leone completed their family. His middle name would be the only chance she would have to honor her father's memory.

Chi Chi had also considered naming their son Saverio, but she guessed her husband wouldn't have liked the idea. They had attempted to discuss names for a baby boy several times, but he was always pulled away by work, obligations—so she wasn't sure where he stood on the matter. He liked the name Cheryl for a girl, but feminine names did not matter now. Tony had been on the road for so much of this pregnancy, she had no idea what he was thinking.

Success should bring gratitude and humility, but in the Arma household, it instilled a panic to hold on to it. Tony accepted every club date offered to him and every movie role. He sent Chi Chi the scripts in advance but no longer took her advice about the quality of the screenwriting to heart. She worried that he was too eager to be a movie star and less committed to being a good actor.

Chi Chi hoped the new baby would change things. What man doesn't want a son? Leone Mariano Arma could be the catalyst to reunite them as a family and bring Tony home to her for good.

Chi Chi rolled over in bed and looked at the clock. It was three o'clock in the morning and time to feed the baby. She threw her legs over the side of the bed, slipped into her house shoes, stood up, and headed down the hall to the nursery.

She stopped in the doorway when she saw Tony holding their baby, kissing him. The infant cooed blissfully in the arms of his father. Chi Chi was elated. The sight of her husband, so long on the road, made her feel complete.

Chi Chi put her arms around her husband and son. Tony placed the baby gently back in the crib before turning and kissing his wife, holding her in his arms for a long time. She relaxed there, allowing him to hold her up.

"You gave me a son, Cheech."

"Are you crying, Sav?"

"It's a dream for a man, you know."

"He's a good baby. Of course he is. He looks just like you."

"You think so?"

"From the moment that cranky doctor put him in my arms."

"How are the girls?"

"Bossy. They love having a new baby in the house."

"I'll have to come home and make sure they don't henpeck my boy."

"Would you?"

Chi Chi took Tony's hand as they walked across the hall to the twins' room. Sunny and Rosie had bunk beds, but the pair was curled up together in the bottom bunk with every stuffed animal they owned. Tony shook his head. He knelt down and kissed each of his daughters before following Chi Chi downstairs to the kitchen.

While Chi Chi warmed a bottle for the baby, she made her husband a sandwich.

"So, what are we going to name the baby?" he said. "I like something simple. Like Nick. Nick is a good, strong name."

"I didn't name him Nick, honey," Chi Chi said softly. She usually tried to defer to his wishes as the head of the household, in the manner she was raised, but in this instance, she could not go along with naming their son after no one in particular. There was tradition to think about after all.

"What did you name him?" he asked casually.

"I wanted to wait. I tried. Lee tried to reach you. And I wasn't sure when you were coming home, and they wouldn't let me leave the hospital until I named him," she explained.

"Okay, so what name did you pick?"

"Leone Mariano Arma."

"We're not naming this kid after my father."

"But, Sav—"

"No, absolutely not. He doesn't talk to me. I don't need a constant reminder of him anywhere in this house, in my life."

"Constant reminder? You're never here!"

Tony looked around the kitchen as if there were an audience watching him argue with his wife. "I knew this would happen. You would go to Detroit and visit them and get chummy, and he'd turn you against me."

"I am not some dope who can be turned. I have my own ideas about things. About people."

"Well, so do I," Tony said. "And you're going to change my son's name."

Tony's self-importance angered Chi Chi. "I am not."

"You will change it. Or I will."

"Our son will be named for his grandfathers. That's it."

"I want him to have a name that is all his own. That belongs to him and only to him."

"You know what? I'd almost let you name that kid Nick if I thought for one second you'd be around long enough to call him by it. But you won't be. And you know what else? I want to do this for your mother and father. They deserve respect."

"Not after what my father did to me."

"Forgive him already, Sav."

"You don't understand this. You have a block about it. Well, get ready, Cheech, because I have a block about that name. It will not stand."

"I can't believe that you, an Italian man, would fight me on this," Chi Chi said. "This is tradition. This is who we are."

"It's who *you* are. I don't claim him anymore. And if you respected me in my own home, you would never have gone against my wishes and named my son after him."

Tony shoved the plate with the sandwich away, got up, and left the kitchen. Chi Chi threw the sandwich in the sink and grabbed the bottle. She climbed the stairs. She went into the master bedroom to confront Tony, but he was not there.

In the nursery, Leone was fast asleep. She placed the bottle on the nightstand before going back down the hallway and opening the door of the guest room. She found Tony in the bed.

"This is where you're sleeping?"

"Change his name, Chi Chi."

Chi Chi closed the door. She went back into the nursery, picked up her infant son, woke him gently, and fed him the bottle, as she had done every night when Tony wasn't there, and would continue to do when he left again. She sat in the rocker as Leone took his bottle. What a racket she ran. The few nights of the month that Tony was home, they tiptoed around so he might rest. She took care of the children. She took care of the house. She paid the bills. She did everything but sing and write songs, which she gave up so her husband might have *his* voice, *his* career, *his* life. Her hand began to shake as she held the bottle. This was not the life she had planned, nor was it the one she had signed on for when she married Tony Arma. Something had to change. As she placed Leone back in the crib, she had a chilling thought. It was too late. While she had been busy hoping something would change, it already had.

The next morning Chi Chi woke to the scents of buttery pancakes and bacon filling the house. She stopped in the nursery to check on Leone, who was still asleep. She went downstairs and watched as Tony made breakfast for the twins, who were already dressed in their school uniforms. He flipped a pancake, and the girls squealed with laughter.

"You girls look nice," Chi Chi said.

"Daddy said not to wake you up," Sunny said.

"That was kind."

"You look tired, Mom." Rosie dumped maple syrup on her pancakes. Chi Chi looked down at her old bathrobe, and imagined how ratty her hair must look. Of course she was tired. Of course she looked awful. She was up at all hours of the night and had no time to rest during the day. She was certain the showgirls in Lake Tahoe didn't have dark circles under their eyes and bloat from childbirth. "What do you girls want for lunch?"

"Daddy made our lunches already." Rosie stood and grabbed her lunchbox.

"Let's go, girls, time for the bus," Tony said.

"Walk them down the driveway." Chi Chi kissed the girls.

"I know the drill." Tony ushered the girls out the door. Chi Chi chewed on a slice of bacon, looked out the window, and watched as the girls boarded the bus. The driver, middle-aged Dicie Sturgill, a woman with a tight perm and smile, flirted with Tony before closing the bus door. Even the school bus driver made a play for Tony Arma.

By the time Tony returned, Chi Chi was already doing the breakfast dishes.

"I can take care of that."

Chi Chi dropped the sponge into the sink. "Fine." She was walking out of the kitchen when Tony stopped her.

"I have to get the baby," she said.

"Name him whatever you want."

"How kind of you when I named him after your father."

The phone rang. Chi Chi reached for it. "Hello, Mama, yes, he's here."

She handed the phone to Tony. "It's your mother."

"*Ciao*, Mama . . . Yes . . . Yes. I'll be there." He hung up the phone.

"Everything all right?"

"My father died."

Tony sat down in a kitchen chair, stunned. Tony had the sad countenance of someone who is lost, not of a person who had lost someone.

"Let's go to Detroit," Chi Chi said.

"What about the kids?"

"We'll take them with us. Come upstairs. You rest. I'll pack." Chi Chi led her husband up the stairs and helped him back to bed. She walked down the hall to the nursery and lifted baby Leone out of his crib. She brought their son into the master bedroom and placed him next to her husband. Tony cradled the baby in their bed. "Leone," he said. After he said his son's name aloud, a tear fell, which Tony quickly wiped away.

Chi Chi and Tony slipped into their seats on the aisle in the auditorium of the Toluca Lake Elementary School. Rosie turned and waved to her parents from the sixth-grade section. Next to her, Sunny breathed a sigh of relief; she had been certain her parents would miss their baby brother's stage debut. The auditorium was standing room only, packed with the parents and siblings of the stars of the school talent show.

The red velvet curtain raised on the auditorium stage. A girl of six, with blond braids plaited tightly, stepped forward. "Ladies and gentlemen," she announced, "Leone Arma and his big brass band."

Leone, age five, wore a bow tie, white shirt, and navy pants. He tilted his bugle toward heaven, sounding out a perfect sliding scale that blew the clouds out of the sky. Sunny and Rosie rose from their seats, rooting for their brother. The audience applauded. Chi Chi grabbed Tony's arm.

"He's got the gift," Tony whispered proudly.

Chi Chi observed how Tony relished Leone in the spotlight. She leaned over and kissed her husband.

"What was that for?" Tony asked.

"I just love you. That's all."

Tony took her hand and kissed it. He held it tightly through the rest of the show. How funny, she thought. She had known Tony since she was young, married him, given him three children, and through all of it, she had never felt closer to him than she did in this moment.

Chi Chi sat with her feet in the swimming pool, reading the newspaper, when the phone rang.

"Cheech, I don't want to be the one to tell you this," Barbara began. "But you know Charlie stops at O'Hurley's on B Street for a beer on the way home? There's a fellow there who works as a reporter for the *Newark Star-Ledger.*"

"Yeah. So?" Chi Chi checked the clock. Her sister had gotten up in Jersey at dawn to call her. "Is this important, Barb?"

"Charlie said this reporter had one too many, and confided that it's going to hit the paper tomorrow. Tony is going to ask you for a divorce."

"It's a press stunt," Chi Chi assured her.

"I'm trying to help you save face."

"Is it my face you're worried about or your own? I'm okay. I'm in a good place."

"Don't be defensive. What good place? You walk around in a state of misery. Tony's never home. You're carrying the load. Don't you see what's happening? You've given Tony a life where he does whatever he wants. No one holds him accountable. He has permission to wander the world like a bachelor, while you're home taking care of business and taking care of the family. It's wrong. Where is Lee Bowman on all of this?"

"Lee sees what is going on."

"What is she doing about it?"

"She's his agent, not his priest."

"Isn't she your agent too? Who is taking care of you and your interests?" Barbara wanted to know.

It was true, Lee had been *their* agent; they'd signed on for her to represent them together as a duo. But as the children needed her more, the team got less of her attention, and Tony received

more. It was all about Tony Arma, the singer, actor, and entertainer. *Tony and Chi Chi* was no longer the name of their act, but
a phrase embossed in gold on their Christmas cards.

"He needs to see a priest," Barbara continued. "Tony is terribly
misguided when it comes to your welfare and what you need."

"And what is it that I need, exactly?"

"Fidelity, for starters."

"Who doesn't?" Chi Chi said without irony.

"You have children. Think of them! They see what goes on. They
hear every phone conversation. The kids at school fill in whatever blanks you don't. And they don't like what they're finding out
about their parents. It's hurting them."

"According to you, we had a weak father, and we turned out all
right. So they will too."

"Our dad was not practical, but his hobby wasn't women."

"I can't keep the ladies away from my husband. It's part of the
job. He's charismatic. He sings like a dream. And every day, all
day, he is surrounded by beautiful women. When I was young,
the women that went after him were older and experienced and
sophisticated, and now that I'm older, they're young and fresh and
willing, and they're still going after him. There's not a lot I can do
about it."

"Tony could fix it."

"I married a singer who has to sell records."

"He doesn't have to sell out his wife in the process. He forgets
you every time he takes a role in one of those B movies or goes on
the road."

"Barbara, you are not helping me. I know all about life on the
road. It is not what you think. It's hard. And it's lonely."

"Why are you defending him, when he's making a fool of you?"

"Is he? Or is he making a fool of you and Lucille and anyone
else who is related to me, because we don't live a life you can un-

derstand? Are you really worried about me, or are you worried about you and how this reflects on your image and the sanctity of whatever you hold precious? Do you look stupid once removed because you're the sister of Tony Arma's wife, who hasn't got a clue?"

"I'm worried about you." Barbara became emotional. "I've worried about you all of your life. You don't think things through. You just barrel into things willy-nilly and hope for the best. Whatever you're thinking now, think twice!"

"What is it about me that needs protection? I do all right."

"I guess I have it all wrong."

"It's not about being wrong or right. It can't be. It's about coping. I will handle this distasteful situation with my husband my way. I will handle my children. I ask that you proceed as normally as you would if you didn't know my husband was cavorting with a firecracker out of East Chicago, Indiana, on a Saturday night after two shows and three whiskeys. If he is going to divorce me, I'll handle it."

"Do you want to know her name?"

"Barbara, I'll see you at the shore after we do the *Sullivan Show*. Goodbye."

Chi Chi hung up the phone.

She didn't need Barbara or anyone else to share the name of her husband's lover. She knew plenty about Tammy Twiford, the sexy siren with the contralto voice. The chanteuse and dancer had set her cap for Tony Arma, and the gossip was, she had hooked him. Chi Chi knew all about the affair: when they first met, hotel rooms where they continued to meet, and the gifts he gave her to keep it going, including a pair of sapphire and diamond drop earrings, which would look fetching with her auburn hair. Always the auburn hair, what was it with the auburn hair? Tony was a slave to it!

It was time to talk to her husband. If the story had gotten as far as Barbara and as deep as Walter Winchell's column, there was no getting past it. She could not hope it would eventually burn out like a candle at the shrine of Saint Teresa, where she stopped to light one, inside the Church of Perpetual Help, whenever she felt most deeply in despair.

Miss Twiford's perfume was the type that lingered: expensive, alluring, and French, the three ingredients that built the grenade to trigger Tony Arma's midlife crisis—and designed, once it detonated, to blow up everything he had worked for, everything he and Chi Chi had built.

Chi Chi had called the movers in Toluca Lake before she had confirmed the rumors about Tammy Twiford. Her plan was to let Tony know that she was moving the children back home to New Jersey because she needed the family around her again. It was not good for the children to be away from their grandmother, aunts, uncles, and cousins. Besides, as they were getting bigger, Chi Chi was finding time to write songs again. She missed her creative life, and for her, that meant New York City, and all it had to offer.

Chi Chi had enjoyed the California house, and there was nothing wrong with the weather, but no matter how hard she tried, it never really felt like home. Tony had moved the family out west so they could be together as he worked in the movies. It was a wonderful idea that had never come to fruition. Tony's roles were taking him away on location for longer periods of time. Tony and Chi Chi might go weeks without having any substantial conversations with one another, if he was on location in a remote venue. As time went by, it pained her to see what he was missing at home, but it hurt her more to know what her children were missing. This was not a life, it was a holding pattern. Chi Chi had demonstrated guts when she was a girl, but she would need to search deep within herself to find them now. She felt she had no choice. She had a family to support, and things had to change.

After Chi Chi dropped the children off at school, she returned home and paced in the Toluca Lake kitchen, waiting until the East Coast offices returned from lunch so she could make her calls. Her first was to Lee Bowman, the woman who made their work lives possible.

"I need a job, Lee."

"There's a variety show out there that's looking for a writer. I could get you in for a meeting. They hired a girl writer on the last show, so they may again. They're looking for someone young, but you're so talented, I think we can fudge on the age issue."

"I'm forty years old, Lee. I'm a mother and a wife. I can't hide the facts. I'd like to get an office job. Something with regular hours."

"Are you and Tony moving back east?"

"I'm moving back east with the children." Chi Chi's voice broke. "I don't know about Tony."

"I'm sorry."

"You had to know."

"I thought he'd straighten up," Lee said softly.

"Maybe he will. In the meantime, I've got to think about the kids. I need to be close to my mother and my sisters."

"Got it. Cheech, I was going to talk to you about this." Lee lowered her voice. "I'm going to leave the agency and open up my own management firm. Put out my own shingle. I want to be my own boss. I want to work in a boutique instead of a conglomerate. I want to sign and manage my own client lists. Very select list. The Ray Coniff Singers almost put me in the hospital."

"I know. How can I help you?"

"I'm not sure yet. Let me think about it."

"Lee, I'm serious about this. I'm going to keep the apartment at the Melody for now. I mean, I have a place. And I could do lots of things. I could help in the studio when your clients make records."

"I have a couple of orchestras on my roster. A few solo acts. And I have Tony. Do you want me to drop him as a client?"

"Oh heavens, no."

"You're still loyal to him?"

"He's the father of my children. And the truth is, if you're managing him, at least I can keep tight control on the business. He's a disaster with all that. And if he leaves me and marries her—" Saying it out loud to Lee made it a real possibility to Chi Chi, which galvanized her to face the crisis head-on. "I have to be smart about this."

"I understand. I've always liked this about you, Chi Chi. You're an artist, but you're practical. Tony may be an idiot when it comes to women, but you will be tied to him financially for the rest of your life. You cannot afford to fall apart."

"I won't. And, I can't let the kids see anything but my affection for him."

"Let's meet when you return. Let me know how I can help the move."

"I will."

"You're going be all right, Chi Chi. I'm sure of that. I knew that the day I saw you shake that jar of jelly beans."

11

1957–1965

Teneramente

(Tenderly)

Snow fell in dizzy silver pinwheels over New York City on the Sunday before Christmas. Lee Bowman hustled Tony and Chi Chi through the crowds, out of the cold, and into the wings of the Ed Sullivan Theater in time for the run-through before the live broadcast of the 1957 holiday show on national television.

The Tony Arma Orchestra had come off the road after a long tour in the west, culminating with a month-long stint in Las Vegas. Chi Chi was looking forward to having her husband home for the holidays. She planned to talk to him about their future together, her prospects, and the children. But, as usual, show business came first, and Tony Arma had to take advantage of a lucky break.

The stage door of the theater was propped open, blowing gusts of cold wind into the hot studio. The air was filled with cigarette smoke, the scent of fresh coffee, and the scent of VapoRub. The roster of talent that would be featured on the *Sullivan Show* that night waited in the wings, warming up, making adjustments, and applying their makeup before the rehearsal. The acts went in order of appearance: singers, jugglers, dancers, comedians, and musicians vied for a moment with the maestro, Ed Sullivan, who stage-managed the show expertly, moving acts through like passengers through a turnstile in a train station during rush hour. He was the conductor, stone-faced but energetic and firm, driving the machine.

Onstage, the crew rolled in holiday set pieces, hoisting artificial Christmas trees flocked with snow. Stage flats painted with scenes of the North Pole flew in from the rafters. The lighting crew focused beams of gold, pink, and white light on the talent as the cameras rolled into their rehearsal positions on the stage floor.

Tony, Lee, and Chi Chi maneuvered through the talent backstage. The young, strapping men of the University of Notre Dame Glee Club, wearing black cutaway tuxedos, reeked of Vitalis, and stood calmly against the wall vocalizing. Nearby, the plate spinners from the Austrian National Circus balanced china dishes on long sticks, while their gymnasts flipped like human dolphins, their jugglers spinning bowling pins in midair. Through the stage curtain in the wings, Tony watched Bobby Darin and his band rehearse centerstage, oblivious to the frenzy around them.

"He's so smooth," Tony said with awe.

"We'll take Mr. Arma from here," the stage manager said. "Do you have charts?"

Chi Chi handed him the sheet music.

"Good luck, Sav." Chi Chi gave her husband a quick kiss.

"This is a miracle," Lee said as she watched Tony and the stage manager go behind the curtain. "Tony's finally on *Sullivan*. I've been trying to get him on this show forever."

"Where can we watch?" Chi Chi asked.

"I'll check. Wait here."

Tammy Twiford, a twenty-four-year-old beauty of the classic midwestern variety—small turned-up nose, light brown eyes, and hair the color of ripe cherries—walked by in a hot pink chiffon evening gown drizzled in dangling crystals. Chi Chi felt sandbagged, but she also knew that Tammy had joined the Tony Arma Orchestra as the lead girl singer before Vegas, and while he had not mentioned she would appear on the television show with him, Chi Chi should have realized it was a possibility. She took a good look at her rival, seizing the opportunity to study her up close. Chi Chi shoved her hands into the pockets of her black-velvet dress coat, which she wore with a matching headband anchored with a brooch, a spray of amethysts Tony had given her for Mother's Day. Chi Chi felt confident. "Miss Twiford?"

"Yes?"

"I'm Tony's wife. I understand you've been touring with the band. Are you doing the southern leg this winter?"

A look of panic crossed the young woman's face. "I'm excited about it."

"Excited about the work, or excited about my husband?"

Tammy Twiford might have been fifteen years younger than Chi Chi, but she wasn't lacking in experience or cunning. "Is there a wrong answer?" she said tersely.

"Of course there is, Tammy. Don't be silly. What's going on here?"

"Ask your husband."

"What exactly shall I ask him?"

Tammy shrugged.

"I see." Chi Chi took a deep breath. "It's been going on that long, has it?"

"Over a year," Tammy said.

Barbara had sent Chi Chi plenty of articles about Tony and Tammy she had torn out of the magazines found in beauty parlors, doctors' offices, and other places where women had long waits. There had been mentions of Tony and Tammy at the tables of Hollywood producers, or out on the town in a nightclub in Vegas, or on the road in cities like Chicago in swank places like the Drake Hotel. Chi Chi had tormented herself enough with the facts. She had confronted her husband, who made the believable argument that it was all business, and that Chi Chi, above all women, should understand. But Tony wasn't a woman; he didn't understand the feelings involved; he probably didn't understand Tammy. But Chi Chi did. She understood her all the way back to Gladys Overby.

"Are you in love with him?" Chi Chi wanted to know.

"Yes."

"Well, Tammy, we will have to figure something out, won't we?"

"What do you mean?"

"This can't go on."

Tammy pursed her lips. "No, it shouldn't. Not this way."

"Do you think you could give him up?"

Tammy looked down at her gloved hands. "Why should I?"

"He's married."

"But you've had him long enough," Tammy said bluntly.

"This isn't a ride at Coney Island. Everybody doesn't get a turn just because they want one."

"It's not like that. He loves me."

"What would you know about that?"

"Plenty."

"Listen to me. Tony and I, we have built a life. We have a family together. Three children. Here's an idea. Be an original, create your own life with your own man. Go and find a nice fella and work hard and put in the time, the years, and create your own home and children instead of destroying mine."

Chi Chi must have raised her voice, because Tammy turned on her heel and walked away, throwing her pink-gloved hands in the air. Tony came through the curtain from the stage. He stopped to talk to Tammy, who was suddenly in tears, before she stormed off to the dressing room.

"What did you do?" Tony walked over to Chi Chi.

"What did I do?"

She paused for a moment, looked closely at her husband, and saw something new. The young man she had fallen in love with was now a middle-aged father of three, only he didn't know it. Chi Chi had made it possible for him to remain young and pursue his career as though nothing had changed since the days at the Cronecker Hotel. Why should anything have changed when she made sure it wouldn't? She had thought about her role in his infidelity, but facing her rival that night made her less conciliatory. She no longer felt responsible for his actions or apologetic for his sins. She had kept their home, children, and accounts in fine fashion. It was she who had sacrificed everything for him. Why should she accept his lack of discipline and his weakness for women? This, she believed, was not her problem.

"You know what, Tony? You can go straight to hell."

Lee joined them, having missed Tammy and the argument. "Chi Chi, let's go." She waved the blue tickets. "I got front-row seats."

"If it's not a seat on the train home to Sea Isle, I'm not interested." Chi Chi turned and headed to the stage door. As soon as she made it outside into the cold and blended into the crowd of holiday shoppers on Broadway, she burst into tears.

Chi Chi sat on the porch of the Sea Isle house and inhaled the fresh air, pulling up the collar on her coat. She had arranged for Lucille to take the children for the day. When Tony pulled up in front of the house and parked, Chi Chi studied him as he came up the walk. He wore a fedora, a wool coat, and around his neck he had looped a silk scarf she had never seen before. A gift from Tammy, Chi Chi assumed.

"We could've met in the city at the apartment," Tony said.

"I don't think so."

"Obviously." He removed his sunglasses, folded them into the breast pocket of the coat. "Aren't you going to invite me in?"

"I need air."

He tapped the coat pockets for his pack of cigarettes and matches. When he found them, he lit a cigarette. "You made a scene at the *Sullivan Show*."

"I apologize."

"What's going on with you, Cheech? You've turned into a hysteric. I mean, you patrol the backstage of the *Sullivan Show* and accuse my singer of an affair?"

"Oh, come on, Sav. You're involved with Tammy Twiford. She told me about it. Not that she needed to."

"And you believed her?"

"Why shouldn't I?"

"I don't want anything to mess up my home life."

"What home life? Oh, that's right. That fantasy you have about spaghetti and meatballs, mass and Sunday dinner, and singing Italian songs by the fire to the kids while you play on your mandolin? The only thing our kids know about a mandolin is that it's that instrument that sits in the closet, covered in dust. They don't know the stories of their grandparents in Detroit unless I share them, they don't visit them unless I take them. And as far as you're concerned, I have created the idea of you to them. I've made you a hero to your children because I know how important a father is in a family. And you can rest easy, because I always will. But I'm finished as your wife, Saverio. I'll give you a divorce."

"I don't want a divorce, Cheech. We're a family."

"That word had a lot of power when it meant something to you."

"It means everything to me. It always has."

"No, the children and I are a family. You're a satellite that circles around us. We want you home, but you've made a life without us. With another woman. You know, when you asked me to marry you, I told you that you liked too many girls, and you said they meant nothing to you. I thought, this is swell, I'm the special one. I was different. But I wasn't. I was just another girl in a long line of them."

"You were different. You *are* different. Why are you doing this to me?"

"I didn't do anything but try to hold us together."

"You didn't try hard enough. Why do you have to work with Lee? Why did you take a job?"

"Because in the event of a divorce, the money gets cut in half, and I can't count on you to put these kids through college. All three of them are smart. They all have potential."

"I'll uphold my responsibilities."

"Oh, Sav, but you don't. You're the prince you were the day I met you. You kept trading one girl to iron your shirts for another. I stuck it out because I love you and we're from the same tribe. But you need to be honest with yourself. We'd be sitting in the dark if it weren't for me."

"Go ahead, say everything cruel you can think of. Hand me my manhood in a sack."

"Keep it. You'll need it for the next Mrs. Arma."

"There will never be another Mrs. Arma. You're it for me. I have a hard time with things, you knew that."

"Really, Saverio? Are you going to drag out that old tale of woe? You're all bottled up inside? Your feelings overwhelm you? Your father threw you out at sixteen on a cold Christmas Eve, and that's why you chase women? I'm tired of the excuses. You're making choices every single time."

"The wrong ones," Tony admitted.

"And yet you persist. That makes you either an idiot or evil. You choose."

"You knew what you were getting into."

"Did I? Did I really know? I don't think so. If I'd have known where this was going, I wouldn't have gotten on the ride at all."

"You don't mean it," he said quietly.

Did she mean it? she wondered. Would she, given all she knew, choose Tony again? From the beginning of their friendship, she recognized the potential. Together they were a creative team, a force. She wrote, he rewrote, he sang, she sang, they entertained, it worked. They could communicate with one another and, in turn, read an audience with the same clarity. When the children arrived in their lives, it was not as simple as she stayed home and he went on the road; it was deeper than the obvious. He returned to the life he led before he met her, and she became a woman that she did not recognize. There was the chasm, and deep within it was her responsibility in this marriage. She gave up who she was, her creative self, her highest dreams, deepest desires, and purpose in order to love him. In exchange, he retreated to the past, before his dreams had come true, before he loved her.

"Cheech, do you mean it? Do you want me to go?"

"I don't believe in divorce, Savvy."

"Good Catholic girl."

"Who married a good Catholic boy. Or so I thought."

"Labels. Just labels." He put out his cigarette and lit another quickly.

"Labels don't matter when you don't follow the rules."

"I guess they don't."

"Why can't you be true?"

Tony shrugged. "If I could answer that—"

"You have to."

"I miss you."

"Come on."

"I can't be alone, Cheech."

"I know that," Chi Chi exhaled, "but this one matters to you, doesn't she?"

"Not like you. But if you cut me loose, I'll go to her."

"Are you serious?"

Tony nodded that he was.

"You'd leave us for her?"

"If you kicked me out for good. Yes, I would."

"So it's my decision?" Chi Chi held up her hands like the sculpture of the strong man who held the world.

He nodded that it was.

"You want me to make this decision too? You have some crust. Some genuine crust. You want me to hold us together, but in the event I don't want to, you expect me to be the one to end it too. You don't have the strength of purpose to quit this marriage and outright choose that girl over me and your children?"

"I don't. I can't."

"But you want me to do it? Even when every day on the road you choose her over me? When you buy her dinner after the show. When you take her back to your room afterwards. When you make a place for her on the bus next to you. When you buy her a mink coat. When you buy her jewelry. When you introduce her to the new players in the band as your girl when they all know you have a wife at home. When you let Walter Winchell run a byline that says you and the missus are through—that's choosing her over me and you know it. Every time you make her feel special, or you take her in, or you show her off, it's another hurt I have to haul around, and after all these years, I have train cars full of them."

Tony sat on the porch steps. Chi Chi stood and went to him.

"I'm not done. Now let me tell you how I choose you every day and why I stay. I consider your feelings. I am no saint but I honored the vows I made to you even when some nice-looking fellas looked my way. I take care of your children like the priceless jewels they are and I don't expect a thank-you for my efforts. You never have to worry about our kids because you know no harm will come to them in my care. Do you have any idea what a burden I have taken off of your shoulders? The ability to relieve another human being of worry and anxiety is the single greatest act of love one can do for another and I do it for you. I also make your life easier because I meet you on that bridge of understanding. I don't expect perfection, I just hope you'll try. I am grateful to you. You work hard and I know what it is because I was there with you, toe to toe, from the rehearsal hall to the stage, making the music. I know what it is to serve people as an entertainer, so I always gave you room to rest and recharge and recalibrate."

"You have been a good wife."

"Thank you."

"And I have not been a good husband."

"You're honest."

"But I love you."

"Love is an interesting thing, Sav. It doesn't fix anything and it can't make you do the right thing even when you want to. You have to choose love over everything else, and the person you love above all others. The girl you're with now? That one is just another step on that ladder to wherever it is you think you're going. You don't love her. You possess her. And like a Packard or alligator shoes or that Bulova watch with the diamond hand you covet, she'll become obsolete or she'll break down, wear out, bore you, or all of them at once. She just doesn't know it yet. Because right now, she's standing in Tony's light. And when you pay attention to a woman, it's like the moon and the sun conspired to bring day and night into the sky in a single moment and blind the stars. I know it because you made that happen for me. I was dazzled. I admit it. I believed nothing would or could ever end who we were and what we had. Boy," she whistled, "was I duped."

"You're angry at me and I understand why."

"Good."

"What's the verdict?"

Chi Chi tried not to laugh. A verdict implied this was a trial and that she was his judge. But if that were true, where was the jury, and why, in such an important moment, was she alone?

"I want you to go, Sav."

Tony put out his cigarette. "I don't want another man raising my children."

"That's not your decision, is it?"

He nodded that it wasn't.

"I will always respect the father of my children."

"And I will always love their mother."

Tony walked back to his car. The crunch of the sand underneath his feet reminded her of the day he first visited, but those old memories had become faded and frayed, like the sun-bleached awnings over the windows of their home by the shore. Chi Chi had told her husband one lie so many years ago. She believed she could handle whatever life would throw at them. She thought she was bigger than the hurt, the pain caused by his philandering, but over time, she realized that she was no match for it. She couldn't turn away from it, nor could she justify it, even when she understood its origins, which were also pain. So much had changed in their marriage, so much had transpired, that she wondered if there was love in her heart for him any longer. She wasn't sure, and for that reason, she knew it was time to end her marriage to Tony Arma.

Chi Chi pulled up to the curb in front of St. Joseph's School. She waved to Sister Elizabeth from the car as the children scooted out of the back seat with their lunchboxes.

"Do we have to go to Daddy's wedding?" Rosie asked.

"I don't think there will be a wedding," Chi Chi said. "They're eloping."

"Why is Daddy a cantelope?" Leone asked.

"Eloping, Leone," Sunny corrected him. "Listen with your giant ears."

"Tammy Twiford's a dumb name," Sunny said. "She sounds like a plastic doll in the bin at the Ben Franklin."

Because she is, Chi Chi thought. But she would never say a word against her children's father, and the new woman in his life. "Sunny, you are not to speak poorly of your father or his new wife, ever."

"I'm sorry," Sunny grumbled. "But it's still a stupid name."

"Don't test me, Sunny." Chi Chi got out of the car to kiss her children goodbye. "Daddy loves us. We are going to be just fine. Now go and have a good day at school."

Chi Chi waved to the nun and thought about running up the steps and explaining what was happening at home but she was pretty sure the Salesians read the *Star-Ledger*. In his favor, Tony had waited almost a year before he called his ex-wife to tell her he had decided to remarry, choosing the woman who had come between them.

Chi Chi had different plans for 1958. She had hoped to take the children to Detroit to visit their grandmother; instead they would meet their new stepmother on the road.

At least Tony had let the situation breathe with Tammy, like a cheap wine, so Chi Chi had time to prepare the children. She could not complain. Chi Chi pulled out of the school parking lot, promising herself she would visit Sister later with a full explanation. She was barely on the way to accepting this turn of events herself. How would she ever explain it to a nun?

Chi Chi stood on the sidewalk in front of St. Joseph's Church, holding her Brownie camera. "Okay, everybody squeeze in tight." She looked down at the lens and snapped as her niece Chiara's First Holy Communion veil fluttered in the breeze. The white eyelet dress had bell sleeves, and a wide white satin ribbon tied at the waist.

"Take another one," Lucille insisted. "Chiara's veil was all over the place."

"I've got it." Isotta adjusted her granddaughter's veil.

Chi Chi snapped another group picture before they dispersed.

Rosie and Sunny ran up to their mother. "Can we ride with Aunt Lucille to the party?"

"As long as you take your brother."

"Ma, he's an anchor," Sunny said grimly.

"No, he's your brother," Chi Chi corrected her. "And he looks up to you."

"He's obnoxious."

"You girls have each other. Imagine how he feels."

"You should've had a boy for him," Sunny said breezily before jumping into Lucille's car.

Chi Chi watched her son run up and down the church steps with his cousins.

"He's fine, Ma," Rosie observed. "I'll make sure he goes with us."

"Thanks, honey."

Chi Chi walked to her car, removing the bobby pin that held her lace mantilla to her head. She carefully folded the mantilla and was about to put it into her purse when she was interrupted.

"Hello, Chiara."

Chi Chi looked up. Jim LaMarca waited for her next to her car.

"Jim, how are you?" He looked sharp in a navy suit and white silk tie.

"I'm muddling along."

"I was so sorry to hear about your wife," Chi Chi said. "Mama told me, and I meant to write, but—"

"You've been going through your own sad time." Jim finished her sentence, but not her thought.

"Your situation is worse, Jim. Your wife was sick, and you took care of her."

"It was my honor to do so. She was a good one."

"So I understand. I am so sorry for your loss."

"How are you holding up?"

"Well, I moved back to the shore."

"I heard. I saw your sister Barbara at the K of C picnic."

"So you know all about it. The kids are doing okay. Tony is on the road. He comes to visit when he can. Day to day, my life hasn't changed much. I'm divorced, and I never thought that would happen. But here we are."

"I thought when I got through the war, that was it, I'd seen the worst," Jim said. "I figured the rest of life would be smooth sailing."

"You know what? I thought so too, Jim."

"What happened?"

"It's all out of our control. All of it."

"It doesn't have to be." Jim tipped his hat back off his forehead. "Old friendships matter. It's important to reconnect. I've been thinking about you."

Chi Chi looked up at him, shielding her eyes from the sun. Barbara and Lucille and every woman she knew thought Jim LaMarca was the best-looking guy to ever come out of Jersey. And after more than twenty years, it was still true. "I hope nice thoughts."

"Absolutely. I'd like to take you to dinner sometime."

Chi Chi closed her eyes for a few seconds, hoping when she opened them that it would be 1938 again, before she met Saverio, before the war, before she knew better. "Jim, thanks for the lovely invitation, but I'm not ready. I hope you understand."

Jim nodded. "I do. Should I hold out hope?" He smiled.

"You know, it's a funny thing about divorce. It's important to be truthful. After all we went through, I still love him." Chi Chi realized that she had nervously balled up the lace mantilla. "I'm sorry."

"You should never apologize for loving someone," Jim said. "It's what makes life worth living."

Chi Chi stood up on her toes and gave Jim LaMarca a kiss. She was reminded in one kiss of what might have been a different life for her, a better one, with a man who respected her, and loved her so much that no other woman who came across his path could turn his head. That was not what fate had provided, and now, it seemed almost silly to try again, to prove that what had not been could be.

Jim opened her car door and helped her inside, closing the door behind her. She watched him walk down the street, and for a moment she wondered if she had made the same mistake twice.

Lucille stood at the front window of Chi Chi's living room. "They're here."

"Let's all paste fake smiles on our faces," Barbara said.

Lucille kept her eyes peeled out the window. "Cheech, Tammy is wearing very tight clamdiggers and an even tighter blouse. Ugh. My God, woman. Go up a size, will ya?"

Chi Chi removed the Saran wrap off the sandwich platter. "The word of the day is tight, and I haven't had a drink yet."

"I can't believe you've invited her." Barbara stacked hot dog buns on a tray.

"I don't want to be that kind of ex-wife. And, I expect my sisters to be nice to her, too."

"I'll need a mug of Brioschi to pull that off," Lucille said. "Because frankly, I'd like to throw up."

"Hey. Not allowed! Class act. That's what we are. The Donatelli Sisters. Nothing short of perfection." Chi Chi lifted the platter to carry it to the backyard, and watched as her ex-husband and his new wife took the path down the side of the house. It was as if she were watching someone else's life happen outside her window.

"Let's go," Lucille said, lifting the platter of cold cuts. "I'm on my best behavior."

"Me, too." Barbara said.

"That leaves me," Chi Chi joked.

The summer of 1961 had been one of Chi Chi's best. The children were settled, her mother was in good health, and her sisters and their husbands and families were close. No arguments. Even the ex-husband front had been calm; Tammy Twiford was nice to the children, and on the road with Tony. The sky over Sea Isle Beach was sapphire-blue and the ocean was calm; the waves unfurled like a bolt of peacock-blue velvet.

Chi Chi stood at the bluff and watched Tony play with their son. Leone ran down the beach as Tony lobbed a football toward him, then ran it back to his father. When a group of Leone's friends charged over the bluff to join him, Leone took the ball and ran down the beach with his pals. He stopped and turned to his father.

"Thanks, Pop!" he hollered before running off.

Chi Chi shimmied down the bluff and walked across the beach to join Tony. Maybe it was the sand, or the sky, or the warmth of the sun, but whenever Chi Chi was on the beach with Tony, it didn't matter where in the world the ocean might be, somehow he still belonged to her. She would chase away the feelings, but somehow they would hover in the distance like the low clouds over the water.

Tony watched Chi Chi walk toward him on the beach. She was barefoot, as she was most of the summer. She wore a white sundress, and her hair was loose around her shoulders.

"I left your wife with my sisters."

"Will she make it out alive?" Tony joked.

"You never know."

"You look good, Cheech," Tony said sincerely.

"So how's it going? How's Tammy?"

"Expensive."

"I know, Savvy. I see the bills."

"Was it wise of me to let my ex-wife remain my business manager?"

"Yes," they said in unison, and laughed.

"That feels good," he said.

"To laugh?"

"To hear someone call me *Savvy*."

Chi Chi didn't know how to respond. The moment felt intimate, but how could it not be? They had known each other for most of their lives.

Tony looked down the beach. "Leone is doing all right, isn't he?"

"He has good friends. He's doing fine in school."

"I mean, without me around."

"He doesn't remember much," Chi Chi said. "Or he doesn't talk about it."

Tony looked hurt. "How about the girls?"

"Sunny is bitter, and Rosie is a saint."

"As it should be with twins." Tony moved some seaweed on the sand with the toe of his sneaker. "You seeing anybody?"

"Honestly, Saverio," Chi Chi said dismissively. "Let's get back to the house. I need help making the ice cream."

"I know I don't have any right."

"No, you don't. But the answer is, I'm not. I thought I might, and then I didn't."

"Anybody interesting?"

"I wish Leone had a brother. The twins have each other, and he's all alone."

"I was an only child, and I did okay."

Chi Chi turned and looked at her ex-husband in disbelief. "You have struggled every step of the way."

"So I struggle. That doesn't mean things didn't turn out all right. Our son will be fine, won't he?"

"I think so. You know, I thought Leone would fix our marriage," Chi Chi admitted. "But he's actually bigger than that. He's going to fix the world. He can talk to anybody. When a child cries on the playground, he's the first one on the scene to comfort him. I've never seen anything quite like him. He has a pure heart. But he's a boy, and he needs his father."

"I could take him," Tony offered. "I'm sure Tammy would agree."

"Your schedule is nuts. Maybe you could get down to see him more often?"

"Sure. Is Leone keeping up with his music?"

"I'm teaching him the piano, but he likes the drums. I bought earplugs for the girls and me."

"He still plays the trumpet?"

"Blows it like Gabriel. It's a noisy house."

"I miss the noise."

"Do you and Tammy have any plans for Christmas?"

"We'll be in Florida. I have a gig at the Fontainebleau."

"Nice. When are you planning on seeing the children?"

"Before I go. I thought we'd do Christmas a little early."

"When do you leave?"

"December first."

"That's not Christmas, Savvy, it's Thanksgiving."

Chi Chi could see that any discussion of a schedule perturbed him. "I can't do anything right," he said.

"Sure you could. You could tell the hotel you have three children you need to see during the holidays."

"I'm trying to make bank for the kids. You know that."

"I understand. But you know I do all right with the songs. And the investments. You don't have to drive yourself into the ground."

"You don't understand."

"What's the matter, Saverio?"

"I can't control Tammy. She spends every penny I make."

"That's the problem with wives—they are allowed to spend every penny you make. When you marry, the spouse becomes your blood relative."

"No kidding."

"That's the law."

"There won't be anything left for the kids."

Chi Chi understood. "Ah. Okay. Now it's my business."

"I want you to manage my money."

"Why would I do that?"

"Because you handled it when we were married, and you're

good at it. You can take a cut so our kids will be secure. And you can put the kid on a budget."

"By 'kid,' you mean Tammy."

"Of course."

"She told Dorothy Kilgallen you were planning to have a family."

"I can't control what she says to reporters. Besides, we can't have children. I mean, I can't."

"What do you mean, you can't? You have three children with me."

"After Leone, I had the procedure."

Chi Chi felt faint. She sat down in the sand. Tony sat down next to her. "What's the matter, Cheech?"

"Why did you do that?"

"We had our family: three children is perfect."

"But we didn't discuss it."

"You had your hands full with the kids, and I could see you were done with me."

Chi Chi began to cry. Tony fished out his handkerchief.

"All the things I've done, and this makes you cry?"

"It's the end of something. I don't know. It's sad."

"I thought the information would please you. To know that our family was it. The twins and Leone. Done."

Chi Chi was surprised by her reaction as much as Tony was. "I don't know why this gets me," she admitted as she pulled her knees to her chest. And then a thought struck her. "Wait a second. You didn't tell Tammy."

Tony nodded that he hadn't.

"But she's your wife. She needs to know."

Tony looked away.

"It's not right, Sav."

Tony shrugged. "I have my reasons. Believe me."

"A marriage without trust isn't a marriage. Haven't you learned that? You should talk to someone. I mean it."

"A head shrinker? No, thank you. I have all the answers, Cheech. I just don't like them." Tony stood up and extended his hand to his wife. She stood next to him.

He couldn't let go of her hand. "This is the beach where we met."

"Not here, Sav. You have a terrible sense of direction." She pointed. "All the way down there. See the Ferris wheel?"

"It's all the same."

"Yes, but the scene of the crime was about a mile away," Chi Chi insisted. "I did your nails, and it was the nail in my coffin."

"You're funny," he said. "Funniest girl I ever met." A gust of wind blew Chi Chi's hair into her eyes, and Tony brushed it away. "Do you really feel that way? Because I don't."

His hand lingered on her face. Chi Chi thought that he might kiss her, so she stepped back. "Oh, no, no, no." She shook her head. "Step away, Savvy."

Tony grinned. "What?"

"You know exactly what."

When Tony, Chi Chi, and Leone returned from the beach, the backyard was empty.

"Where are the girls?" Chi Chi asked Barbara.

"In the house," Barbara reported. "Tammy wanted to see their room."

The bedroom Sunny and Rosie shared was decorated in pink and purple paisley. The café curtains were trimmed in rickrack; the bedspreads had layers of ruffles, and each twin bed had a pillow with their initials monogrammed on the headboards.

Tammy Twiford Arma stood back and surveyed the books on Rosie and Sunny's shelves. "You girls read an awful lot."

"It can't hurt," Rosie said.

"I guess not."

"You should come down one Saturday when we go to the library," Sunny suggested. "They have guest lectures."

"You're inviting me?" Tammy sounded surprised.

The twins exchanged a glance. "Sure."

"Thank you, Sunny."

Lucille poked her head in the door, delivering two bowls of ice cream to her nieces. "Tammy, would you like to come down to the pool? We're having dessert. Tony is back from the beach. Leone too. Chi Chi is making s'mores."

"Sounds great." Tammy followed Lucille down the stairs.

Sunny sat up on her bed to make sure Tammy was out of earshot. "Can you believe how nonchalant Mom is acting? How about the aunts?"

"They have to get along," Rosie said practically. "They don't want to upset us."

"Maybe they really like her."

"Not a chance. It's all an act. I can't believe you like that woman," Rosie said, keeping her eyes on the bracelet she was weaving out of ribbons.

"She's Pop's wife." Sunny plunged a spoon into the ice cream. "We can't just shun her. We have to be nice."

"Wait until she has a bunch of kids and we get put out on the curb like an old sofa. See how you like her then."

"That would never happen. Besides, we'll be in college in a couple of years and what will we care?"

"You're so naive."

"Family is forever."

"I don't think she is. Tammy is not a keeper. Look at the blouse she's wearing. That bra looks like it's made out of party hats. Mom would never wear something like that."

Sunny shrugged. "Maybe she should."

"I don't want a mother like that. I don't want a stepmother either."

"Well, guess what? You got one. I know a lot more about divorce than you do."

"What does that even mean?"

"I read the decree. Mom and Dad's."

"What did it say?" Rosie asked in a voice that inferred she both wanted and didn't want to know the contents of the document.

"Mom has full custody. I think she forced Pop to give up custody because he had the girlfriend."

"I don't want to talk about this," Rosie said. "And getting chummy with Tammy isn't going to help you. She got Mom out of the way, and it's much easier to get rid of his kids."

"It will not happen. I'll fake it. I'll be really nice. When I want to see Dad, I'll call her. And she'll make arrangements. She won't help if we treat her like dirt."

Rosie thought for a moment. "You have a point."

"Rosie, listen to me. Mom is not going to let us do anything. We need Dad. And she cut him out completely. Our only hope is to cut him back in somehow."

"I could use some help in the kitchen. What are you girls whispering about?" Chi Chi asked as she walked to the closet with the girls' laundry on hangers. She hung their skirts and blouses on the rack and closed the doors.

"Nothing," the twins said in unison.

Chi Chi sat down on Sunny's bed. "You invited Tammy upstairs to talk. That was nice of you."

"Glad you approve." Sunny opened her book and turned away from her mother on the bed, but she couldn't settle down yet. "You should have never let her steal Daddy. She's not even that pretty. Or that smart. How could you let this happen?"

"Watch your mouth, Sunny," Chi Chi said.

"She doesn't mean it, Mom," Rosie said.

"Don't speak for me," Sunny said.

"Mom needs to know you read the divorce decree, and you know that Dad has been denied custody of us."

Chi Chi sighed. "Sunny, why do you snoop? No good comes from it."

"You don't tell us anything. None of the good parts anyway."

"I was waiting until you were older."

"We're sixteen. Now is the time."

"Sorry, honey. I'm new at this, too."

"That's not an excuse," Sunny said grudgingly.

"You're right. It isn't. But I'm not going to take any lip from you either. You were raised to have respect and good manners, and I'm not going to let everything fall apart."

"Because everything has?" Sunny flipped around. "Our lives are ruined."

"I don't think so, Mom." Rosie glared at her twin. "We're okay."

"I want my girls to be better than okay," Chi Chi said.

"What's wrong with Dad?"

Chi Chi hesitated before she answered. "He has a stressful life."

"Terri's dad works in a slate quarry and handles the explosives," Sunny said. "Handling dynamite in a cave is more stressful than singing songs about rolling pins."

"You win," Chi Chi said. "You have all the answers. Why don't you be the mother and I'll be the daughter and you run the world?"

"I wouldn't do things like you do them. When I have a family, I won't drive the family into the ground like you and Dad did. What are we even doing back in Jersey? Who even wants to live here when they can live in California? I miss my friends and my school. This is the worst."

"When you grow up and graduate from college, you can move back to California, if you still feel that way."

"You better believe I will."

"You're so rude to Mom," Rosie said. "Can't you see Mom's suffering too?"

"She's not suffering. She pushed Dad out the door like he had wheels on his shoes."

Chi Chi had had enough. "Sunny, I put up with a lot from you, but it ends here. Your father and I loved each other, and we still do. But he wants a life on the road. And that's no place to raise a family. Try and have a little empathy for him and a little compassion for me. Where is your Christian charity? That tuition I'm paying to the Salesian nuns might as well be going to make fertilizer." Chi Chi got up and left their room.

"You're evil," Rosie said to her twin, pulling an Oh Henry! bar out of her nightstand drawer.

"She's ridiculous."

"She's trying."

Sunny rolled over. "She needs to try harder."

Rosie munched on her candy bar and opened *Giant* by Edna Ferber. As she read and chewed, she got lost in the story of the Texas oil family. It did not take much to distract her from anything unpleasant.

Sunny turned away from her sister and pretended to sleep, keeping her face to the wall. That way, her twin couldn't see the tears fall.

Chi Chi mastered the art of coparenting by becoming an expert traveler out of necessity. Tony had relocated to Rome when offers in the States dried up. In the early 1960s, Italy offered sanctuary for American artists in need of reinvention, including singing actors like Tony Arma.

Chi Chi peered out the window of the Pan Am jet as it began its descent into Rome. Leone, thirteen, anxiously clutched both arms of the seat. Chi Chi looked over at her son and gave him a reassuring smile. She knew it was only a matter of time before her son would pretend to be fearless, so she treasured these final moments of his boyhood when he still needed her.

"There's nothing to be afraid of, Leone," she promised as she pulled on her gloves.

"Whatever you say, Ma." Leone leaned forward and looked straight ahead. "I'm sure that rumbling means we haven't lost an engine." His dark curls and eyes were like his father's, but he had the Donatelli profile, which pleased Chi Chi. "Ma, why did Pop get married again?"

"Well, after things didn't work out with Tammy, he came to Rome to make a movie, and he was lonely. He made friends with an actress in the movie. After a time, he fell in love with her. If it helps, I like Dora Alfedena a lot."

"Do I have to like her?"

"I think you will. But you can take your time."

"Why does Pop get married so much?"

"You'd have to ask him."

"Are you going to remarry?"

Chi Chi smiled. "I don't think so."

"Why not?"

"I don't want to."

"Good." Leone sat back in his seat. "One less new person for me to meet."

"Now, let's go over the rules. You're going to be kind to your new stepmother. You're going to help Nonna Rosaria and listen to your sisters."

"You have me answering to everybody but the Pope," Leone joked.

"You have to answer to him too."

"Wherever I am, I'm always the only boy. Why is that?"

"It's not true. You'll be with your father."

"Sort of. He's always busy getting married."

"I know you might find this a little funny, but your dad thinks it's important for you to see him in a stable relationship. He's actually being responsible."

As the jet touched down, the wheels hit the runway, and bounced on the ground, until the airplane steadied itself. The roar of the engines and the screech of the rubber wheels on the pavement was deafening. Leone gripped the arm of the seat more.

"It's almost over, Leone. Just the landing."

Leone had a fear of fast cars and airplanes, which his parents had tried to assuage by making the boy travel. He was relieved as he followed his mother off the plane, disembarking down a set of exterior metal stairs to the tarmac. Rosie, Sunny, and their grandmother were waiting inside the terminal. The twins ran to their mother when they saw her hat in the crowd.

"Ma, you made it!" Sunny said, as she hugged her.

"Ciao, Mama! We're so happy you're here!" Rosie threw her arms around Chi Chi. "Wait until you see the apartment. It's so nice. We love it."

"We do," Sunny agreed. "It's so cosmopolitan."

Chi Chi stopped and looked at her girls. "They used to call your dad the Cosmopolitan Neapolitan. Funny. But, look at you. So sophisticated. My college girls." Rosie wore a sundress and sandals, while Sunny wore a flowing skirt and a peasant blouse. Both had discovered Roman gold and wore sparkling hoop earrings. "Tell me about school."

"I love Sapienza. The art classes are amazing. We go to the places da Vinci and Michelangelo and Tiepolo painted," Sunny said.

"I got straight A's in my business classes, Ma," Rosie said proudly.

"Great, I can turn the books over to you someday."

"We go to a lot of parties," Sunny told her.

"Ma, the Italian boys are only after one thing," Rosie said.

"You don't have to tell Ma," Sunny said, nudging her sister. "She married one."

"How's your *nonna*?"

"She loves it here, too. I don't think she'll ever leave. And Dora likes her. Leone, look, there's your *nonna*."

Leone ran and embraced his grandmother Rosaria, who stood by the entrance. She was dressed simply in a black linen skirt and white blouse. She looked as though she hadn't aged a day since Chi Chi had last seen her before Rosaria moved to Rome.

"We live in Trastevere," Sunny said. "It's where all the actresses and movie stars and writers live. You know, the courant people."

"We fit right in," Rosie said.

"You girls are getting quite an education in Rome." Chi Chi hugged Rosaria, her former mother-in-law. "You look beautiful, Mama."

Rosaria tried not to cry.

"Now, none of that, Mama."

"I feel badly, that's all." Rosaria dug into her pocket for her handkerchief. "That your life with Saverio . . ."

"Girls, take Leone and get the luggage," Chi Chi said. "He knows which bags belong to us. I'm going to walk with Nonna."

Chi Chi put her arm around Rosaria and sat down with her. "The girls say you love it here."

"I'm home again, Chi Chi. I'm back where I started. I go up to the Veneto in the summer, but I'm here the rest of the year with Saverio. It's wonderful."

"Do you like Dora?"

"She's very nice," Rosaria said. "But marriage number three?"

"Show business!" Chi Chi threw up her hands.

Rosaria looked at Chi Chi. "I don't understand."

"I can't judge, Mama. I want Saverio to be happy, with or without me. When he's happy, and I'm happy, the children have a chance at happiness. They have no chance if we're miserable."

"What happened with the second one?" Rosaria asked.

"Tammy wanted a baby and Sav said he was done."

"That's not what he told me."

"That's what he told me," Chi Chi said.

"He said that he had made a mistake. They had nothing in common."

"Mama, you can have everything in common with a man and he still leaves you."

"*Capisce.* I wish it hadn't been my son that left you."

Tony stood outside the terminal beside a four-door canary-yellow Mercedes with a midnight-blue leather interior. He embraced his son and couldn't let go. "You're a giant, Leone! What are you feeding this kid?" he asked Chi Chi.

"Macaroni. What do you think?" Chi Chi said, giving Tony a

peck on the cheek. In the years of their relationship, she'd always been able to take the temperature of where they were with one another from Tony's reaction to her kiss. Today she could tell he had moved on, and they were once again good friends.

The twins, Leone, and Rosaria settled into the back seat as Tony helped Chi Chi around to the front passenger seat and opened the door. She squinted at his head.

"What do you think?" he asked.

"New piece?"

"Yeah. Had it done in a little place in Rome. They get the hair in Sicily."

"You know what, Sav? It's better than the American toupee ever was."

"I think so too!" he said enthusiastically. "It's good to have you here, Cheech."

Chi Chi sat across the table from Dora Alfedena in the kitchen of the Armas' apartment, Tony's ex-wife in awe of the good taste of his current one. The apartment was spacious, with high ceilings, stucco walls, and thick monastery doors. Dora's decorating style was simple and elegant: neutral colors, textured fabrics, and soft rugs.

Tony's third wife had furnished it with low-slung leather chairs, tile worktables, and long wooden benches instead of chairs at the dining table. The floors were highly polished terracotta tile. The walls were painted grapefruit pink, as if to bring in the tones of the sun rising and setting over the Eternal City's sandstone walls.

Dora was a petite brunette with classic Roman features. Her aquiline nose, wide-set brown eyes, and golden skin were made for the camera. Her successful screen career had more to do with her acting talent than her appearance, but her beauty was undeniable. She had a warm way with the children and Rosaria, which Chi Chi appreciated. She imagined they would have been friends had they met somewhere else at a different time. Chi Chi believed that Tony could not have made a better choice for a mate.

"What is this, Chiara?" Dora asked, looking over her reading glasses as she pointed out a line on the contract.

Dora was around Chi Chi's age, in her late-forties, and unlike Tammy, she was wise to the Italian ways, having been raised in the world of it. She understood Tony Arma and was more philosophical about his nature than Chi Chi had been.

"It explains what you get if Tony precedes you in death."

"This is too much." Dora removed her reading glasses and placed them on the table.

"It's only fair. It's important to know that you are taken care of in the long term. I want you to have a full understanding of his portfolio, because he never took much of an interest."

"I know. When he sees something, he buys it. Like a child."

"Not to worry. Tony has investments. I manage them. He has an allowance. It's his money, but I'm the gatekeeper. That's his choice. But I want you to understand that it is also your money now that you're married to him. If you ever need anything or have any questions, just call or write to me, and I will explain."

"In case of divorce, I get this?" Dora pointed.

"Yes."

"But if there are no children, why so much?"

"Dora, it's based on the United States laws."

"No wonder you people get divorced there."

Chi Chi laughed. "I know. Not a lot of incentive to stay in a marriage."

"How about you?" Dora leaned in. "You have a nice man in your life?"

"I don't."

"Too busy?"

Chi Chi smiled. "Work and children. I'm on the run."

"Slow down before you run out of time."

Chi Chi pulled a small envelope out of her purse and handed it to Dora. "Here is all my information. If Leone, Sunny, or Rosie needs anything, call me. You're Leone's stepmother, and you have permission to be the adult in his life in addition to his father and me. I don't believe in children running the home."

Dora smiled. "I agree."

"If Tony needs something, or you do, I can wire money to you in a matter of hours. I want you to let me know if Rosaria needs anything. Medical care, a new dress, tickets to the Veneto—it doesn't matter. Whatever she needs, whatever she wants, you let me know. She is to be deprived of nothing."

Dora nodded. "Mama. I understand."

Chi Chi stood in the Piazza San Pietro in Rome, covered her head with a lace mantilla, and pulled on her black gloves before entering the Basilica of Saint Peter in the Vatican. As she entered, she heard the echo of her footsteps on the terrazzo floor, and was overwhelmed by the height of the ceilings. She stopped as tourists flowed past her and looked up. She took in the splendid altars, the majestic archways, vaulted ceilings, and inlaid duomos.

As she walked up the main aisle, shards of golden light cut across the pews, reminding her of the churches of her youth on the sacred days that had mattered to her. As a divorced woman, she no longer belonged inside a Catholic church; her failure had expelled her from the beauty of the faith, and because Chi Chi was honest, she felt shame. The frescoes told the stories of the saints in painted tiles. As she stood back from them, she mourned the moments in her own life when she fell short and failed to do her best for those she loved. The smooth marble of the sculptures was a reminder of the role of patience over time leading to truth and ultimately beauty. The bronze details on the doors were layered filigree, tangled skeins of the artist's intention, depicting man's rejection of God. Everywhere she looked, Chi Chi was reminded that she had not measured up and didn't belong.

Chiara Donatelli had not made a success of her marriage; for a Catholic girl, this wasn't simply a personal failure, but a spiritual one. While she had a thousand reasons to explain the demise of it, there had not been a single good one she could find to stay in it. Yet she still attended mass, though she did not take communion, hoping to find some answers, or perhaps even peace.

Alone in the mother church, without her children or ex-husband or ex-mother-in-law, she wandered through the home of her lifelong faith like a stranger. How she loved Pope John XXIII. As an Italian American, she appreciated the pope's origins and life story. He had lived in a family as one of the many children of an impoverished farmer at the foot of the Italian Alps. With the installation of this pope in 1958, she could relate personally to her religion, because its leader was a simple priest from a humble background, not a prince from an exalted one. But as she walked through the basilica, none of that mattered because she was in exile from her faith, cut loose from the ties of the sacraments she had cherished. Just as her marriage had ended, so had her relationship with the church of her birthright. Tony Arma, it turned out, had taken that away from her, too, but what Chi Chi still had to figure out was why she had let him.

Tony stood in a follow spot on the stage of the Treasure Cove nightclub in Naples, Florida, in a beige leisure suit. He wore a floral dress shirt, an ascot, and eggshell loafers with tassels.

By the spring of 1968, Tony was fifty-two years old. The movie offers had dried up for him in Italy, the major tours with the orchestra named for him had dissolved from lack of ticket sales, so Lee booked him in hotels where audiences had nostalgia for the music of the big-band era.

Dora sat backstage reading the *Corriere della Serra* as she sipped a cup of hot espresso. Dutiful and supportive, she had gone on the road with her husband and had found ways to amuse herself as he played two shows a night in the side rooms of fine hotels along the coastline of Florida. Whenever she heard Tony say the word "wife" from the stage, Dora would stop whatever she was doing and listen.

It turned out that she, too, found Tony Arma a mystery to be solved.

Tony walked to the piano, the beam of soft blue light following him to the curve of the glistening black Steinway grand. The pianist underscored his patter before the song with the opening riff of the new ballad he was introducing into the show that night.

"Every song is a story, you know. After I divorced my second wife—a nice girl, by the way, we just couldn't make it work—my agent sent me to Italy to work in a genre of films called spaghetti westerns. It was there that I met a real doll, my wife Dora Alfedena. She is a respected actress in Italy, and she won my heart. Now, you all know that I had three children with a great lady, Chi Chi Donatelli."

A smattering of applause was heard in the club.

"Tony and Chi Chi had a good run. Chi Chi wrote a lot of the songs I recorded, and when my beautiful mother passed away last month, honest to God, I thought it was the end of the world. She was kind and decent and beautiful. She lived in Rome with Dora and me. I got on the phone with Chi Chi, and over the course of a few hours, I expressed my thoughts, and we wrote this song together. It's a little ballad called *Rosaria il mio cuore.*"

> The light in the world changed today
> The reds were dull, the blues were gray
> The sun itself seemed to fade away
> Rosaria my heart, Rosaria my heart
>
> La luce nel mondo e cambiata oggi
> I rossi erano opachi, i blu erano grigio
> Il sole stesso sembrava svanire
> Rosaria, il mio cuore, Rosaria, il mio cuore

12

1978–1987

Inquieto

(Restless)

Leone Arma, at twenty-six years old, entered his mother's dressing room at *The Tonight Show* with a bouquet of sunflowers and red roses. "For you, Ma. Burbank's finest florist. You look beautiful."

"You lie. But I'll take it. And I'll take them," Chi Chi said as she sat at the mirror in a long robe.

"Where's Pop?"

"He's talking with the producer. Peter Lasally? Is that right?"

"That's right." Leone lived up to his name. He had a full head of dark leonine curls, his mother's eyes, and his father's old nose. He also had their musical talent combined. "See, you fit right back in the scene."

"Not really. It's a good thing I'm out of the business—this end of it, anyway. I can't remember anything anymore. I'll be lucky if I remember the right key to sing in. I hope I don't kill Mr. Carson's ratings. Half of America will tune in and take one look at this old broad and flip the channel and watch Dick Cavett." Chi Chi powdered her face. "As they should. Nothing to see here but the decline of civilization."

Leone laughed. "Ma, just be yourself. You're more hilarious than any comedian."

"Just what a woman wants to hear, Leo."

"I like funny women."

Tony rapped on the dressing room door before opening it. "You decent?" he asked through the door.

"Come in already."

"Hey, Pop." Leone gave his father a hug.

"Okay, Cheech, you'll be stage right most of this thing. They're putting down pink tape for you, black for me. When we dance, stay within the blue tape." Tony yanked the cummerbund of his black tux and adjusted his pinkie ring. The scent of Brut cologne filled the small room. Tony was perspiring and throwing scent.

Chi Chi looked at him in the mirror. "You're leading. *You* stay within the tape."

"You get grand when you dance. You flail. If you flail, your arm, your leg, something, will be cut off on camera."

"Hallelujah. Cut me off, cut me out." Chi Chi raised her arms in the air like an Olympian.

Tony looked panicked. "Don't blow this for me."

"Leone, take the lint roller to your father. He looks like he did somersaults in a cat box." Chi Chi handed her son the lint roller.

"I don't go near cat houses. I'm married."

"I said cat *box*. As in litter box. And I caught you. Again. But what else is new?"

"Ma, save this for the act. When Johnny invites you over to the couch. It's gold."

"There's no guarantee we'll be invited over." Tony adjusted his collar. "If your mother dances outside the sightlines, we'll never be invited back, period. So let's not get our hopes up."

"That's the last thing you need to worry about. No hopes left here, Tony." Chi Chi sighed as she sprayed Aqua Net onto her hair.

"Cripes almighty, Cheech. You'll give us all first-degree cancer with that stuff."

"You want my hair falling out when we sing?"

"No."

"So, don't breathe." Chi Chi sprayed more Aqua Net onto her hair.

"What are you wearing?" Tony demanded.

"It's a surprise," Chi Chi barked back.

"Do we match?"

"Match? You're in a tuxedo. Why do we have to match?"

"Because when we used to do the act, we matched. The audience expects us to match."

"They're not paying. This is TV. It's like a telethon, except nobody's benefiting from it except you."

"You got issues, Cheech," Tony said. "Big ones."

"Wonder why?"

"Would you two please stop?" Leone said firmly. "Think about this moment. Think about how far you've both come. This is so cool. You're going to be on TV with Johnny Carson singing the song that started it all. Be happy, would you, please? Life is short."

"Especially when you're old," Chi Chi commented.

"We're not old," Tony countered.

Chi Chi looked at her ex-husband. Waves of compassion rolled over her like a hormonal hot flash He had a paunch, a toupee, and hands with liver spots the size of Milk Duds. He was not only old, he could be in the advertisement for the pill to cure it. "Okay, Tony. Whatever you say."

"I want my parents to get along. Can you do that for me?"

"I can do that, son," Tony said.

"So can I," Chi Chi agreed.

"Good. I'm going to warm up with the band. You two behave yourselves. And Dad, stay away from the couch. It's a lint factory."

Tony began to pace. "Stay within the tape, Cheech. Just stay within the tape." He cracked his knuckles.

Chi Chi put down her lipstick. "Would you please stop? If you don't stop, I'm going to pull off this shoe, if I can pry it off my foot, and beat you about the head with it. I will stay within the tape. I know how to hit a mark."

Tony smiled in relief. "That makes me feel better."

"Where's Dora?"

"She's not coming."

"Why not?"

"She said I make her nervous. All of a sudden I'm like an annoyance to people."

"I'm joining her club."

"You'd like that. Gang up all the wives against me, three against one."

"Your second wife, no one can find her. I hear she joined a cult and is working in a Dairy Queen in Mequon, Wisconsin. There's just Dora and me."

"I don't want to go down this road."

"Because whenever we do, you get lost, Tony."

"I'm going back to my dressing room. You're beginning to piss me off."

"That only took forty years," Chi Chi called out after him. The door slammed shut behind him.

Chi Chi sat in front of the mirror and put on her lipstick. When she was done, she smiled in the mirror. "I'm sixty years old. I want to kill myself. I got more lines on my face than Act One of *Hamlet*. I barely smoked a cigarette, and I look like I inhaled a pack a day. How is that fair?"

Chi Chi slipped out of her robe and into her Clovis Ruffin caftan. It was a loaner from I. Magnin, so she was careful to tuck the tags into the back of the dress.

Sunny peeked into the dressing room. "Ma, you look like a star!" She pushed through the door, followed by Rosie. The twins wore peasant blouses, long skirts, flat sandals, and their hair cropped short.

"Ma, the hair is cool," Rosie said.

"I love you girls, giving me confidence when I could throw up."

"It's been a while since you've sung with Dad."

"Do you think you can do it without falling apart?" Sunny asked.

"I don't know. But either way, it'll be good television." Chi Chi snapped on her earrings.

"It's a pleasure to welcome Tony and Chi Chi Arma to our show," Johnny Carson began. "This legendary act worked the circuit in the days of the big-band era, when they were kids. They've agreed to come on the show tonight for a little reunion. Please welcome Tony and Chi Chi."

The curtains, bold stripes of cobalt blue, salmon, emerald green, ruby red, gold, and purple, parted like a circus tent before the entrance of the ringleader.

The Armas entered holding hands. Tony headed stage left, Chi Chi went stage right. Chi Chi's caftan in swirls of pink, fuchsia, and orange was off-set by her jet-black hair in an updo. She carried a rolling pin.

A soft drum brush underscored their dialogue.

> Where you been, Tony?
> Around, Chi Chi.
> Around who?
> Just around.
> What do I gotta do, Tony? Follow you everywhere?
> Not a bad idea, Cheech.
> The rolling pin don't scare you no more?
> Not much.
> Not much. But you still love me, don't you, baby?
> Not much.

Horns. Strings.
Tony wagged his finger at his ex-wife, and they began to sing.
Wife sang:

> I make dough

Husband sang:

> She makes dough

Wife sang:

> He makes dough

Together they sang:

We make dough—with Mama's Rolling Pin

Wife sang:

We got married, the church was nice

Husband sang:

She wore a veil and a chunk of ice

Wife sang:

Preacher said are you out or are you in

Together they sang:

She said yes and I said yes—To Mama's Rolling Pin

Chi Chi's heart began to race in that old way it used to. She was long over her ex-husband in the romantic sense. This moment was a lot like visiting a house you sold years ago, a home where you once were happy. You walk through the rooms filled with another family's things, the walls painted different colors, the scent different, and it is at once familiar and yet completely unknown.

Chi Chi looked into her husband's eyes and saw something new, and she thought she had seen it all. Tony Arma was grateful. That's what moved her, what made her heart beat faster. They had meant something to each other once, and he remembered.

"Say hello to our son, Leone!" Tony yelled over the orchestra.

The cameras swiveled to take in Leone as he blew his trumpet like he was blasting the gates of heaven open.

"That's my kid," Tony said proudly.

"He gets his talent from me," Chi Chi said.

"Says who?"

"Says me."

"He gets his looks from me."

"Says who?"

"Says my schnoz," Leone said from the orchestra as he turned in profile and blew the horn.

Johnny laughed appreciatively, and the studio audience, mostly around their age, appreciated the old routine. It was their youth, too, returning in a song from the days before the war. They relaxed into the music, the mood conjured days gone by when one of those low, hot Jersey shore summer suns in a cloudless sky was so bright, it left nothing in shadow, not even their memories.

Chi Chi and Tony brought it all back once more, all the living that had transpired between World War II and the present, and for many, the song placed them smack dab in the middle of the past when they first fell in love, mourned the loss of his mother, and held high hopes, in the days when they believed there was still time to make dreams come true. Tony felt that energy surge through the studio as the bold brass section stood up and blew the music of the big-band era. Was the sound better then? Or was everything better because they had been young?

Tony hated the word *nostalgia*. It meant he was a has-been, a crooner who had hit it and never would again. The comeback he'd dreamed of, planned for, and needed would never be. He had finessed every angle, called every contact, worked every room, and had taken every shot, and he was still just a mid-list singer who could open solid but kept the needle tight on the sales chart at 500K and not one album more, stateside and international combined. Great for a year-rounder, an opening act in Vegas. Just fine. Lucrative even, if you showed up, stayed in shape, were in good voice, laid off the sauce, worked the crowd, and goosed those old feelings. But it wasn't enough—not good enough for Tony Arma.

As Tony sang, Chi Chi pounded the rolling pin in her hand like a billy club when he upstaged her, the audience roared when she went to slug him with it, quickly pulling it back when he turned to face her, rolling it innocently in the air as though she was making him fresh macaroni for Sunday dinner or a piecrust to be filled with sweet Michigan cherries. It was an act, a comedy routine. But it was still funny, and it had sustained them.

Chi Chi was surprised when Tony took her into his arms during the bridge. He hadn't done that in years, and certainly not since they had their troubles. As he whirled her around the polished linoleum, their bodies in sync, her feet barely touched the ground. She felt weightless as they floated over the musical notes, like a veil of smoke.

Chi Chi closed her eyes and allowed herself the pure joy of the brass, of Doc's trumpet as it blew fierce in a solo line and kicked back in with the orchestra in a seamless revelry. How she loved swing music, and always had.

When they broke to sing the final stanza, Tony went stage left, Chi Chi moved stage right. They harmonized:

> If you want your love to be true
> Don't hesitate to follow our rule
> Once you marry and become kin
> Keep him on a short leash
> With Mama's Rolling Pin!

Chi Chi was about to take a bow when Tony stepped downstage. They had not rehearsed this move. She froze, her hand in midair, and waited.

The *Tonight Show* orchestra vamped with a phrase of music from the song.

Chi Chi didn't know where to go; the song was supposed to be over. They had not rehearsed an interlude. She looked over at the producers in the wings, who seemed to be enjoying their number.

She was unsure whether to stay or go. Tony's back was to her, so she stood and forced a smile as Tony swayed to the music. At this stage of life, thoughts ran through her head like a ticker tape. *Is he having a stroke? Did he forget the ending? What's he waiting for? We're live on television coast to coast. This was a terrible idea!*

Desperate, Chi Chi looked over at Johnny Carson, who was blowing smoke rings casually from his cigarette, as though nothing were wrong. Ed McMahon was looking over some notes. Fred De Cordova was in the wings, smiling. Chi Chi thought perhaps it was her own health that should be questioned. Had *she* forgotten something?

The B camera wheeled in closer to Tony as the music underscored his speech.

"Ladies and gentlemen, I don't know if you remember how I met the mother of my children. But it was over some macaroni in Sea Isle, New Jersey, when we were very young."

The drummer hit the snare and then the cymbal.

"We are still young at heart," he continued.

Chi Chi shook her head. Tony was doing some shtick. Okay. She could handle it.

"There's been a lot of macaroni and gravy since then . . ."

"You been talking to your cummerbund?" Chi Chi ad-libbed.

The audience roared.

Tony shot her a look. "But what you don't know"—Tony worked the lip of the downstage camera area—"is that we had a little help on *Mama's Rolling Pin* from an act that was known far and wide on that little strip of sand in Sea Isle City, a trio of the prettiest sisters God ever made this side of the Eternal City, and I'm not talkin'. Newark. Ladies and gentlemen, for the first time since the last time, join me in welcoming Barbara and Lucille, who, along with Chi Chi, were and ever shall be *the Donatelli Sisters!*"

The buildup had been so tasty, the audience responded with wild applause. Johnny sat up in his seat as the rainbow curtains parted once again. Barbara and Lucille joined hands and walked toward their sister.

Chi Chi stayed in position, in her light, and shook her head as she admonished her ex-husband with her microphone as though it were a rolling pin.

Barbara wore a flowing lime-green Qiana caftan and matching turban, while Lucille wore turquoise palazzo pants and a hot-pink bolero, which was lovely against her dove-gray wedge haircut.

"Surprise," Barbara said under her breath as the *Tonight Show* orchestra vamped.

"We practiced, I swear," Lucille whispered. She was already sweating under the lights.

The stage crew whisked out standing microphones and placed them on marks on the stage floor. Barbara and Lucille took their positions.

Before Chi Chi could run backstage, Tony joined them. All three cameras faced them. "You sonofabitch," Chi Chi said to Tony through a clenched smile. He threw his head back and laughed. "Just sing, Cheech."

Tony took her hand. The cameras rolled back into position downstage and focused on Tony and Chi Chi. Camera C widened out and stayed on Lucille and Barbara.

As the band started, it was as though forty years had come and gone, taking with it, like a low rolling tide, all the sadness.

The remnants of their pain washed away all the should'ves and would'ves and might-have-beens, for as long as the band played. What did they sing? Another chorus of *Mama's Rolling Pin*.

The audience seemed hungry for the touchstones of the past, for the validation of their gleaming youth. The swing era, after all, had belonged to them, and there had been nothing like it since. They had won a war, built a way of life, and survived. When the song finished, the applause was deafening.

The stage manager escorted Lucille and Barbara offstage. They waved to the audience, who applauded as they made their exit. Johnny indicated that Chi Chi and Tony should join him on the couch.

Tony insisted Chi Chi take the lead chair. She refused, so Tony sat in it, but not before he made sure that Cheech sat in first position on the sofa. As they went to commercial, Johnny shook his head in admiration. "The definition of hip," he said.

They thanked him before he was pulled away by his producer.

Tony turned to Chi Chi. "Never sat down for an interview."

Chi Chi smiled and looked out over the studio audience. "Enjoy it. Because when this is over, I'm going to kill you."

Tony grinned, reached over, and patted her hand. He was sweating profusely from the dance number. Chi Chi had already waved the makeup girl over to blot him. As she mopped his brow, he said to the young woman, "Aren't you a knockout. You look like Connie Stevens."

The makeup artist laughed uncomfortably.

"Enough, Grandpop," Chi Chi said. She winked at the girl as she powdered Chi Chi down. When the makeup artist left the stage, Chi Chi called after her, "Don't worry about him, he can't see and he can't hear and he's up all night tinkling."

"You never let me have any fun," Tony said.

Chi Chi didn't answer him. She looked straight ahead as Carson took his seat and welcomed the audience back from the commercial break.

Tony opened the segment with a crack, shaking his thumb at Chi Chi, and repeated, "She never lets me have any fun."

"You had so much fun they sold out of it," Chi Chi said dryly.

The audience—particularly the women, Chi Chi noticed—laughed at that.

"Now everybody will know why we got divorced," Tony said.

"But will they care?" Chi Chi tapped her cheek with her finger. "I don't think so, Tony."

"I care," Johnny interjected.

"Isn't that lovely," Chi Chi deadpanned into the camera. "Ask him what he's been up to. That will tell you everything."

"Tell us what you've been up to, Tony," Johnny said.

"I've got a room at the Sands in Vegas."

"For about ten years now?"

"On and off. It's a good show. We have some of the guys from the old tour, and some of the ladies."

"Always the ladies," Chi Chi purred as she smoothed her gown.

"I'm glad props took the rolling pin away," Johnny joked.

"Smart move," Chi Chi said.

"I understand there are rumblings that you two may reunite and bring back the old act," Johnny said.

"Yes," Tony said.

"No," Chi Chi said. "Here's the problem, John . . ." Chi Chi began.

"Just one problem, John . . ." Tony said.

"Just one?" Chi Chi interrupted Tony.

"Really, Cheech? You're going to do this on national television?"

"Why not? The nice people at home are in bed, and who doesn't like having their evening ruined by a good fight?" She smiled.

"Folks at home are trying to relax."

"They'll be plenty relaxed when I'm done with you," Chi Chi cut in.

"What is your problem?" Tony asked.

"It's not my problem."

"It is your problem."

"That's your opinion."

"What is the problem, Chi Chi?" Johnny asked her.

"Tony's problem has many names, John: Doris. Sheila. Connie. Nancy. Didi. Should I keep going?"

"I wish you wouldn't," Tony said.

"My ex-husband likes the ladies, and that's fine, now that he's my ex-husband."

"That's why I'm her ex-husband, or so she says."

"It was the only reason. He's a lovely father, and except for the extracurriculars, a pretty good husband. Not very handy, but I am, so it worked."

"You remarried, didn't you?" Johnny asked Tony.

"Twice," Chi Chi answered for him.

"He asked me." Tony turned to Chi Chi.

"Three if you count me," Chi Chi interjected.

The audience laughed.

"I'm never counting you again."

"Don't," Chi Chi said breezily. "But I'm the one who keeps the checkbook."

"You do?" Johnny asked in surprise.

"She does," Tony admitted.

"How does that work?" Johnny wanted to know.

"She has always been good with numbers. We've got the kids. And we wanted to make sure that all our hard work didn't go up in smoke."

"So, this is a kind of modern arrangement." Johnny was intrigued.

"We're family, John," Chi Chi said. "Family is forever."

The audience cheered and applauded. Chi Chi had touched a nerve: people understood the message. She looked at her ex-husband, who wore the expression of a man who had been driving lost for hours and refused to stop and ask for directions. She reached over and took his hand.

"I'm all right," he said. "I'm all right."

A month after their appearance, Chi Chi opened a large envelope filled with fan letters addressed to "Tony & Chi Chi" in care of *The Tonight Show Starring Johnny Carson*. She dumped the contents on her dining room table when the phone rang.

"Are you Mrs. Armandando?" a voice asked.

"Armandonada. Yes, I am."

"This is the emergency room at Saint Vincent's Hospital in Greenwich Village."

Chi Chi's heart fluttered. "Is something wrong with Tony?"

"No, ma'am, it's about your son, Leone."

Chi Chi was so distraught, she grabbed her purse and keys and left her apartment on Gramercy Park without locking the doors. When she arrived at the hospital a few minutes later, she handed the cab driver a $50 bill and didn't wait for the change. She pushed through the entrance doors and ran to the front desk.

"I was called about my son, Leone Armandonada."

Chi Chi was escorted to a conference room on the second floor. A nun entered, escorted by a New York City policeman.

"What happened to my son?" Chi Chi cried.

The nun poured a glass of water for Chi Chi and guided her to sit at a table. The policeman sat across from her.

"Mrs. Arma, there's construction on the West Side Highway.

And there was an accident around West Fifty-Seventh and the underpass there. It was pretty bad. Our guys were on the way, and so was an ambulance. But your son, who was driving north, was turning off on the Fifty-Seventh Street exit, and he saw the accident and pulled over. He saw that there were people hurt, and he got out to help. He helped two of the passengers to safety. Had them climb up on some scaffolding to keep them out of harm's way. He had gone back down to the street to help with the driver when your son was hit by another car. He died instantly."

Chi Chi couldn't breathe. The nun thanked the policeman and asked him to go.

When she regained her breath, Chi Chi said, "I want to see my son."

She said it with such certainty that the nun didn't argue. Instead she accompanied Chi Chi to the morgue in the basement of the hospital. When they arrived at the glass door into the morgue, Chi Chi stopped outside and stood against the wall, letting it hold her up. She began to weep and slid to the floor. The nun knelt next to her.

"You don't have to see him," she said quietly.

"No, I want to." Chi Chi summoned her strength, and with the help of the nun, she stood up.

"He hasn't been cleaned up yet, Mrs. Arma."

"I understand," Chi Chi said, pulling herself together.

Inside the morgue, all of the examining tables were empty, except for one. The nun summoned the attendant, who joined them. He carefully folded down the sheet so Chi Chi could see Leone. His face was covered in streaks of blood, but his teeth and nose were intact. He had a beatific expression on his face—it was strangely serene. He had died doing the right thing. He had died trying to save someone else.

"My boy," she cried, and kissed his face as many times as she could, as much as they would allow. She took time to look at him, to study him, so she might remember every detail. He looked as he did when he emerged from her the day he was born, covered in the stuff of being born, which was the irony of it: Leone looked as though he had just arrived in the world. But as it was on that day, it was the same as this one: mother and son, alone together, just the two of them.

This was the child who had never been any trouble. He was a peacemaker. He might have wanted to learn to play the piano for his own reasons, but Chi Chi knew better. It was a way to be close to Saverio, to be a part of his father's life, to stay close to his parents, first by learning how to play from her, and later, sitting through long hours of rehearsals as Tony sang the same songs over and over again, and his loyal son, without complaint, accompanied him. When the piano wasn't enough to stay close, he picked up the strings, and so it went, until their son had a command of every instrument in the band.

Leone tried every day of his life to pull his family together. He instinctively knew that his mother and father should love each other, that family should stay connected, that they should shore one another up, never tear each other down, but pull together as one and thrive.

"It was an honor to be your mother," Chi Chi whispered. She knelt next to her son's body and made the sign of the cross, praying with everything within her that her father was there to hold her son on the other side. She did not have to ask God to take him in, because she understood that he had loaned this boy for a short time to help their family, their flawed and hurting family, find joy whenever it was possible and healing whenever it was necessary. He had done so much work in that regard in his short time on earth. He had made them laugh and helped them find the goodness in one another.

The nun placed her hand on Chi Chi's shoulder.

"It's time," she said softly.

As Chi Chi left the room with the nun, she looked up at the clock. She had stayed with her son for close to three hours, and she would have stayed the rest of her life, had the nun allowed it.

The doorbell rang again. Chi Chi lay in bed, refusing to answer it. She had ignored the phone, the buzz of the intercom from the doorman, the annoying knocks at the door, and now the doorbell that sounded like the elevator chimes at Saks during the holiday rush. She feared the fire department would enter with an ax.

"Go away," she shouted from her bed.

The ringing stopped.

Chi Chi sat up in bed. Her mother guilt kicked in. What if Rosie or Sunny needed her? What kind of a mother ignores the phone and the doorbell and knocking? She grabbed her robe from the end of the bed and answered the door.

"Oh my God. Jim?"

"I'm sorry, Chiara."

"Was that you calling?"

"Yes. And knocking and buzzing. I was afraid something happened to you."

Chi Chi looked at her old friend. "Well, Jim, something has. Would you like to come in?"

"Sure."

Jim's thick hair had gone white, but there were few signs of aging other than that.

"I look awful," Chi Chi apologized.

"You look beautiful," Jim corrected her.

"Jim, you're a good man but a bad liar."

Jim laughed. "I'm sorry I wasn't here when Leone died."

"I'm glad you weren't. We had a small service and he was cre-mated. I have to take his ashes to Italy at some point, but I don't know when. No rush."

"No rush."

"He left behind a list of things he wanted done. A will, I guess you would call it. And in six months"—Chi Chi put her head in her hands and wept—"In six months there will be a party in his honor at a restaurant. Can you imagine? He thought of that. And he had no idea he was going to die."

"Maybe he did."

"I wonder. You know, I knew. From the day he was born, I knew. Isn't it strange? How that goes. You know everything when your children are born. You can see what they'll become, though you will do everything in your power to change certain things, or think you can change the course of their lives by giving them pi-ano lessons or making them take a summer job or forcing them to get a haircut. But none of that matters. They are on their own path and fate will play out the way it will and there is no mother love that can change it."

"I wish it could."

"He was such a fine young man."

"He had to be. He was your son."

"My only son."

"You'll see him again."

"Do you think so?"

"I believe it."

"I cry out for him. You know, when a child comes through you, he takes a little of your soul with him when he emerges out into the world. I think so anyhow. And I pray he finds me again. That he'll know me. That I'll get one more chance to hold him."

Jim took Chi Chi into his arms.

"You will get the chance, I promise."

"I've made so many mistakes, Jim."

"I don't think so."

"I should've married you."

"Well, I tried."

"I know you did."

"I'm seeing a lovely lady now. Elizabeth Finelli. You know her? She works at the bank in Sea Isle."

"Yes. Nice woman." Chi Chi smiled.

"Very nice."

"Thank you for coming over."

"I'm sorry I was so persistent, but I worry."

"No, no, I'm glad you checked on me."

Chi Chi walked Jim to the door. She reached up to kiss him on the cheek, but he took her hand and kissed it instead. She closed the door behind him and walked to the window. "Leone? This is your mother talking. I'm getting out of bed. It's been six months, that's three months shy of how long I carried you inside of me. But I can't do this anymore. I can't live in the dark. Nobody is waiting around for me to be happy again. Nobody is waiting around for me to heal. But I am sick of myself. I have to do something with whatever time I have left. But I'm going to need your help."

Chi Chi went into her bathroom. She turned on the lights and ran the water into the tub. She leaned into the mirror and looked at her face. "Chi Chi Donatelli. Today, we begin again."

One year after Leone's death, and per his handwritten instructions, Chi Chi and Tony hosted a luncheon in Greenwich Village in his favorite restaurant, the Pink Teacup. There wasn't nearly enough room in the place for the crowd that attended, but it didn't matter. The reception poured out into the street, and for a moment Manhattan became a small town like Sea Isle City celebrating the life of a young man who had good friends and a family who loved him.

Dora, dressed in an elegant black suit and hat, said goodbye to Lucille and Barbara before turning to her husband. "I'm going back to the apartment."

Dora kissed Chi Chi. "I'm so sorry, Chiara. He was a wonderful son. I miss him."

"Thank you, Dora. You were a lovely stepmother to him."

Tony went outside and helped Dora into a cab.

From the restaurant's doorway, Barbara looked at Lucille. "What's going on there?"

"I think his third wife is getting rid of him," Lucille whispered.

"Not another one," Barbara said. "How can you tell?"

Lucille pointed in the direction of the table by the door with her head.

"Yeah, so?"

"He's taken up with his masseuse."

"Are you serious?"

"That's her. Over there. In the white skirt."

Barbara looked at the birdlike woman in her early sixties. She had large blue eyes, thin blond hair, and wore wire-framed glasses.

"That is not his type."

"Barb, at a certain point, you take whoever will take you."

"I guess."

"What are you talking about?" Chi Chi joined them.

"Tony, who else?"

"He's with the masseuse," Chi Chi confirmed.

"What an idiot." Barbara shook her head.

Tony joined them inside. "This was beautiful," he said to them. "He was a special kid."

"He must've known he wasn't going to grow old," Lucille said.

"Did he say something to you?" Tony asked.

"Who plans their memorial service when they're not yet thirty? And how did he know to wait to have the service one year after his passing? He said after a year his mother wouldn't cry through it. And you didn't."

"Not all the way through." Chi Chi smiled. "But I'll always cry for Leone."

Barbara nodded. "We will too, sis."

"You want to come upstairs, Sav?" Chi Chi asked. "I won't be good company."

"Hey, we're all we got." Tony put his arms around her. "We're the only two people in this world who knew our son the way we did and let's face it, we loved him the most."

"Leone worried about you. I tried to assuage him on that front."

"And I thought I'd find the place where I fit. Where I'd open the door and I'd say, 'Ah, okay, I'm complete, fulfilled, and what's inside is enough.'"

"And it wasn't?"

"For a time. And then whatever it is that makes me tick, stops. And I have to go. For reasons I don't understand. Never will, I guess."

Chi Chi and Tony got off the elevator. Chi Chi unlocked the door to her apartment and invited Tony inside.

"Are you going to divorce Dora?"

"She wants out."

"Because you're with your masseuse."

"That's just a sidebar, kid."

"No, Sav, it's not a sidebar, it's a barbell that you dropped on

Dora. You cheated on her and she caught you, and for whatever reason, she is kicking you out the door this time."

"I feel terrible about it."

"Do you?"

"Yeah."

"I can't fix everything for you, Saverio."

"You always did."

"Not this time. Your marriage is your problem."

"You saved me plenty."

"Not really. I only helped save one life. And that was many years ago." She sat on the sofa. "You know, I dream about the boy sometimes. I see him in the water. And last night I had the dream again. I'm back on Sea Isle Beach. I swim out. I'm twenty years old. I move like a marlin, and when I get there in the dream, when I reach the raft, it's always the boy I saved. But last night, I got to the body and it was our Leone. And I couldn't save him."

"I want to come home," Tony said.

"You have a home with Dora."

"It's not working. I want to come home and put our family back together again. I have it in me, Cheech. I know it."

"By the time we get you unpacked and I put on the coffee, you'll be agitated and want out."

"I'm different. I'm older now."

"Age doesn't make us wiser, it just makes us older. I'm tired. And it would just figure, after all we've been through, that we'd lose our son."

"What do you mean?"

"I am being punished for my ambivalence. I had other dreams. I didn't want to be a mother at first. Remember?"

"But that changed. You love the kids."

"Oh, I'd die for them. And I was a good mother because I had a good mother. But I knew somewhere down the line, I'd pay for my ambition. And here it is. The marker is paid in full. I hope whoever stands to gain from this is satisfied."

"It was an accident, Cheech. What happened to our son was an accident."

"No such thing."

"You think this was all destined to happen? Losing our son?"

"From the day he was born."

"I can't believe what you're saying."

"You're floundering, Saverio. You like to think you control things, but even when your hand is on the wheel, you're not in control."

"I don't want to be apart anymore," Tony said. "We made him together. I remember the night we made him, don't you?"

"Yes, I do. But we don't know how to be happy together. We cling to each other in grief, and that's love to you?"

"It's part of it. But we were happy together too."

"Sometimes." Chi Chi looked away. "But it always comes down to the same thing. You think you want me, us, all of us, but you don't want the life. If you did, if you ever had, you would have never let us go. You never made the big decision."

"To be home?"

"You never decided what was sacred to you. And when you don't decide, in the end, nothing is."

He put his hands in his pockets. He was Tony now, and had been for so many years, but whenever he was with Chi Chi, the tuxedo fell away, the orchestra disappeared, the lights faded to black, the microphone went silent, and he was just Saverio, the kid he was the day she met him.

Everything that came after Chiara Donatelli was to push her away. He didn't want to love her too much, because he believed he was, deep down, *no damn good*.

"Are you headed back to Vegas?"

"I have a booking." Tony nodded. "I thank God for it. It keeps me sane."

"You love to sing, nothing wrong with that."

"Do you think I can make it right with Dora?"

"Sure."

"She loves me."

"We all love you, Sav."

"I know."

"Go back to the apartment tonight and tell her you've been an old fool and you want another chance. She's an Italian girl. We've been dealing with this nonsense since Hannibal's Army came over the Alps. She'll be all right."

"She'll stay?"

"Who can resist you?"

Tony laughed. "You always say the right thing."

Tony fumbled with his hotel room key.

"Gimme that. You're nervous!" the woman whispered. She took the key, unlocked the door, and went inside his room. Tony followed her.

The suite was Vegas chic. It was decorated in dark blue and cranberry, with a California king-sized bed facing floor-to-ceiling windows with a view of the strip. The woman yanked the drapery cords to reveal the flashing neon below.

"How much time do you have?" Tony asked as he turned on the lights, lowering the dimmer.

"The bus leaves in two hours," Cheryl said. She went to Tony and put her arms around him. "I was going to play blackjack after the show, but this is better." She fiddled with his bow tie but could not loosen it. He helped her.

Tony removed his tuxedo jacket. "I haven't stopped thinking about you."

"You must've had a stroke when you saw me sitting ringside."

"It was more like death by drowning. I was flooded with memories."

"You always had a way with words." Cheryl Dombroski stood back and looked at Tony, trying to reconcile the entertainer with the boy she recalled from the choir loft at Holy Family Church. "It's no shocker you made it."

"Come here." Tony took her hands.

"You still think about me?"

"Sure I do, Cheryl. For years. You broke my heart. When we were kids, the night you got engaged, I was ruined." Tony still had vivid memories of Cheryl Dombroski. It was kismet that she had shown up in Vegas. Tony often saw people from his days on the road, but it was rare that anyone from Detroit came to one of his shows. He'd often wondered what had happened to his first love.

"I'm so sorry." Her perfume had the scent of lilies, but as she slipped out of her shoes, Tony got a strong whiff of Bengay. "About that night all those years ago. And sorry about the Bengay. We went to the zoo, and I must've walked ten miles. My feet are killing me, and my calves are like cinder blocks. I must've laid it on thick." She rubbed her feet.

"It's a trek." Tony made Cheryl a drink. "Did you see the exotic animals?"

"Once my feet hurt, I stopped looking at the animals."

Tony handed her a rum and coke.

"So funny how life plays out," she said. "Do you ever get back to Detroit?"

"Not much," Tony said. "A job here and there. But it's not the same. How was South Bend?"

Cheryl had to think. "Oh, Ricky lasted at Packard about five years, and then we went west. He worked for Boeing in California for eighteen years, and that's when he got sick."

"I'm sorry."

"They're a cancer family. All the boys got it. The girls in that crew last forever, but the boys all get clipped by the Big C. My Ricky got lung. Died slowly. It was awful. I took care of him until the end. And after about five years, the kids said, 'Ma, look at you. You still got your shape, and you love people, you should go out.' That's when I met Phil."

"What does Phil do?"

"Golfs. He's retired. He was a parts man for TWA for years. I met him at Catholic singles."

"Do you still sing?"

"When I've had a few." She rattled the ice in her glass. "I've been following you all these years. I saw you on *Mike Douglas*, and I didn't know you were going to be on, and I was doing my chores, and I had a huge pile of ironing to do, and I saw you on the TV and I ironed my hand. I was so excited. Thrilled, really."

"I know how you felt." Tony sat on the edge of the bed and patted the spot next to him. Cheryl sat down.

"You do?"

"The thrilled part. It's how I felt about you when I was sixteen. It was Christmas. I had bought you a gold chain."

"You never gave it to me." She winked at him slyly.

"It was the Christmas Eve you told me you were engaged."

"That was a wild night."

"Not for me."

"No, I mean, in terms of how it changed my life."

"If you mean that, it was a wild night for me too. My father threw me out, and it began . . . this." He indicated the room. "This career. I don't know if you can call it one, it's something else. Something you do because you have to, not because you want to."

"You look like you're having fun up there under the lights."

"I do have fun when I'm working. It's the rest of the time. It's lonely."

"Oh, baby," Cheryl said as she rubbed the part of Tony's leg that went to sleep the most often, the side of his thigh.

He took his cue. Tony kissed Cheryl. He had wanted to kiss her for almost fifty years. He couldn't believe it had been that long. Sometimes it seemed like Detroit was ten minutes ago, and other times, it seemed like everything that happened before his fiftieth birthday had happened to another guy. Her kiss was nice enough, but she withheld. He wondered if she was thinking of Phil.

"What happened to it?" Cheryl nuzzled his cheek.

"To what?"

"To my chain. The chain you never gave me. Did you pawn it?"

"I carried it around a long time."

"You must've really loved me." Cheryl slipped off her jacket.

"As much as boys can love girls at sixteen." Tony noticed Cheryl's bust was high and firm, like a showgirl's.

"Right, right." Cheryl massaged his shoulders.

"Years later, I gave the chain to a hotel maid in Bemidji, Minnesota."

"Was she pretty?"

"Old enough to be my mother."

"I imagine you service fans of all ages." She laughed, but realized quickly that she had offended Tony. "I didn't mean that."

"It wasn't like that, Cheryl. We were talking, and she had lost her daughter. And I listened, and I felt like I had nothing to offer her, nothing to give. And then I remembered the chain. So I gave it to her, and I said, 'The man who sold me this chain told me that this gold came from the mountains of Lebanon and that he crossed oceans and continents to bring it to me, and that meant it was special in some way. And I had a hard time letting go of it because I thought of that old peddler every time I tried.' Well, this woman understood what I was trying to do, and she accepted it with great humility in honor of her daughter."

Cheryl and Tony sat on the edge of the bed, sipping their drinks. Tony put his drink down. Cheryl had already placed hers on the television table. Cheryl pounced on Tony.

Tony's cummerbund snapped off; so went his shirt, shoes, socks, belt, and pants. Cheryl's clothes fell away like a wild wind had kicked up and blown them off a clothesline. She had quite a figure for a woman in her midsixties. She could've passed for forty—and without his glasses, Tony could even pretend they were back in Detroit in high school. He could have imagined anything. Her hair, now strawberry blond, was styled in a lacquered upsweep, which Tony found difficult to navigate, but the desire in her blue eyes made up for the hardness of her hair.

Tony remembered that Cheryl had been on the upper school drill team and had been adept at high kicks and physical stunts, like splits and a midair jump called the Herkie. In that regard, she remained agile. She did a lot of nibbling and gnawing, which reminded him that room service closed at 1:00 a.m., and he hoped he could order a meal à deux before the kitchen closed.

Cheryl was eager to envelop and please in saddle style, which conjured Tony's favorite Westerns starring Tom Mix. He remembered going to one with Cheryl and the CYO from Holy Family. He wondered if she remembered, but he couldn't ask her, as his mouth was otherwise engaged.

After a while—and there was no telling on Tony's part how long that was—Cheryl had expended a lot of energy working hard to please him. She moved on top of him north to south like a well-oiled bicycle pump as she repeated, "There it is. There it is, there it is, there it is," a kind of mantra that went from coaxing, to coaching, to flat-out navigation. But he never quite got where he needed to be; the destination remained in his head. Cheryl slid off of him, lying next to him on the enormous bed. She panted as though she had just run up the stairs to his suite on the thirteenth floor two at a time.

"What's the matter?" she asked, gulping for air.

"It's not you."

"I'm not young anymore," Cheryl admitted.

"Wouldn't help if you were." Tony reached for the cigarettes on the nightstand.

"I see. Because I'm in shape. I do water aerobics at the Y. I could crack walnuts between my knees. I've still got power in my thighs."

"Without a doubt." He offered her a cigarette.

Cheryl declined. "It's psychological, Saverio."

"You think?"

She rolled over on her side, the curves of her body reminiscent of the Roman goddess in repose positioned in the infinity pool behind the hotel, who, in a feat of engineering excellence, had water spitting from a clamshell crown on her marble head. "Payback. I hurt you back then, and you harbored all this pain and rejection, and now you can't . . . because I wouldn't then."

Tony didn't know what to say, so he said nothing.

Cheryl rolled over on her back. "It's fine. We're in our sixties. Every encounter isn't the Fourth of July. This is life. Do you want me to try again?"

"I don't think so."

"I didn't think so. It's too much in one night."

Tony watched as Cheryl collected her clothing from every corner of the room. "You look good, Cheryl. Really good."

"I know." She shrugged. "Genetics. And Weight Watchers."

Room service arrived with an order of waffles, crispy bacon, black coffee, orange juice, and hash browns promptly at 11:00 p.m. Tony had ordered breakfast as soon as Cheryl departed; to make the time fly, he pretended that it was the next morning so he might put the painful events of the evening behind him. He was also starving because he had exerted a great deal of energy with no finale. It was like arriving in Paris pulling a rickshaw and finding out there's no Eiffel Tower.

As he poured the syrup on his waffles, he picked up the phone.

"Hey, Cheech."

Chi Chi put down the book she was reading in her New York apartment and checked the clock. "You all right, Saverio?"

"I don't know."

"What do you mean? Are you sick? It's late, you know."

"I know. Did I wake you?"

"No, I'm reading. Judith Krantz has a new one out. I can't put it down."

"You never could."

"Is there a problem with your credit card?"

"No, everything is fine. In that regard."

"So what is it?"

"It finally happened, babe."

"What are you talking about?"

He took a bite of his waffle. The butter and syrup dripped onto the napkin he had stuffed into the neck of his undershirt. He chewed. "I couldn't perform."

"You lost your voice?"

"No, I can sing."

It took Chi Chi a moment to understand. She closed her book.

After a few moments, Tony asked, "Are you still there?"

"I'm here. I'm grappling."

"So am I."

"I don't know what to say."

"I don't either."

"Except maybe you had it coming."

"On a night when I couldn't possibly feel worse, you make me feel worse."

"Except, of course, I'm your only real friend." Chi Chi sighed and propped her feet on a pillow. "Who was she? A showgirl?"

"No, as a matter of fact, she was older than you."

"Has it come to this, Savvy?"

Tony laughed. "Evidently."

"I can't see you perusing the audience in the Orchid Room for women that look like Mrs. Santa Claus. You must know the lady."

"How did you know?"

"At this stage of life, strangers don't hold the same allure. The past is what interests us. Holding on to what we knew," Chi Chi said softly.

"I knew her back in Michigan. She sang with me at Holy Family Church."

Chi Chi sighed. "That's a long time ago."

"She was beautiful. Polish girl. And I was sixteen, and she was seventeen, and she married another fella."

Chi Chi yawned. "What do you want me to say?"

"You know everything about me, and this is part of the picture," Tony said quietly.

"Saverio. You don't have to make love to every woman who wants to make love to you. You can have dinner and a nice conversation and a good-night kiss or not. You can take a walk down memory lane and not wind up in bed. You don't have anything to prove anymore."

"I must. But I can't prove it."

"You're under no obligation to meet a woman's needs, even when she demands it. Buy them a drink. Fine. Spin them around the dance floor. Okay. Then say good night, put her on the bus, and go up to your room and order pancakes."

"Waffles."

"Whatever. You can sing in the Orchid Room and enjoy your life. You can even retire if you want. I've made a nice nest for you. You have enough money. And with that cover of *Gravy*, you'll be making good money for the next few years. We've been all through this. Where's Dora?"

"At the house."

"Where are you?"

"The hotel."

Chi Chi checked the clock on her nightstand and quickly calculated the time difference. "Have you changed out of your tux?"

"Not yet."

"Have you had something to eat?"

"I ordered room service. Waffles. Bacon."

"Too heavy."

"I think you're right. I'm a little sick to my stomach," Tony admitted.

"You need to eat something lighter. There's usually crackers in the minibar. Go look. And have a Coke. No ice. I'll wait."

Tony went to the minibar, shuffled through the drawer, and poured a bottle of Coca-Cola without the ice. "I'm back," he said into the phone. "They had crackers. And a Coke."

"A miracle."

"You're a witch," he said as he chewed a cracker. "How do you know everything? Don't answer that." He swigged the Coca-Cola. "You can read me from three thousand miles away."

"Your stomach will settle in a minute. But your ego, that'll be bruised for a while."

"Nothing in the minibar for that?"

Tony began to laugh, and soon Chi Chi was laughing with him. They laughed so hard, it was as though they were rehearsing a sketch for the act.

"This would be hilarious if it wasn't my life, too," Chi Chi said.

"I really dragged you down, didn't I?"

Chi Chi didn't answer him. "Take a shower, change into fresh clothes, and go home. Put this behind you."

"What if it happens again?"

"Even Cadillacs break down eventually."

"You think I'm a Cadillac?"

"I did."

"Do you still?"

"After all we've been through, you want to know if I've still got it for you?" Chi Chi asked.

"Why not?" he said quietly. "I'm very vulnerable right now. I could use some shoring up."

"You're a married man. You have a wife for that."

"Right." He sighed.

"You belong to Dora. A very nice lady, by the way. And she takes excellent care of you."

"You like Dora more than me."

Chi Chi laughed. "I'm grateful to her. She's been good for you."

"She has."

"Maybe one of these times, before you invite a lady to your room, maybe you sit down, by yourself, and think: Why am I doing this? Why am I doing this when I have a good woman at home waiting for me?"

"Why would I do that?" Tony asked her.

"Because the answer might surprise you."

Chi Chi hung up the phone. She hadn't thought about Saverio Armandonada in a long time. Why had he called her out of the blue and asked her if she still cared about him? Why would her feelings even matter to him now, when they hadn't along the way, when they should have? Chi Chi had found solace elsewhere. Like many women before her, she made a life alone that worked. When her marriage ended, the loss of her husband brought other gifts forward: a sweeter connection to her children, her work, and now her grandchildren. She had found ways to make her life rich without Tony in it.

Duty-bound love is the Italian girl's area of expertise. The Italian woman is a master craftsman at the art of sacrifice. But love, romantic, wild, impetuous, unguarded, and free? Chi Chi had never experienced it. Love had always been about him: making his life better, shoring up his confidence, pushing him out into the world to succeed. Any feelings of abandon, surprise, and fulfillment were reserved for her work, for the creation of the music, for the process of making something from nothing, and for the creative enterprise that had never let her down. The music had been a faithful companion.

13

1987–1988

Calando

(Slowing down)

Chi Chi walked along the serene moss-carpeted streets of Treviso, Italy, feeling at home. The silver canals hemmed by walls of soft pink stucco were as her grandmother had described them. Now that Chi Chi was older than her grandmother had been when she shared those stories with her, she could appreciate the enchantments of the Veneto, and understand their longing for home after they emigrated. The Venetian springtime held the colors of a Tiepolo painting: vivid blues, soft greens, and gold with swirls of magenta.

Chi Chi carried her son's ashes in a box, carefully set in a leather case. She planned to leave his ashes in the fields outside the city, where Leone had spent a summer studying the violin. He had meant to return to the Veneto someday, but he died before he could make his dream come true. It had been nine years since Leone died, and his mother wanted to honor his wishes before it was impossible for her to do so.

She booked a room in a small inn at the foot of the Dolomites. She hired a driver to take her from the city and through the countryside. The bright green farm fields rolled out in patchwork velvet squares, while the mountains with their salt-colored peaks blended into the sky. There were small ponds along the road like scattered mirrors that reflected the clouds.

"Per favore, accosta qui, l'autista."

Chi Chi picked up the leather case and got out of the car. She trudged across the field to a serene pond, hemmed by glorious cypress trees. She made the sign of the cross, opened the box, and interred her son at the roots of an old cypress tree.

When she was finished, she wept quietly for his memory and all he had missed, but as soon as she had completed the task and honored his wishes, she dried her tears and returned to the car.

When Chi Chi arrived at the inn, a porter helped her with her luggage outside. She climbed the steps to the lobby.

"Your room has been taken care of, madam," the clerk said.

"By whom?"

"By your ex-husband," the familiar voice said from behind her.

"What?" She turned.

"I couldn't let you come here alone."

"I already put our boy to rest."

Tony put his arms around her. "So we'll visit him."

It was the velvets of Fortuny, that legendary Venetian textile maker, that spoke to Chi Chi. Standing in the showroom in the Giudecca section of Florence, Chi Chi held the weightless saffron fabric etched with fingers of peacock blue. She remembered the colors of summer on the beach in Sea Isle. Yellow light, teal waves, a sun so bright she was blinded, and when she opened her eyes, all she saw were stars.

Had Fortuny seen the same ocean tide, or a similar saturation of color at the same time of day? Had he observed a similar palette on the beaches of the Lido or Santa Margherita or Positano? He must have. This was her youth in texture, color, and form. The shroud material could serve as representing the day she met Saverio Armandonada. This fabric spoke of the time it was, the moment it had been.

"Babe, you want that for something?" Tony asked as he nestled his head into the crook of Chi Chi's neck, so their cheeks touched. His skin had the scent of cedar, lemon, and tobacco. More memories were conjured for her. She held some, felt others, and now his scent.

"What does this look like to you?" Chi Chi asked. She held the fabric up to the light.

"Am I supposed to know that fabric from somewhere?" he asked.

"What does it remind you of?"

"The curtains in Mount Airy Lodge in the Poconos, 1946."

"I'm not joking."

"I'm not either."

"It looks like the beach at Sea Isle. The day we met."

Tony squinted. "The blue?"

"Yeah, the blue."

"Yeah, I see it."

"Madame, posso aiutarti con il tessuto?" The salesgirl wanted to know how much fabric Chi Chi wanted to purchase.

"*Due*." Tony held up two fingers. "You know, *Due*. Give her a couple yards," Tony said. As the shopgirl draped the fabric over the table, set the metal ruler, and cut the velvet, Chi Chi observed the process with delight. The girl smiled at Chi Chi. "Che cosa hai intenzione di fare con esso?"

"Yeah, I want to know too. What are you going to make with it, babe?" Tony asked.

Chi Chi leaned on the table and looked at the design. "Something grand."

The girl folded the fabric carefully. "Va bene. Che bella," she said.

As Tony paid the bill, Chi Chi sorted through the fabric samples hanging on dowels. She was in awe of Fortuny's creations— gold velvet etched in pale blue, violet burned with a soft green, a regal red damask. Fabric, she believed, too exquisite to become a gown, a drapery, or a coverlet, almost too glorious to be used for any common purpose. Sometimes it is enough to be near something lovely. It doesn't require possession; nothing has to come of it, nothing need be created from it. Let its purpose be to exist solely as a thing of beauty and provide joy.

The details of the design and the execution of the patterning inspired her. Chi Chi understood how that same craftsmanship could intimidate and therefore cause the opposite reaction. It might cause a person to lash out and attempt to destroy it, just because it was so stunning. The stories of Fortuny's competitors looking to put him out of business were legendary. Jealousy almost took down the House of Fortuny.

When Tony Arma took a lover or a wife, it wasn't because he was inspired by the woman, it was about possessing beauty and the possibilities of what something new might bring. It wasn't love, after all; it was a man trying to surround himself with beauty in order to feel something, in hopes that beauty would reveal the truth. So far, it hadn't for Tony. But beauty had, in every way, fueled Chi Chi's creativity.

"What do you think of this place?" she asked.

"Italy?"

"Fortuny."

He scanned the room. "Velvet is velvet."

"But it's not."

"You see things I don't."

"That's always been true."

"And that's why we're friends. You see for me, and I see for you." Tony shrugged.

"What do you see for me exactly?" Chi Chi asked.

"I push you to write music."

"I was writing before I met you."

"But not as much and not as well."

"You're taking credit for that?"

"Not for your talent, no. But I will take credit for knowing how magnificent you are and making sure you knew it, too. Fair enough?"

Chi Chi didn't answer. Tony handed her the artfully wrapped yardage, folded into a neat rectangle and tied with an embossed silk ribbon. She held it close to her breast, like a schoolgirl clings to her favorite book.

"Thank you," she said.

"I like to see you smile, kid."

Chi Chi stood on the terrace of her hotel room, with a view of the Dolomites. The salt-covered peaks were so white, they appeared lit from within. The moon hung low and pale pink, like a pearl. There was a knock on the door.

"You have got to be kidding," Chi Chi said when she opened it.

Tony stood in the doorway with two glasses and a bottle of prosecco. "That's how you greet your lover? You're not inspiring much confidence."

"Go back to your room, old man."

Chi Chi was about to close the door, but Tony stopped her. "That's not how this story is going to go."

"This isn't a story, Sav. We have already lived it. You already wrote the ending. This is the sequel. We're good friends, with a lovely family to share. And that's all we're going to share."

"They wouldn't be here without us."

Chi Chi looked at Tony. She thought about it. Here she was, in the Veneto, at the foot of the mountains that had so much meaning to her. This was the place her mother's people were from, the place of her dreams as a girl. Now that she was a grandmother, she had fewer years ahead of her than behind her, and there was no full circle, just a life of fits and starts, mostly because of the man who stood before her. She had been curious through the years why he hadn't returned to her and begged her forgiveness. She knew he'd tried—there was that moment on the beach after he'd married Tammy, and another time in Rome, when the twins graduated from college, and when Leone played his first professional gig in Los Angeles and he had taken her in his arms impetuously and danced, and she thought for sure he would spend the night. But he hadn't, and she did not invite him, and that was that. But now that they were alone, just the two of them, the past seemed to dissolve like a chalk message on a stone wall in the rain, as if it had never been written. Whatever was left in her heart for him remained; it had not left with the bitterness that she had released long ago. Under all that pain, disappointment, and regret was love. Love remained when everything else had disappointed them. For the life of her, she could not imagine why. She still loved this man, and while it was completely without logic, it was as real as he was standing before her. Her conscience was clear. Tony was not married; neither was she. So, Chi Chi said, "Come in, Savvy."

She closed the door gently behind him.

He put the glasses and the bottle down on the table. "Come here."

"For what?"

"What do you think?"

"I want you to state your intentions."

"Talking takes the starch out of it, kid."

"I don't care."

"I want to make love to the only girl I've ever really loved."

"That's a pretty good opener." Chi Chi went out on the terrace. Tony followed her.

"You know my problem, all these years, is that I believed you," she said.

"I figured. You never married anyone else. Why not?"

"That's a personal question."

"I'm about to go to bed with you. I think we can get personal."

"I never remarried because I could never figure out why we couldn't make it work."

Chi Chi got that funny feeling in her legs, a weakness she hadn't felt in years. Her muscles were turning to cake batter. At sixty-nine, she worried; it was hardening of the arteries, the precursor to heart attack and strokes, or perhaps it was a nerve issue. She went back inside and sat down on the bed.

Tony joined her. "What do you say?" He leaned over and kissed her tenderly.

Chi Chi laughed.

"What is so funny?"

She held up her hand. "When our eyes are closed, we're not old."

Tony laughed. He kissed her again. "I'll show you old."

"I give up."

On the forty-third anniversary of their wedding, or the twenty-sixth anniversary of their divorce, however they wanted to look at the numbers, Tony and Chi Chi reunited and made love at the foot of the mountains, in the Veneto in the country of their people. And in what would forever be known as the Miracle of the Dolomites, neither of them broke a hip in the process.

Lee Bowman jogged through the first floor of Bergdorf Goodman on Fifth Avenue like a young girl, inhaling the scents of expensive perfumes, kid leather, and the petals of the long-stemmed fresh roses stuffed into giant crystal urns near the elevators.

Chi Chi waited for her friend and business partner on a stand in front of a three-way mirror in the private shopping area on the eighth floor. Reserved for the most wealthy clientele, the dressing room was a throwback to the halcyon days of custom fittings and design, before women bought lovely couture clothing off the racks.

Chi Chi studied herself in the mirror. She had come around on her looks, deciding not to get a face-lift. She liked the way time had played out on her features; besides, she liked her lips and eyes, they had stood the test of time. When you're happy, you don't need a plastic surgeon, but she didn't want to hurt her sister Lucille's feelings, who had an eye and neck lift. The great beauties always have the most to lose as they get older. Obviously Tony was still enchanted by her charms, as they were set to remarry at St. Joseph's in Sea Isle. A proper mass and ceremony. Mort and Betty Luck agreed to come all the way from Milwaukee to stand up for them again. Their children would be their wedding party. Chi Chi's life had taken a new turn, and she was following the path. All the pain and struggle had somehow been worth it. She thought about writing a song.

Chi Chi heard Lee calling for her in the area outside the dressing room.

"Room seven, Lee!"

Lee made her way down the hallway and pushed the door open. "Oh, Chi Chi," she said, taking in the dress. "You look gorgeous."

"Do you think Tony will like it?"

"Absolutely."

Chi Chi stepped off the platform. Lee helped her with the zipper. Chi Chi stepped out of the dress carefully and hung it on the padded hanger. She stepped back into her skirt and buttoned her blouse. "You know, Lee, you dodged a bullet, never getting married."

"Did I?"

"Yup."

"How so?"

"It's all so unpredictable."

"I had enough unpredictable in our business." Lee chuckled. "But I've never missed a husband. I had some very nice beaus."

"You sure did."

"That was enough for me. Happiness is all about accepting what's enough."

Chi Chi gathered up the dress that she would wear as she promised her life to Tony Arma once more. And as dresses go, this one would live up to the moment. Another Italian artist, Giorgio Armani, had made sure of it.

Three weeks later, Chi Chi pulled on her bathrobe and went to the front door of her apartment in Gramercy Park to collect the newspapers. She put on the coffee, turned on *The Today Show*, and unfolded the newspapers on the table. As she flipped through the *New York Post*, an item caught her eye.

OLD-SCHOOL CROONER TONY ARMA GETS HITCHED TO COCKTAIL WAITRESS GINGER WHEEDLE IN ATLANTIC CITY. NEW BRIDE IS 23, OLD GROOM 72

Chi Chi's phone rang. Barbara shouted into the phone about Tony's disgraceful wedding. She cursed, railed, and yelled about how Tony Arma had done nothing but embarrass their family from day one.

Chi Chi hung up the phone. It rang again.

It was Lee Bowman. "I hope to God he was thinking with something besides his crotch! Did she sign a prenup?"

Rosie called. Sunny called. Lucille screamed into the phone. They were shocked. Stunned. But, no one, it seemed, was concerned about Chi Chi's feelings.

"Why aren't you angry? I'd kill him!" Rita railed.

"I've already been through the worst. Losing my son," Chi Chi reminded her.

Chi Chi went into her bedroom. She opened the closet door. On the hook on the back of the door, in a dress bag, was the dress she was to wear when she remarried Tony: the gorgeous chiffon chemise in magenta with a seed-pearl collar from Bergdorf's, Armani privé. Chi Chi stared at it. "Glad I didn't cut the tags off."

Chi Chi sat at her desk in the offices of the BowDon Company on Fifth Avenue, filing paperwork. Lee and Chi Chi had turned their management business into an unexpectedly profitable booking agency for musical acts and orchestras. Even in the era of disco, there remained a demand for swing orchestras.

The receptionist buzzed her. "Mrs. Arma is here to see you."

"Send her in. And Pam, make the arrangements we discussed immediately, please."

A pretty young woman in her early twenties, with wild curls, permed brown hair, a trim, small figure, and a high, hoisted bust entered Chi Chi's office. The shoulder pads inside her silk blouse overpowered her small frame, making it look as if she were wearing shoeboxes under her clothes.

"I'm Tony's wife," the young woman announced.

"Ginger, is it?"

"That's right. You were his first wife?" she blurted nervously.

"I was."

"He divorced you long ago."

"Long, long ago. Three wives ago."

"He's only my second husband," Ginger said.

"But you're twenty-three. What happened to your first husband?"

"He's in Gracedale."

"What happened?"

"He had a stroke when he was seventy-six and had to go in a home, and his family turned on me."

"I'll bet they did. How did you meet Mr. Arma?" Chi Chi arranged the pencils in the cup on her desk.

"At the bar at the Isle of Capri."

"In Italy?"

"No, the Isle of Capri restaurant on Third Avenue."

"Were you a patron?"

"A cocktail waitress. The tips were good. I was sad to quit," she admitted.

"You quit when you married Tony?"

"He wanted me at home." She shrugged.

"Mr. Arma is at that stage of life. He needs serenity. He needs naps. Let's face it. He could use a nurse."

"That's cool. It was good at first. The first month was nice. Then he went on the road, and my mother moved into the spare room."

"You couldn't be alone."

"I don't like it. Ma gets along great with Tony. She plays that record *Pacific Songbook* every night when she has her highball."

"I imagine she'll move on to Jack Jones now that you've moved on from Mr. Arma," Chi Chi said.

"I don't know about that. She is a big fan of his records. She loves *Gravy, Gravy, Gravy.* She's of your generation." Ginger swallowed nervously. "I'm here for my settlement."

"What settlement?"

Ginger's lip quivered. "The money paid to one spouse by the other in cases of abandonment."

"You've been abandoned?"

"In a permanent way. He left me. He said he'd be in Vegas."

"Why didn't you go with him?"

"I'm from Queens."

"I think New Yorkers can travel outside the city limits."

"But I don't want to."

"So Mr. Arma said the marriage was over?"

"He didn't tell me directly. I just got the papers."

Chi Chi nodded. "I know."

"You do?"

"This isn't the first time." Chi Chi sat back in her chair. "Where's your mother?"

"She's outside in the waiting room."

"Ginger, if you don't mind, I'd be more comfortable speaking with your mother. Could you send her in? I'd like to talk to her privately. There's a small refrigerator with soda in it out in the reception area. If you're thirsty. Help yourself."

"Thank you."

Kloris Wheedle Rinhoffer had a cap of short black hair, and her skin glistened with self-tanner. Her face had a pumpkin sheen. She wore false eyelashes as thick as the bristles on a push broom. She resembled the orange ceramic Siamese-cat ring holder the twins had bought Chi Chi one Christmas, down to the flinty black rhinestone eyes.

"Mrs. Wheedle?" Chi Chi stood and indicated Kloris should take a seat.

"Technically it's Mrs. Rinhoffer." She sat down.

"Mrs. Rinhoffer, I've just met your daughter for the first time, and I would assume the last."

"I don't want to eat up your time," Kloris said. "What's your offer?"

"What are you looking for?" Chi Chi asked.

"One million dollars and the New York City apartment at the Melody."

"Mr. Arma doesn't have a million dollars, and he doesn't own the New York apartment," Chi Chi said.

"Well, he'll have to come up with it."

"Mr. Arma doesn't have it," Chi Chi repeated.

Kloris smiled. "Then you go get it."

"I'm his ex-wife, not his mother. And even if I were his mother, I wouldn't be responsible for his flimflam marriages."

Kloris ignored the swipe at her daughter. "He sold millions of records."

"Thousands," Chi Chi corrected.

"A lot." Kloris raised her voice. "And he's been touring since he was sixteen. That's a lot of dough."

"Under the rolling pin."

Kloris's eyes narrowed. "What kind of a racket are you running here?" She looked around the office speculatively, as if she were calculating the rent, the bills, and the commissions Chi Chi must be collecting.

"Mrs. Rinhoffer, your daughter is Tony's fourth wife, and they've spent less than a year together as a married couple—eight months, to be exact. Four of that, Tony was on tour. So that leaves four months. How do you figure a million in compensation?"

"He's rich."

"That money is all gone," Chi Chi said.

"What do you mean, gone?"

"Gone. Three children, three marriages. Career in decline. A tax bill with such enormous penalties, it still isn't paid off. There's no money for your daughter or for you. None."

"Ginger is pregnant."

"Congratulations."

"One million, and the apartment."

"I suggest you ask the father of the baby for the money."

"That's why I'm here! Tony Arma is the father!"

"It would be impossible. Tony has been sterile since 1953."

Kloris was undeterred by facts. "Sometimes accidents happen."

"With the bartender at the Isle of Capri, maybe. But not with Tony. That would be a miracle. Last time I checked, Sunnyside, Queens, is not Lourdes, France."

"I'll go to the papers with everything I know. He drinks, and he wears a toupee!"

"Say whatever you want. You're not getting a penny."

"He's impotent!"

"Hard to get a young lady pregnant if he's impotent."

"Not all the time. Here and there, I'm told." Kloris stared at Chi Chi, her eyes turned as cold as black coal at the other woman's imperturbability. "All right," she said. "Two hundred and fifty thousand."

"Not a penny."

"Listen here, you old bag—"

Chi Chi smiled. "I've been called worse, and from the looks of it, so have you."

"You can't get away with this."

"And neither will you. Let me be clear, Mrs. Rinhoffer. If you think that you can come in here and scare me, after what I've lived through, you're mistaken. I came up in the clubs and I dealt with real gangsters. You're an old-fashioned thug. You're here to shake me down. You want something for nothing, or in this case, money in exchange for your daughter's body."

"My daughter is not a prostitute!"

"You named her price. One million dollars and a piece of real estate. What do you call that, if not prostitution?"

"She was his wife. There was true affection between them. She loved him!"

"Love. That's a big word coming from a small person."

"You're just jealous! She's young and beautiful, and he left you for not one, not two, but three women."

"Who Mr. Arma chooses to bed or wed is not my concern or my responsibility. I'm a busy lady. But mother to mother, I see what you're thinking. The clock is ticking. Your daughter's youth is slipping through your hands like ice. Your business will dry up in a few years. When Miss Wheedle's charms go, and they will, so will your opportunity to extort money from old men. So you have to beat it to the bank, and fast."

"You have some nerve!"

"Between us old girls, you'd have given Tony a tumble yourself if you thought he'd bite."

"I wasn't interested in him in that way," Kloris sniffed, sticking out her chest.

"But you were. That's why you play *Songs from the Pacific* on your hi-fi on a loop."

Kloris shrugged. "I'll get a lawyer."

"It won't matter. I own everything. When you listen to *Gravy, Gravy, Gravy*, picture my face, because I wrote it, and I own the copyright. I own the copyright on every song Tony Arma sings." Chi Chi pulled a large black checkbook ledger out of her desk drawer, opened it, and wrote a check. She tore it out of the book and handed it to Kloris.

Kloris looked at the amount. "Three hundred dollars? You're insane." She threw it back on the desk.

"Moving expenses for Ginger." Chi Chi opened her wallet and placed a five-dollar bill on the check.

"What's that for?"

"A cab to the apartment. When you get there, you'll find all of Ginger's things and yours packed to go in the lobby. The locks have been changed, and security has been instructed not to let you or your daughter past the bellman post. If you try anything funny, the police at the fourth precinct will escort you back to Queens personally."

"Where do you get off treating us like criminals? We've been taking care of Tony. What do you do? Nothing! You're a bitch!"

Chi Chi sighed. "I imagine I can be."

Rinhoffer grabbed the check and the five-dollar bill. "I will be back."

"You can come back as often as you like. Your extortion attempts won't work any better in the future. And next time, you'll have to pay your own cab fare."

Kloris began to argue with Chi Chi again, but it was too late:

the phone rang. Chi Chi picked up the phone as Kloris left the office, pushing Lee aside.

"What was that all about?"

"Another woman who wanted something for nothing. Tony runs his love life like it's a two-for-one sale at Loehmann's."

"Are you all right?"

"I never get used to it," Chi Chi admitted, her voice suddenly tired. "Poor kid."

"His fourth wife?"

"She doesn't have a mother."

"I just saw the woman. Lousy face-lift. Fooling no one."

"That's no mother," Chi Chi said. "I'm crying because I was lucky. I have a good mother who loves me. I still need her, even at my age. So when I meet a terrible mother like that one, I know the difference."

"You're a better woman than I am. I don't want to understand people like that."

"You've never had to, Lee. You didn't marry Tony Arma. Oh, the parade of characters he has brought into my life." Chi Chi closed the black ledger and slipped it back into her desk drawer.

"Do you think he'll marry again?"

"He can't bear to be alone."

"Then keep that checkbook handy."

"If the good Lord takes me first, there will be problems. Men lose their way when they get old. We find ourselves, they get lost."

Chi Chi walked to her apartment on Gramercy Park. She kept a good pace in the thick of the rush-hour traffic as commuters poured down into the subway stations like moles disappearing into the earth. She was grateful for her job, and pleased she still had the energy to do it.

At seventy, Chi Chi had stamina and strong legs. She had a few minor health glitches along the way, cataracts, an issue with the bones in her neck, and a female problem that was easily fixed once it was identified. Barbara and Lucille had their own health scares, but all in all, the Donatelli girls figured they were lucky. Isotta was still with them. Now in her nineties, she lived with Barbara and still made homemade macaroni for Sunday dinner.

New York City at twilight remained Chi Chi's favorite time of day. She tried to time her walk home to be at the Flatiron Building and the Twenty-Third Street Park during the moment the peach sun slipped into the streaks of purple that hovered over the horizon in New Jersey. There was something about the blues and violets of twilight, at the confluence of the park, Fifth Avenue, and lower Broadway, with the looming majesty of the Empire State Building behind her, that gave her a sense of her place in the world. Chi Chi walked along East Nineteenth Street when she heard someone call her name.

An older man stood under the awning of the Union Square Café. He took the last drag off a cigarette before putting it out in the brass ashcan. Chi Chi squinted at him.

"Cheech?" he said.

"Hello, Saverio." Chi Chi stepped closer to him, to get a good look. He had stopped wearing the hairpiece. He wore a navy suit, a hot pink Italian tie, and a striped blue and white dress shirt. She had sent him paperwork, weeks earlier, which he had not signed and returned. "I understand you're divorcing Miss Wheedle?"

"Ginger. You can call her Ginger."

"I'll call her Miss Wheedle. The least you can do is sign the paperwork." Chi Chi tucked her purse under her arm. She was glad she had put on lipstick before leaving the office, and that her hair had been done that morning. She wore a sage-green bouclé suit with brass buttons and black suede pumps. She liked wearing the color of money; after all, she had earned it.

"You look good," he called after her.

She turned back. "Save it. I prefer honesty, I think I deserve that courtesy."

"You do look good," he said sheepishly.

"Better than you."

"That's cruel."

"Sav, you know what's cruel? Following me to Italy, where I've gone to inter my son, seduce me, tell me you want to marry me again, only to return home and marry a young woman the age of your granddaughter instead. Worse? Instead of telling me yourself, you let me read about it in the paper. How do you live with yourself? I used to think you'd lost your mind every time you made a stupid choice, but that's too easy. I am tired of taking care of you, cleaning up your messes, letting your children believe you were a good man, supporting you to them unconditionally, keeping the books, making pots of gravy when you were hungry, fretting about the minutiae, and agonizing about the big stuff. When are you going to be an adult? I even have your funeral expenses paid, your headstone engraved, and your suit picked out for when the time comes.

"I have done everything I could to make your life easier, to take the pain away. And in return, you hurt me time and time again. I have my theories about why, but they don't matter anymore. I wake up every morning wondering how I got here. Before I put on the coffee and brush my teeth, I have to convince myself that I'm worth the cup of coffee and the dollop of toothpaste I am treating myself to, because I spent my life loving a man who valued me less than either of those things.

"And here's the irony, Saverio: you are alive today because of me. You have money in your pocket and children and grandchildren who love you because I made sure they did. Every birthday there was a card from you, and every Christmas a gift from you. Look at me. Take a good long look. The next time you see me on Fifth Avenue, don't call my name and don't act like you know who I am, because you don't. That diamond heart you gave me when you asked me to marry you, I get it now. You gave me a diamond heart because you never had any intention of giving me the real thing."

Chi Chi turned and walked down the street. The city was bathed in sound; she did not hear Tony call her name.

14

NOVEMBER 2000

Triste

(Sorrowful)

The nurse opened the window in Tony Arma's hospital room. A crisp autumn breeze blew through the room. Tony tried to inhale the fresh air, but he could only manage small, shallow breaths.

"I'm going to close it now, Mr. Arma."

Tony waved his hand. "Thank you, that's enough."

"Can I get you something to drink, Father?" the nurse asked Father Joe O'Brien, the new chaplain of St. Vincent's Hospital, as she adjusted Tony's blanket.

The priest was young, Irish, and eager to be of service.

"No, thank you."

ADRIANA TRIGIANI

"You know you're on your way out when the combined ages of your nurse, your doctor, and your priest are less than your own," Tony said.

Father O'Brien laughed. "I'm sorry I missed your act. I'll get the CD."

"There are several." Tony folded the hem of the sheet neatly over the blanket. "I never officially retired. My agent is still in business. Lee Bowman. The last of an ilk, Padre."

"You can call me Joe."

"I can't do that. I was taught to never call a priest anything but Father."

"Your choice."

"Just my upbringing, Father. Where are you from?"

"Scranton, Pennsylvania."

"I played your burg. Very early on. Spring 1938. Hotel Casey. Home to Billy Lustig and the Scranton Sirens. Billy hired Tommy and Jimmy Dorsey out of Shenandoah, Pennsylvania, when they were teenagers. We were all teenagers. We used to pack in the coal miners, and I used to think, Sing, boy, sing, or that will be you underground busting rock and your back. I had a lot of respect for those men."

"Who was your favorite singer?"

"When I was coming up, the best of the best was Sinatra. Of course. The rest of us were footmen on the gold carriage of the king. You know the guys that run alongside and jump on the moving vehicle and do their best to hold on? That was us, all of us because Sinatra was in a class by himself. None of the rules applied to him. Nobody could tell him what to do. Harry James, the story went, wanted Sinatra to change his name to Frankie Satin. Sinatra refused. And that's the difference between a star, a headliner, and the sap that sings under a blinking bulb in a side room in Vegas. The star says *no*."

"Did you?" the priest asked.

"I wanted fame and fortune too much, so I agreed to everything to get them. I did what I was told. So Saverio Armandonada became Tony Arma. The name had just enough swing and sounded like a dish of macaroni. That's what they told me at the time. But I never felt like Tony Arma—I never became him. The name didn't mean anything to me, and if something doesn't mean anything to you, it won't matter to anybody else either. When they made me change my name, I gave up four thousand years of my family history—or that's how it felt. When they take away a man's name, they might as well cart away his conscience with it. You're up for grabs. I did the best I could wearing another man's shoes, but they never fit."

"Do you want forgiveness, Tony?"

"Saverio, Father. I was baptized Saverio."

"Do you want forgiveness for your sins, Saverio?"

"Yes, Father."

"I give you absolution for everything," the priest said, blessing him.

Tony sighed. "Let me ask you something. Is it true? Has a place been made for me there?"

"In my Father's house, there are many rooms." The priest smiled.

"Yeah, but for real and true, is there a room for me?"

"Yes, there is."

"And how do you know for sure?"

"It's been promised."

"So there is a promise that will go unbroken."

"Saverio, it's the only one that is guaranteed. It's the one between you and your God."

Saverio Armandonada began to weep.

"It's not good for your lungs to cry."

"Tell you the truth, it feels good, Padre. Feels like I'm purging."

"Then cry."

He wiped his eyes on the bedsheet. "I want to see my mother again."

"You will."

"She said she'd be there, but I thought she only said it when she was dying so I wouldn't be afraid when my time came."

"She might have, but she meant it."

Tony looked off into the distance. "I made love to a lot of women, Padre."

"Should we say an act of contrition or a prayer of gratitude?" the priest joked.

Tony shook his finger at the priest. "Things have changed in the Holy Church of Rome since I was a kid. I might have shown up for mass more often if I had a priest like you. I do need some forgiveness. I didn't put the women first."

"It sounds as though you are truly contrite."

"I never meant to hurt anybody."

"Most of us don't."

"I can't remember a lot of it. Funny how that goes. When you're in love, you think that's all there is, that's your unlimited universe of contentment. When it turns on you, and it always does, you can't remember the happy times. They're erased. Sometimes you can't remember their names, but you see things and you're reminded of a particular pleasure. A nightie. A stocking. A velvet ribbon. Something will trigger a memory, and the time you spent together rolls over you like a truck. I don't remember names so much now. Times and places are better. And if they help me remember the women, that's not half bad."

"I imagine it isn't." The priest smiled.

"I didn't learn a damn thing. Well, maybe one thing. No matter how many women you marry, every new wife wants a new kitchen. Could never figure that one out. Even when she couldn't cook, she wanted the kitchen. Kitchens are the most expensive rooms in a house. Bathrooms are a close second. But women, they have to have a kitchen of their own."

"There are some mysteries that we can never solve."

"You got that right, Padre. Not in this lifetime. There's no jam like the one you get in with a woman. They know things. They demand effort and excellence from you—more than any man. Which means you can never win. Devious connivers of the fourth degree. But I could never find a way to live without one."

"What did your father do?"

Tony's expression went blank. "Do?"

"For a living. His profession."

"He made the glass that became the windshields and the windows in Ford automobiles."

"How interesting." The priest leaned in.

"He started in 1915, a year before I was born. And he died before he retired from Rouge. He was still working when he died. True story."

"What was his name?"

"You writing a book?"

"No, I'd like to pray for him."

"Leone."

"The lion."

"Yes. He was a lion."

"What's your favorite memory of your father?"

"Oh, that's a tough one."

"Too many?"

"Nah. Not enough." Tony closed his eyes. "He used to make a fire pit in the winter. In the snow. Hell, it snowed from September to June back then in Michigan. It wasn't the rust belt, it was the ice bag. Anyhow, my father would dig a pit in the snow, build a fire, and roast chestnuts in an iron skillet. And the aroma of that had the scent of the earth, but sweet. Wherever I go in the world, if someone is roasting chestnuts, I think of my father."

"You must miss him."

"My son was named after him."

"You had a son?"

"One boy. A good boy. Toured with me when he turned eighteen. You're too young to know my music, I guess."

"I grew up on Springsteen, Southside Johnny, and Bon Jovi—you know, the shore bands. Hair bands too."

"Good for you. Every generation has their own music. That's how it should be. My wife is from down the shore. Chi Chi Donatelli."

"You married an Italian girl."

"Divorced her too. Chiara Donatelli. She sang too. Wrote songs. We were of the time of singers like Dick Haymes, Jack Leonard, Dinah Shore: Chi Chi wrote a big hit that Dinah recorded. Yeah, the singers back then, you can't top them today. You should take a listen sometime. There was Ethel Waters and Ella Fitzgerald. Sinatra of course, and Tony Bennett, Louis Prima and Keely Smith, Perry Como, Dean Martin out of Mingo Junction, Ohio. Let's see. Jerry Vale. Steve and Eydie, they were a lot of fun, and they came along later. Bandleaders like the Dorsey brothers, Harry James, Vaughn Monroe. Henry Mancini, Jimmie Lunceford, someday take a listen to him. Cab Calloway. Duke Ellington. Nobody should leave this life without dancing to *String of Pearls*."

"Tell me about your son."

"Leone could play any instrument he picked up from the age of five. No bull. Settled on the sax eventually, could play the piano and the trumpet, and he hit the skins with ferocity. But he died young, too young, in an accident. He was helping other people on the side of the road. Not far from here, on the West Side Highway.

He died in this hospital. How's that for irony? They brought him here. After he died, I walked to mass here every Sunday in the chapel. It helped me cope. I can't say that I joined in. I sat in the back. Never went to Communion."

"Why not?"

"Didn't feel worthy."

"Because you were divorced from Chi Chi?"

"She was the first. I had four marriages altogether. And four divorces altogether. Padre, a bachelor lies before you."

The priest whistled. Tony wanted to laugh, but didn't have the breath. The machine over his head beeped.

"I'm sorry, Saverio."

"That was funny." Tony shook his finger at the priest again. "The well-timed whistle. It kills every time."

"You only had children with your first wife?"

"Correct. Three with Cheech. I loved that girl from the start. Just liked being around her. There are people like that. They bring you up just by showing up. First as a friend. That's why I married her. I trusted her. I didn't have to do a lot of explaining. I think that's where men step in it. Women want to understand why we do the things we do. If we could explain it, we'd be women. I have a newsflash for the ladies: most of the time, there's no reason for any of it. I just lived. Men don't pick things apart—maybe we should. Every woman I ever loved wanted me to explain my feelings, and every time I did, every time I was honest, calamity ensued."

"Why was that?"

"The truth tastes like wine that's turned. You see, Father, a man lives in debt to a woman who loves him and takes him in, because we know we're unworthy. But the day comes when we're presented with a bill, we know we owe the woman and we have to pay, and there's only a couple ways to do that. One is to give them your life, with the ring, the house, you know: the whole

shot, kids, family. And the other is to do them the favor of staying away. That's right, the big scram. I did it a lot, and I did it in
every marriage. I found if I lingered too long, I got on everyone's
nerves, including my own."

"So far, Mr. Arma, I don't see any sin in that."

"There isn't until you step outside your word."

"You mean lie?"

"If you want to call it that. Usually I was just sparing the woman's feelings."

"Chi Chi's?"

"I tried not to hurt her."

"But you did."

Tony nodded. "If you would've told me that anger and regret
are the two strongest emotions at the end of life, I'd have told
you you're crazy. But it's true. I'm more alive in here"—he tapped
his head—"than I've ever been. I'm like a caged animal in a body
that doesn't work anymore, with a sharp mind that does. And
now that I'm old and supposedly wise, everybody wants answers.
I got twin daughters who want to understand why their father
did the things he did, but it's awful hard to explain the navigation of the human heart to your children, who would prefer you
didn't have such thoughts about anyone but their mother, and
even then, they only want you together in peace. I love my kids,
I'd die for them, but I don't live for them any more than they'd
live for me."

"In my line of work, we like to gently suggest that you live for
God."

"I fell short on that, too, Padre. I'm a man of this world. I tried
to make people happy. Sometimes I hit the bull's-eye, and sometimes I got a dart in the neck for my efforts."

"Isn't that true of all of us?"

"I don't know about that. Chi Chi saw me a certain way, and I told her, you may see me in that light, but that light fades. It moves with the sun and disappears with the moon, so don't count on it, kid."

"She held out hope for you."

"I bet she still does. She's what I call an optimist."

"Saverio, you have had last rites and your final confession. Would you like to take Holy Communion?"

Tony sighed. "It would make my mother happy."

"Would it make you happy?"

"Whatever made my mother happy would make me happy too," Tony said softly.

The young priest opened the leather case in which he carried a bottle of holy water, a vial of chrism, the blessed oil, and the pyx, a small gold bowl with a lid containing the consecrated hosts.

"How are you feeling, Sav?" Chi Chi said, as she entered the room. "Good afternoon, Father."

Tony looked up at Chi Chi. "Your hair is white."

"I stopped dyeing it." Chi Chi, still trim at eighty-two, wore a black pantsuit and white pearls.

"Why?" Tony squinted at her.

"The same reason you stopped wearing a toupee."

"Too much maintenance."

"Of course. It got old, Sav."

"Padre was about to give me Communion."

"And he wants it?" Chi Chi turned to the priest.

"May I offer it to you?"

Chi Chi thought about it.

"Cheech, take the wafer, will you?" Tony said in a raspy voice.

Chi Chi held the plastic cup with a straw on the nightstand up to Tony's lips. He took a sip.

"I was thinking that we didn't have a mass when we got married." Chi Chi placed the cup on the table.

"The war was on," Tony reasoned.

"I should have insisted."

"We were in a rush, as I remember." Tony winked at her. "You couldn't wait."

"One of us was." Chi Chi turned back to the priest. "Yes, I'd like to have Communion, Father."

The priest removed the lid from the pyx and gave Communion to Chi Chi. He placed the small white wafer on her tongue. She bowed her head and made the sign of the cross. The priest turned to Saverio and did the same. The three sat in silence for a few moments.

"Thank you, Father," Chi Chi said.

"Where are the girls?" Tony asked.

Chi Chi looked at her wristwatch. "They will be here any minute."

"Nice. Padre can meet them too."

"Sav, I want you to do something for me."

"Sure."

"I want you to tell your daughters that you love them and you're proud of them."

"I don't need a script, Cheech."

"You were terrible at improvisation. You always needed a script."

The priest tried not to laugh as he listened to the old couple bicker. He packed up his sacred kit and placed his prayer book on top of it.

A bunch of silver helium balloons embossed with the message "Get Well Soon" in purple floated into the room, carried by Rosie, who held the strings. Sunny followed her sister inside. Rosie let go of the balloons when she saw the condition of her father. The balloons floated to the ceiling and gently tapped against it, as though they were trying to escape.

"What happened, Dad?" Sunny asked.

"A little heart attack."

"Are they fixing you up?"

"Sure, sure." He turned to the priest. "These are my daughters. Rosie and Sunny, Father."

The priest shook each woman's hand. He had pictured them much younger, as Tony had called them girls, but the twins were fifty-five years old.

"Is the priest here to give you last rites?" Sunny wanted to know.

"Of course," Tony said. "He'll give them to you too, if you sit here long enough. Relax, girls. It's strictly routine."

"A sponge bath is routine. Last rites are for the dying," Sunny said, her eyes filling with tears.

"Come here, Sunny."

Sunny moved close to her father. "You were a funny kid," he said. "Made me laugh all the time. Not because you were trying to be funny, but because you were trying to seek justice in this world. Well, guess what? The joke was on you. There is no fairness and no justice but I love you for trying. You were adamant that this or that had to be fixed, or that your sister got the better shoes or your brother the better bicycle. But it wasn't because you wanted the stuff. You wanted everything to be fair. And that makes you wise. I like your husband. And I love you, and I'm proud of you."

Sunny kissed her father and sat next to him on the bed, wiping her eyes on her sleeve. Chi Chi stood behind her.

Tony turned to Rosie. "Rosaria, you were named for my mother. That got you some points out front. You were like her. Beautiful. Too accommodating. Too nice. But that's a good thing. If there were no angels walking around on this earth, nobody would want to go to heaven. Thank you for my grandson and granddaughter. And for my great-grandson. I love you too, and I'm proud of you."

Rosie kissed her father and sat on the other side of him, taking his hand as Sunny held the other.

"Dad, do you want to say something to Mom?" Sunny said softly.

"What for?"

Chi Chi laughed.

"No, Dad, really."

"If you girls need an example of how to be, you look to your mother. She knew me best, and she never held it against me. Not much."

The priest stood at the end of Tony's hospital bed. He had already given Tony Arma everything in his kit, so he offered a final prayer to the family. When he was done, Tony closed his eyes and fell asleep.

As the sun set, Greenwich Village was bathed in violet light. Chi Chi and her daughters held vigil through the cold November afternoon as Tony lay dying.

Around nine o'clock that night, Chi Chi stood up to stretch. Rosie was curled up on the end of her father's bed, while Sunny sat holding Tony's hand as she sat upright in the chair next to him observing his breathing. The room was quiet except for the whirl of the monitors on the machines.

Tony opened his eyes. Rosie sat up on the bed, and Sunny stood up. Chi Chi leaned in. "Do you need something, Savvy?"

"Leone," he said softly. "Leone." And, as surely as he had been alive, he was gone.

The three women stood in silence, holding the moment of his passing.

"Mom, he saw Leone," Rosie said with wonder.

"He's with our brother!" Sunny whispered.

Chi Chi embraced her daughters. "Isn't it wonderful? He's not alone."

The twins believed that their father had been reunited with their brother.

But Chi Chi knew differently. It wasn't her son who was on the other side to greet her husband. She was certain that when Saverio arrived in the place of all understanding, there was only one man he needed to see, only one soul who could end his suffering, and that man was his father, Leone Armandonada.

The monitor began to beep, another machine buzzed. Soon the nurse ran into the room. She shut off the machines, checked Tony, and turned to them. "I'm so sorry."

Chi Chi sent Rosie and Sunny out of the room when the nurses arrived to bathe and dress Tony. She sat by the window as the nurses prepared him for the undertaker.

"Mrs. Arma?" The nurse touched her gently on the arm. "You're Tony's wife, aren't you?" The nurse gave Chi Chi the miraculous medal that Tony had worn since their engagement. "He was wearing this. The Blessed Mother never lets me down either."

"What's your name?"

"Mary Ann Sullivan Whalen."

"A lot of names for a good Irish girl. Are you devoted to her?"

"I say my rosary every day."

"Not easy—what you do. Here, please take it."

The nurse was surprised. "I couldn't."

"There aren't a lot of young people who appreciate these medals anymore." Chi Chi pressed it into her hand. "They only work if you believe in them."

"Thank you. I will take good care of it."

"Thank you for taking such good care of him."

The nurse looked over at Tony. "Would you like to remove his wedding ring yourself?" Chi Chi got up from the chair by the window and followed her to Tony's side. "May I have a moment with him, please?"

Mary Ann left the room as Chi Chi fumbled for her reading glasses in her coat pockets. As usual, she found them dangling from her neck on a gold chain. She placed the readers on the end of her nose, leaned in to take a close look at her ex-husband. She ran her hand over the top of his head and down the side of his face. She tenderly kissed his cheek. It was cold. It felt like it had when he went outside and had a cigarette with the boys between sets in a place like Chisholm on the Iron Range of Minnesota, places so cold even the thermometers froze.

She held Tony's left hand and peered down at his wedding ring, then slid it off his finger. Her own hand began to tremble as she held it up to the light. The inscription read:

Chi Chi's Husband

"I'll be damned," Chi Chi said softly to herself.

Three wives later, and he was wearing *her* ring at the end of his life. She felt plenty, but she could not cry. She slipped the ring onto her thumb and sat down on the bed next to him. He was beginning to transform in those minutes after life has ended and death takes hold. Tony's color was changing rapidly; his face no longer showed human emotion. His soul had lifted away. Beauty, truth, integrity, and hope were gone now, his body abandoned by its spirit like any machine that has lost its purpose.

Chi Chi continued to hold his hand, remembering that day on the beach so many years ago when he offered it to her and she didn't want to let go. She slipped out of her shoes, climbed into the bed, and lay next to him, as she had done so many times when he crawled home late from a show in the early days, when they found it painful to spend even one night apart. She remembered how he would quickly fall asleep, exhausted from the gig, and how she would try not to move, so as not to disturb him, knowing he needed his rest. When they were young, she would hold him as he slept, just to be near him. Those days had become the nights that had become years that were lost after he left her, or she kicked him out, who could remember? The middle and the end of their marriage was muddy now; only the beginning was clear, when they were happy. Their life together had not been easy. If it were a song, it most certainly was not a ditty, as the band called requests from the audience, tunes that were so simple they required no rehearsal. Nor had their journey together been a chart topper, a song everybody knows but no one much performs anymore. Commitment had not come easily to either them, if she were being truthful. Their song was neither a novelty nor a humoresque. They had meant everything to one another, but like all masterpieces created from nothing, what they had was flawed. A work of art? Sometimes. But not to everyone's taste. Mistakes? Plenty. Too many to list, and they would cause overtime in a confessional. There was no need for absolution now. She had given it. All was forgiven. All of it.

Chi Chi closed the window in her bedroom, shutting out the cold and the sound of the sirens of the fire trucks on Lexington Avenue. She flipped on the light and stood at the mirror of her vanity and brushed her hair. She leaned in close to the glass and took a good, hard look at her face.

She opened the jar of expensive night cream that made more

promises than Tony Arma before she married him, and gently applied it to her face. She rubbed her hands together to work the cream into them when she saw Tony's wedding band on her vanity tray where she had left it earlier.

Chi Chi opened her jewelry case. Lifting out the top tray, she found the rings from her past that chronicled, in gemstones and gold, the important days of her life. She found the diamond chip in a gold chevron her father had given her on her Sweet Sixteenth birthday, the class ring from St. Joseph High School, the engagement ring from Sav with the diamond pavé heart, and finally, her polished yellow-gold wedding band.

When Tony and Chi Chi had their first hit, Tony took their original bands that he purchased from the shop in California and had them melted into fine gold bands.

Chi Chi slipped on her reading glasses and checked the inside of the band. It was inscribed:

Tony's Wife

She slipped the wedding ring onto her finger. It had been years since she had worn it. She clasped her left hand as though it were injured, but she was simply protecting it—from all that had gone wrong, couldn't be made right, and now wouldn't be. She slid into bed and pulled the coverlet up to her chin. She had the chills. Chi Chi had the same funny feeling she had when she first fell in love with Saverio Armandonada. She was afraid.

Chi Chi hadn't set foot in the Melody since Tony moved in permanently in 1981 after his divorce from Dora. There was no other wife left to clean it out, or to be truthful, one who felt it was her responsibility. She shook her head at the irony of *that*. Their game of musical chairs had ended with Chi Chi still standing. She turned the key in the lock and entered the apartment.

The place was neat but shabby, in need of redecoration. There was evidence that wives along the way had fought to remove certain colors, furniture, and rugs, and won. But for the most part, Tony had held on to Chi Chi's decor, which meant he had, in his own way, also held on to the original intent for the place.

She opened the windows to air out the rooms. The scent of tobacco lingered in the air, which meant Tony smoked after he was diagnosed with lung cancer. It wasn't just a hunch; she confirmed it as she emptied an ashtray into the garbage can in the kitchen. Sunny had been by to pick up the mail and left behind several copies of the Long Island newspaper with Tony's obituary on the kitchen table.

OBITUARY
November 10, 2000

Crooner Tony Arma, best known for hits sung with first wife Chi Chi Donatelli (*Mama's Rolling Pin*) and went on to international success with *Gravy, Gravy, Gravy*, died in St. Vincent's Hospital in Greenwich Village after a long illness. The singer was also a featured actor in spaghetti westerns, including *Frankie Fedora*, where he played Joey "The Foot" Casciole, and had a top 20 *Billboard* rank with the movie's theme song. Arma lived the last thirty years of his life in Rome, Italy, before returning to New York City. Son Leone preceded him in death. Twin daughters Rosaria and Isotta survive him, as well as several grandchildren and former wives: collaborator Chiara "Chi Chi" Donatelli, singer Tammy Twiford, actress Dora Alfedena, and restaurant hostess Ginger Weevil.

November 11, 2000

Correction: Because of an editing error, the spelling of Mr. Arma's fourth wife was incorrect. Her name is Ginger Wheedle Arma.

Chi Chi chuckled to herself. The twins had called Ginger a boll weevil, so perhaps there was a smattering of justice in this weary world.

Chi Chi went through the apartment slowly. She peered into closets and drawers and cabinets. She found herself in the master bedroom, inside the walk-in closet flipping through hangers holding Tony's suits, jackets, and pants. There were six tuxedos, one for every decade since the Dorsey Brothers. She spent time pulling out boxes, opening them, and sorting through plastic bins. One of the wives must have hired a professional organizer along the way because bins were labeled with specific items: dress socks, pocket squares, and another was marked *Swim trunks*.

A cedar chest full of his neatly folded wool sweaters carried the scent of his Fabergé cologne. His silk bow tie collection lay flat on tissue paper in an Hermès box like puzzle pieces.

She found a box on the floor of his closet next to his shoes marked *Chi Chi*. Inside, she found props from the old act. Relics. The original rolling pin she believed to be long gone was wrapped in a Fontainebleau Hotel beach towel. Funny hats, fake teeth, wigs, and eyeglasses, the stuff of sketch characters and stagecraft were jammed into the box. She let out a gasp when she found her paper piano in a roll tied with a velvet ribbon. She placed it on the bed next to her. Maybe one of her grandchildren would appreciate the old thing.

She made her way back to the living room to get her purse to go. There was too much stuff, bringing up too much of the past, and she was overwhelmed. She was annoyed that he had left all this junk for her to sort through, and that he knew for certain that he could count on her to clean up any mess in the end because she had spent her life taking care of him.

Chi Chi went into the kitchen and poured herself a glass of water. She took a few sips and walked into the living room. She sat down at the piano and tickled the keys. At least he had kept it tuned. She wondered why.

Chi Chi had been writing a song she started when she was thirty-seven that she had not been able to finish. Other songs had come into her consciousness since then, and she composed many of them without impediment, but not this one. She remembered Tony pressed her to get it done, but she had never found the right words. And now, she heard the words and music in her head, but she didn't have the right instrument.

Chi Chi got up from the piano and went back to the bedroom closet. She searched through it, emptying it, box by box, until the bed was covered with stuff. She flipped open the lids of the storage boxes, hauled the stool from Tony's desk to the closet, and stood on it, peering at the contents on the top shelf. She sorted through her ex-husband's hatboxes, marked *Borsalino*, and pushed them out of the way.

Her face broke into a grin. She found what she had been looking for without much fuss. She lifted Tony's old mandolin off the shelf. The wood had aged to a soft burgundy, the color of her mouth when her lipstick had faded after she had spent the day talking and failed to reapply it. She tucked the mandolin under her arm.

By the time Chi Chi made it back to the living room, night had fallen. Outside the windows, the city was draped in black velvet. The moon shimmered in the night sky like a shard of a seashell, delicate and silver.

She found a paper and pen and sat down at the table with

her tools and the mandolin. She plucked a tune on the strings,
tightening them as she played. She heard the music in her head,
wrote the notes down on the paper, and soon the lyrics flowed.
Her thoughts moved her hands between the paper, pen, and the
strings. She wrote:

> Wait for me
> We need one more chance to talk things through
> Wait for me
> Where time does not rule me and you
> The sand, the sea, the sun, and the snow
> We owned them all, don't you know
> Stop and think what we once had
> Can't even imagine it now, all gone so sad
> If there's a heaven, and you would know
> Might you wait by the gate until I show?
> I may wear lavender or gold or gray
> Will you reach for me then and ask me to stay?
> I want to hold you again, where we live in nothing but
> light
> This time we'll be kind and do everything right
> You'll be true and I'll show grace
> And when the music plays, I'll see your face
> Wait for me—Saverio.
> Wait.

Chi Chi put down the pen. She reached for the mandolin to
play the song from the beginning, as was her technique, but she
stopped when she felt an odd pain travel down her left arm. Perhaps she had pulled a muscle hauling those boxes from the closet.
She rubbed her wrist and forearm, but the pain did not subside.
She had butterflies—excitement, no doubt, from having finally fin-

ished the song it took nearly fifty years to write. Chi Chi felt a fluttering in her chest as her heart skipped a beat. She put her hand to her heart and left it there, waiting to feel its rhythm resume.

"Saverio," she whispered.

And she smiled.

The End

Discography

INTRODUCING TONY ARMA (1948)
Haven't We Met
It Was So Cold, He Proposed
Samson & Denial
Jelly Bean Beach (with Chi Chi Donatelli)
Mama's Rolling Pin (with Chi Chi Donatelli)
A Girl I Can Talk To
Gravy, Gravy, Gravy (with Chi Chi Donatelli)
One Gold Chain
The Italian Girl Samba
Midtown Blues

TONY ARMA: THE PACIFIC SONGBOOK (1950)
Nothing But Ocean (with Thoughts of You)
A Tiki Hut for Two
The Pineapple and Mango Drag
Ration Our Love
Baby Call Me from Home
Island Dream
Miss My Wife
Violet Sunrise

CHRISTMAS WITH TONY & CHI CHI (1955)
Silent Night
O Holy Night
Away in a Manger
The Little Drummer Boy

O Come, All Ye Faithful
Santa Claus Is Comin' to Town
Joy to the World
Mama's Rolling Pin (Make the Cannoli)

TONY ARMA SINGS IN THE ETERNAL CITY (1962)
Panis Angelicus
Kyrie
Ave Maria
Macaroni Bomboloni
Meet Me in Roma
The Hills of Roseto Valfortore
On the Road to Naples
Prayer of Saint Francis

MOVIES FEATURING TONY ARMA
Frankie Fedora
Mr. Mondo
The Jive Makers of Jersey
Venus di Vegas
Serena of Staten Island
Cocktails, Nibbles & Me
The Inner Sanctum
Follies Bare All

Acknowledgments

The Perin sisters of Delabole farm outside Pen Argyl, Pennsylvania, were of Venetian descent, born in America and named for Italian queens. Viola (Yolanda), Edith (Enes), Helen (Eliana), and Lavinia are my Mount Rushmore. Ambitious, strong, and emotional, they moved through the world like silver arrows in a blue sky. My grandmother, Viola, mother of four, worked in a factory from the age of fourteen, and eventually owned her own mill with my grandfather. Edith, mother of two, operated a lovely restaurant called the Little Venice with her husband, Tony Romano. Helen Blackton, married to Don, was a beautician who ran her own shop after she served in World War II. Lavinia Spadoni, mother of three, wife of Frank, worked with Viola in her mill, Helen in her shop, and eventually for the people of the state of Pennsylvania as a prison matron (as the position was called when she began). With the passing of Aunt Lavinia this year, I revel in their beauty, strength, faith, and daring. Farm girls fear nothing. They appreciated style, glamour, and nice things. They aspired to the good life but had their own definitions. Viola loved travel; Edith was a fabulous baker and cook; Helen embraced adventure; and Lavinia loved people, whether it was having friends over for a weekly card game or dropping by for a visit. The swing music of the big band era kept the sisters company through their romances, hopes, work lives, and a world war.

My evermore thanks to the glorious team at Harper led by two of my favorite men: Brian Murray and Jonathan Burnham. Sara Nelson is a total joy, an astute and hardworking editor, and a champion for a good story. Thank you to the team: Dorian Randall, Amber Oliver, Jennifer Civiletto, and Mary Gaule.

My gratitude to the tireless Kate D'Esmond and Emily VanDerwerken; our marketing wiz Leah Wasielewski; the fabulous Katie O'Callaghan; Jennifer Murphy; Mary Ann Petyak; Tom Hopke Jr.; the queen of the libraries: Virginia Stanley; Lainey Mays; Chris Connolly; and Tina Andreadis.

The design team is superb: Robin Bilardello crushes the cover art again with a glorious Louise Dahl-Wolfe creation featuring the exquisite Mary Jane Russell; thank you, Jillian Verillo, Joanne O'Neill, Gregg Kulick, Sarah Brody, and Bonni Leon-Berman.

The most excellent sales force is led by Doug Jones, and I'm grateful to: Mary Beth Thomas, Josh Marwell, Andy LeCount, Kathryn Walker, Michael Morris, Kristin Bowers, Brendan Keating, Carla Parker, Austin Tripp, Christy Johnson, Brian Grogan, Tobly McSmith, Lillie Walsh, Rachel Levenberg, Frank Albanese, David Wolfson, and Samantha Hagerbaumer. Mary Sasso and Amy Baker are the best in paperback, Tara Weikum in YA; the video and studio team are spectacular, thank you: Marisa Benedetto, Lisa Sharkey, Alex Kuciw, and Jeffrey "Scooter" Kaplan.

I am thrilled that Edoardo Ballerini is the voice of this novel, produced by the great Katie Ostrowka. I adore Danielle Kolodkin, Natalie Duncan, and Andrea Rosen.

At William Morris Endeavor, I thank the dazzling, darling Suzanne Gluck, the bold and beautiful Nancy Josephson, and the gorgeous and hilarious Laurie Pozmantier, and the best team any-where: thank you: Andrea Blatt, Ellen Sushko, Eve Attermann, Jill Holwager Gillett, Ilayda Yigit, Jonathan Lomma, Gretchen Burke, Elizabeth Wachtel, Tracy Fisher, Alyssa Eatherly, Fiona Smith, Ja-nine Kamouh, Gwen Beal, Matilda Forbes Watson, Alina Flint, Siobhan O'Neill, Fiona Baird, Jamie Carr, Caitlin Mahony, Tan-ner Cusumano, Graham Taylor, Will Maxfield, Michelle Bohan, Joanna Korshak, Chris Slager, Liesl Coplan, Alli McArdle, Hilary Savit, Kathleen Nishimoto.

Thank you, ladies of The Glory of Everything: you are all stars: Lucy Beuchert, Jillian Fata, Alexa Casavecchia, and Emily Metcafe. Thank you to our interns: Oona Intemann and Gabrielle Ho. Thank you, Jake and Jean Morrissey, for your wisdom in all matters from books to movies to parenting. At the Origin Project thank you to the angel, cofounder and executive director: Nancy Bolmeier Fisher; her right arm Ian Fisher; and her wings, Ryan Fisher; thank you, Linda Woodward, for your hard work and vision!

Evermore thanks to: Richard Thompson, Kim Hovey, Ian Chap-man, Suzanne Baboneau, Gina Casella, Mary Ellen Fedeli, Beth Vechiarelli Cooper, Caroline Giovannini, Kenny Sarfin, Phoebe Curran, Christine Freglette, Ron Block, Liz Bartek, Catherine Brennan, Lora Minichillo, Candy Purdum, Debbie Hoffman, Dan-iel Goldin, Carrie Robb, Kimberly Daniels, Rene Martin, Gary Parkes, Robin Homonoff, Candyce Williams, Robyn Lee, Glen Moody, Jillian Bullock, Glenda Hall, and Nita Leftwich

My gratitude and devotion to: Ed and Chris Muranksy, Hoda Kotb, Jennifer Miller, Kathie Lee Gifford, Christine Gardner, Kathy Ryan, Tony Krantz, Kristin Dornig, Brian Balthazar, Doro-thy and Bob Isaac, Jennifer Bloom and Andrew Kravis, Christine Onorati, Dianne and Andy Lerner, Betty Fleenor, Spencer Salley, Dana Chidekel, Jayne Muir, Connie Shulman, Evadean Church,

Larry Sanitsky, Kathryn Drew, Nigel Stoneman and Charles Fotheringham, Monique Gibson, Bunny Grossinger, Kathy McElyea, Mary Murphy, Lou and Berta Pitt, Doris Gluck, Mary Pipino, Tom Dyja, Liz Travis, Dagmara Domincyzk and Patrick Wilson, Dan and Robin Napoli, Sharon Ewing, Eugenie Furniss, Philip Grenz, Christina Geist, Joyce Sharkey, Gail Berman, Cate Magennis Wyatt, Carol, Dominic and Gina Vechiarelli, Jim and Mary Deese Hampton, Jackie and Paul Wilson, Greg D'Alessandro, Mark Amato, Meryl Poster, Sister Robbie Pentecost, Heather and Peter Rooney, Aaron Hill and Susan Fales-Hill, Mary K. and John Wilson, Jim and Kate Benton Doughan, Ruth Pomerance, Bill Persky and Joanna Patton, Angelina Fiordellisi and Matt Williams, Michael La Hart and F. Todd Johnson, Richard and Dana Kirshenbaum, Marisa Acocella Marchetto, Violetta Acocella, Emma and Tony Cowell, Hugh and Jody Friedman O'Neill, Nelle Fortenberry, Cara Stein, Whoopi Goldberg, Tom Leonardis, Dolores and Dr. Emil Pascarelli, Eleanor "Fitz" King and daughters Eileen, Ellen and Patti. Sharon Hall and Todd Kessler, Aimee Bell, Rosanne Cash, Charles Randolph Wright, Constance Marks, Jasmine Guy, Mario Cantone, Jerry Dixon, Judy Rutledge, Greg and Tracy Kress, Father John Rausch, Judith Ivey, Mary Ellen Keating, Nancy Ringham Smith, Sharon Watroba Burns, Dee Emmerson, Elaine Martinelli, Sister Karol Jackowski, Jane Cline Higgins, Nancy Toney, Betty Cline, Max and Robyn Westler, Tom and Barbara Sullivan, Brownie and Connie Polly, Karen Fink, Norma Born, Beata and Steven Baker, Todd Doughty and Randy Losapio, Craig Fisse, Steve and Anemone Kaplan, Christina Avis Krauss and Sonny, Eleanor Jones, Veronica Kilcullen, Lisa Ryskoski, Mary Ellinger, Iva Lou Johnson, Cynthia Rutledge Olson, Mary Testa, David and Michelle Baldacci, Dottie Frank, Joanna LaMarca, Sheila Mara, Louisa Ermelino, Jenna Elfman,

Janet Leahy, Susie Essman, Wendy Luck, Elena Nachmanoff, Dianne Festa, Miles Fisher, Becky Browder, and Samantha Rowe.

Michael Patrick King, I always leave the light on for you.

My evermore thanks to my brothers and sisters and the Stephenson family. It is a wonder to see my nieces and nephews, the Stephensons: Mallory, Brad, Julianna, and Gabriel; the Noones: Anna, Matt, Ally, and Anthony; and the Trigianis, Luca and Ella take flight.

Welcome Colette "Coco" Thompson, Willoughby Cash Knobler, and Zoya Lena Athar, rays of light and might.

With the publication of every book, I will miss Marion Cantone, my honorary sister, who waited for each one and read them into the night; Bill Bombeck, Erma's tall, handsome, steady husband, was a great guy, and is now with the funniest writer of our times in heaven. Jim Abe Fleenor was a handsome, high-spirited, hilarious boy who grew up to be a wonderful teacher, father, husband, and writer. Karen Watkins Snow was beautiful, funny, and smart, and a fabulous sister. Faith Cox was a great educator, and a dear friend. Lorraine Stampone Coyne was the first friend I ever made, and there's no replacing her ever. Danny Galloway was hilarious, smart, and a great friend and writer. Ingrid Josephson was a beautiful mother and friend. Terri Albright was a loving mom and a perfect St. Mary's sister.

Tim and Lucia, thanks for not changing the locks: *Sono la persona più fortunate che abbia.*

My mother, Ida Bonicelli Trigiani, taught me until the final moment of her life. Librarians never leave a task undone. Nothing will ever be the same without her. When I miss her, and I do, and I miss my dad, and I always will, I listen to *String of Pearls* and remember them . . . dancing.

About the Author

ADRIANA TRIGIANI is the *New York Times* bestselling author of eighteen books in fiction and nonfiction that have been published in thirty-six countries around the world. She is an award-winning playwright, television writer/producer, and filmmaker. She wrote and directed the film version of her novel *Big Stone Gap*, which was shot entirely on location in her Virginia hometown. She is cofounder of the Origin Project, an in-school writing program that serves more than a thousand students in Appalachia. She lives in Greenwich Village with her family.

**From the bestselling author of *The Shoemaker's Wife*,
comes an exhilarating story of friendship, family,
love and loyalty, told against a backdrop of
Shakespeare's greatest comedies ...**

Kiss Carlo

In 1949, South Philadelphia is bursting with possibility. When an urgent telegram from Italy upends the ordinary life of Nicky Castone, he begins to wonder whether there's more to life than a steady job in the family business and a sweet-natured fiancée.

Discovering in secret the draw of the local Shakespeare theatre company, Nicky quickly becomes enchanted by the stage, its colourful players and the feisty Calla Borelli, who runs the show. But before long, Nicky finds himself on the horns of a dilemma. Will he return to his conventional life and family, or does he have what it takes to risk everything and chart a new course?

AVAILABLE NOW IN PAPERBACK AND EBOOK

**SIMON &
SCHUSTER**

Overture

MAY 1, 1949

ROSETO VALFORTORE, ITALY

A cool breeze shook the old wind chimes on the balcony outside the ambassador's bedroom. The peal of the delicate glass bells sounded like the tings of crystal after a wedding toast.

The stone palazzo had been grand before the war, with its terra-cotta-tiled roof, marble floors, and carved monastery doors. Positioned on the highest peak in Roseto Valfortore, it was also imposing, like a bell tower, save the bell or the tower. It was named Palazzo Fico Regale because the hills that cascaded down to the road that led north to Rome were speckled with fig trees. In summer the trees were lush and green, loaded with purple fruit; in winter the barren branches, wrapped in turbans of burlap, looked like the raised fists of Mussolini's blackshirts.

Inside, the official consort, Signora Elisabetta Guardinfante, packed her husband's dress uniform with care. Elisabetta was small and dark, her eyes like thumbprints of black ink, more iris than whites. Her fine bones and lips were delicate, like those of her relatives of French descent from the north of Italy.

She rolled the red, white, and green sash tightly into the shape of a snail shell, so that when he unfurled it, the silk would lay flat across his chest without a crease. She pinned the chevalier ribbon and the gold satin braid across the breast of the royal-blue jacket before buttoning the beaded cuffs to the sleeves. She hung the jacket on a hanger padded with cotton batting and placed it in a soft muslin dress bag, as though she were laying an infant in his bunting. She turned her attention to the trousers, folding them over a wooden hanger and straightening the military stripes that ran down the outside of each pant leg before slipping them into a separate muslin sack.

The wife hung the garments in an open standing trunk, took inventory of its contents, and counted out six pairs of socks, including three she had mended before packing. She checked the black patent dress shoes, each in its own chamois bag, and pulled out the left one. Finding a smudge on the toe, she buffed it with the hem of her apron until it shone. She rolled a wooden shaving cup and brush, a small circle of soap, and a straight razor tightly in a linen towel, then tucked the bundle into the dress shoe before placing it inside the trunk.

Elisabetta examined the impeccable stitchwork on the hem of her husband's undershirt, where she had used the silk trim of her own camisole to bind the frayed fabric. Satisfied that her husband had everything he needed for the journey ahead, she hung a small net pouch filled with fragrant lavender buds and cedar shavings inside the trunk, securing it tightly with two knots. The little things she did for her husband went unnoticed, but she did them anyway, because she knew they mattered.

She snapped the lids shut on a series of velvet jewelry cases containing regulation Italian Army gold cuff links, a matching tie bar, and two medals awarded to the ambassador's father from World War I, *al valor militare* and *merito di guerra*. She left the solid gold *aiutante* medal from World War II on the nightstand. It had been a gift from the previous ambassador, who was eager to unload it, as it bore the profile of Benito Mussolini etched on one side, with the symbol indicating a rank of major in the Italian Army on the other.

The winter of 1949 had been the worst in memory. A mudslide caused by a flash flood of the Fortore River marooned the locals high in the hills for several months. The Italian Army had dispatched a rescue party to bring supplies and medicine up to them, but the burro and cart regiment failed to reach the town because Via Capella della Consolazione, the only road with access to the village, had been washed out. Instead of saving the Rosetani, the regiment nearly lost their own lives as they slid back down the steep incline in a gloppy trough of deep mud.

The people of the village had lost all hope until spring arrived. The sun, which had disappeared for most of the winter, suddenly exploded in white streams over the town like the rays of gold on the monstrance in the tabernacle inside the church of Santa Maria Assunta.

"It's time, Bette." Carlo Guardinfante stood in the doorway of their bedroom wearing the only other suit he owned, a brown wool custom cut with wide lapels, his best pale blue dress shirt, and a rose-and-cream-striped tie. His wife fixed the knot and slipped his round-trip ticket and the telegram confirming his arrival into the breast pocket of his jacket.

Carlo was a southern Italian, typical in temperament but not in appearance. He possessed the passionate disposition of his neighbors but did not share their dark Mediterranean coloring. He had the freckled face of a farmer to the north, the large hands of a man who could handle a plow, and the height that gave him, at six foot two, the stature of a general. His broad shoulders had earned him the nickname Spadone.

"Everything is ready for you." Bette looked into her husband's eyes. In the bright morning light, they were the color of the soft waves in the port of Genoa, more green than blue. His reddish brown hair had flecks of white, too soon on a man of thirty-eight, and a reminder of all he had been through. Carlo had spent the last few years worried about the citizens of his province, frustrated by the lack of progress on their behalf, and the anxiety had taken a toll on him. Carlo was so thin, Elisabetta had punched two extra holes in the leather of his belt and attached the grommets herself. She'd adhered a small brass bar to the long end of the loop, so it wouldn't look as though she had made any adjustments.

"How's the belt?" She tugged on the loop.

He patted the brass plate and smiled. Carlo's front teeth had a space between them, known in the village as lucky teeth because, in theory, he could fit a coin between them, which meant good fortune would be his all his life. But Carlo didn't feel lucky, and any hope of prosperity had washed away with the road to Rome.

So Carlo looked for luck wherever he could find it.

"Am I supposed to pass this off as a new Italian style?"

"Why not?"

Carlo kissed his wife on the cheek. He picked up his billfold, opened it, and counted the lire. "There's more here. Did you club the priest?"

"The smart wife puts aside money and doesn't tell her husband."

"Your mother taught you well."

"Not my mother." Bette smiled. "Yours."

Carlo patted his wife on the fanny. "Pack the Il Duce."

"Oh, Carlo. Americans hated him."

"I'll show the symbol side. His *faccia* will face my heart. Maybe the brute bastard will finally do some good for us."

"He'll do better melted down and sold."

"The more gold I wear, the more important I seem. My chest should rattle like a tambourine." Carlo snapped the case shut and handed it to his wife. "*La bella figura.*"

"*Va bene.*" Elisabetta picked up the medal from the nightstand

and placed it in with the others, locking them into the safe box of the trunk.

Carlo pulled his wife close. "When I come home, we paint the villa."

"It needs more than paint." Elisabetta looked around the suite. As the lady of the house, she saw the failure to meet her obligations. There were the cracks in the plaster, rusty streaks where the ceiling leaked, frayed hems on the damask drapes, and most disturbing to her, squares of plywood covered the windows to replace the glass that had shattered in the heavy winds. Elisabetta sighed. The windows had been the most dazzling aspect of their residence, their rippled glass carted from Venice, but now the missing panes looked like teeth long gone from a lovely smile. "Our home needs a miracle."

"Put it on the list, Bette." Carlo embraced her.

"We won't live long enough to fix everything that needs repair."

Carlo did not take his appointment as *Ambasciatore da Provincia di Foggia e Provincia di Capitanata da Apulia* lightly, nor did he see his role simply as a figurehead. He wanted to do some good, but there were no funds attached to the honor and few favors. All across Italy, from the Mediterranean to the Adriatic and from north to south, reparations went to replace waterlines, restore electrical plants, and rebuild essential factories.

There was little concern for Roseto Valfortore and small villages like it. Stranded during the winter months, Carlo had not been able to go to Rome and plead for help. The letters that had made it through had been met with the curt response that there was greater need elsewhere.

The Holy Roman Church advised him to rally the townspeople to do the work themselves, but Roseto Valfortore had been deserted by the young; some had died in the war, and the rest migrated to Naples to find jobs along the Amalfi coast or east to the Adriatic to work on the trade ships. Most Rosetani, however, emigrated to America, where there were plenty of jobs in steel mills, factories, and construction. The families that stayed behind were too poor to take a risk, and too old to want to. Everywhere Carlo looked, life was bleak. He had hoped for a sign that their luck would change, and when none appeared, he hatched one final scheme to save his village.

The sun bathed the town in white light as Carlo, in his suit and fedora, and Elisabetta, who had put on a straw hat, linen coat, and her best black leather shoes, emerged from their home. The polished couple inspired confidence against the backdrop of the ravaged village where the tile roof tops had been mended hastily with mismatched planks of wood, ancient stone walls had crumbled to rubble, and deep potholes pitted the stone streets.

As the old houseman followed them out, he kept his head down and chewed on snuff, balancing Carlo's trunk on his back with ease as though it were light and he were still young.

The townspeople filled the winding streets for the ambassador's send-off, waving long green cypress branches high in the air like flags. Carlo tipped his hat and bowed to the people, taking in their cheers and affection like sips of cool water for his parched soul. Women rushed forward holding letters in sealed envelopes, which Elisabetta collected for her husband, promising them he would deliver them in person once he arrived at his destination.

The houseman placed the trunk in the cart, freshly painted in bright yellow partly to draw attention away from the decrepit donkey hitched to the carriage. The animal, too, was decorated in honor of the important passenger, his bridle festooned with colorful ribbons in pink and green. Carlo smiled, reflecting that the decorations on the donkey were a lot like a new hat on an old woman, a temporary distraction from a permanent problem.

The ambassador hoisted himself up into the open bench of the carriage. A cheer of great jubilation echoed through the streets as

Elisabetta handed her husband the stack of letters, which he held high in the air. Carlo leaned down to kiss his wife good-bye.

The crowd parted as the cart lumbered down the street followed by Elisabetta on foot. The Rosetani fell into place behind her as the cart moved through the village. A small contingent of girls threw rose petals chanting "Kiss Carlo!" as their mothers ran alongside the cart, reaching for him. The women were thrilled when Carlo chose them, took their hands, and kissed them.

Father DeNisco, wearing a black cassock, stood on the white marble steps of the church and made the sign of the cross as the carriage passed. The driver and Carlo bowed their heads and blessed themselves.

As they reached the entrance of the town, a new mother stepped forward and lifted her baby up to the carriage. Carlo reached for the infant and gently cradled the bundle swaddled in white in his arms. He pulled the baby close and kissed his cheek.

Elisabetta brushed away a tear at the sight of her husband holding the baby. It was the picture of her highest dream.

There was a time in Roseto Valfortore when the streets had been filled with prams. There were a hundred babies in the village before the war; now, they were as rare as this one infant. The thought of that galvanized Carlo to move forward with his plan.

As the carriage went through the gated entrance of the town, the throng stopped and cheered.

"The people love you," the driver said.

"They love you when they need you."

"And when they don't?"

"They find someone new." The ambassador pulled the brim of his hat over his eyes. "How's the road?"

"If we are careful, we'll make it."

"On time?"

"I think so. The car is waiting for you in Foggia."

"Does it have enough petrol?" Carlo asked wryly.

"Depends on his gratuity."

"And yours." Carlo smiled.

"I don't work for fun, *Ambasciatore*."

"No one does."

"Italy forgot about us. All the money goes to Roma. Milano. Even Bologna took a slice of the reparations."

"For railways." Carlo was not interested in talking politics with the driver; he knew all too well that his people had been forgotten. "The station in Bologna is important."

"Of course. But so are we. The farmers feed the people, but they starve us. They forget the villages and save the cities."

"Can you pick up speed?"

"Not if I want to keep the wheels on the carriage. Your road is the worst I've seen."

"I appreciate your assessment," Carlo said, and checked his pocket watch. "I can't miss the boat in Naples."

"How's your luck?"

"The sun is shining, when I thought it never would again, so I would say my luck is good."

The ambassador was on his way to America, and he would need it.

Carlo turned to take one last look at his village. The hillsides were mounds of wet black mud, smattered with a few hopeful sprigs of green. The spindly trunks of the fig trees had survived, stubbornly pushing up through the earth like markers of hope itself. The clutter of stone houses on the hilltop stood against the powder blue sky like a stack of cracked plates on a shelf. All was not lost, but what remained might not be enough to save his home.

Carlo watched as his wife pushed through the crowd to get a final glimpse of the carriage. Carlo waved to her. Elisabetta placed her hand on her heart, which made him feel more pressure to return a hero and gave him an ache in his gut.

Elisabetta's face was the final image Carlo would take with him on the road to Naples to board the ship that would take him to America, where he would make his way to a small village in Pennsylvania that he believed held the key to saving Roseto Valfortore. He had heard that in America, all that was broken could be mended; there was a solution to every problem, and money flowed like the sweetest wine at a party that had no end.

Ambassador Carlo Guardinfante was about to see for himself what was true, and whether the land of hopes and dreams would provide either for him so he might save the village and the people he loved.

FIRST CLASS
HOLIDAYS

Booking your dream holiday is not a decision to be taken lightly, whether that be a touring holiday, a luxury honeymoon or a holiday to celebrate a special occasion.

That's where award-winning First Class Holidays come in. Specialising in tailor-made holidays to Canada & Alaska, America, Australia, New Zealand, South Africa and the Pacific Islands, they take away the hard work when it comes to planning the trip you've always imagined and provide an outstanding level of service while doing so, and with over 750 years' experience between the team, over 100,000 satisfied customers and 23 years delivering exceptional service, they'll plan your journey to absolute perfection, offering first-hand advice with the knowledge they've garnered throughout their own travels.